SIMON SAYS

Linda Williams Stirling

Midnight Garden
PRESS

Midnight Garden Press
Elmira, NY
www.midnightgardenpress.com

ISBN: 9798988591214

Cover Design: MiblArt at www.miblart.com
Interior Design: JDStirling at Midnight Garden Press

Credits:
Yacine Boubred, owner of YASDesignerGB, Designer for Celtic Trees
Jay Madison, owner of Seaquint Design, Designer for Celtic Knots
Oxee Treex, owner of TreeX, Designer of Oak Leaves
Commercial Licenses Held

Library of Congress Control Number: 2023913713

First Edition: September 2023
Printed in the United States of America

***Dedicated to** my children Joseph, Benjamin, and Rebecca
who have been a part of Simon Says their entire lives,
and who have always supported and encouraged me.*

*Whoops! I mean Benjamin, Rebecca, and Joseph, because
Rebecca is tired of always being last since she's the youngest,
and Benjamin is tired of always being in the middle. Joseph is just tired, so
I got him a chair and ottoman, and now he's happy.
Fixed that problem.*

In Loving Memory

*For my dad, John Parks Williams,
who believed I could do anything
and was the best man I've ever
known.*

*For JP, who was a better person
than I am,
even though he was a dog.*

*My short-legged Welsh dog, named after my
short-legged Welsh dad.
I love and miss them both.*

Acknowledgments

I'd like to thank Dianna Horst of Ridgewriters who provided invaluable guidance and encouragement on story development and editing. She believed in Simon from the start.

Much gratitude to Christina Desotell Smith who asked all the right questions and helped me finalize and sharpen everything up, from timelines to character development. She has been a wonderful and supportive friend, and always up for our crazy adventures.

Thanks also to Diane Butler for transcribing my manuscript and giving additional feedback, along with Jamie Lane and several others.

Hopping on the Wayback Machine, I'd like to thank my High School teachers: Mrs. Alice L. Clawson, who nominated me to participate in the National Council of Teachers of English (NCTE) writing competition, which I won, and Ms. Helen Bancroft, who, after my win, would accept no other answer from me than a promise I was going to be a writer. Also, my Sixth Grade teacher Mrs. Lord, who noticed, encouraged, and rewarded my love of books and reading.

Finally, thank you to my children Joseph, Benjamin, and Rebecca, who grew up with my original verbal tale of Simon, which became a short story, and finally became a novel. They found the process exciting, gave me writing time, loved and supported me, and always believed that just producing a completed manuscript was a cause to celebrate, but knew I would truly bring Simon to life one day. Love you to infinity and beyond! Also, thanks Ben, for being the face of Simon!

Table of Contents

SILENCE abruptly descended on the crowd in the playhouse as darkness engulfed them. A blue light cut a sudden swath between their tensed bodies, highlighting a mist spilling across the floor. People looked around with expectant faces. The vapor snaked and swirled among them, wrapping around their legs, catching them like flies in a spider's web.

Women nervously gripped at the folds of their long skirts. Others clutched at their rough cloaks, pulling them tightly over their bodies. Still, the sudden chill cut through the layers of fabric. It wormed its way through their tunics and chemises and lay damply against their skin. Mouths fell open in noiseless gasps. Eyes widened in fear and anticipation.

Distant music floated above their heads echoing the strains of moon shadows. Near the edge of the crowd, a figure emerged from the swirling blue. A sudden intake of breath passed like a ripple in a pond through the crowd as everyone turned to stare. Tall and sturdy, the man strode boldly through the misty beam. The air seemed to spark and dance with streaks of lightning as he moved.

Throughout the hall members of the audience rubbed their arms at the sudden prickling on their skin and the raised gooseflesh that came with it. Others quickly moved out of his path, darting glances at him, unsure whether to be scared or elated. The music intensified as the powerful man swung his great cape around and climbed the stage steps, then faded away as he sat in the lone chair, a pointed hat balanced on his head.

The weaver of magic, the teller of tales had arrived. Some in the crowd blinked several times or rubbed their eyes in amazement. They would later swear they could see his stories following behind him, breaking free of the mist. Alive in the blue light they danced up the steps to await the call of their master. The storyteller leaned comfortably back in his chair slowly surveying the ordinary lives thronging below him.

"Simon," a voice whispered breathlessly.

The man's head inclined slightly in acknowledgment, his sandy hair falling about his shoulders. With a shift of his blue eyes, he saw the pompous and overfed who sat in the upstairs galleries. There was a man in a richly embroidered coat straining over his plump belly, a mug of the best ale in his clutching hand. Next to him, a woman laced so tightly into her fancy brocade bodice Simon wondered how she could breathe. Their money could buy them a cushioned seat, but not a soul. Truly, some rich proved decent folks, Simon conceded, though it took great patience to find them.

His eyes moved on with the briefest flicker of dismissal. He looked below him and a small smile crossed his face. On the hard dirt floor of the courtyard stood the people who caught his interest. Hardworking and hopeful, they typified the mass of humanity who struggled for survival, living and dying with equal passion. He nodded his head in satisfaction. He had accepted this role so very many years ago because of people like them. What he accomplished here tonight, as on so many other nights, would reaffirm his own people had not died in vain.

He looked to the rear of the crowd and focused on one woman in particular. A softness settled across his countenance as he smiled again. What a beautiful spirit she had and such a kind heart. To his eyes, she shone like a bright light in the darkness. What a joy it would be to have such a woman by one's side. He examined her life with reverence, beginning to imagine how it could blend with his own.

No. He shook his head slightly in irritation at his mind's wanderings. Thoughts such as those had no place in his life. Still, he was glad to have found her. *I will give her a wonderful story. She deserves that much from me.* He smiled again. Tonight would be most worthwhile.

In the front row, a woman rubbed her eyes and squinted at the stage. So strong was Simon's aura, she thought she could see the shapes of his stories undulating about him. They moved to and fro, caressing him, caressing the audience, heightening anticipation. Suddenly, Simon sat up straight, raising an arm out in front of him. Startled, the woman made a small sound and leaned back. The audience moved with her. He made a slow sweeping motion above their heads. The spell was cast; the story began.

"There once lived, in a place not so different from our London, in a time not unlike our own 1630s, a raven-haired woman with translucent skin and a tiny, ever-so-small birthmark below her right ear. She was a small thing, barely reaching the shoulders of a normal man. But a single look into her deep brown eyes and one knew immediately her size was deceiving. Inside she had the strength and determination of a giant." Simon paused, again staring intently towards the rear of the crowd.

A young woman standing at the back of the audience slowly lifted her hand and placed it over the right side of her neck. The description in this story was merely a coincidence, but still, she adjusted her dark hair to cover a small mark below her ear. Barely moving her head, she shifted her eyes nervously to see if anyone noticed.

No one had. Hunching lower among the crowd, she peered up at Simon between the heads of the people before her, eyes narrowed in wariness but feeling a sense of curiosity as well. What kind of story could this be? The man couldn't really be talking about her. That was impossible. She'd never even seen him before. Unnerved, she fought the compulsion to run away. The story wasn't about her, she insisted to herself, but she couldn't resist the urge to hear about a woman portrayed so similarly.

Simon sat on stage weaving his magic. The story continued.

"As with so many villagers and townsfolk today, her family struggled to survive. Her father was called into service for King James I to defend our beautiful England. Like so many others, he died fulfilling his charge, leaving this young lass as the only member of her family with any hope of keeping them together and alive; a blind old grandfather, a younger sister and brother, and a baby, not yet two years old. The mother had died during her last birthing."

He leaned forward, his eyes wide, his face a picture of determination, and in a booming voice continued. "Our young friend had no choice but to do all her family required. Cooking, cleaning, mending and making clothes, growing and harvesting food, taking care of the animals; all the while caring for the three young ones and the old man. It was no life, only a struggle for survival."

"But, you may say, this is the way of life. This is not any different from what we all live with every day. This is our story, too. What makes this young woman any different?"

The dark-haired woman rose on her tiptoes now, too shocked to be cautious. Her mind worked frantically, full of questions about how this man could possibly know so much about her. It was too much her own story to be a mere coincidence. She scowled at the storyteller until he looked her way again. Gasping, she dropped back out of sight.

Simon stared after her, a smile playing about his lips. He deliberately used her name now, confirming her fears. "Katherine, as we shall call her, was different. She did what necessity demanded, but her heart and her soul soared beyond her limited world." He could almost hear her moaning softly in the back. Although this was a difficult moment for her, he knew it would soon pass if he continued to press forward.

He leaned back contentedly in his chair, his soft voice floating almost like a caress through the audience. "Young Katherine understood her lot in life to be no more than a drudge, performing a daily routine of backbreaking work. She also understood the future lay ahead and time always promised change. She lived for that future and for the promise it held for the children she raised as her own. Katherine loved them all, but the young baby, Samuel, she held dearest. She had great dreams for his future."

"So, she worked hard to provide for their needs. And she watched. And she listened. She paid attention to what happened in the world, in the country, in the town. She learned reading and writing, numbers and music, absorbing everything she could. Then she went home and taught the children. The future meant changes and she would see her family prepared for them. That Samuel, in particular, would be ready for a better life."

Simon leaned forward again and looked around, taking a moment to stare directly into people's eyes. Across the audience, some swallowed hard or took a step back from the intensity of his gaze. Some looked away but many of them stared back, mesmerized by his presence and his words, puzzled by the feeling in the pits of their stomachs that spread through their beings as the story progressed. A feeling they could not yet put into words.

"You see," Simon said, "her dreams for the children kept her going and gave her hope. Visions of a better life for them beyond her own drudgery."

Katherine's face contorted in agony. Simon had done it. He'd told her story...her entire life. She felt no remaining doubt about that possibility. *How does he know? My name, my family, Samuel.* She took a step to run away, then hesitated. Running would draw unwanted attention. No. Best to stand very quietly and hope she blended in with the others. She forced herself to unclench her hands and realized she tasted blood from biting her lip.

She closed her eyes and took a deep breath. She could not bear the thought of continuing to endure listening to a stranger who knew and was telling every detail of her life. Katherine's hands involuntarily pressed against her mouth to keep from screaming at Simon to stop but knew it would only make things worse. If the others found out, they'd think she'd bewitched the man and stone her.

Katherine hugged her arms around herself, trying to muffle the sound of her pounding heart, hoping to dissolve into the ground. Her face drained of color. The air grew so thick she had difficulty breathing and the pounding in her ears increased. As her knees started to buckle, she caught hold of the person's arm next to her. Steadying herself, she could see the other woman's questioning eyes glinting in the semi-darkness and with great effort let go of the sturdy arm. With a weak apologetic smile, Katherine turned away before the woman got too close a look at her. Better there be no questions, for she had no answers.

Taking another deep breath, she ground her teeth and forced her hands down to her sides as the Storyteller continued his saga on the stage. She stood silently, rooted in place, reliving her life as it drifted about the room. Her legs shook and she visualized herself falling to the ground like a withered plant and crumbling away. What kind of sorcerer is this Simon? How can he know all these things? Her jaw tightened and her hands clenched back into white-knuckled fists. She used every ounce of willpower she possessed to stand still, but her eyes gave her away. They shone with the fervor of a caged animal waiting for the slaughter it knew must come.

Simon continued his narration. Her life was an open book to him. He knew her intimately, though he'd never met her before. For a moment, in a particularly touching passage extolling Katherine's many virtues, his eyes looked into the distance and, almost unawares, a look of tenderness stole across his face. Katherine. She was like a rare and priceless jewel he had only heard of but never seen. Her heart, her soul, her very essence were beautiful, precious, and to be cherished. A feeling of love washed over him and once again he could see a life with her.

The sensation surprised him and his breath caught as he stumbled over his next few words. In a rare moment of panic, he beat the feelings down, a mental hammer pounding sharp blows on the crystalline emotions. They shattered and disappeared, but the fragments cut him inside, jagged splinters working their way through his flesh.

Simon felt their lingering, aching pain. For the audience, the fleeting moment passed, virtually unnoticed. Just part of the story, and Simon was a true master at his craft. But Simon knew, as did a lone man with a lantern carefully watching from the back, exactly what damage was done in that brief moment.

The unwelcome feelings buried, Simon got back to work, his face now a smooth careful mask reflecting only the story. He would not make another mistake. He scrutinized the crowd, his eye movements quick and sharp. Ah yes, he knew them all. One look sufficed.

He observed the smiling woman in front, her drab clothes showing wear, but clean and worn contentedly. Off to the side stood a man and his young son, who had not yet grown into the clothing he wore. And then...Katherine. Flesh and bone folks who scraped together their coin to stand and listen. He told his stories for them.

Bringing his concentration back to the story in progress, Simon searched the back audience until he could see her scrunched figure once more. Yes, Katherine definitely knew his tale belonged to her. It was a relief to know she intended to remain. The possibility always existed during one of his performances that his subject could simply walk out. And the story wouldn't work if they didn't stay to hear it.

So far throughout his many appearances, he had managed to keep all his targets in place, though some required extra concentration. Tough ones he stared down with a look that chilled their bones, or if necessary, resorted to mental forces that simply did not allow them to leave. Eventually, all quit resisting and stayed. Fear of the power and knowledge he possessed did not allow them to do otherwise.

Simon smiled. Katherine had stayed. He'd shared her life up to that very point in time, but he would not stop there.

He knew she'd want to hear his surprise ending. *What a shock it must be,* he mused, *to have your future held out for all the world to see, like laundry strung along a rope.*

He presented the remainder of her tale. "Katherine's bright spirit and tenaciousness did not go unnoticed. A kindly physician in the town, who often made calls only to find his patients already well tended by the young lass, soon realized her great strength and intelligence. Discreet questioning revealed to him her station in life and the circumstances of her household. A chance encounter upon her return from an outing allowed him to find her disposition and temperament as sweet as he believed, and to see how she might react towards him. It was not long before he courted Katherine in earnest."

"The two wed and Katherine became his assistant. A well-suited couple, they shared years of joy and contentment in each other's company. The doctor cared for her family as his own, ensuring they had everything they needed. Her brothers and sister were formally educated and a good job secured for the older boy and a happy marriage for the girl. Her beloved brother, Samuel, grew up to study medicine under his brother-in-law and became a well-known and respected physician in his own right."

Simon sat back and smiled. "It would not surprise me if you soon all heard of a young lady like our Katherine." The smile faded and he stared earnestly at the crowd. "Then you will remember my words and know their truth. Faith is always rewarded."

The crowd murmured in appreciation. Simon allowed them a moment to mull over his statements, his eyes seeking out Katherine's. He needed to be sure she understood the gift he was giving her. He couldn't quite comprehend his concern, but it existed nonetheless. He located her in the back standing quite still, deep in thought. She appeared to be fine. His body relaxed slightly and his gaze moved on, resting briefly on the young boy and his father. He smiled again. A perfect pair. He sat forward and his audience hushed in anticipation.

"I once met a brave young lad blessed with good and loving parents. Hard workers, yet poor all the same. Bad luck seemed to live on their doorstep. Their chickens wouldn't lay eggs, their crops failed to produce, one unending tragedy after the other. But a stubborn lot, they kept trying long after others would have given up. His father's clothing had been mended so many times only patches remained. The boy, forced to wear britches much too large for him, had to tie them on with a cord of leather to keep them up..."

Over to the side, the young boy hitched up his pants and looked up at his father with wide eyes and open mouth. "Da. Is he talking about us, Da?"

His father pulled him close. "Hush, boy," he whispered, listening to the story. "I don't know what's going on, but let's not have finger-pointing. It sounds like us, but how can that be? It's a story, lad," he said. "Just a story."

"I don't know. But, Da? The first story ended good. If our story ends good, too, maybe that means things will be getting better."

"That's a fine thought, lad. I don't see how that can be, with your Mum hurt like she is. But it sure is a fine thought." Simon watched from the corner of his eye as the two straightened back up and stared at him expectantly. They were ready, if not eager, to hear whatever he had to say. He almost chuckled. This pair would definitely stay for the ending.

"That day turned out to be the hardest day they had yet faced. Not much was left to even try starting again, and the mother now lay in bed with a broken, twisted leg. The father arranged for a neighbor to look in and care for her as he made a trip into town to search for some work, or at least a chance to barter for food and help for his wife. He took the boy along, a good strong lad eager to help. In an attempt to cheer the young one, they entered a hall for an evening's entertainment."

"The night left them much refreshed and with reason to hope the bad luck had ended. And it was indeed done with them. By the time they arrived home, a miracle had occurred. The mother greeted them at their door with many tears of joy and thanksgiving, her leg twisted no more. The following morning brought fresh eggs from the hens and milk from the goats. In the fields, green shoots thrived where only barren land had lain before. The family was more than saved, they prospered, their faith rewarded."

A sudden flurry of activity took place at the side of the stage. Simon smiled as the boy dashed quickly from the hall, his father close behind. At the door the father paused and looked back at Simon with a grin, tipping his flat cap in thanks.

Dipping his head slightly in return, Simon's gaze shifted and settled upon the woman standing in the front. His eyes glistened in anticipation. Looking around the room at his audience, he began his next story.

"This is the tale of a loving, faithful wife. As in our earlier story, her husband had also been called into the King's service a few years past and she had not heard from him since. Most thought he had been killed in some distant land, though no word ever came to clearly state that as truth. Years passed, yet the faithful wife refused to give up hope. Each night she lit a candle and placed it near the window, hoping its light would lead her husband home to her."

"It became a joke of sorts. People laughed at her foolishness. If not dead, they claimed, then he had run away with a new love. The wife only smiled and went about her work. She knew her husband, and she knew the love they shared to be true. Whatever kept him from her would someday end and he would return."

"Although usually a cheerful and content woman, a day came when the burden became almost too much to bear. She longed desperately for her husband, but her neighbors had almost convinced her she waited in vain. In an effort to escape her pain, she went to an inn to listen to the entertainment. The respite worked, for as the evening wore on she could smile again and hold her head high."

"Her faith renewed, she went home and lit the candle one more time. That very night a man appeared at her door. So thin and ragged and dust covered she barely recognized him until she looked deep into his tired eyes and saw her husband. He had been held captive in a foreign land, sick and starving, waiting for an opportunity to escape. Once free, he traveled the vast distance mostly by foot, thinking only he must return to his love."

Simon's voice dropped to a hush. "Such a joyous homecoming you have never seen. Theirs was a deep and abiding love, the kind most folks only dream about." He paused for a moment looking distractedly towards the back of the room. With a sharp intake of breath, he returned to the story. "She never stopped believing and her faith was rewarded."

He looked down at the woman in front. She stood with her head high, a trembling smile, and a face wet with tears. In a soft voice Simon finished, "After all her years of waiting, she had only to go home and light that candle one more time. Faith is always rewarded." He nodded encouragingly at her and she smiled at him in triumph. *She understands*, he thought. *She will light her candle one last time...tonight.*

With a quick movement, Simon stood up. He was done with his stories for the night. Down the steps and through the blue mist, he strode towards the back of the hall as jugglers took over the stage. Nearly there, he stopped and looked to the right. Directly where Katherine stood with pounding heart and sweaty palms. Fearfully, she raised her wide eyes to look into his narrowed ones. Her hand moved to her throat and fluttered there for a moment before settling to rest on the cross she wore.

"Simon says, remember my words. Faith is always rewarded." His voice was very quiet and gentle, for her ears alone.

Like that brief moment on stage, love seemed to radiate from him. Katherine's brow smoothed and her heart quieted. The fear vanished almost of its own will, leaving anticipation and joy in its stead. Yes, he spoke the truth, she realized in wonderment. What other explanation could there be for what had happened that night? She believed him. Everything he said. Katherine believed it all, though she couldn't say exactly why.

She was mesmerized by his eyes as if she could see the heart of him in their blue depths. Kindness, sadness, love, longing, beauty, and something more...indefinable. The urge to go to him, hold him, comfort him became almost overwhelming. He loved her. It would be so easy to love him back. Yet, Katherine also saw within him a barrier. Something held him apart from her. Her instincts told her no matter what they might each feel for the other, they could never be together. Whether it was fate or destiny, something else pulled Simon away.

He must go on alone. But she, because of his gift, because he wanted her to have love and a good life and to be taken care of, she would have everything. Another love waited for her. It would have to be enough. A smile spread across her face and she gave him a tiny nod.

Simon tilted his head slightly in return. He closed his

eyes briefly, feeling all her thoughts and desires. He wavered a moment thinking his heart would shatter. Why was this happening? How was it happening? He loved her and she returned that love. How could he live with knowing what he had to walk away from? It was almost more than he could bear. With a great wave of his cape, he turned away. In the next blink of an eye he vanished, the blue light fading as quickly as the story shapes that hurried after their master.

Complete silence befell the hall as all eyes strained to see through the mist that suddenly thickened at Simon's departure. A cold draft soon dissipated the cloud and as if on cue the people surged, voice and body, into an exclamation of surprise and wonderment.

"Could the stories be true? Are there such people?" asked an older lady.

"Of course they're true," answered another woman. "My aunt knows someone who's heard wonderful things from another town Simon stopped at. Somewhere soon, this Katherine and the others will have their miracles." She beamed at the thought of the blessings that would be coming.

"I'm sure I saw the boy and his father. They arrived in town yesterday afternoon," a voice said.

"I know Katherine." called out a man. "I'm sure I know the young woman. I pass her in town almost every day."

"Yes, yes...I've seen her too. She helped an old man who fell in the street."

"I saw her this very morning, standing in front of the bread shop."

The tide of voices rose quickly into a frenzy as each tried to assert their claims on her existence.

Amid the cacophony, Katherine quietly and with determination picked her way through the crowd. The woman whose sturdy arm she had grasped looked thoughtfully after her, sudden recognition and understanding answering the questions in her eyes. She looked around at the noisy crowd, shaking her head slowly, and watched silently as Katherine made her way to the door. Katherine glanced back and caught the woman staring at her, knowing instantly she was found out. Just as quickly, she knew her secret was safe. Smiling, she blew the woman a grateful kiss and escaped the hall.

Simon's story had to be true. He couldn't feel that way about her and not have the story be true. She would make sure to be worthy of his gift and live a life that honored it. Katherine wanted it so badly she could taste the flavor of it in her mouth. No longer to be a drudge. A future for her family. Such an impossible dream yet so close within her grasp. If only the story could come true. She would work very hard to help the doctor cure and care for people. It would still be taxing work but it would not be drudgery.

She repeated the words in her mind over and over, *please let it be true, please let it be true. Simon's story must come to pass.* Part of her eagerly awaited the foretold meeting, yet a persuasive voice persistently intruded with words of gloom. Fairy tales didn't come true. Desperately she cast the doubt away. *It must come true.* She had to believe, she wanted to believe. What else did she have to look forward to? She paused then, remembering the emotions pulsing from Simon. He loved her. To her memory they had never met, yet she knew the passion emanating from him as well as she knew her own feelings.

He loved her, yet he sent her to another man. She could only believe he did so to ensure she would be well taken care of. Simon would not be cruel to her. The story would come true.

The doctor Simon spoke of must be a wonderful man. Not only would he want her, but her grandfather and the children, as well. With his help, she could properly take care of them all And Samuel. She lifted her head and gave a quiet chuckle of pleasure. Her very own Samuel a physician, too. She never dared hope for so much.

Katherine turned down the narrow street that led to her cottage and walked right into a gentleman approaching the corner. He steadied her, then swept his hat off in a polite gesture.

"Your pardon, Miss."

"I'm so sorry, Sir. I wasn't paying any attention. Please forgive my clumsiness." Her cheeks flushed with embarrassment.

The gentleman looked a bit flushed himself, nervously shifting from one foot to the other. "I should be the one apologizing. It was entirely my fault. I am Dr. John Torrence," he gave a small bow with the introduction. "I hope I haven't caused you any discomfort, Miss...?

Katherine gave a start and looked closely at him, her eyes wide in amazement. "Miss...Peterson. Katherine Peterson." She curtsied in return.

"Ah, Miss Peterson. I believe I've heard your name before. I understand you tend the sick most admirably."

Katherine found it difficult to keep her mouth from falling open. She snapped it shut and swallowed hard, barely squeaking out a reply. "Thank you, Dr. Torrence. I do my best."

"I happen to be down this way because of your neighbor, Mistress Wainwright. Her baby is due any day and she's having some difficulty moving about. If it's not too presumptuous, would you consider checking in on her tomorrow morning? I'll be over by midday."

"Certainly. I don't mind at all. I've been helping her here and there as I could, anyways."

"Thank you. I can't seem to be everywhere I need." He

shook his head sadly. "Seems there's more and more sickness going around."

Katherine felt her heart pounding. Could this be mere coincidence? What were the chances such a meeting would occur on this very night? It had to be Simon's story. Her legs quivered and her knees felt weak again, but she forced herself to speak calmly. "I have my own family to care for, but if you need assistance, I'm sure I could help a bit."

Dr. Torrence's face brightened as he smiled. "Could you really? That would be wonderful. Of course, I'll try not to take too much of your time, but anything is greatly appreciated. This was a most fortunate meeting, Miss Peterson." He glanced around at the darkening surroundings. "It's quite late in the day. I don't like the idea of letting you continue on alone. May I escort you home?"

"I don't live much farther from here. I wouldn't want to trouble you when you're already on your way home." Her words protested, but she could feel her heart racing and her skin tingling at the very thought of walking along with him.

"I must insist then. If you're willing to give of your time to my cause, I can surely spare a few minutes of my time to see you home safely." He held his elbow out to her. "Shall we?"

Katherine gave another small curtsy then took his elbow with a smile. A shiver ran through her as her hand made contact with his arm.

"Are you cold, Miss? Shall I give you my coat?

"No, I'm fine. Thank you." She pretended to adjust her cloak. "It slipped a bit."

They continued on to Katherine's house, making small talk of herbs and medicine and the good work of caring for people. When they reached her door Dr. Torrence took her hand and kissed it lightly. The twinkle in his eyes as he smiled at her was easy to see in the rising moonlight.

Katherine felt her skin tingling again.

"I'll stop by tomorrow when I look in on Mistress Wainwright if that's agreeable to you."

"Indeed, Dr. Torrence. I look forward to it."

He tipped his hat again. "Goodnight then, Miss Peterson. Until tomorrow." Whistling, he walked into the night.

Katherine stared after him, her mind awhirl in thoughts. It wasn't a coincidence. Simon had told the truth. She clasped the cross at her throat and looked up at the stars, whispering a prayer of thanks before entering her home.

She quietly slipped in the door, her thoughts still focused on Simon. What was happening now, the new life unfolding before her, was all because of him. She hung up her cloak and leaned against the wall, eyes closed and a smile on her face. It was a rare man who could step away from his own love in order to ensure a better life for his beloved. A good and wise man. She would never forget what Simon had done for her and her family. If there was ever a chance to cross paths again, she wanted to thank him face to face and let him know how honored and grateful she was. One day, after she and Dr. Torrence were married, she wanted her family to know of this miracle, too.

CHAPTER TWO

THE carriage was waiting beside the hall as Simon rushed out. He climbed in quickly, his weight causing the vehicle to sway and creak in protest. He settled into his seat with a weary sigh of relief, roughly massaging his temples.

"Now, Marcus. Let us go before they come thundering out, pushing and pulling and pleading with me to save their respective lives."

Marcus quickly stowed away a lantern and placed a large blue crystal into the pouch he carried at his waist. Unlike any stone he had ever seen, it always amazed him to see the eerie blue glow it cast when he held it to the lantern during Simon's performances. Marcus had asked Simon about the stone. More than once, in fact. But Simon always gave him an odd look and muttered about distant times and old friends and promptly changed the subject, as he did when asked about the bag of powder that made the mist. More secrets to heap on top of this mystery called Simon. Although technically his servant, Marcus and Simon had long been friends. Yet for all they shared, Simon still kept many secrets locked away.

But no time to ponder. Marcus jumped onto the driver's seat and snapped the reins. The carriage jerked forward. They hurried down the road and made a turn as people began pouring from the building. Like so many ants, they hurried here and there searching for the Seer. Simon didn't look back. He had escaped once more.

He removed his hat and settled back into the soft leather seat of his coach. Almost involuntarily, his eyes closed. *These appearances are so damned tiring,* he thought. To a certain extent they had always been so, but the years wore on and on, and decades passed into centuries, and now he could feel a difference in how the use of his powers affected him. He shifted in his seat, weariness seeping into his bones. On other days like this, he had let himself imagine what it would have been like to live as other men do. To be born, live his few years as best he could, love and be loved, and then be laid to rest in his grave. Maybe even have children to mourn over his passing. But, not today.

Simon felt again the sharp pains that had come during his story. Katherine. *Why did I ever choose you for my tale? If I'd only known the feelings you would bring to life in me, I would have passed you by. But, no.* He shook his head. *That wouldn't have been fair to you, Katherine. You are so beautiful and strong and brave. You deserved every good thing in life I could think of for you. Even if that life can't include me.*

He sighed loudly, his hand pressing against his chest, trying to push away the odd pain he felt there. Katherine. She was exactly the kind of woman he would have wanted to spend his life with. When he looked at her and saw the gentleness of her soul and the beauty of her spirit, he understood for the first time the meaning of love. For him it meant pain. Pain and longing for the unreachable, throughout all of time.

Simon forced a smile that barely touched his lips. It could have been wonderful. They could have shared such joy together. He paused and the smile faded. It could never be, so best not to dwell on it. Why nurture a pain he had no power to heal? This was his life. He had accepted that from the start. He must accept it now.

Simon's course had been chosen from the beginning. His beginning. Their ending. He had been honored and touched by their sacrifice. Their lives for his. Although a young man at the time, he possessed great wisdom. Still, he had not seen what they saw. Now as he recalled the sadness in their eyes, he understood. The greatest sacrifice was his. He had the gift. Or, the curse, depending on which way you looked at it. Through the years he went on. He could not ignore the gift. It would not let him ignore it.

So indeed, one look sufficed. One look and he knew more than he wanted to know...a past, a future, the essence of a soul. He saw their joys and tragedies, all the tiny threads and knots that made up the fabric of their lives. And if he so wished it, he could tie a knot here or move a thread there, and a life changed forever. Whatever Simon said, they lived.

His life alone could not be touched.

"Excuse me, Simon." The voice gently prodded him from his reverie. Simon's eyes opened to see Marcus looking back at him. "I am sorry to disturb you, but we're getting close on to the tavern. You'd best change into your everyday cloak now."

Simon smiled. "Thank you, Marcus. What would I do without you to assist me?"

"Work yourself harder than you already do, I don't doubt. Keep up this pace and you'll put yourself into an early grave."

"An early grave, Marcus?" Simon shook his head with a sad chuckle. "No, I'm afraid there is no early grave for me. I shall be telling my stories for a long, long time yet."

Marcus looked back again, puzzled, a question ready to escape his lips. He hesitated as he watched Simon's sad face, then turned slowly to the front. He would save his questions until later. What happened on stage tonight hurt Simon badly. Marcus had seen the pain, despite how well he covered it up. He rubbed his chin, wishing he could think of some way to help.

Inside the coach, Simon took off his tall hat and great cape and folded them up on his lap. He turned in his seat and removed the back portion of leather to reveal a hidden compartment. From within it, he took out an ordinary-looking cloak and plain brown hat, refilling the vacancy with his distinctive stage attire.

Sneaking glances over his shoulder, Marcus observed this regular ritual of change from awe-inspiring to ordinary with the same amazement he always felt. "Simon, I find it unbelievable that with such a simple change of appearance, you become virtually invisible to everyone you meet. Once out of costume, people ignore you. They walk by you on the street without so much as a glance in your direction, when only hours before they clamored at your feet. I always wondered how that can be?"

"It's really very easy to explain, Marcus. The people who come to hear Simon don't see me either. They see a great, wise sorcerer in a pointed hat and sweeping cape. A very vivid image. If they look for Simon on the streets, it's that image they search for. Not an ordinary man in a plain cloak and hat who looks like a dozen other fellows. Therefore, I appear and disappear as if by magic. If I'm lucky, in between I have a few blessed moments of peace."

Marcus gave him a worried look as he pulled to a stop in front of their night's lodging. Simon often had low spells, but he hadn't been this melancholy for quite some time. Marcus had watched him avoid relationships and push people away for years. He knew him better than anyone, but even he had reached a wall in their friendship that couldn't be breached. Somehow, this Katherine seemed to have touched Simon's very core. The raw wound she left would not heal easily.

"Go in and get settled, Simon. I'll be in with the bags as soon as I stable the horses."

"You'll find me by the fire, Marcus. I'll order our dinner. Come along when you're able."

Marcus is a good fellow, Simon thought as he stepped out of the carriage. *I'm lucky to have found him.* It was so much easier when one had a companion of sorts. At least for a while, he could share a portion of his existence, though he dared not share too much.

Simon entered the tavern through a creaking door and found himself in a silent common room. He enjoyed his peace and quiet, but to find a common room of that description was unusual. He beckoned a nicely dressed man in an apron who barely came up to his armpits. "Good evening, Innkeeper. Two rooms for the night, please, and bring us some supper and ale by the fire."

"By all means, Sir." The short, plump man who bore the title of Innkeep hovered anxiously by Simon. "First, Sir, I must ask you...mind, if it were only me I wouldn't bother, but the Missus, Sir. Well, Sir, the Missus will be wanting to see your money first, Sir. I hope you take no offense, Sir. The Missus has her reasoning, Sir; she don't mean nothing by it."

Simon had several pouches attached to his belt and

more well buried elsewhere. They contained enough wealth for a frugal man to live on for hundreds of years. He pulled out a smaller bag that contained coins of English currency and handed the trembling man a few. "I trust this will keep the 'Missus' happy."

"Yes, Sir. Thank you, Sir. She'll be most pleased, Sir."

"Good." Simon paused and looked intently at the cowering man. The Innkeeper's life story unfolded in Simon's mind. It was no wonder the room stayed so quiet. Obviously, this reflected the effect the 'Missus' had on folks. No one dared breathe a word in this place. The uncomfortable atmosphere discouraged business, and Simon knew the short man and his Missus were sad and unhappy people.

"I recall a story I want to share with you. I once knew an Innkeep. Went by the name of George."

The Innkeeper's head snapped up and his eyes opened wide. "G...George, you say?"

"Yes," Simon replied. "George. A good sort, though a bit timid. A large part had to do with his loud, overbearing wife. He had no peace in his house; his days filled with the dread of upsetting her. Despite her attitude, he still loved her, for the memory of what she used to be had not died within him. One day he decided he could not go on as he had. Life being too short, he wanted to share it with a wife who loved and respected him."

The Innkeeper's eyes stayed wide and unblinking, his head nodding in amazed agreement.

"That very same day, he confronted her. He stood up for himself and decided he would not let her browbeat him any longer. When his wife saw George meant what he said, she relaxed and let him take charge. It seems all along she really wanted him to take enough interest in her to stand up to her. Their love blossomed anew and their inn flourished because of the peace and tranquility found there."

Simon smiled down at the wide-eyed rotund man who, so shocked, forgot to tremble. "Nice story, don't you think? Why don't you go see the Missus about my dinner now."

"Yes, Sir. I'll be right out with your food, Sir." Nodding, the man walked away, sneaking puzzled glances over his shoulder.

Behind a far door, a woman's voice thundered. "George! Where have you gone to, you lazy good-for-nothin'? Get back in this kitchen now, George."

The short timid man paused like a bird ready to take flight. Once more he looked back at Simon, emotions fighting for a place to settle on his face. Suddenly, he squared his shoulders and, walking taller than he had in years, marched into the kitchen.

"Missus, you and me are going to have a talk. There are a few things I want to set straight around here."

His wife looked up at him in surprise, then her eyes narrowed angrily. "Don't you be talking that way to me. Who do you think you are?"

George didn't back down. He stuck out his chin and looked her in the eye. "I'm your husband, Elsbeth. Things are going to be different around here. No more yellin'. From now on we talk, not holler, you hear? You treat me with respect. I will still listen to you, as long as you listen back. We work this Inn together. We share this life. Understand? So from now on we will act kindly to one another."

Elsbeth planted her hands on her bony hips and moved closer. She stood a good four inches taller than George, making it easy to look down on him. "Is that so? Why should I?" she growled.

"Because I said so. I love you, Elsbeth, but I won't put up with any more of this hollerin' and orderin' me around like I'm a hired stableman. It stops now. I mean it, Elsbeth." His knees quivered slightly, but he held his ground.

His wife looked taken aback. She paused for a moment, thinking. "I believe you do," she answered slowly, giving him an appraising look. She took another step closer, a sudden earnestness in her eyes. "What else did you say? Besides the yellin' part."

"I said I love you, Elsbeth."

She seemed to melt in front of him as a tear slid from the corner of one eye. "Do you really, George? Do you love me?"

"Oh, Elsbeth," he smiled, "I always have."

"I love you, too, George." She folded her arms around him, bending her head to rest near his shoulder. "I'll try so hard, George. Wait and see. I can make you happy. I promise I'll make you happy."

"We'll make each other happy, love."

Simon shook his head as he watched the kitchen door close behind the Innkeep, then made his way over to one of the smaller tables. He could not begrudge his fate. Lives changed for the better tonight because of what he had done. He could not even count the numbers he had touched over the many, many years. He had accomplished much good.

Even so, the questions always haunted him. *Is it enough? Do I choose the right people? Do I make the right changes?* He sat down heavily, his shoulders sagging, his hands covering his face. The world had so many deserving out there, why had he been chosen to pick them out? Who was he to be making these choices for them? He found the questions disturbing, even more so for the fact he had no answers.

"And there is no one to ask," Simon murmured.

"Ask what?" Marcus queried as he took the seat opposite.

Simon sat up abruptly. "Ask when they might get some food in front of these tired, hungry men. Innkeeper," he called out. "We are awaiting your service."

Promptly, George arrived and presented the Missus. The beaming woman smiled broadly at them, setting tankards of ale on the table. "Be sure they don't run out of this here ale," he said, "and get two big plates of that fine cooking of yours for them."

"Oh, to be sure. Just as you say, George." With a wink at her husband, she scurried back to the kitchen for their food. George adjusted his coat and, looking very content, sauntered casually away.

"Simon, you've been telling tales again."

"Whatever makes you say that, Marcus."

"Because whenever you tell a story someone's walking around with this strange happy grin, you're ready for a nap, and your eyes," he paused. "Your eyes..."

"What about my eyes," asked Simon quickly, his face now a guarded mask.

"I don't rightly know, but I can see something...an odd lightness...in your eyes. It only happens when you've told a story." Marcus studied Simon, trying to look deep into his soul's windows. The mask was thorough, however, and Simon's shielded eyes no longer revealed anything. Marcus gazed down and smiled. "What do you do, anyways? Entrance them or cast a spell of some sort?"

Simon sat back with a chuckle. "Neither. Let's say I give very powerful suggestions."

"To be sure. I've seen some marvelous things during my time with you. What's it been, twenty years?" Marcus shook his head. "Whew, that's quite a long time roaming."

"Is it? Twenty years a long time? Well, I suppose it must seem like that to you. You were all of fourteen when we joined up. Are you tired of the life, lad?" Simon leaned close to his friend's dark head. He had tried often, but he never could see the boy's life. The threads bound them too closely, Marus' life too intertwined with his own. To change Marcus' life would affect his own and so, it could not be done.

"I never said you had to spend your entire life with me. If it's time to settle down in a cottage and find a good woman, you're free to go, Marcus. With my blessings and enough to live comfortably on for years. You've been a good friend and a faithful companion."

The two pairs of blue eyes locked on each other...one narrowed in concern, one opened wide in surprise.

The Missus appeared again, bearing two heavy plates piled high with thick slices of fragrant mutton and steaming vegetables. More than enough for two hungry men. She maneuvered the plates onto the table, pausing as if to comment. Seeing the intent look on the men's faces, she thought better of her words and hurried away.

Marcus' mind raced. He knew the evening upset Simon, but he hadn't expected this. The man offered him the opportunity to have the very thing Simon wanted most, but would never have. Why? For the chance to see one of them have a happy home life? Did he think of finally ending his storytelling days and had no more use for him? Or did he simply feel guilty? Simon had sacrificed everything because the life he led required it. In traveling with him, Marcus had made the sacrifices as well. No home, no wife, no family. Just him and Simon.

The thoughts made Marcus pause, and he considered again his past choices and the future that lay before him. Simon sensed his friend's contemplations and awaited Marcus' decision with trepidation. His hands wanted to clench, but he forced them to lie still upon the table. *What do I do if Marcus chooses to go,* he thought.

When younger, Marcus actually had dreamed of finding a loving wife, raising some strapping young lads, and maybe a dainty lass or two. After all, this had been simply a position at the beginning. A way to have a roof over his head, food in his belly, some coin in his pocket, and a bit of adventure to boot. He could have left at any time. Truthfully, he had considered it on lonely nights when he had no home to go to, only another room at another Inn. A look of joyful welcome, a glowing hearthside, gleeful cries of 'Papa, Papa', and a woman's warm embrace proved inviting thoughts.

But some men's destinies led them down other paths. As he came to know Simon and understand the task he had set upon, Marcus found fulfillment in accomplishing this 'greater good', as he now thought of it. He belonged here with Simon. It didn't erase the occasional longing or regret, emotions the two of them would always have in common, but Marcus found contentment with his choice. He'd had a good life with many joys and he'd seen many miracles. Very few men could say that. And he'd certainly had his adventures.

Simon was no ordinary man. Saint or sorcerer, Marcus couldn't be sure, but he had powers and knowledge unknown to earthly beings. Sometimes, Marcus could feel the immense raw energy barely contained in the fragile wrappings of this person he called friend. Simon could have done anything with that power, but he had chosen to reward the good and kind souls of mankind. Marcus smiled softly. Could there be a better life, after all, than helping a miracle worker? To be an integral part of this wondrous 'greater good'?

His focus shifted back to the man sitting opposite and he started in surprise. Simon's face was white with tension. "Simon...I didn't mean to imply I wanted to leave." Marcus groped for words, flustered now. "I appreciate your concern and generosity, but if you've no objections, I'd just as soon keep things the way they are."

Simon leaned back, relieved. "Of course I've no objections, lad. I simply wanted to be sure you were content with your choice." Silently, the storyteller willed his pounding heart to settle down. He had, indeed, become attached to the boy; though really a boy no longer. To be honest, he was even dependent on Marcus to help fill the void that loomed in his soul. Seldom had he been lucky enough to find such a person.

Marcus took a swig of ale and braced himself. "Simon, are you going to be all right? About Katherine?"

Simon looked at him with wide eyes. "How did you know?"

"I have been your servant and friend for twenty years. You may hide many things from me yet, but you can't hide it all. I know you well enough to be able to see your pain. I recognize it because I have felt it myself."

Simon glanced down and murmured softly. "I can never have Katherine or anyone like her. I made the choice for this life of mine. I will deal with the consequences of that choice." His jaw tightened and he looked up again, his expression firm. "Some things are better left alone, and this is one of them. Katherine is in the past already and I am fine. There is still much work to be done and that is where my focus lies."

"Indeed, Simon." Marcus knew it best not to continue. Another time perhaps, when the ache had dulled. Better to talk of other things now and let Simon's mind get some distance from his pain. He pulled a moist piece of mutton off the plate in front of him, chewing thoughtfully as he pondered. "I've often wondered, Simon, why you can't see my life as you see others. Or have you seen it and you're afraid to tell me?" He shook the piece of meat at Simon and chuckled.

"No, Marcus," Simon answered quickly, grateful for the change of subject, "yours is one of the few lives I've been unable to see. We, like it or not, have to take our lives as they come. Manage things as they happen." He seemed to notice the food in front of him for the first time and began eating.

"Well, so far it hasn't been too bad, has it?"

Simon reached over and patted the other man's shoulder. "No, my friend. These past twenty years in particular haven't been too bad at all."

"Do you remember the day we met?" Marcus shook his head in amusement. "It was right here in London on Candlewick Street. I came flying out of the candlemaker's shop and landed right at your feet."

Simon laughed as he motioned the Innkeeper for more ale. "Flying because of a kick in the seat of your pants, as I recall."

"Beeswax everywhere. I spilled the whole damn kettle. Not a very good start for a candlemaker's apprentice."

"But it provided an excellent opportunity for me."

"Right," Marcus laughed. "You looked straight down at me without even blinking an eye. 'Will you be needing a job?' you asked."

"And you said, 'May I start this very minute? I seem to have no fire in me for candlesticks.'" Simon choked out the words, his face red with laughter.

"Seems I got here at the right time, good Sirs," George said, holding up the pitcher in his hands as he approached. He filled their mugs to the brim, then set the pitcher down heavily. "Why don't I be leavin' this here so you can help yourselves. Plenty more where this come from. Is the supper pleasin' to you? The Missus, she's always been a good cook."

"Excellent repast. Very tasty," chorused the men patting their filling bellies.

"Ah, the Missus will be so happy to hear it. You must be tryin' some of her bread pudding next. Best in the County, they say." George walked back to the kitchen, calling out as he went. "Missus, my love. I'll be having two bowls of your best bread pudding out here."

"Yes, my dearest George. Right away."

Marcus leaned back, a serious look on his face. "That, Simon," he motioned towards the kitchen door, "is what makes these years of roaming worthwhile. I doubt I'll ever understand how you make it happen, but happen it does, and I guess the how isn't so important. Not too many people in life have a chance to be witness to the miracles I've seen with you."

"You think I've done good, then? Picked the right people, set the right paths? Do you think I've done the right things?" Simon leaned forward intently, his brow creased.

"Most definitely. One man can only do so much, Simon. You couldn't possibly reach every deserving person on this earth. But the ones you have reached are good people who will do good things. And others will benefit through them. Your stories are like the drop of rain that falls into a puddle. After it splashes in, we can see the rings of its influence spread out until the whole puddle has been affected. You reach so many more than the person whose story you tell. The entire community benefits. You have done the right things, my friend." Marcus looked at Simon and smiled. He had made the right decision himself. A few sacrifices were worth being part of this greater good.

A shadow seemed to pass from Simon's face as he whispered, "Thank you."

By the time the pink in the sky had turned golden yellow with the rising of the sun, the carriage waited at the front gate. Two men approached it from the tavern. The younger man, still the servant, carried the bags with a smile. He had a good life and no real regrets for accepting this position so many years ago. The older man, still the master, walked straighter and with a lighter step than he had arrived with the previous night. His regrets, for the present, lay at rest and his heart warmed with the thought he truly had a friend to depend on. For a few more years at least.

CHAPTER THREE

TIME passed swiftly for Marcus, like the fleeting life of a moth compelled to throw itself into the irresistible flame. His twenty years with Simon had grown to more than fifty. A happy old man, with a sprinkling of white hair and blue eyes that sparkled, he found pleasure in each new day.

"Ah, Simon." Marcus breathed in deeply as the two walked along a village street together. "Isn't it a glorious day? I think this is one of the most amiable villages we've stayed in. Good food, comfortable lodgings, and friendly folks." He smiled at a passing gentleman who bobbed his head respectfully to him. A deference to age, for Simon now appeared the younger of the two.

"Should I be jealous?" Simon asked with a smile of his own.

"Jealous?" Marcus laughed. "Why? Are there hordes of

young lassies following me?" He stopped and looked quizzically about. "Horsefeathers. They're gone already. Young things move much too quickly for an old man like me."

"No, no," Simon chuckled back. "I'm referring to all this bowing and scraping you receive. I'm supposed to be the great sorcerer, but I'm lucky to get a 'good day' from someone."

"That's because I'm a kindly old gentleman, and you're merely some young pup."

"A pup?" Simon stopped abruptly. "I...am a pup?"

Marcus turned and eyed him. "Well, look at yourself. I've acquired dignity, refinement, and white hair. I think you must be running backwards." He peered closer at Simon's face. "Don't think you're old enough to even have whiskers anymore."

Simon pulled himself up straight. "You know very well I am your elder, Marcus. I deserve some respect at least from you. And I do too have whiskers. However, I'm very skilled with a blade from my many years of experience." He rubbed his chin and leaned close to his friend, a mischievous twinkle in his eye as he whispered. "I shaved long before your existence even began to be contemplated."

"And how long would that be?" Marcus whispered loudly back. "Fifty years? One hundred? Five hundred? How old are you?" He put a hand to his ear playfully. "Speak up, I'm a deaf old man."

"Shhh." Simon looked nervously at the other people on the street. "Someone could hear you."

Marcus laughed. "Hah! Who would listen? They'll think I'm not only deaf but daft, as well. Another babbling old man.

"Have you forgotten already? You're the kindly old gentleman they all respect and bow to. Of course they'd listen to you. My, you really must be getting old." He shook his head in mock sadness.

Marcus looked at him casually out of the corner of his eyes. "So, how old did you say you were?"

"I didn't, and you should know better than to ask." Simon wagged a finger at him.

"Is there no way to catch you off your guard?" Marcus sighed. "I did manage once..."

"It was a simple mistake," Simon said quickly. He picked up the pace of his steps, forcing Marcus to do a half-jog to keep pace.

"I enticed you to say you had been in France...," he paused his speech to take some deep breaths.

"Many people have traveled to France. We have even been to France."

"In 1502?"

Simon shrugged. "There's nothing special about that year."

Marcus put a hand on Simon's shoulder to slow him down, panting. "It's over...one hundred and fifty years ago."

"A mathematical error," Simon scowled as he slowed to a stop. "It'll never happen again."

"Well," Marcus mused, hands on his hips as he caught his breath, "didn't you mention another time..."

Simon threw up his hands. "That's quite enough, young man. You should be old enough to start forgetting these things by now." He ignored the odd stare of a woman passing by. "You're not going to trick me into saying anything more, you hear? You know far more about me than you should already. Aren't you tired of asking me questions after all these years?"

"Not half as tired as you are of sidestepping them. Pup." Marcus smiled and sauntered into their tavern.

He would have liked more answers, obviously. But

Marcus had long ago learned to live with the questions because he believed himself to be the closest connection to one of the few enchanted beings to ever walk the earth. Many nights he sat in his tavern room faithfully recording the day's events, hoping his words would someday pay tribute to his master's greatness.

Several months and many towns later, they once again entered a quaint new village. As a practice, Simon found it best to be well out of reach before people realized his stories came true, always rushing off to the next destination. He paid the new Innkeeper and the men each went to their new rooms. Simon placed his leather bag on the bed and settled into the uncomfortable wooden chair next to it. The difficulty of always being on the move weighed heavily on him. Never able to get too comfortable for too long. It tended to make the soul weary.

Simon leaned his head into his hands, thoughts plaguing him like mosquitoes. He gave everything. His whole life he gave and gave. What did he ever get in return? Not even a simple 'thank you.' Maybe a little head nod here and there. He paused, his hand moving to his chest, searching for an object hidden beneath the fabric. His fingers closed around a small worn cross. There had been one thank you. A smile flitted across his face, chased away by a scowl. A cold cross held scant comfort on a lonely night.

He yanked the gift free of his neck and threw it onto the bed. It glinted there dully, a symbol of the giver and the creator. Both beyond his reach. Simon stood up and paced to the window. He stared at the heavens, pain etched on his face.

"I know you're out there. I have seen enough things in my life to know you are there. Why won't you show yourself to me? I have worked so hard. My miracles benefit you as much as them. Why can't I find you? You're like the fading scent of perfume. I know where you've been. I can find the traces of your passing. But I can never find you."

He pushed away from the window with a wry smile. Another cruel twist of fate. He could not be with the creator, nor with the created. He dangled somewhere between. Enticed by both. Closed off from both. Trapped by his own choice, freely and naively given.

At the end of the hall Marcus, too, paced his room restlessly. The tempo of their travel had picked up recently. They moved around constantly. He felt on edge, and Marcus knew if it had grown difficult for him, it was more so for Simon. Simon, who seemed to have no beginning, and possibly no ending. He would recommend they stay put for a while. A holiday, so to speak. God knows they could both use one.

He could see Simon sagging into another of his low periods. Marcus knew the signs very well. It never stopped him from telling his stories, but it took more out of him. Marcus gritted his teeth in concern. He sat down, his fingers drumming on his knee. What could he do? How could he ease the building tension?

His reverie ended as a knock sounded at the door. Before he could speak Simon walked in, his face a smooth, controlled mask. He walked past Marcus and warmed his hands at the fire.

"How are you, Simon?"

"I am well, thank you. Very well." Simon shrugged but did not turn to face his friend.

"Yes, I can see that." Marcus stood and joined him at the fire. Maybe drawing him out in conversation would be good.

"Have you never done a story with an unhappy ending, Simon? In all our years together, I don't believe I've ever heard one."

"I've been tempted many times, believe me. But I took a

sacred oath years ago. My mission has been to reward the good, not punish the bad. There is One greater than I who will take care of them at the ending of time."

"So. After all these years, I find you do believe in God. Why haven't you told me this before?"

"I don't recall your asking before," Simon answered dryly. "You've asked about almost everything else, but not that. However, yes. I do believe in a Higher Power. If I've learned anything these many years, it is the fact we are not here through an accident of nature. There is One we call Be'al, the source of all beings, who stands over us all. I have seen their handiwork." Simon turned away, deep longing in his whisper. "But search as I may, I cannot see them."

"I used to think you were him, back in the early years," Marcus smiled. "It took a long time before I realized your stories weren't about religion. They were simply about hope. A simple message to keep folks going and make life better." Shaking his head, Marcus mused, "Though you didn't turn out to be him, you're really not one of us either."

A flash of pain crossed Simon's face. Marcus saw the shadow and hurried his words on.

"I mean, you aren't ordinary like us. You're special, like a wizard. You're a messenger, bringing peace and goodwill."

"Peace for whom!" Simon thundered. "Where's my peace? Is the messenger never allowed to see his Master? I am not man; I am not God. What am I then? Where do I belong? When will there be peace for me?" Simon strode past Marcus and out the door.

Left alone, Marcus quietly sat on the edge of the chair. He had not seen this side of Simon in all their time together. He understood great pressures rested on Simon because of whom, or what, he was. He couldn't begin to comprehend everything, but he understood more than Simon realized. He had seen the brooding, the searching, the constant questioning. He had worried through great depressions with him and rejoiced at the triumph of stories come true. Good or bad times, an air of sadness always existed around Simon, reflecting some great loss for which he could not find compensation.

But despair and anger? He had not seen those before, did not quite know what to do about them. If Simon despaired, if he finally gave up, what hope remained for the rest of them? He brought their hope. Without him...Marcus couldn't help shivering at the thought.

Rising quickly, he hurried from the room. He'd realized soon after Simon chose him he now had a life's mission. He had worked hard to fulfill it. Anything needed to keep Simon and his wonderful stories going. He knew the importance of those stories, and therefore, his own importance in helping to make them happen.

Tonight appeared to be his ultimate test. He could not let Simon give up. As he hurried down the hall past his friend's empty room, he looked through the open door. With a shake of his head, he retrieved the discarded cross and placed it in his pocket. Simon would want it when he came to his senses. Marcus ran out of the Inn and instinctively turned towards the woods behind the building. His friend would likely have gone there, a place to be alone and closer to nature. Swiftly, he followed after him.

Back and forth, back and forth. The Storyteller's footsteps crunched through the gravel, back and forth. His pacing kept cadence with the pounding in his head.

Why am I behaving like this? Síomón, he counseled himself, *regain control. You know why it has to be this way.*

He stopped, pounding his fist into a tree trunk. "I had the choice. I didn't have to be here. I made the choice." he shouted into the air. His only answer came from the growing, howling wind.

"My choice!" he shouted again.

The wind ripped at his coat and tangled his hair. The trees rattled and bent with its force. Far off, townspeople ran for shelter, puzzled by this sudden storm. Mothers screamed for their children. Men hurried for livestock or shuttered storefronts and windows.

A sense of panic filled the air. An overwhelming feeling of their lives drastically shifting. Just as the grayness enveloped the countryside, so did fear settle on the people like a dank fog.

Out in the woods, Marcus took refuge behind a large tree. The wind seemed to grow stronger here. He felt sure Simon must be nearby.

A mighty crack sounded over his head. Marcus instinctively raised his arms to cover himself. The broken limb brushed down his side as it fell, knocking him to the ground.

I must get to Simon. I must help him before it's too late. Marcus dragged his injured body upright. With effort, he pushed once more through the wind. It seemed to carry traces of the familiar voice he searched for.

"My choice, yes. But not my last. I still have choices. I can choose to end this here, now. To finish this once and for all. I can still have my freedom. Even if it is only the freedom of death."

"No!"

Simon spun around to face his faithful companion.

"Simon, you mustn't. Think. Stop and think what you're doing." Marcus stumbled forward. Blood clotted at the scratches on his face, his old body bruised and torn. "Look around you. Can't you see what's happening? As you suffer, so do we all. If you kill yourself, you kill us as well."

Simon looked at Marcus in horror. The truth showed in every bleeding line of his face.

"I understand the pain, Simon. I've seen the questions you live with. But you must know by now how much we all need you. You must realize the wonderful good you've done in this world. The hundreds...no, thousands of people whose lives you have touched and improved."

The wind eased and the world seemed to steady itself. Marcus reached out and grasped his friend's arm.

"Your reward will come, Simon. It will take longer than most because you have so much more to accomplish, so much more to give. But it will come. I don't doubt when the time is right, God himself will hang the banner and escort you home."

Simon clasped him to his heart. "Marcus. Marcus, my friend. What would I do without you?" He stopped, puzzled, and wiped unexpected wetness from his eyes. "Tears? I've never cried a tear in my entire life. It is an unusual sensation, not entirely unpleasant."

"Hah. Maybe you're more one of us than I thought. Come, Simon. The hearthside is calling to us. My weary bones need a rest. A few bandages here and there wouldn't hurt either. And you, I think, need this." He held out the old cross. Simon took it tenderly and replaced it around his neck. Another tear escaped his eye as he nodded his mute thanks.

The two men walked out from the trees, which now stood still and silent. Marcus favored his left leg and kept his left hand curled protectively at his chest. Simon caught him as he suddenly stumbled, wincing at the look of pain that crossed his friend's face. Carefully, he placed his arm around Marcus to support him and help him walk easier. It made progress slow and awkward, yet did nothing to prevent Marcus' limp from worsening. As they reached the town the streets filled with people examining the damage and comparing notes on the mysterious storm.

Simon flinched as he surveyed what he had caused. *They've done nothing to deserve this,* he thought. *I had no right. I cannot afford to be so selfish again.*

"It will be all right, Simon. Don't let this haunt you. Remember, you have the power to fix this."

Simon nodded and they continued moving through the people.

"Oh my, those poor men," a large rolling woman cried out. "Were you caught out in that horrible storm?"

Some folks hurried towards them, clucking over their misfortune. A few women armed themselves with water and cloth for bandages.

"You're hurt," the rolling woman said as she caught sight of Marcus' scratched and bruised face. "Let me get a look at those wounds."

"I'm fine. But please, take care of my good friend here. I fear he received the worst of it." Simon looked with great concern towards Marcus, who now looked very poorly. His heart hurt to know he had caused the injuries but could not heal them. Because of their closeness, his stories held no power for Marcus.

"Oh my, yes. You've lodging at the tavern, haven't you?" She waited for no reply. "Edward. Peter. Let's help these gentlemen to the Inn."

With great ceremony, the townspeople clustered towards the tavern. Some truly wanted to help. Mostly, they all wanted to hear how the strangers survived the storm. It held more appeal than dealing with the reality of putting the town back in order again.

"Simon," Marcus whispered. "The story, Simon. Tell them the story."

"All in due time. I need to see you taken care of first."

The group crowded into the tavern's common room, Simon and Marcus given priority seating by the fireside. The outspoken woman washed away the blood and tended to the wounds personally, making quite a fuss about it while maintaining a running commentary. The Innkeeper graciously supplied bowls of stew and mugs of ale to fortify the two wayward travelers.

Simon watched carefully as she bandaged Marcus and wrapped him in a warm blanket. Others brought a stool for his feet, a pillow for his back. He really had aged into an old man. It surprised Simon. For all his jokes, he never believed it until now. He had never allowed himself to become so close to a person before, so dependent. There would be a price to pay for this. Meanwhile, he had a new role to learn. He would be Marcus' helper.

The Innkeeper reappeared, bearing pitchers of ale. He happily passed them around to all, Simon's coins jingling in his pocket. As talk drifted back around to the storm damage, Simon gave a nod to Marcus and began.

"If you don't mind me joining in, maybe I can lighten your moods a bit."

Murmured ascension ran through the room.

"I think this ale has already lightened the mood wonderfully. What can you do to lighten the work?" A sarcastic young man laughed near the edge of the crowd.

"Ah." Simon appeared to ponder for a moment as he stared at the young man. "I actually had in mind to share a story about another small town that had to deal with a disaster very similar to yours. I thought you might want to hear how they took a tragic situation and made the town even better."

"Horseshit."

The group turned as one to glare or scowl at the troublemaker.

"Why doesn't he go home?"

"He's always makin' trouble."

"His father should 'ave beat his mouth shut when he 'ad the chance."

The young man's angry gaze swept the room and came to rest on Simon. Their eyes locked.

"I think you, particularly, will find this story interesting. A young man saved this town, went by the name of Bartholomew." Simon glanced at his audience.

"Ha, hah. Hey, Bart. You're a hero." The townsfolk joined in laughter.

"I don't have to listen to this." The young man stood, ready for flight.

"Bartholomew is your name as well? How odd." Simon stared intently into his eyes. The man's tensed body relaxed and he slowly sat. "But that has nothing to do with my story. Just an interesting coincidence."

The group chuckled again, but their attention shifted back to Simon. Bart sat quietly. Almost as if held in his seat by force.

"The small town I speak of had the misfortune of being caught in a terrible storm that crept up so suddenly they had no time to prepare. It devastated the people. Houses lay in ruin, crops destroyed, their livelihoods apparently lost. That, of course," he leaned forward, "is why I happened to recall this story. It's so much like your problem."

Heads nodded in agreement.

"All would have been lost if it weren't for Bartholomew's shrewd thinking. Others looked down on this lad as worthless and mistreated him most of his life. Folks around his town never figured he'd amount to much. The constant questioning and exploring of his younger years, the pulling apart to see if he could put things back together, were viewed as stupidity and destructiveness. Actually, those were signs of an exceptionally bright and inventive boy. His father reacted with abuse. The neighbors, tired of Bart's questions and his getting into everything, followed the father's example."

The room grew quiet, save for an uncomfortable shifting of chairs by people who felt the story, indeed, hit too close to home. A peaceful look occupied Bart's face now. A spark of hope glimmered in his eyes.

"As the years passed, Bart's inquisitiveness turned into hostility. He rebelled against anything or anyone who tried to harness him. Avoiding work became his new pastime. He gained nothing from it anyways. The townsfolk met all his attempts with derision and scorn. So, he settled for passing his time at the local tavern, nursing a pitcher of ale throughout the day."

Uneasy glances shifted towards Bart, who grinned broadly, thoroughly enjoying himself now. He knew this story belonged to him. As Simon said, he had intelligence. Grateful for the magic that had kept him in his seat, he savored the reactions of his neighbors. He had no idea what made this sorcerer choose to defend him, but he would take this miracle. Deep satisfaction spread through him. Surging upward burst forth a feeling he had never had cause to experience before. Hope. He may be different, but given the opportunity, he knew he could contribute. He had all sorts of ideas to improve things if they'd only listen. Maybe now they would.

With shining eyes, Bartholomew watched the storyteller. Simon felt his gratitude. It soothed like a balm to his turbulent soul. He glanced at Marcus who smiled and nodded his head knowingly.

"After the great storm passed, the townspeople seemed at a loss. It had been so sudden, so damaging, they didn't know where to start. In the midst of this chaos sat Bartholomew. To the town's good fortune, he had not become overly jaded. When the need became evident, he took the risk once again to speak out. This time, people listened."

"Good people at heart, once a few of them began to see the value of his ideas, the others found them less threatening as well. Soon the town worked together under Bartholomew's direction. Oh my," Simon smiled and shook his head, "you should have seen that place. The things they accomplished were remarkable."

He stood, stretching his hands at the fire to warm, glancing back over his shoulder at the room full of people. No one said a word; no one moved from his chair. Simon smiled to himself. He knew they wanted more.

"Do ya be knowin' why these grand things could a' happen?" Simon turned quickly, purposefully startling them as he momentarily lapsed back into an old Irish brogue. "Because they gave Bartholomew the simple courtesy every living creature deserves. Respect. For the first time in his life, they treated him with respect. Bart simply responded in kind."

With help, Marcus got on his feet, Simon ready to guide him upstairs to their rooms. "You'll all be hearing of this town, I'm sure. It's destined to become quite well-known in these parts. You see, eventually, faith is always rewarded."

He walked through the group, carefully easing Marcus along, pausing almost imperceptibly by Bart. "Simon says, remember my words," he whispered.

Dawn found the carriage once more on its way. This morning, however, proved different from all the previous mornings. On the front bench, trying his best to drive the horses, sat Simon. Bundled warmly inside, Marcus grinned and chuckled, trying desperately hard not to laugh aloud at his master's inexperience.

"Marcus," puffed Simon through gritted teeth, "are you doing all right in there?" His gloved hands clenched the reins tightly as he attempted a quick glance to the back. This caused the short reins to pull as well, and horses followed by carriage veered to the right.

"Whoa, Whoa. Blasted horses, where do you think you're going?" Simon brought everything to an abrupt halt.

Marcus could contain himself no longer and burst into laughter. He buried his head into the blanket in a feeble attempt to muffle the noise.

Simon glared back. "Let me know when you're quite finished and we'll resume our journey."

"You," Marcus gasped, "you told me you knew how to drive this thing." The laughter continued.

"Well, it looked easy enough. I'm sure I'd have done much better if it weren't for these temperamental horses. They keep turning every which way."

Marcus let out another roar and doubled over.

Simon turned around in genuine alarm. "Marcus, you're going to injure yourself. Do be careful."

"These old bones," he gulped for air, "are definitely too sore for such exercise. Why don't you let me up there so I'll be able to get a proper rest."

"I told you this morning when we left I would drive. You're in no shape to be doing anything. I wouldn't have moved you out of your bed at all if it had been feasible for us to remain in town."

"I know, Simon. But you had to tell the story. That Bartholomew...what a perfect subject. You could see him come to life." Marcus winced as he adjusted his body. "This is worth it, Simon. I can manage until we come to another good town."

Sitting quietly, Simon stared at his friend. "I want to thank you for what you did yesterday." He held up a hand to stop Marcus' protests. "We both know what the outcome could have been. I let my emotions rule me and I cannot allow that to happen. You reminded me of why I'm here, why I made this choice. You, Marcus, gave me back my hope."

Simon's intense look took on an exaggerated air of alarm as he turned around and picked up the reins. "Now, tell me how to drive this blasted thing."

With a few instructions, Simon finally managed to keep the horses moving at a fairly steady pace and in the right direction. As the rhythmic clop-clop of hooves marked the passing time, Marcus drifted off to sleep. Simon continued driving through the long roads of the quiet countryside, but his mind drifted too. He recalled his home in Ireland, and the first day he began to realize his whole world was changing.

"Síomón. Síomón." The voice echoed down through his memory. "It is time to join the circle."

Simon stood up, adjusting the hood of his roughly woven brown wool robe so his face became a shadow. He left his stone house under the ground and joined the others walking deasil, or clockwise, through the Oak grove towards the sacred site. They walked following the setting of the sun, the path of the seasons. They walked the way their kind had always walked. Tonight marked Yule, the Winter Solstice. The darkest point of night approached. The ceremony would soon start.

As they reached a clearing by the Sacred Oak, three columns of cloaked figures paused. The Stallir, leading the middle column, faced a pile of wood in the clearing and remained in place to mark the center. At the head of the columns on either side stood the Bard and the Seer, who continued leading all the figures on until a half-circle, a crescent as in the shape of the waning moon, formed. As they looked up at the zenith of the new moon, the chant began. The sound of their voices blended with the waves crashing off the cliff beyond the tree line. Three times they repeated the words. They ended as their chief, the Stallir, stepped forth with the sacred fire. The flame that would not die. He touched it to the pile of wood and bracken, all eyes watching as the bonfire burst into flames.

Later, Simon stood with a few of the others, finishing off a piece of freshly roasted lamb. His eyes avoided the flat, red-stained stone to the side, one of their ways he had never quite been able to accept. The lamb tasted good, though, and he licked his fingers. From the corner of his eye he could see the Stallir approaching. Always an honor to be singled out by him, and doubly so on this special night.

"Síomón." The voice resonated in his head. He could hear it though the older man never moved his lips. He simply stood there smiling.

Simon nodded his head in acknowledgment. *"Yes, Liam?"* His thoughts answered.

"This is a special night, Síomón. Take it in, draw strength from it. Things will be changing soon." A troubled look came to his eyes and he glanced away. When he looked back, Simon could see affection for him there, mixed with sadness. *"Patric has returned, as we knew he would. It is only a matter of time."*

Liam moved away, leaving Simon to stare after him. Time until what? Clearly, they all knew about Patric. They had spent many a night discussing the unusual slave who had escaped to France after a short six years with them in Ériu. They knew he would someday come back as a Christian priest. There had been new religions before, why should this one be any different? Or did Liam know a future closed to them?

Tomorrow, he decided, *I will join with Diarmuid and together we will vision. Maybe with our combined strength, we can see what Patric is up to.*

"We're still moving in an upright position. That's a good sign." Marcus' voice pulled Simon back to the present.

"Ah, my friend. You're awake." Simon started to turn around to look, but Marcus stopped him.

"Keep your eyes forward, Simon. I've had enough excitement for a time."

The two continued their light banter throughout the day, Marcus drifting in and out of sleep. Darkness had long fallen when Simon pulled the carriage to a halt.

"Very well done, Simon. We've actually made it in one piece. I told you, simply relaxing on the reins would make a world of difference."

"I did do rather well, didn't I?" Simon climbed down and opened the coach door. "Careful now. Let me help you, Marcus. You're bound to be fairly stiff."

"That, I surely am. I never dreamed the thought of bed could be so lovely. Would you mind terribly if I took supper in my room tonight?"

"I'd be very angry with you if you did otherwise," Simon replied. "Let me get you settled and I'll have some ale, hot tea, and beef broth brought up. Rest and quiet are what you need. Hot food, a warm bed, plenty of ale. Maybe even a young lass to do the nursing. You'll be back on your feet in no time."

It turned out to be almost two weeks before Marcus again ventured from his room. Age made the healing process slow. They spent another week wandering the town, building his strength back up. By that time rumors had reached the village from a neighboring town concerning a miracle of some sort. It seemed there had been a freak storm, and out of the destruction had risen a new leader who had the most astonishing ideas. The town would undoubtedly prosper beyond anyone's dreams. Most amazing of all, a wandering prophet who had appeared magically in the midst of the storm had foretold everything.

"Are you well, Marcus?

"I am, Simon."

"Then, it's time to move on. My stories are catching up to us."

Once more the carriage started its journey. Simon sat gratefully in the back admiring the skill with which Marcus handled the horses.

"Marcus?"

"Yes?"

"I wanted you to know...I appreciate you, Marcus."

"I already knew that."

"You did, eh? Well, let's take good care of you. I'd like your company a few more years yet."

"That's why I'm out here. It's safer for me."

Simon chuckled quietly. Staring out the window into the distance his expression sobered. "I need you, Marcus."

"I knew that, too. But thank you anyways."

They traveled almost non-stop for several days. A precaution to keep distance between them and the stories. Evenings they usually sought a small clearing in the woods and slept in the carriage. It left a harder trail to follow if anyone should ever think to search them out. They kept to themselves as much as possible, which became easier and easier the further they traveled.

It passed briefly through Simon's mind that people seemed to be avoiding them. Traffic on the road increased, though it all seemed to be headed in the opposite direction they traveled.

"Have you heard any rumors of a war ahead of us, Marcus?"

"None. The most I've heard is there's been some sickness and the Lords and Ladies are retreating early to their summer homes in the country for a taste of sweet air and recreation."

"Sickness? Anything we should be concerned about?"

"Not that I can tell."

"Let's turn south, just to be safe. We haven't been in that area for some time."

Another seven days later their travels brought them to London. They had not returned there since Katherine's story. Simon pulled out the small worn cross and looked at it fondly, remembering Katherine's sweet face. He had her memory, at least. He could almost convince himself a glimmer of love made for a better life than never knowing love at all. With a smile, he turned back towards the coach window and peered out. He always enjoyed seeing the changes time had brought about, some of them with his help. Today, his enjoyment soon turned into uneasiness.

"This doesn't feel right, Marcus."

"What do you mean, Simon? Everything looks nice and quiet to me."

"That's the problem. This isn't a nice quiet town. Where are all the people? Where are the children running through the streets? This is definitely wrong. I feel danger here."

A nearby door opened briefly as a dark-cloaked woman came out. The men heard wailing from inside. She did not seem to notice the coach at first, not until Simon called out. At the sound of his voice, she gave a frightened look. Hurrying around the corner, she glanced back to make sure they weren't following.

"Quickly, Marcus. One of the old taverns we stayed in before should be on the next street over. The King's Grille I believe it's called. We shall seek our answers there."

Simon looked at the buildings as they drove past. He felt a sense of familiarity about all of this. Why couldn't he put his finger on it?

They stopped in front of the King's Grille and Marcus climbed quickly down. "I'll go in and see if there's anything they can tell us."

Simon, brooding, nodded his head and continued staring about him. London had always been an exceptionally dirty place, but by 1665 the population had increased drastically, as had the filth. The rats had also increased, he noticed. There seemed no end to them as they rooted through the garbage-strewn streets.

The rats. Stories of a sickness. Suddenly, Simon knew. His body tensed as he hurriedly leaned his head out the window, calling loudly. "Marcus. Marcus, get out of there quickly."

Marcus already ran for the carriage, his face ashen.

"Simon. It's the Plague, Simon. It's everywhere. They said people are dying by the hundreds."

"I know." Simon snapped, angry with himself. "Swiftly now, get in the carriage and get us out of here."

"I didn't touch anything." Marcus cracked his whip at the horses and set them running. "I was very careful. I didn't touch a thing. The Innkeeper didn't come anywhere near me, either."

Simon didn't reply. He watched Marcus intently.

"Why do you keep scratching your leg, Marcus?"

"Oh, those ridiculous rats. Didn't you see them? They ran all over the place. I think a couple of fleas must have bit me. If that's the worst I got out of there with," he laughed nervously, "I guess I can't complain."

All color drained from Simon's face. He sat back and closed his eyes. Nausea, anger, and fear swept over him like a tidal wave. He knew. He knew very well.

The rats. The fleas. The Plague. Marcus.

CHAPTER FOUR

"**Stop**, Marcus." Simon's voice sounded flat. Lifeless.

"Here? We're not even out of town yet. Let me go a bit farther."

"No, Marcus. My friend. Stop here."

Marcus checked the horses and pulled them to a stop. He watched Simon slowly open his door and climb out, his movements stiff and wooden as if moving through a fog. A sickening sense of dread began gnawing away inside the man as he climbed down from his bench.

"Simon? What is it? Are you all right?"

"Marcus, take my hand. Look into my eyes. Look hard."

"Wha...? Simon, are you trying to see my life? You know it doesn't work on me. We've tried this before."

"We must try again. Look hard, Marcus. Concentrate on me." For several minutes, Simon's narrowed eyes stared intently into Marcus'. His face reddened with the strain. Tears of sweat worked their way down his brow.

"It's no use," he monotoned and turned away.

"Simon. You must tell me what's going on." Marcus' voice edged with terror. He grabbed Simon by the arm and forced him to turn back. "This can't be about the Plague. I stayed in there only a moment. It can't be the Plague." His head shook in denial.

Simon put his hand to his forehead, clenching his hair, unable to answer.

"I stayed only a moment. I didn't even touch anything."

Finally, Simon looked up, grasping his friend by both shoulders. "You didn't have to touch anything. It's the fleas, Marcus. The Plague is carried by the fleas."

Both pairs of eyes looked down at Marcus' leg, his stocking saggy and crinkled at the spot he had furiously scratched the small, itching bites.

"Oh my God," Marcus whispered. "Oh my God." He fell back against the carriage.

Simon grabbed him again. "We can't give up yet, Marcus. Maybe those fleas weren't infected. There's still a possibility. There's still...hope."

"Hope? You can give me hope, Simon. Tell a story, quickly. You can stop this from happening. You have the power to change things."

"Marcus. Marcus." He pulled away. "You know I can't. I tried. It doesn't work with you. It never works for you. Your life is too close to my own. You know that, Marcus. If there was any way I could do it, you know I would," he ended quietly.

"I know, Simon," he whispered back, closing his eyes. "What am I to do now?"

Simon embraced his old friend, trying to impart strength. "We can't leave now. We'll have to find a place here to stay. We should know by tomorrow morning whether you have the sickness."

He guided Marcus to the carriage door. "I'll drive us back to the King's Grille."

The two men settled quickly into their rooms. The Innkeeper, though puzzled by their return, happily gave them the best rooms in the house. His first paying customers in days. The title 'best rooms' didn't amount to much. They sat closer to the quieter back side of the building, had maybe a bit more padding in the sleeping mats. But they were clean and each had a fireplace laid with fresh kindling, ready for a warming blaze.

"Try not to worry, Marcus. It's likely nothing's going to happen. By this time tomorrow, we'll be well on our way to a new town. And you," he pointed at his friend, "will be driving that blasted carriage again."

Marcus laughed despite his concerns. "Such a short jog back here. I don't see how you had time to have so much trouble. I thought you would overturn the whole thing."

"It was the dog. I did fine until that bloody cur came yipping and yapping, trying to play tag with the horses' hooves. You should be thanking your lucky stars we're still alive."

"No," Marcus answered slowly, "I don't think I will thank them, yet. It probably would've been an easier way to go." He walked to Simon and looked him in the eye. "Do you know, Simon? Have you seen how it happens? I haven't. But I've heard the stories." Abruptly, he turned away.

"Yes, I've seen it," Simon answered slowly, reluctantly. "Long ago. More times than I care to admit. Whatever happens, Marcus, I'll be here. If that is what's to come, I'll stay with you. I'll take care of you, old friend."

"With a heavy pillow, I hope," Marcus said under his breath. But he smiled and nodded his head, taking what comfort he could from Simon's words.

"Now, let us put this aside for tonight. There's music and ale awaiting us downstairs and, I've heard, the best loaf of bread you'll taste this side of the Channel to go with our stew. Tomorrow will be here soon enough. But tonight...this moment...belongs to you, Marcus."

The morning dawned bright and sunny. A rare occurrence in that part of the world. A good omen, Simon thought. He dressed quickly and hurried next door to Marcus' room. Once at the door, he hesitated. Was he prepared for what he might find on the other side? Taking a deep breath he knocked.

The door opened almost immediately. Marcus stood there fully dressed and smiling. "I'm ravenous. Let's go down and eat. I want a bowl of hot porridge with fresh cream and maybe some berries." He headed towards the stairs, pulling an astonished Simon along with him. "A couple of poached eggs, surrounded by golden potatoes fried up with bacon fat and onions. A thick juicy slab of ham. Oh. The bread. It was wonderful sustenance. I'll have a good chunk of that with sweet creamy butter."

"Marcus." Simon stopped and grasped his friend. "You're well."

"I am not just well; I am completely well. Perfectly well. Totally well. My bones didn't even creak when I got out of bed. It's a wonderful morning and I have the appetite of a horse."

"Then don't let me stand in your way." Simon waved his friend forward. "Lead me to the feed, oh healthy one."

The men soon ate heartily, the food hot and satisfying. They washed it down with plenty of strong, fragrant tea, chatting lightly, happily, as the food came and went. As he worked his way through his potatoes though, Simon realized Marcus had become increasingly quiet. He looked over at his friend's plate and watched the food being pushed back and forth. Marcus lifted a forkful to his lips only to set it down again, untouched.

"Full so soon, Marcus? You haven't even tasted your bread."

"I guess I'm not as hungry as I thought." He gave a weak smile. "Would you excuse me? I think I'd like a taste of fresh air."

He stood and moved towards the door, suddenly breaking into a wobbly run. Simon jumped up, knocking over his chair, and followed. He found Marcus near the narrow alley at the side of the tavern, forcefully vomiting.

"No, Marcus. No. You were well. This can't be happening." He held his friend as the heaving gradually tapered off.

Marcus stood up breathing heavily. Tears seeped from his eyes. "It's starting, Simon. I have the Plague."

The tears matched Simon's. "I'm sorry, Marcus. I'm so, so sorry."

Marcus' shoulders slumped and he sagged forlornly against the building. Massaging his aching rib cage, he leaned over and spit the bile from his mouth. Simon watched, feeling a part of his own life seep away. A sense of horror grew within him. He had no control over the events now taking place. For the first time, he felt helpless. It terrified him. Marcus began to shiver, although the morning sun blazed above.

"Are you cold, my friend? Here, put on my cloak." Simon wrapped the thick cloth around him, his hand brushing Marcus' face. He stopped in consternation and felt his face again. "Your skin is hot. The fever is growing. We must get you back to bed."

The two slowly climbed up the stairs they had so joyfully descended one short hour before. At the sound of hurrying footsteps, they paused and turned.

The Innkeeper looked up at them in fear, maintaining a safe distance. "Where are you going? What's wrong with this man? Is it the Plague? If it's the Plague you must leave right now. You're not to go upstairs. If he has the Plague, you must turn around and get out. I have a family. I have to keep them safe. You must leave."

Simon's eyes narrowed. "My friend is sick and I will take him upstairs and put him to bed. You will keep me supplied with water, ale, kindling, and rags. I'll also want a good-sized flat stone and some wild cabbage, plus the leaves of burdock, mullein, plantain...as many of them as you can find. No one need enter the room; you may leave everything at the door. Take no more guests. I will pay you for the rooms. I'll let you know of anything else I may need later."

The Innkeeper backed away, bewildered. "Well, yes...of course. Whatever you say."

Simon turned and guided Marcus on up. "As long as my friend receives everything he needs, you and your family will be safe from the Plague. If he is not treated well I guarantee you nothing. Do you understand?" Simon glared back over his shoulder.

"Completely. I understand completely, Sir. You'll have everything you request." The Innkeeper's eyes flashed wide and bright in his colorless face as he watched the two men turn into the bedroom.

"Here, Marcus. Lay down and rest." Simon helped him strip to his undergarments and got him comfortably settled in his bed, the blankets pulled up warmly over his shivering body. Once the Black Death struck, it struck quickly.

At the sound of movement outside, Simon opened the door. The Innkeeper looked up from his scrunched position depositing items on the floor. Besides the things he had asked for, Simon noticed extra sheeting lying there along with a bucket.

"It's for the vomiting, Sir. The ale will help ease his pain all right, but most of it will come right back up. And...and the sheets, well, they're bound to get soiled. I thought you'd want to keep him as comfortable as possible." He stood, nodding his head meekly. "We found a stone and some wild cabbage behind the Inn. They're all washed and ready. The Missus and our lasses are out gathering the rest of the plants you asked for."

"Thank you for your consideration. Here." He pulled a small pouch from his pocket and dropped it in the man's hand. "That should be more than enough to make up for your troubles these next few days."

The man's mouth hung open as he felt the weight of the bag, his head still nodding furiously. "Yes, Sir. Whatever you need, let me know. We'll take good care of you, Sir." He continued muttering to himself as he walked away, his hands clawing to open the bag and reveal the riches within.

Simon checked Marcus, then moved the items inside. The kindling got stacked by the hearth with the stone. The sheets and cabbage waited on the side table. Ale and water went bedside with the rags, the bucket nearby. More noise at the door and Simon opened it to find a softly padded chair. The Innkeep backed away, keeping his distance.

"That there is for you. If you're going to stay in there and tend to him, you'll need a chair that's easy to sit on." He disappeared once more down the stairs.

Simon pulled the chair in and positioned it next to the bed. "Marcus. Are you still with me, lad?" He reached over and placed his hand on the burning forehead.

Marcus tried to focus his glazed eyes. "It's so cold. Can you build me a fire, Simon?" He moved his head painfully to the side.

"Certainly. Whatever you want." Simon let his hand

drop, taking note of the swelling lymph glands in Marcus' neck. If the buboes there had begun to swell then he could assume those in his armpits and groin would be doing the same. To lie still would be painful. Any movement at all would intensify the feeling.

He turned away, angry at his helplessness. For all his ability to live throughout the passing of time, for all his power to change and rearrange lives, he could do absolutely nothing for this dying man. If he had been a stranger, yes. But because he had let him become a friend, he could do nothing to ease his pain, let alone save him from death.

Simon's whole body shook with rage and frustration. He leaned his head against the cool stone of the fireplace, trying to regain control. He must not dwell on what he could not do but rather focus on the things that could be done to ease Marcus' suffering. For the few hours he had left, he could provide him with the comfort of not having to die alone. Simon let the coolness of the stones soothe him as he remembered the first choice he had been given. The first sacrifice.

Tadhg hurried over to Simon, his face flushed. "The Stallir sent me for you. He's waiting by the Sacred Oak." He patted his friend on the back. "Liam has always liked you, Síomón, but he seems to be showing even more interest lately. Maybe you are to be the next Stallir?" A smile sat upon his lips but it didn't reach his cold eyes.

"Don't worry, Tadhg. The Stallir will be with us for many years yet." Simon laughed it off but hurried to find Liam all the same. For some time he had sensed strangeness in the air. An odd vibration, unlike anything he had felt before. He had even spoken to the Seer about it, hoping he would use his ability to see through the future to find what was happening. To his surprise, the Seer made excuses and put him off, seemingly flustered by Simon's questioning.

Liam saw him approaching and motioned Simon to sit beside him under the tree. Immediately he felt the resonance of the voice in his head. *"The time has come, Síomón. We must talk."*

A wave of fear washed over him. Liam's summons had nothing to do with who might be the next Stallir. No, it reached much farther and deeper. He had been called here to talk about the ending of life as they had known it.

"Yes, Síomón." The words drifted through his mind. *"You are right. This is concerning the end of our race."*

"But Stallir...Liam, how can this be? Our lives are so much longer than ordinary people's. Many of us are still very young. We have special gifts and abilities. How can it just end?"

"The times are changing, as they always have. But they will begin to change much faster now. Soon there will be no place for our kind. Remember Patric?"

Simon nodded.

"He has brought Christianity to Ériu and the people are embracing it. In all honesty, I can't blame them. It is full of goodness, of hope. A hope they so desperately need. However, it leaves no room for us. Patric will soon drive our people out of this country and there will be no other country that will take us in. We will be lost."

He looked at Simon and spoke aloud for the first time. "I have been meeting with the Stallir of all the clans for some years now in preparation for this time. We have agreed on a plan to preserve the essence of our kind, and in doing so, to leave a wondrous gift for the human race." He placed his powerful hand on Simon's shoulder. "That gift is to be you, Síomón."

Simon's mouth dropped open in shock. He had not expected this. "Me?" he stammered, barely able to get the word out.

"I understand your confusion. There is much I still need to explain to you. This is what I have been preparing you for since your beginnings. It will be a wondrous thing. But, like all wondrous things, it will demand sacrifices as well."

Simon took a deep breath and straightened up from the fireplace. His own pain should remain unimportant. He must do what he could for Marcus. He lit the kindling, stoking the fire until he had a good flame crackling in the hearth. He took the large, smooth stone and placed it at the edge of the fire to heat. As gently as possible he pushed the bed across the floor until close enough for Marcus to easily feel the warmth.

"Yes...yes. That's much better. Thank you, Simon," Marcus mumbled, barely coherent. His body shivered and his sleep shirt lay damp across his chest as it soaked up the sweat of the fever. Simon poured some water into a basin and moistened a cloth. He wiped the flushed face then left the cooling rag on his forehead.

He pulled out a small knife and cut at Marcus' remaining clothes. He knew the swelling glands would soon press upon the material and cause even more pain. They commonly became open sores and Simon wanted to prevent any unnecessary chafing. As careful as he tried, he couldn't help but move the swollen body. Marcus moaned.

"I'm sorry, friend. I need to get these off you or it will hurt worse. I'm almost finished and then you can rest again." He took another damp rag and washed Marcus' body, then covered him again with the blankets.

"I'm going to try the cabbage poultice, Marcus. See if we can draw some of the pus out and take the swelling down. When the other plant leaves get here, I can add them. Hopefully, we can reduce your pain." Marcus didn't answer. Simon felt for heat from the stone. Nodding his head in approval, he tore leaves off the wild cabbage and placed them on the stone. After watching them sizzle and wilt a bit he picked the hot leaves up, replacing them with fresh ones. He laid the heated leaves over the buboes, continuing until they were all covered four or five layers deep. He used more cloth to cover and hold them all down and pulled the blankets back up to help keep the heat in.

By the time they had cooled and sat on Marcus' skin a while, the Innkeeper had brought the other cleaned plants Simon had asked for. He plucked off the leaves and began the process again with a mix of the new ones, a rotation he would continue every couple of hours.

"Do you want to try some ale while these sit, Marcus? It could help soothe the pain."

"Yes," came the whispered reply.

Simon took the bottle and emptied a small portion into one of the mugs. He carefully raised Marcus' head, putting the mug to his lips. He swallowed with difficulty. Half the liquid ran down his front but some made it down the parched throat.

"Very good. We'll try some more in a while." Simon cleaned him up again. Suddenly Marcus clutched at his stomach. Simon grabbed the bucket in time to catch the fresh stream of vomit. When the heaving subsided he laid Marcus back on the pillow and wiped his mouth.

"I'm sorry. I had hoped the ale would stay down. We don't have to try again, Marcus. Just lay quietly."

Simon settled him as comfortably as possible and

rearranged the poultice. Then he pulled the chair close and sat down. Marcus looked bad. Perspiration damply matted his white hair. A glaze shadowed his unseeing blue eyes in a pale, drawn face. The glands in his neck, as in the rest of his body, had already swollen badly. They looked ugly and sore under the poultice leaves. Such a horrible ending to such a selfless and giving life.

Exhaling a large sigh, Simon switched the warm cloth on Marcus' forehead for a fresh cool one. He took his friend's hand gently. "Free your mind, Marcus. Let it go. Your body can give you nothing but pain now. Let your mind wander to other places, other times, when life brought you comfort and joy."

"Remember Devonshire, Marcus? What a lovely time we had there. They were celebrating the festival. Flowers and ribbons hung everywhere. Remember? We stayed for several days and joined in the festivities. They had some good ale but, ahh, could they make a nice strong cup of tea. And the scones. We couldn't eat enough of them. Morning, noon, and night we ate scones. Scones with currents, scones with jam, scones with clotted cream. We even bought a basketful to take with us when we left. We had so many I believe a few hardened to stone before we could eat them all."

He chuckled at the memory. Watching Marcus, he noticed a small smile flickering about his pale lips. He could do some good after all. A bit of the heaviness in his heart lifted.

"Besides the scones, I remember you to be particularly fond of their clotted cream. It really was wonderful. 'Richest in all the land,' I think you said. Oh, but the worst clotted cream we ever had came from that tiny village to the east. Do you remember that one? So bad we had to spit it out. At least two weeks past its prime, I'd say."

The hours limped slowly on as if time itself had been

wounded. Simon left the bedside only when the fire required wood, to pick up more supplies from outside their door, or to pour fresh water in a basin to bathe and freshen Marcus. Every couple of hours he switched out the cabbage poultice for the mixed leaf poultice and back again. He kept a fresh cloth on Marcus' head and used another to drip water and moisten his mouth. But he never stopped his monologue of their times together.

They had so many good memories from past years. Simon told them all, pausing only to moisten his throat with some liquid. A time or two Marcus responded with a smile. Once, he even managed a small chuckle about the day they lost a carriage wheel.

Marcus had been smoothly driving the carriage along at a brisk pace when it hit a rock in the road. The pin holding the wheel snapped and the whole wheel went rolling off on its own. The carriage tipped to the right, digging itself to a sudden stop. Marcus flew through the air and landed head-first in a bush. Simon was tossed about and ended halfway out of the window, hanging like a rag doll. They both cursed at the time, but what a comical sight. It made a fine memory.

But memories could not hold Marcus. As the hours passed he slipped further and further away. Still, Simon didn't quit. He held Marcus' hand, squeezing and patting it occasionally, and kept the stories going. If any spark of consciousness flared through his friend, he wanted him to know he remained at his side.

Daylight came and Simon's voice grew hoarse and ragged. He paused to gulp down a cup of hot tea and for a chance to stretch his aching limbs. Marcus seemed quieter now as if he finally got some real sleep. Simon stood, his back creaking almost as much as the chair he rose from. He walked to the window shaking out his legs. He could hear the sound of birds chirping outside.

As he approached a flock took to the air. He glanced at them and almost turned away. Then the pattern of their flight caught his eye. A coldness went through his heart as memories of the Old Ways returned. The birds flew in a crescent shape from the west...the Sluagh. The Spirit Host to forecast a death. He quickly closed the shutters to bar their entrance. With apprehension, he turned around to face the bed.

Marcus looked at him with tired eyes. "Simon?" he whispered.

Simon hurried to his side, unnerved by both Marcus' sudden awakening and the sign in the sky. "I'm here, old friend. I've been here the whole time."

"I know. I could feel you holding on to life for me." He paused, gathering his strength. "You could never read my life. Simon, because we've been such good friends...like family. For that very same reason, I could read yours better than you realized. Even if your powers worked on me, this is an event you couldn't have changed. It is my time to die, Simon. You will have to let me go. If it hadn't been Plague, it would have been something else. Simple old age, perhaps. Don't abuse yourself over it. You have been a great friend to me and you have given me a life full of adventure, wonders, and miracles."

He paused again, his breath shallow and labored, clasping Simon's hand in his own weak one. "My time is up. But you must go on. There is much work left to be done. You have, I believe, an old Promise you must keep. A task you must fulfill."

Simon looked at him strangely. He opened his mouth to speak but Marcus continued.

"Such wisdom from a mere mortal, eh?" He tried to laugh but the effort resulted in a spasm of pain crossing his face. "I have had a good life with you, Simon. There are no regrets. But now it is time for me to leave. I wanted you to know you have been a true friend. My best friend."

"Marcus," Simon's voice rang with panic. He knew Marcus must die. But not yet. He couldn't let go of him yet. "I haven't had people I could be close to for hundreds of years. Not until you, Marcus. I have loved you like a brother. Like a son."

"I know, Simon. And I have loved you," he whispered. His eyes closed then briefly fluttered open again. He pushed his hand towards Simon. "My ring. Keep my ring. So you will always remember me."

"Marcus. As if I could forget you, my friend."

Marcus smiled softly. "I shall never forget you either. It has been an honor to serve so great a man." His breath escaped as the smile faded, his spirit free of its painful confinement.

Tears spilled from Simon's eyes as he softly replied, "Yes, Marcus, my friend. It has indeed been an honor."

The sun was setting when Simon finally stood up and laid down the cold hand. He now wore a simple gold band on his smallest finger, which he clutched to his heart as if afraid it too would slip away. The fire had long since burned out; the used rags and sheets laid in a pile on the floor. The bottle of ale stood untouched save for Marcus' first sip. Simon seemed oblivious to it all.

Opening the door he called to the Innkeeper. "I'll need a wagon and horse. Let me know when they're ready."

"Is it over then, Sir?"

"Yes...it's over."

The Innkeeper paused, "I...I'm sorry, Sir."

The tall figure sagged a bit as he sighed. "I'm sorry too."

Simon went back into the room and prepared Marcus for the trip. He carefully bathed him one last time, then crossed his arms gently across his chest. He used the remaining clean sheets to softly wrap him, like a babe in a swaddling cloth. Enfolded in the coils of fabric he placed fresh flower petals gathered from a vine growing outside his window. When the Innkeeper announced the wagon ready, he cradled his friend tenderly in his arms and carried him down.

The Innkeep waited at the door. His family stood in the back halls watching and whispering in hushed voices.

"You've filled the wagon with fresh straw. Thank you." Simon stepped outside. He laid Marcus down on the fragrant bed, arranging him comfortably.

"Will you be bringing back the wagon, Sir?"

"No."

"I thought not. You'll be needing this, then." He placed a saddle and bridle near Marcus' feet.

Simon nodded. "The room is safe to clean. Be assured no harm will come to anyone from it."

"Yes, Sir. Will you be returning for your room? Or are you going home now?"

Simon paused, a distant, haunted look on his face. He had no home. No place to go. "I will be returning," he answered slowly.

Nodding his head, the Innkeeper went back inside his tavern. Simon walked reluctantly over to the carriage Marcus navigated so skillfully. He stared at the empty driver's seat, willing Marcus to appear there. He wanted him to laugh and tell him it had all been a bad dream.

Nothing happened. With a sigh, he opened the door and climbed in. He sat on the comfortable old cushions and closed his eyes, inhaling the warm leather scent, his mind wandering to happier days.

"Oh, Marcus. We've had some grand times together. If only I could have made your departure an easier one." He shook his head as if he could shake the pain and guilt away.

"Time, they say, heals all wounds. I have more time than I know what to do with."

He turned in his seat and pulled open the back compartment. Reaching into its hidden recesses he removed his great cloak and hat. He replaced the seat and carried his bundle to the wagon. Carefully, he laid it near Marcus. He must finish the task.

The drive took some time. He searched for a clearing in the woods far away from any town or village. He did not want to be bothered. The darkness lay as heavy as his heart, the bright light of the moon partially obscured by drifting clouds.

Finally, he stopped, satisfied. He unhitched the horse and tied him to a tree well away from the wagon. Glancing up, Simon realized the moon's zenith would soon be reached. He smiled at the coincidence. In the old days, it had been considered the sacred hour. A fitting way to say goodbye to a dear friend.

He lovingly unfurled the great old cape. It had been with him for many years now and had served its purpose well. With the passage of time, the cape no longer seemed appropriate. As the years changed, Simon changed also. He knew the days of the magician storyteller had come to an end. He must find a new way to tell his tales.

Tonight, the grand cloak made its final performance in a tribute to Marcus. Simon draped the velvety cloth around the body, using the old pointed hat as a cushion for his head. With a final farewell, he lit the straw. He watched with overwhelming sadness as the wagon and its contents went up in flames. Tears came unbidden and streamed down his face. He tried to stop them, to regain control, but could not. Any more than he could stop the wail that tore itself from his heart and echoed through the woods.

Simon stood alone...again. He could find no comfort.

Simon Says

CHAPTER FIVE

THE dancing lights and flickering shadows jumped hypnotically. Simon's tears had finally ceased and his voice had silenced. Still, he stood there, mesmerized by the flames. He had no strength left in him to move. He was well acquainted with loss, of course. He had lost all his people, after all. But that was centuries ago, mutually decided as a gift to mankind.

But this. This was a fresh and new and all-consuming pain. There was no benefit to offset the loss. No one's life was made better by Marcus' absence. Simon's life was infinitely worse for it. How was he to bear it?

Throughout his many years, he had been so careful to never allow himself to form any close relationships. The others had advised him against it long ago. Now he knew too clearly the reason why. There would have been too many painful goodbyes. His heart still ached when he thought of Katherine, and he never actually spent time with her. He'd only seen her life story. It was enough, though, to light a fire within that had never completely gone out. But Marcus...Marcus who was like a son to him...whom he had spent years side-by-side with, he could not even begin to fathom how he would survive without.

Simon shook his head angrily. The cost came too high. He would not make this mistake again. They had discouraged him from this to protect him. He had chosen to ignore that counsel and now he would pay the price forever. Even worse, Marcus had paid the price for his choice as well. He could blame no one else. Liam's warning echoed in his memory.

"We have never attempted this before, Síomón. We're not quite sure what will occur. But we have agreed we must try. All our wisdom, our power, magic...our very lives will meld into yours. You will go forth throughout the ages as a Guardian of the good in men. You will seek it out and reward it. You will move among them but you must never be one with them. The danger would be too great. If your powers should be exposed, men with depraved hearts would try to force you into their service. Or," the Stallir paused, glancing sideways at Simon, "they might hunt you down like an animal and destroy you.

"The other possibility is you may become too attached to people. With their lives so very short compared to yours, well, you would always be leaving them behind." Liam nodded his head knowingly. "It would be very hard to continually live with the loss of loved ones. Believe me,

Síomón. If you choose to accept this journey you will have to accept it must be alone."

Simon tried to stifle the fear he felt. "Alone? For how long?"

"As long as it takes, my son. From the end of our times into long beyond." He placed a hand on the younger man's arm. "I know, Síomón. It is frightening. I can't promise you it'll be easy. I can tell you great things can be accomplished through you that will last throughout time."

"Why me, Liam? Why have you chosen me?"

"You're different, Síomón. Even for us. I knew it from your very beginnings and that is why your name is as it is."

Simon had to smile. "My name? I don't understand."

"It is a name that will transcend time. A name like Sliabh would've made it a bit harder to blend into other places, other ages." The old Stallir turned to look into Simon's eyes. "But your name, like you, can adapt to what the future may hold. Eventually, you'll be known as Simon, which will become the common spelling and pronunciation. Surprisingly, even your wheat-colored hair will help you blend in more easily than all the shades of red most of us bear."

Liam paused, looking into the distance. "I know you have always been uncomfortable with some of our ways, Síomón. Searching. Reaching for points beyond us. Eager for change. Sure of a future that can improve life for all of mankind. You have a love for the human race. A desire to help. Do you know what your name means?"

"To hear?"

"Yes, as in to hear your calling," Liam's smile reached his eyes this time. "But, also, it means to be heard. You will find that when you hear the needs of the lives you see, and then the stories of change you tell are heard by them in return, is when you will have the power to effect change. I am giving you the chance to make a difference, Síomón. But you must make the choice."

Simon stood up, a troubled look on his face. "I must think about this, Liam. But answer me one more question first. What happens to us if I decide not to do this?"

"Then we must all perish and even no memories will remain to live on."

Rude laughter suddenly interrupted Simon's mourning.

"Hey, lookee here. Dis nice genleman's made a grand fire to warm our backsides at." Three men stumbled into the clearing. They staggered and bumped each other, obviously having overindulged in the contents of the flasks they carried.

"Eey, Missterr," one slurred as he approached Simon. "I'm thirsty. Gimme somethin' ta drink." He turned his tankard over to show its empty state.

Simon stared coldly at them. "This is not a good time for you to be here. Tonight, this clearing is sacred ground. I strongly suggest you leave. Now."

The dirty, foul-smelling man continued to stand in front of Simon as if he hadn't heard. The other two laughed near the shell of the burning wagon.

"Missterr, I said I wants a drink. Where ya be hidin' yer ale?" He pushed his face close to Simon's, a dangerous glint in his eyes.

Simon could see the pockmark scarring on his face, the yellow and brown stumps making up the few teeth left in his mouth. "And I said, leave this place while you can."

The man stopped, staring at Simon. Suddenly he broke out with a loud laugh. "Eey, mates. Dis 'ere gent says we gots ta leave. What ya tink of dat?"

"I'll show ya what I tink," replied one as he pulled down his pants and began to urinate on the burial fire. "I've drunk enough ta put dis whole damn fire out."

"No!" roared Simon. "How dare you!" Anger beyond anything he had ever experienced surged through him, layered on his grief. Eyes wide, lips pulled tight over his teeth in a snarl, he let go of his last vestige of control. His fist lashed out, knocking over the first man. He rushed at the other two who quickly scattered.

Hands clenched to the point of making the veins on their backs bulge and his knuckles white he shouted, "Stop! Now!" He could feel the power seething out of him. The men stopped, full of fear. They wanted to run away, but their bodies wouldn't move.

"I gave all of you the chance to leave. Instead, you defiled this place. I came here to burn away the Plague. Now, I take it and give it to each of you." Simon spat the words at them. "It will come on quickly, painfully. There will be no quick release. You will lie awake for days in your own filth, begging to die. But die, you won't. Thirty days you will pay the terrible price for what you have done tonight." He took a step forward, the urge to kill strong within him. "Now go. Quickly."

The men disappeared into the dark, like rabbits with the hounds of hell at their heels. Simon watched them go with a growing sense of shock and realization. Slack-jawed and shoulders sagging he sank to his knees, all anger and strength gone. *What have I done,* he thought.

"Liam. Liam." He cried out desperately. "Please forgive me. I have betrayed the Trust. I have broken my Promise."

He collapsed into the dirt near the fire in anguish, a trembling hand reaching out to the flames. "Marcus, my friend. What am I to do now?"

No answer came as he lay alone in the clearing. Hours later when the sun came up, he lay there still. Nothing remained of the fire but char and glowing embers. Slowly, Simon raised himself to his feet and with great effort saddled and mounted his horse. Head down, his gaze carefully avoiding the pile of black ashes, he headed back to the King's Grille, a broken man. He could not go home. The only home he had ever known, he left behind over twelve hundred years ago.

The Innkeeper kept a respectful distance when he entered. Simon went straight upstairs, his step faltering slightly as he passed the room where Marcus died. He hurried on to his own room. They had left Marcus' few remaining possessions in a neat pile on his table. Simon picked up his friend's travel bag and sat on the edge of the bed clasping it to his chest. He stroked the soft leather but couldn't bring himself to look inside.

Downstairs the Innkeeper berated his wife. "Where's your head at, woman? How could you think to take chattel that wasn't your own? He's probably looking for it this very minute."

"Oh shush, he isn't. I'll wager he didn't even know the poor man kept any writings. If he asks about it, I'll tell him we only now found it and were about to return it to him."

"There's a different bearing about him. He's a powerful man. You don't want to cross him. There'll be trouble, take my word for it."

"You worry too much. Nothing will come of this, you'll see."

"What do you need the blasted book for anyways? You can't read a whit."

"I know, but Constance what works at the millinery can. She'll read it to me. I just know it's full of secrets. Traveling men like them always have adventures and secrets to keep."

"Some secrets are better kept. Aye, woman. You'll be the death of me yet. Keep the book if you must, but I'll not be helping you if he comes for it."

Simon did not come for it. Two days passed and he never stirred from his room. The Innkeeper's wife kept the book handy, in case he did. As the hours passed, she felt confident he knew nothing of Marcus' missing journal. She paraded past her husband, patting the book and smiling smugly.

When the third morning came, Simon still sat in his room. Worry etched the Mistress' face now. What if he, too, had died of Plague? All alone in his room with no one to help. No one to hear his final whispered secrets. She approached his door nervously and gave a timid knock. It would be a fine mess if he had died. Hopefully, he left his money on the table. She knew he carried many coins in those bags at his belt, but she clearly wouldn't go near a body with Plague. They'd very likely have to pack up and leave, for the tavern would surely be foul now.

Perhaps, she pondered, *I could pay a coin to some street boy to take the bags off the body. He won't care about no sickness if it puts a coin in his pocket. Me and my husband deserve the man's money now the tavern is done for...*

"Come in." The voice was low.

The woman frowned, a bit disappointed at being deprived her due. She cautiously opened the door and peered in. Simon sat on the hard wooden chair by the window, staring outside. She saw no traces of Plague.

"I worried for you, Sir. You haven't been down to eat for days. I thought you might have took sick."

"No. I'm afraid I'm perfectly healthy."

"Well, if you want to stay that way I think you should be coming down for some of my mutton stew. You'll soon be losing your strength if you don't."

Simon turned and looked at her. She felt a flash of fear as

their eyes met. Her husband had been right. A mere look from this man raised the hackles at the back of her neck. She dropped her eyes quickly from his gaze and curtsied back out of the room.

"I will be down," he told her retreating figure. "Dish me up the stew."

Simon stood and took a deep breath. Maybe food would help to clear his head. It had been so long since he had mourned the loss of someone he had forgotten how painful and draining it was. How it seemed to use up every fiber of his being. How it required all his time and concentration. He did not know how to get beyond it. For three days he sat and stared out his window, searching for a sign. He watched the birds, scrutinized the stars, the moon, the sun. He called out to Liam. He called out to God. He asked for strength and wisdom. He begged for forgiveness and a way out of the pit he found himself in.

He received no answers.

He started downstairs, not allowing his body to react to the empty room nearby. Everything seemed off-balance. Simon placed one hand on the wall to steady himself, rubbing his eyes with the other. His mind wouldn't function properly. He had no clarity, no focus. Only the words echoing in his mind existed, repeating like a mantra...*Marcus is dead. The Trust is broken.* He could see no way to resolve his dilemma. *Marcus is dead.* The world he treasured so deeply shut itself off from him. Simon could feel it shift and distance itself. *The Trust is broken.* Would he ever find a way back?

The savory aroma of mutton mixed with herbs and spices greeted his nostrils as he entered the main room. *Rosemary,* he thought, *and garlic.* It came to him suddenly, he had grown very hungry. He sat down to the steaming bowl placed on the table, gratefully noting the chunk of fresh bread sitting there as well. He licked his lips in anticipation.

He savored each bite, his tongue exalting in each flavor. He could not remember a time when food tasted so splendid. Maybe he should consider going without eating every so often so he could have this pleasure of reentry. *Marcus will love this,* crossed his mind. *I must make sure she saves some for him.*

Marcus is dead. Simon's spoon clattered to the table. *The Trust is broken.* He had forgotten. His eyes opened wide in surprise and guilt. He looked around desperately, feeling suddenly disjointed. How could he have forgotten, even for a moment?

"It's all right, you know."

Simon shifted his eyes quickly, searching, and saw the barmaid.

She smiled sadly. "I know how you be feelin'. I lost me Mum not so long ago. It gets better after a while. Still, I sometimes think she's waitin' in the next room for me. In a way, it's comfortin' to feel they're still with us." She paused, tipping her head to the side. "Don't be gettin' upset over it. It's the only way we can keep them alive."

Simon slowly looked away, absorbing her words. Ordinary folk like her had taught him so much. Even after all these years he still had much to learn. How did they possibly manage on the short amount of time allotted them?

He nodded his head. "Thank you. It...the feeling...caught me unprepared."

"It will get better," she repeated. "In the meantime, let me get you some more stew."

She reached for his bowl but he put a hand up and waved her away, his appetite gone. The stew looked nothing more than cold, brown, coagulated lumps. He quickly grabbed his ale, thinking perhaps he could survive on that instead. He sat a while, trying to wash away the pain. Gradually his attention turned to a conversation nearby.

"It be the strangest thing ever I heard," remarked a short man sitting with his back to Simon.

"I'll say," replied his companion. "There's no doubt it be Plague, but they ain't dying."

"I heard they all three came a runnin' into town a few nights ago, rantin' and ravin' about some man who cursed them with the Plague. Evan be the one who talked with them first, you know."

"Really? Evan? What'd he say 'bout it?"

"He said it be the liquor talkin'. Either that or the fever. The Plague already sat heavy on them."

"Well, I heard this man not only put the Plague on them but told them they'd live for days just to be makin' them suffer."

The color leached from Simon's face until he looked ill and ashen, his mug of ale poised at his lips. He knew the agony of the Plague. How could he have condemned anyone to live with it? Shame and remorse washed over him like a wave in a storm. No prayers or signs could help him now. He truly had failed the Promise he'd made. He had taken the Trust bestowed on him and crushed it under his heel like garbage. *Marcus is dead. The Trust is broken.*

"They be sufferin' all right. No doubt it's Plague though. They be all swelled up and crazed with fever. Keep talking 'bout that strange man and some fire."

"Poor lads. Their minds are prob'ly gone from the pain."

Simon could bear it no longer. He slid back his chair with a clatter and stood. The two men turned to look.

"Where are these three men?" he asked.

"Why you be wantin' to know?" came the suspicious reply.

"It's very important I find them. I have a message to

deliver before they die." The men exchanged glances as Simon continued, "It's an apology of sorts...from someone who wronged them...and a pledge to their kin."

"Well," said the short man, "if it be to make amends." The two men exchanged looks again, the second one nodding approval. "They be at one of the lad's uncles, name of Clifton, off the Old Brompton Road. It be an old cottage with broken wagon parts laying 'bout."

"Don't know how much good it be doin'," added the second man. "The fever's got them right bad."

Simon's face looked cast in stone and the two men shriveled under his stare. "It will do some good," he stated.

Calling for his horse to be saddled, he quickly departed. The pounding hooves matched his own pounding heart. His great haste came not from fear the men would die before he could reach them, for he knew they had days to go yet, but rather the knowledge that so much suffering lay before them. He had to try to rectify his mistake to whatever extent possible.

It didn't take much to convince the household to let him in. Some coins in their pockets and a promise to end the men's pain. They sent him around to the sickroom, really an old lean-to against the outside of the house. Simon approached the moaning figures, ignoring the overwhelming stench filling the air. He stopped at the first. It was the man with the pockmarked face.

Leaning over he whispered, "Do not be afraid. I have come to help you."

The man opened his eyes. As he focused on Simon they widened in fear. "Have ya come ta be heapin' more curses on us? Haven't we paid enough?" He looked around as if searching for a place to escape. "What are ya, a demon? Why do ya want ta be torturin' us more?" The last few words squeaked out, pleading.

Simon stepped back as if struck. People called him many things throughout the years, but all in reflection of the good he'd done. Never before had he earned the name of demon. Marcus, Liam, the others; they would be so disappointed. "I've come to end the pain and suffering I've caused you and your friends. I cannot take back this horrible thing I've done. But I can end it and give you the peace you deserve."

"Do ya be sayin' you'll release us? You'll be lettin' us die?" Hope sprang to his face.

Simon's heart seemed to stop beating and became a leaden thing in his chest. His breath escaped him and he had to forcibly drag it back in. How thrilling it used to be to see hope shine in someone's eyes. But not like this.

"Yes, I release you." He got down on his knees beside the pile of straw that served as the sick man's resting place. "I need very much to beg your forgiveness. I should not have acted in anger and done this terrible thing." He shook his head sadly.

The dying man looked at his two companions, now dead, and knew himself to be close behind. With a hard glint in his eyes, he looked back at Simon and whispered harshly, "After livin' wit da pain of dese last days now ya come and be askin' fer forgiveness, so ya can live on and be easy in yer soul. Ain't goin' ta happen. Ya put us in hell. Now ya can go dere too."

Simon stared back at him in shock, their gazes locked. "I...I'm sorry. So sorry," he stammered. The man did not reply, only continued to stare.

"I'm sorry," Simon repeated as he realized he looked into the eyes of a dead man.

CHAPTER SIX

A half-eaten bowl of cold porridge sat on the floor outside Simon's sleeping room. The Mistress of the King's Grille walked by and almost tripped over it, same as she did every day. She stooped to pick it up, muttering and shaking her head.

"Doesn't eat enough to feed a bird. The man will be withering away to nothing. At least he's paying us well enough." Shaking her head again she went downstairs. In the kitchen she found her husband testing the quality of the ale, as he regularly did each afternoon about that time.

He put down the mug, wiping his mouth with the back of his hand as she came in. "What you got there?"

"It's the Wizard's. Since he doesn't come out anymore I've been setting his food by his door. Hardly touches a thing. It's a shame, that's what it is."

"Since when have you been so concerned about the man? Let him live in peace. Or die in peace if he likes. If he wants to be alone, let him be. He's already paid another month in advance either way."

"It's not right, I tell you. The Wizard's special people. We can't let him waste away up there."

"Sarah, why do you keep calling him the Wizard? He's just a bloke who's got nowhere else to go."

"He is a Wizard, I say. You know I've been reading those papers his manservant kept."

"Constance has been reading," her husband corrected.

"You know what I mean well enough. Anyways, the writing tells about all these stories Simon, that's his given name, tells to people. And they all come true. All kinds of good stories with money and jobs and love."

The Innkeeper scowled at her. "What rubbish. I'll tell you who's been making up stories. His manservant, that's who."

Sarah sat down and stared her husband in the eyes. "It's true. You know it's true. You told me yourself what a strange and powerful man he is. All those things he told you to do...you had to do them. Said you couldn't seem not to. He is a Wizard all right and you know it."

He grumbled at her, taking another swig of ale. Simon had changed now his friend was dead. He no longer loomed above everyone, unfathomable, untouchable. He seemed reduced to a tired old man. So much older than when he first darkened their door a few weeks ago. The Innkeeper didn't want to be reminded that some old bloke had had him jumping like a toad every time he raised an eyebrow.

His wife looked at him slyly. "If we take care of him, when he's done with his grieving, maybe we'll get one of those stories. Be able to have one of those high-class places with servants to run it and do all the hard labor. If he dies all we get is whatever coin he might have left in his bags. If he lives we can have everything." She nodded encouragingly.

Her husband stopped and stared at her, eyebrows lifted, mind working, A smile snaked its way across his face. "Be sure to leave him plenty of food at his door," he said finally.

Simon sat in the quiet darkness of his room. He didn't bother to light a fire, let alone a candle. He rarely bothered to eat. He sat, all day, on the hard wooden chair by the window. Sometimes at night he moved over to the bed and lay there on the covers, staring at the ceiling. He had indeed gone to hell. The moment they entered this blasted city. No peace existed. No rest could be found.

He failed them all. It stood like a giant mountain before him. He couldn't find a road to lead him past. No seething anger this time. Just disappointment and resignation. In his heart, he knew it was finished. He could do no more. *Marcus is dead. The Trust is broken.*

The days of his unchanging routine slowly plodded on, turning into weeks. The new year came and went. The Innkeeper's wife left food regularly at his door and clucked as she picked it up later, virtually untouched. She would never get a story if he didn't start eating. In his room, Simon sat and mentally replayed Marcus' death and his own downfall, oblivious to the passing time. Not until he heard shouting and the sound of running feet did he rouse from his dark reverie. The noise grew and soon running feet drummed inside the tavern. Simon noted an acrid scent in the air. He jumped as someone pounded on his door.

"Sir. Sir. You must get out. The City's on fire."

Simon strode across the room and yanked the door open. "Whatever are you talking about? The whole City can't possibly be on fire."

The Innkeeper stood there with an ashen face. "It's the truth, Sir. Come to the street and look." He pulled at Simon's arm, then quickly let go. "Everyone's leaving." The man told the truth.

Simon grabbed Marcus' bag. Quickly putting on his belt of pouches and coat, he pushed past the Innkeep and ran down the stairs. People streamed through the streets, belongings strapped on their backs or piled into wagons. The sky clotted dark with smoke. Oily black clouds highlighted the flickering orange reflection of flames. London in 1666 proved a city of kindling. Filled with tight-packed, dry wood structures, it needed scant prodding to light up the sky. The Innkeeper's family spilled out of the tavern, their arms full of precious memories.

"Here." Simon motioned. "Take my carriage. There's plenty of room. Hitch up your horses and get out."

"Come with us. You can't stay here. The fire's spreading too fast." The Innkeeper's face drew tight with fear.

His wife flung herself at Simon. She clutched at his shirt front, eyes wide. "You can stop this, Master Simon. I know all about you. Tell a story, Simon. Save us, save our homes. You have the power."

Simon pulled away, stumbling back away from her.

Sarah grasped at the empty space he left, her hands raking the air. "You can save us, Simon. Why do you wait?"

The Innkeeper watched Simon's worn face keenly. "There's no time, love. He can't help us beyond what he's already done. He's only another old man. We must take his carriage and leave now." He pulled her towards their ride, mumbling soothing words.

"Simon!" she shrieked. "You have the power. Why don't you help us?"

He shook his head and turned quickly away. "I can't," he said. "Your husband is right. I can't help anyone."

He walked swiftly to the back of the Inn and saddled his horse. Mounting, he joined the mass exodus out of London.

He didn't bother returning to his room for the rest of his meager belongings. He kept only what he had on him. The fire burned for almost a week, leaving nearly the entire city in ashes. Simon rode away and didn't look back, ignoring the voices in his head reminding him of the Promise he once made.

"You've reached a decision, my son?" The Stallir stood at the cliff-top observing the unending ocean before him. He looked over at Simon as he approached.

"Yes, Liam. I have decided." Simon's hands twisted nervously in front of him until he forced them to his sides. Straightening his shoulders, he stood tall in front of his elder. "I have decided to accept."

Simon's heart pounded like the waves crashing against the rocks at the shore below. He knew he gave the only possible answer, but the thought of what he agreed to made him faint-headed.

"Very good," answered Liam, smiling though his eyes shone with sadness.

"What do we do now?"

"The other clans are on their way. The full moon is the night after next. We'll do the Joining then." Liam looked around him, taking in the beauty of the Irish countryside, the reassuring presence of his fellowmen. How he would miss it all. But they had chosen the greater good. Taken as a whole they made but a very small sacrifice compared to what they would accomplish.

He looked back at Simon, whose gaze had followed his own and now rested on the cloaked figures who made up his friends and family. Such a difficult task he asked of this young man. Liam would have liked more time to prepare him, but alas, it could not be. He could only pray, yes...pray maybe to this God of Patric's, that Síomón would have the strength to carry him through all that lay before him.

"Yes, Liam." Simon looked at him now. "Pray to Patric's God if it will help. I fear I might fail you. All of you." He waved his hand to include everyone.

"Remember Síomón, you will have all our wisdom, all our power combined into you. You will be able to touch lives, to change them for the better. Your power will be so great we can only imagine it. And your wisdom, hopefully, will be equal. For you must use your powers carefully and only for the betterment of mankind. To resort to evil will mean we have all given ourselves in vain. You have goodness inside you, Síomón. I know I can trust you to follow it."

"I appreciate your trust, Liam. The trust all the elders have placed in me. I promise I'll not let you down. But," he hesitated then embraced the older man roughly. "I shall miss you, Liam. I shall miss all of you."

Liam closed his eyes, his heart heavy. They did the right thing, he had no doubt. But what a difficult thing. Although the boy was somewhat frightened, he could sense his excitement too. Only time would reveal to him the awful responsibility he had accepted and show him who had made the real sacrifice.

"I know, Síomón. Just remember. We will live on inside you. Your memories will keep us alive."

Simon sagged in the saddle, his shoulders drooping in sad resignation. He rode north out of London, working his way west towards Wales. He dared get no closer to Ireland.

He needed some small comfort of his homeland, but he could never go to that lovely green isle again. Not after what he had done.

He wandered aimlessly until he discovered a long abandoned cabin in the woods, perfect for his needs. Totally secluded without a trace of mankind for miles. They would be safe from him.

The solitude did not bother him. Except for Marcus, he had been alone since his journey began. Liam had spoken the truth, though. He should never have allowed himself to get close to anyone. Maybe then he wouldn't hurt so much from Marcus' passing. Maybe then he could have saved him from the Plague. Guilt followed Simon like a faithful dog.

With a sense of relief, he set to work preparing his new home. The physical labor gave his mind a different focus and he gratefully blocked out the pain of his recent past.

Simon first examined the cabin's framework and tested the soundness of the wood. He shoved against the building, grunting in satisfaction when it didn't give. The construction proved solid. As long as the foundation and framework stood strong anything else could be fixed. Looking up at the patches of sky through the roof, Simon easily determined his ensuing priority.

He spent the next few days in nearby fields gathering long grasses, and alongside a large stream-fed pond where he found a supply of rushes. As he squatted by the water tying his dried reeds into bundles with the sweat beading on his brow, Simon could almost feel content. At least he did no harm here. Between his two sources of materials, he soon had enough sheaves to repair the holes and add a fresh layer of thatch all over the roof. It took another week to accomplish but he welcomed the work, grateful for the activity.

Simon's attention then turned to the cracks and gaps in

the walls. He located a large piece of bark for transporting mud from the pond, which he mixed with short pieces of rough grass chopped up with a sharp-edged stone. The resulting stiff mixture he stuffed into the cracks, blocking out shafts of filtered light. Once dried, it held well and kept out the wind. Next, Simon tightened the shutters and rehung the door. He found it a hard-working few weeks, but worthwhile. Now he could truly make this house his home.

Inside, he tied a small bundle of rushes to a stick and used this makeshift broom to sweep away the years of accumulated cobwebs and dust. He cleared out some trash and made a pile of the broken furniture bits that had been left behind. With some ingenuity and elbow grease most of it he could make usable again. He swept the solid-packed dirt floor clear of debris and gathered fresh pine boughs from the woods, which he laid in a corner for his bed. He cleared old leaves and twigs from the sturdy chimney and cleaned out the hearth. Next to it, he piled broken pieces of dead wood for his fire.

Over the following weeks he repaired the furniture. Simple and sturdy, more than sufficient for his needs. He had a chair and table and, by piecing assorted miscellany together, what would suffice as a work counter. A couple fragments of old planks provided some shelves. Simon stood back and looked over his accomplishments, his head nodding approval. A fine cabin.

With surprise, he realized how pleasant the work over these many weeks had been. It felt good to do more than stare at a wall and think. The labor occupied his days and the physical exertion caused him to sleep deeply at night. He badly needed such a diversion and would not willingly give it up and go back to sitting yet.

A garden. That would be his new project. It would take some real work to get a patch of rich brown earth cleared out. A practical yet time-consuming task. The bread and cheese he had picked up while searching for his new home had long ago run out. He had made do with nuts and berries found in the woods, along with some plant greens and tuberous roots. Meat never posed a problem as his snares worked quite well. But it would be pleasant if he could grow a few vegetables and have a nice stew.

Simon picked a likely spot to the side of the cabin and marked it off. Hauling away the stones turned out to be a bigger job than he had expected, but not an impossible one. He started piling them around the plot as a makeshift low fence. He left a couple very large rocks where they lie, thinking he would simply plant around them. However, after spending one long day trying to break up the soil and unearth the bushes and weeds, Simon soon found bare hands and a sharpened stone would not be sufficient to get the job done.

He reluctantly acknowledged that despite his best efforts to find or create the items he needed, he would have to make a trip into a town for some supplies. The realization disturbed him. He had sought to be self-sufficient and eliminate any need for contact with other people. *Just this once,* he grudgingly consoled himself, *and I'll never go back again.*

He made a list and checked it several times. He had to be thorough and careful with his choices for there would be no second trip. He would require some tools, including a pick, an axe, and a shovel. More specific items for woodworking, tanning leather, preparing and spinning yarn. Some water bags, a couple buckets, a pitcher, and a few pots, along with a couple of sturdy plates, bowls, and mugs. Eating and cooking utensils, some blankets. Various seeds for planting, a rooster, some hens, two nanny goats and a buck, the same in ewes and a ram. Not much for a lifetime, but enough for a start.

Simon pulled out one of the pouches he had hidden in his cabin and rehung it on his belt. Saddling his mare he started off reluctantly. He rode all day without coming across another living soul. As he untied the blanket rolled behind his saddle and prepared to spend a night among the trees and stars, he gave a silent prayer of thanks. His cabin proved as isolated as he had hoped. Little fear of civilization encroaching too close to him.

He awoke before dawn and set off again. The mid-day sun blazed when he finally sighted a small village. Circling wide of the town, he started at the far side, buying a small wagon to haul his new belongings home in. He hitched it to his horse and continued on. He received some odd looks, for strangers rarely rode through, but had no difficulty in finding what he needed.

He spread his purchases out, a few things at each stop, so he wouldn't draw too much attention. He bought the animals and seeds from far-spaced outlying farms. The goats and sheep he tied so they could walk along in back, while the chickens rode in rough woven bags. He threw in a few sacks of grain to make sure the animals had enough food until he produced his own. To his surprise and delight, he came across two small books for sale. A rare find in small villages and probably the only ones in the whole area.

He held his tongue and carefully evaded questions. He had no desire to speak to anyone more than necessary. Simon especially avoided looking at people. He did not want to see their lives or know their stories. Unworthy as he had shown himself to be, he should not even walk among them let alone presume to help. He did his business and moved on. He had to step carefully, for he felt a bit light-headed. His chest constricted tightly and he couldn't seem to get enough air. As soon as he had everything loaded up, he swiftly left the area. Not until the village faded well out of sight could Simon breathe properly again. But, he had his supplies. He never had to return.

Simon hurried back to his cabin, driven by the shadows haunting him. At the cabin he was safe. At the cabin he could do no harm. Relief washed over him as the old structure came into view the following evening. *I made it,* he thought. Taking a cloth from his pocket, he mopped the sweat from his neck and brow. He looked at the isolated homestead and nodded his head. His penance. Not much to look at. More than he deserved.

What Simon had been and what he had accomplished no longer had any meaning. His past died with Marcus, burnt away with the fire. He had no more heart left in him to continue the lost quest. He lived with despair built into a high wall around himself, holding his guilt close like a warm blanket. He accepted full blame for all the tragedies that had occurred. He had not kept his Promise. He had broken the Trust.

The seasons came and went, the years passing until once again the warm days lengthened. Simon stepped out of his cabin and walked around to the side. It was the Summer Solstice. He etched a small line on the cabin wall to mark the special day then moved off to complete his chores. The wall was filled with such marks. Simon had stopped counting them long ago, somewhere in the late 1700s. The weathered cabin and surrounding area had a decidedly worn and settled-in appearance. Smoke drifted lazily from the chimney, the aroma of vegetable stew wafting from the windows. A well-tended garden sat off to the side. Small fields of grain sprouted farther away.

A lean-to attached to the cabin covered a dug-out area containing a root cellar for vegetables and a place to hang meats. Nearby sat a small, domed bread oven made from bricks of mud and straw. Inside, the cabin now had a smooth wooden floor covering the hard-packed dirt, scattered with beautiful rugs woven by Simon's own hand. On the rugs stood sturdy, yet attractive furniture which Simon had carved and fashioned himself.

The corner where he had slept on pine boughs now opened into a small bedroom furnished with a comfortable bed with intricately carved posts. They resembled tree trunks with miniature animals scampering up them or peeking out from holes and were covered by twisting vines upon which rested various birds and butterflies. Like all the furnishings in the small cabin, a work of art. A great amount of time had been spent, not only in the creation of the furniture but also in the study of the wildlife they celebrated.

The bed's mattress consisted of a hand-woven sack stuffed with wool trimmed from his sheep over the many years. His old homemade spinning wheel and weaving loom sat near the window, well worn from use, and had balls of wool yarn piled between them in a rough basket. Bundles of dried flowers, herbs, and medicinal plants hung from the rafters.

Out front protruded a small porch upon which a comfortable rocking chair swayed in the gentle breeze. On the side of his home opposite the garden, Simon's animals had a wooden shelter of their own with a fenced paddock enclosing some woods as well as pasture. His original few had reproduced into a nice flock. The sheep and goats romped together and the chickens clucked and scratched near their coop. Simon's horse, however, had long since died and he had not replaced her. If he had the urge to wander the woods, he found it better done on foot anyways.

Simon squatted on his hands and knees in the garden, weeding. He hummed and whistled as he worked the fragrant soil. He had straight rows of cabbages and turnips, carrots and potatoes, some onions, garlic, and a few parsnips. He didn't require much variety, only sufficient bulk to fill his stomach when hungry. His goats supplied fresh milk for drinking, and he made different cheeses from both the goats and the sheep. In exchange, he shared his extra vegetables with them. The older animals eventually wound up smoked or dried to provide Simon with occasional meat.

Sitting up on his haunches, Simon wiped his forehead with the back of his hand leaving a trace of moist earth there. He could hear the voices again. He'd been hearing them inside his head, off and on, for years now. The first few times had been frightening. In the beginning, Simon questioned his sanity. Then he began to wonder about being haunted. Nothing further ever happened, just the vague voices, and after several months he grew used to them. As hard as he tried, he never could understand any individual words, only an impression of many voices calling. If they held a message it couldn't be deciphered. As usual, Simon blocked them out and went about his business.

He smiled at his growing crops in satisfaction and bent back over. One more row to weed and he finished for the day. He worked his way down the patch and stood at the end, rubbing his stiff back.

Leaner, his face quite worn, he had long hair streaked gray and white, tied back out of his way. Both the hair and his beard grew rather shaggy and unkempt from lack of a good cut. He brushed his hands off on his baggy wool pants. After years of practice in spinning yarn, weaving, and sewing, he felt quite adept at creating his own clothing. However, wool could get quite warm no matter how finely spun, so he preferred his clothes on the loose side to allow for some ventilation.

Simon walked back to his cabin rolling his shoulders and shaking his legs, trying to work the kinks out. *I must be getting old,* he thought. *I never used to get so sore from bending over in the garden.* He took a long drink of water before pouring some into a basin. He quickly washed up, enjoying the feel of the cold water on his hot, dusty skin. He patted himself dry with a cloth and stepped up onto the porch. Sighing, he eased himself into the rocker. A squirrel appeared almost immediately on the arm of the chair. Simon chuckled as he pulled some bread crumbs from his pocket and fed him.

"Hello there, my good fellow. Is it treat day already?" He looked up to see a dozen more squirrels approaching as the air filled with the flapping of wings. The birds settled on the porch rails and nearby tree branches.

"Well. That answers the question. I suppose it is treat day. Excuse me then friend. I must get on with it. The masses are waiting."

Simon disappeared into the house briefly and returned with two sacks. From the first, he took handfuls of grains and seeds sweetened with honey and scattered them among the clustered animals. He threw a couple more handfuls off to the side where the birds would feel more comfortable. He looked towards the woods and saw a half-dozen rabbits poised there. Whistling softly, he approached them as he reached into the second sack.

Naturally timid animals, they trusted Simon. However, they still preferred to stay out of the wide-open area and away from the other creatures. He knelt before his downy friends and pulled out some carrots and assorted greens. Distributing the treats, he reached out and gently stroked the silky fur of an older rabbit.

"Good afternoon, Prudence. You look in fine form today. And how is Hubert?" He looked over the remaining rabbits then returned his gaze to Prudence. "Where is Hubert? Is he all right? He never misses treat day."

The rabbit stared intently at Simon, her dark eyes unwavering. Her nose and whiskers twitched rapidly, then her ears jerked suddenly to the right. Simon's eyes followed the direction of her ears and saw his two other guests waiting beside the garden. His eyes narrowed and his jaw tightened as he stood and approached the foxes.

Simon towered over them, his voice low and cold. "You know my rules. It is not that you can't hunt, for hunting is what foxes do. It is that you can't hunt here and make the other members of our family your prey. We have all followed the rules for many, many years and it has benefited all of us. You have thrown it away."

The foxes sank to the ground and rolled over to expose their soft bellies in sorrow and submission.

"It is no use. I trusted you. Now, you have broken that trust." Simon stopped suddenly, the words echoing with thunderous force in his mind. *Broken the Trust.* He hid his face in his hands as he fell to his knees. "Oh, God." *Broken the Trust.* "How can I condemn them for my own sin?"

He sat in the dirt, unmoving, for many minutes. The animals waited, quiet and still, tensed for flight. The way they waited in the woods when they sensed trouble at hand.

Memories flooded over Simon. Memories he had worked hard to keep buried. Thoughts he didn't want to face again.

They came for him. He could hear the footsteps

crunching through the dirt and rocks outside. Simon stood and placed his hood up over his head. The bags of gold, silver, and jewels tied to his belt hung heavy and cumbersome. He carried the wealth of all the Druid clans, saved for this purpose alone. Enough to sustain him through many, many years. Simon thought he'd surely have no opportunity to use even half of it. A separate pouch carried a large clear blue crystal, while his hands gripped blankets tied around food and clothes, his flint, some twine, a sack of powder, and more coins.

His heart raced with excitement, with fear. Out of all the worthy men in all the clans, they had chosen him. Although very proud of this, he had been careful not to act overly important with his friends. Impressed anyways, they treated him with great honor. He had rather enjoyed all the attention and special care. Tonight's ceremony would be the grand finale for all of Liam's preparations.

They waited at the door. Simon walked out to join them. He found Dougal, their own Seer, and a Seer from another clan. A few others stood there, including his friend Tadhg.

"Tadhg. Thank you for coming to walk with me. I regret we haven't had much time together these past days, but I'm glad you're here now." Simon stepped close and embraced his friend. Tadhg stood stiffly, his return embrace half-hearted. Speaking lightly to ease the tension in the air, Simon said, "I guess you were wrong. They didn't want me to be the next Stallir." They all managed a brief chuckle, though Tadhg had only a forced smile.

They started down the path to the circle, the two Seers flanking Simon. Tadhg fell in line last, the forced smile fading quickly from his face. He glared at Simon's back with intense jealousy akin to hatred. With effort, he smoothed his face to a controlled mask.

Simon could see Liam down there waiting with many

others. He didn't realize how many of the People existed until he saw them assembled like this, layer upon layer, circled around the wood prepared for a bonfire. A shiver coursed through him. What would really happen tonight?

They approached the ring and Liam smiled, the same sad smile he had given ever since Simon accepted. Complete fear now took over any feelings of excitement or anticipation present within him. He wanted to run away but his feet, with a power all their own, took him inside the circle. There he stood alone, facing Liam and the other Stallirs.

"It will be all right, Síomón." The words drifted through his mind, reassuring him.

The chant began. Three times they repeated the words. As the voices stopped, Liam took the Sacred Flame and lit the fire. This time he did not withdraw the carrier rod. There would be no more use for it after tonight. He returned to the line, pausing momentarily as he passed Simon.

"You have chosen well, my son. I am proud of you." Their eyes met and held. Even as Liam joined the other Stallirs and the chanting began again they did not break the connection.

The group joined hands. Their voices resounded in unison, growing louder. They moved closer, Simon realized. The fire hissed and spat. Waves crashed in the distance. Even the wind howled in acknowledgment.

He suddenly felt a crushing weight. The very air squeezed out of his body. They kept moving closer and closer. He could see Liam's eyes, large and dark before him. They radiated a power stronger than anything Simon had imagined.

Briefly, to the side, he caught a puzzling glimpse of Tadhg. Why did he sneer that way? He had no time for questions. The chanting roared through his ears. It seared his brain. He could feel the heat of the fire burning at his flesh. The pressure on his body intensified.

He could not breathe at all now. Had they lied to him then? Had they simply wanted to get rid of him for some reason? Did they arrange all this so he would willingly walk in here for them to kill him?

He could bear it no longer. Simon's voice broke loose in a shrill scream of pain and terror. Liam's face floated in front of his own with a sad smile. All faded to blackness.

How long he lay there he had no idea. He slowly came around, his eyes gradually focusing. The clearing stood empty. Nothing remained of the fire but cold ashes. Even the carrier rod seemed consumed. He carefully pushed himself to his feet expecting to be weak and tired. Instead, he found himself full of energy with a strength he did not remember. He called out to the others. No answer came.

Simon looked around, bewildered. Maybe they had told the truth after all. Everyone appeared gone. Could they be here inside him? He felt his arms, his chest, looked at his legs, down his back. He didn't seem to be any different. Only that funny feeling inside.

The dirt. He made a quick examination of the circle. He found all the footprints leading down, circling the fire. He could trace how they had all closed in on him. And then they stopped. Just stopped. No retreating footsteps, no hurried departures. Simply gone. He was truly alone.

Simon stood in the ashes, looking at the emptiness around him. What did he do now? All his friends, his family, the elders, even Liam...all forever gone. If only he could take it back, undo the ceremony. Maybe they could have found a different solution. Maybe they could have selected at least one other to go with him. Too late for choices now. He stood alone. For how many years would he have to live with their loss...and his loneliness? Simon's hands clenched at his sides as he raised his head and gave a mournful wail that echoed throughout the countryside.

Slowly Simon lowered his hands and looked again at the foxes. "It is not your fault. You are only foxes after all. Simply doing what foxes do. There is nothing for me to blame or forgive. I, however, am a man. I should have known better. But that didn't stop me either."

He pushed himself clumsily to his feet and waved the animals away. "Go. Go and be what you are. Be a fox. Be a rabbit. It isn't my place to make you companions for me. I have no right to impose standards of living that are so at odds with what your true life cycles demand. I cannot make you pay for my own mistakes. Go." He waved again and the animals quickly dispersed in a flurry of feathers and fur.

Simon stood alone in the clearing, observing his solitude. "Ah, Liam," he whispered to the sky. "You told the truth. I saw the pain in your eyes that night and I puzzled it shone for me. Now I understand. You did indeed know I would have a hard path to follow. But did you know it would end like this?"

"Look, Liam." He pointed to his fields of wheat and oats. "See the way the wind moves along the top of the grain? It touches each stalk and passes by. It never settles in among them, never stays to see what it's done. It can never truly be a part of the field. It simply keeps moving. On and on and on. I am the wind, Liam." Simon sighed and began shuffling towards his cabin.

"And," he mused, "if the wind stays in one place too long it begins to fade away and die out. Is that what comes next then? I am growing old. I have stopped too long and death is all I have left to do in my life."

The breeze suddenly picked up and a blast of harsh wind

ripped by. Simon stopped in surprise, his eyes following the traces of the wayward gust. It crashed and twisted into the wheat field then fizzled away. Simon hurried over, puzzled by the short but sudden gale, concerned for any damage it had done. Relieved, he could see none. The field looked the same as before. A gentle breeze caressed him, cooling his brow, helping to carry a young bird on its first flight.

Moving away Simon's eyes caught something amiss at the edge of the field. Some damage after all. A few stalks were bent over. He smiled as he walked closer. Just a few...not so bad. A wind so powerful could have destroyed everything, but it didn't. Simon picked up the stalks. Three. He only lost three. Granted it was a shame to lose any, but many more survived. The wind provided more help than harm and he could accept that three stalks had been lost.

The wind killed three. Simon put a hand to his face as if slapped. *I am the wind.* The earth spun beneath him and he staggered to keep from falling. He took deep breaths as he tried to regain his equilibrium. Suddenly he stood straight and looked around.

"Liam. Are you here, Liam? Did you do this?" No answer. Simon still stood alone. "What does it mean, Liam?"

He walked back to his porch and slowly sat in the rocking chair. "What does it mean? The wind had the power to destroy it all, but it only destroyed three. I am responsible for the death of three. But the fact I could have caused the death of many more doesn't excuse the ones I did. No, no...that's not it. I'm sure this is a message for me, but I'm missing it."

He closed his eyes and rubbed his temples, concentrating. "The wind does much good. Its value far exceeds its deficiencies. We don't like or excuse the damage but we can understand it. Maybe forgive it. Or at least live with it. The wind goes on, regardless, and does what it's supposed to do. Is that it? The wind goes on?"

Simon looked around at the first place he could truly call home in many, many years and shook his head. "Could it be that my time to fade away has not yet arrived? That running away wasn't the answer to my failing? Maybe there's still time to make amends. Maybe that is the message in the wind."

He placed a hand on his brow as he recalled the gentle cooling breeze. With closed eyes, he saw the fledgling sail high on a wind current. Despite the destruction, the wind had still provided good. He knew the message. The wind would go on, and so must he.

He must re-enter the world.

CHAPTER SEVEN

THE big store windows gave a clear reflection of the old man as he walked by. Simon stopped in surprise and felt the smooth glass. *Amazing,* he thought. *Everything is amazing. I don't ever recall a time when things advanced this quickly. It's only been what, one hundred and sixty years or so?* He looked at his reflection in puzzlement. Other than in a pool of water, he had never seen what he looked like.

Peering closer, he ran a hand through his long, shaggy white hair. Chopping it occasionally with a knife had done no favors for it. His beard hung scraggly and unkempt, his homespun clothes odd and outdated. He looked around, all too aware of the stir his appearance created. Obviously, clothing styles had changed drastically during his absence as well.

Everything had changed. Simon had avoided civilization

and once he became self-sufficient never returned to a town again. The times he knew existed no longer. He looked back at his reflection. He saw an old man. Worse, he felt like an old man. Time finally seemed to be running out for him after all.

The revelation acted as a catalyst. It had taken some time for him to work up enough nerve to actually come into town. He had even begun to doubt the message in the wind. Now he realized he couldn't let life end on the road he'd been following. A crazy old hermit dying alone in the woods. Determined, he marched down the street until he found a barbershop. He opened the door and went in, a tiny bell tinkling to let the owner know someone entered. Simon jumped at the sound then smiled at the ingenuity. He shook the bell again to enjoy the melodious tone.

"Sir. Sir, please."

Simon chuckled. "I like that...tells you when the door opens, eh? You think that up yourself?"

"No, I'm afraid not." The young man stepped back, looking at Simon in dismay. "Is there something I can do for you?" His tone and expression showed his distaste.

"Well, I'm badly in need of a haircut and shave." Simon chuckled again, ignoring the young man's sneer. "I've been in the country for a while. Didn't realize I'd gotten quite this bad."

The man responded by tapping a price board near the door. "Prices have probably gone up since the last time you've seen the inside of a barbershop. Better check your pockets first."

Simon pulled himself up to his full height, shoulders back, fire in his eyes. He glared his answer.

"Charles." An older man hurried out from the back. "I think that's quite enough," he said angrily. "You've been warned already about your tongue. Maybe you should take the next couple of days off to think about it some more."

"Maybe I'll take the rest of my life off. I don't need to be subjected to the likes of him. I never cared for this position anyways." He stomped towards the back. "Go ahead and take your charity case, it's no concern of mine."

The owner turned apologetically to Simon. "It's hard to get good help nowadays."

"It always has been."

"That is for certain. Well, come over and have a seat. That's quite a head of hair you have there so I best get started. Wish mine had held up as well." He patted his bald top with a smile. "How much do you want taken off?"

"Most of it, I think. Whatever it takes to bring me up to date."

The barber laughed. "If it's up to date you want to be, most of it will have to go. The rest we'll have to fairly plaster to your head. These are modern times, you know. It is 1824, after all."

"Yes, 1824," Simon mused. He looked thoughtfully at the barber, straining to see inside the man. It had been so long. A fading image filtered through his mind of a man looking over his accounts with a worried frown. A small start.

"Do you mind if I tell a quick story while you work?"

"Please do. I love a good story."

"It's nothing much really. Just a barber I heard of who spent his life building up his business and a broad base of regular customers. He went out of his way to make everyone who entered his shop feel special. He treated them all well, young or old, rich or poor. But the times changed and new barbers appeared. The gentleman I speak of grew older and he began to worry at the drop in his business. If things didn't improve he would have no money after he grew too old to run his shop. Many a night he spent looking over his accounts, wondering how he'd pay all his debts and still have money for his family to live on."

The barber clucked in sympathy. "I feel for the gentleman. It's a position I can definitely understand." A look of fear suddenly crossed his face. "He came out all right, didn't he? I'd hate to think of a hard working fellow like that ending up in debtor's prison."

"Oh yes. He came out fine. The fellow put signs out front of his shop stating a shave and a haircut would be half-price for the next three days only. Had a big boom in business. Many new customers tried him out and, being so impressed with his fine treatment and skilled trimmings, he ended up acquiring a new flood of regulars. Paid off all his debts and put away a tidy sum to carry him through the rest of his days."

"What a splendid idea. You don't suppose the gentleman would mind if I tried it out, do you?"

"Certainly not. In fact, I think he would insist. Why don't you make the signs today?"

"I will. As soon as I clean you off and send you on your way."

Simon admired himself in the mirror with a smile, rubbing his bare chin. "Wonderful. How much do I owe you?" he asked, reaching for the pouch at his waist.

"Not a thing. Consider it a trade for the fine story you told me. After all, I am borrowing the idea."

Simon smiled again and nodded his thanks. He walked out of the shop looking like a new man. With a cheery farewell to the barber, he set out in the direction of a tailor the kind gentleman recommended. It felt good to mingle with people again. He had been away far too long.

The clerk in the tailor's shop proved very helpful, making several suggestions to help Simon find the right style for himself. Truly quite a task, since up to this point he'd had no style. Finally, they finished, both satisfied.

Simon left with several purchases, including the tweed outfit he wore complete with a bowler.

He passed the big store window again, pausing once more to look at his reflection. He nodded in satisfaction, adjusting his hat to a jaunty angle. Time to truly join the world again. He spent many, many years mourning his friend, regretting his mistakes. The earth did not open up to swallow him. No spirits came to haunt him. He had paid his penance and wasted many years.

I must salvage what's left, he thought. *If I'm to die soon, then let it be with dignity. Let it be in completing that which they sent me to do. If the power is still here to do it with.*

Simon continued down the street, looking intently at each person who passed. At first, he could pick up nothing. Out of practice, they walked by too quickly for him to break through. Finally, he sat down next to a young man on a bench who stared thoughtfully at a building across the street. Simon turned to him casually, his physical demeanor in contrast with his intense and probing eyes. He caught only a fading glimmer such as he experienced with the barber.

Simon closed his eyes and concentrated. After a moment he felt a wrenching inside himself and the wall that blocked him out began to tumble. His body relaxed against the bench as images of the man's life flooded through. A thought wormed its way into his brain and he turned away briefly. *The wall collapsed from within,* he realized. *They did not block me out. I closed myself in.*

He turned back to the gentleman and took a deep breath. "You seem very distracted, young man. Are you feeling quite well?"

The man glanced at him, then turned his eyes back to the building. "Well enough, I suppose."

"I see. Perhaps I can offer a small respite from your

troubles. Do you mind if I share a bit of a story with you?"

The young man looked at him again, a bit longer this time. Finally he smiled. "Most definitely. A story would be wonderful." He glanced back at the building. "I've nothing better to do today."

"Well then. This is the story of a young man I once met by the name of Robert."

"Robert, really? That's my name as well."

"You don't say. What an odd coincidence. Now I'm sure you'll enjoy this story since you already have so much in common."

"I'm sure I will. Please go on."

"A smart young man, Robert successfully put himself through school. It had been a long, hard struggle, but he persevered against the odds. Once school ended, however, he felt a bit lost. Where to go, what to do next?"

Robert's mouth hung open and his eyes widened. "What did he do next?"

"He heard about a good position with an accounting firm. Robert loved numbers and he loved lining up the columns and having everything balance out at the end. Really quite skilled, you see, and absolutely perfect for the position. Perfect except he lacked confidence. He actually sat outside the accounting firm's office for two days trying to gather the strength to walk in and ask for an interview."

Robert let out a shaky breath and glanced at the building across the street again.

"Finally he could wait no longer. Almost like the sun coming out from behind the clouds, he suddenly realized the value of his skills and how much he had to offer. With this newfound courage, he marched right over to the firm and requested an interview. He outlined his education, training, and skills, and the head of the firm took him in for a meeting immediately. Turns out the firm wanted someone exactly like him."

"He got the position?" Robert's voice squeaked.

Simon leaned closer. "Of course he got the position. He had faith in himself. And Robert, faith is always rewarded."

Robert breathed deeply and looked across the street, deep in thought. He chewed on his lip, then squinted his eyes. Finally, he stood up and straightened his jacket, extending his hand to Simon.

"Thank you very much for sharing your story, Sir. I found it extremely...enlightening. I'd love to stay and chat but I find I've got a task I need to complete."

Simon shook his hand, his gaze following Robert's to the building across the street. "It's been my pleasure, Robert. I'm so glad to see you're feeling better."

Robert smiled. "I feel much better actually. I think the sun coming out must have helped." He tipped his hat and moved towards the street. "Good day, Sir, and thank you once again."

Simon sauntered down the walkway, fairly swaggering. He had done it and he felt good. For over one hundred and sixty years he had hidden away with his mistakes, convinced he had lost it all. But he still had the powers and he hadn't been hit by lightning when he used them. The hope still existed. Joy such as he had not felt for centuries surged through him and he couldn't help but give a cheerful hop as he walked.

He didn't know how many years he had left but for as long as he could, Simon determined to make up for lost time. Maybe he could find forgiveness yet. Telling stories one on one made a good start but he needed more. He needed to find a way to reach a group all at once, like in the old days. At least for a while. Long enough to feel he began to make up for those wasted years and wasted lives.

London. I must return to London, he thought. *That's*

where I fell from grace. That's where I must redeem myself. I'll find a family who would benefit from receiving my cabin and its contents. I've still plenty of gold and coins in my pouches. All I need is a small bag of my personal things, like before. Then I will start telling my stories as I cross the country and head towards London.

The young woman tried to walk past the tiny bookstore without stopping to look, but as usual, she did not succeed. A sigh escaped her lips at sight of the slim volumes and booklets on display. She clenched and unclenched her hands, longing for the day she could walk in and buy something...anything. Setting her jaw in resignation, she took a step to leave when she noticed the sign:

All Welcome
A Reading of Literary Works
By Master Storyteller
Friday 5 October, 7:00 O'clock P.M.
Edmond's Hall
No Charge for Attendance

Katherine Torrence's hands flew to her mouth in excitement. A Master Storyteller at Edmond's Hall. He appeared tonight and it wouldn't cost her a pence. She moved away from the window, then quickly stepped back to look one more time. Yes, it really said 'No Charge'; everyone was welcome to just walk in and listen. With a joyous skip, she hurried home. Finally a genuine reading. No need to pretend this time.

At precisely 7:05 p.m. Simon stepped onto the short

front platform and nodded to the full room with a small smile. His flyers for this final performance had gotten a full response. A good group of people too, from various walks of life. Exactly what he'd hoped for. He purposely chose small neighborhood halls in lesser-known areas such as this one, for he feared he would draw only the upper crust of society with readings. Not that the rich didn't have their own problems and heartaches, but his heart always reached out to the hardworking poor.

Upon his return arrival in this city, Simon saw with relief London had recovered from his last encounter. In fact, he thought it to be better than ever. Coming back to tell his stories had been a good choice. It acted as a balm to soothe his soul and assured him he had a right to hold onto his hopes for forgiveness.

He looked over his audience until his eyes caught sight once more of his final subject for the night. Despite his shock at seeing her, he had known Katherine the moment she walked into the room, just like he had known her ancestor before her. He smiled. Katy. Her family and friends called her Katy.

As her life unfolded in his mind he felt once again the long-buried pain. He had not expected to experience it ever again. Somehow the two women, separated by centuries, shared the same spirit, the same essence. He could see the same beautiful soul in Katy he first saw and loved in Katherine. This unforeseen rebirth of his longing for a love he could not have proved almost more than he could bear.

But Simon well knew the penalty for allowing someone into his life. He would not let it happen again. He attempted to block from his mind the vision of joy and happiness such a love could bring. Like a splinter buried too deep to pluck out, the thought remained and festered. Only twice in his many long years had he found someone who touched his soul this deeply. After tonight he would have passed both on for others to love. Even if he could not have that happiness, he would be sure this special woman, like Katherine before her, would experience all the joy he could not.

He pulled his eyes away from Katy and focused on his first subject, a solemn old gentleman sitting alone in the front.

"My first tale tonight is the sad story of the estranged father. He was raised in a very stern home and, while he did not enjoy his childhood, he believed it the proper way for such things to be. After all, his parents were not evil. Just harsh and unloving. He had grown up fine and had a moderately successful life."

In the audience, an old gentleman's eyes narrowed and he pulled on his collar as if it suddenly choked him. He shifted his weight in the chair uneasy with the story, though he couldn't say why.

"He eventually married a fine wife, chosen partly because she exuded love and warmth and happiness. Qualities at least part of him recognized as sadly lacking in himself. They had only two children, as the wife's doctor instructed her health would be seriously threatened by further childbirth. Most unfortunately, the young daughter died of the fever before she grew to be seven years old. The older brother survived unharmed. The family grieved openly for the loss of their darling. All, except the father. He had been taught grief was a thing to be borne privately, and silently, and shared with none. The pain existed, it is true, but his outward appearance reflected none of it. He even counseled his son to bury his sorrow and act like a man."

Simon looked sadly at the audience as if sharing the family's feeling of loss. His eyes flickered briefly to Katy but he forced them to move on.

"The son felt deeply disturbed at his father's apparent

lack of compassion and feeling. It caused an even deeper rift than already existed between them. As soon as he could the son left home and never spoke to his father again. The mother took it extremely hard. Even though she maintained contact with her child, she could not bring father and son together. Shortly thereafter she passed on, her family still broken."

"The old man lived alone now. Some days the pain of his losses overwhelmed him. He could hide it no longer. One night he found the courage to re-evaluate his life and saw how he had failed himself and his loved ones. With honest eyes, he realized those qualities he loved and received so freely from his wife were the qualities he refused to grow within himself."

"He knew his son had married and had a young girl of his own, now the same age as the old man's daughter when she died. He watched them from afar. His heart skipped a beat when he saw the golden hair of his own daughter gleam brightly on the head of his granddaughter or heard his wife's tinkling laughter flow from the young girl's mouth. He longed for forgiveness and acceptance. Was it too late to make amends? How could he possibly restore his family?"

"He didn't realize his son shared his suffering. His boy wanted to rebuild what they had lost but didn't know how to approach his father after all those years. He feared his father would close the door in his face. He couldn't go through that again...the old man needed to bridge the rift first. Somehow, as if he finally sensed what needed doing, the man knocked timidly on his son's door the following day. His appearance provoked great surprise and hesitation at first, then the son took his father into his arms and held him tight. They were a family again. The mother looked down from heaven above, cradling their daughter in her arms, and smiled."

The audience buzzed with whispered comments.

Families attending the storytelling together looked at each other, patting and smiling, glad for the closeness they shared. The old man near the front sat hunched over, holding his head in his hands. He looked up at Simon, nodded his head, then leaned back over in deep thought. Simon smiled then glanced over at a pretty girl sitting quietly next to her mother. He began his next story.

"There once lived a young girl of nine, very sweet and lovely. Quick, bright, and quite the pride and joy of her parents. A perfect child. Except for one slight impediment. The girl could not talk. Her parents worked with her for years, coaching and prodding and enticing. They took her to doctor after doctor with always the same result. They didn't know why she lacked a voice and they couldn't offer a cure. Finally, the parents decided to stop trying. No more elixirs, no more exercises, no more hot compresses."

Mother and daughter stared at Simon with big eyes. The mother's arm rested protectively around the girl's shoulders. She shook her head as if to say, 'Don't do this to my child. Don't hurt her any more than she's already been hurt.' Simon moved the story quickly along.

"They didn't love their girl any less. Perhaps they loved her even more for the hardships she faced. They had simply and sadly come to accept they would never hear the sweet song of her voice. They would not subject her to any more poking and prodding."

Simon leaned forward and looked intently at his audience. "Maybe because of the release from all the medical intrusions or perhaps because of the great love her parents had for her. Whatever the reason, one night as the little girl and her mother stepped out into the brisk night air, the child looked up at her with large eyes and spoke. In clear and melodious tones the child said simply, 'I love you, Mama.' The parents had a great celebration and all rejoiced over the daughter's miracle." He nodded at his listeners and smiled at the young girl. "Never forget what Simon says. Faith is always rewarded."

Sighs exhaled throughout the room and more than one handkerchief dabbled at an eye. The people appreciated the stories as simple heartwarming tales. Whether true or not they never questioned. Even the slight possibility they could be true uplifted them all.

Simon went through several other tales until he began to tire and his voice grew hoarse. Clearing his throat, he began unfolding his last story. He narrated Katy's life, waiting for signs of recognition.

"This beautiful young woman had large inquisitive eyes and gleaming dark hair that hid a tiny birthmark below her right ear. Although from a well-bred background, her family had fallen on hard times and now lived a meager life. At home she had to care for a sickly mother and a younger sister, quiet and withdrawn, having less fiber than our young lady. The father passed on several years earlier after being swindled out of the family fortune by his friend and partner."

It did not take long for Katy to know. Her mouth compressed to a line and her face bleached white. A trembling gloved hand rested on her cheek. The woman sitting next to her leaned over, gently touching Katy's arm.

"Are you all right, my dear?" she whispered.

"Yes," Katy choked a reply, arranging the trim on her hat to cover a mark on her neck. "I'm a bit warm. It will soon pass." She pulled out a small embroidered handkerchief and began fanning vigorously, telling herself not to panic. Simply a bizarre coincidence. She shifted her eyes nervously. All the others stared at the storyteller with rapt attention. They didn't recognize her. In fact, they paid her no attention, thinking it just another story. As long as she sat quietly no one would ever know he really spoke of her.

"She had a strong spirit though and refused to allow the circumstances of her life to dictate her destiny. Despite her hardships, this young lady, whom we shall call Katy, attempted to enrich her life in whatever little ways she could." Katy choked at the mention of her nickname, quickly covering up the sound with a soft cough. She gave a tight smile and small nod to the woman next to her, then fanned her handkerchief even more furiously.

Simon continued, apparently oblivious to her. "She looked for anything to transport her beyond the back-breaking work of keeping her small family together. Katy collected various booklets and papers to read from people's discards and stood in the alley behind the theater to catch snatches of the music within. She even pretended her plain meal at four o'clock in the afternoon was really an elegant tea like in the old days, with tiny cakes and scones, drinking her cup of tea with her pinkie finger in the air." Simon parodied his descriptions with movements, his palms open for a book, a hand to his ear to listen for music, his finger raised in the air as he held an imaginary tea cup.

Taking a deep breath, Katy steeled herself and stared at Simon with her head high. Her clenched hands now hid in the folds of her dress. Simon allowed himself a brief smile. She knew. Further, she would stay. *She has such strength and courage,* he thought. *And beauty. The way she holds her head...*he quickly buried that thought with his earlier contemplations and continued.

"The course of Katy's weary life was set. Or so it seemed until one fateful night when a stranger entered her life. She returned home from a small outing, where I might add, a startling event happened that left her shaken."

Katy sat straight up. Her eyes opened wide as her clenched hands unfurled to clasp her mouth in shock. The room seemed to shift and waver for a moment and she swallowed hard at the churning in her stomach. Simon told her life up to this very moment in time, and now, she realized with a small shudder, he continued beyond. How could he possibly know her future? Then again how could he possibly have known her past? Katy trembled at her thoughts. The muscles in her legs tensed, fighting the urge to run.

Simon smiled, feeling each expression of her face. Her fear was but a small price to pay for what the future held. "Fortunately, Katy was not so shaken that when faced with an emergency she could not respond. Because of her quick mind and actions, she saved a man's life that night. A wealthy and influential man. In his gratitude, the gentleman presented her his card and extended an invitation to visit his place of business three days following so she might be more properly thanked."

"Katy's life turned from that point. Many wonderful things began to happen to her...an excellent job, a better life for her family, love, and marriage. Her mother saw doctors and soon became well. Her sister, taking heart at all that transpired, became more self-confident and outgoing. With Katy's help, she blossomed into a bright and pretty young lady. A poor young lad who once showed Katy a kindness became a successful and trusted man, touching the lives of thousands throughout many years with his words because of her."

"Katy, with her compassion and willingness to work, brought about several good changes in her town and became loved and respected by all. She felt, you see, her good fortune should be shared with as many as possible."

"A fairytale, you may say. These things don't happen to real people." Simon paused and nodded his head knowingly. "Ah, but they do. Katy's faith was strong and she held on to all her beautiful dreams despite the hopelessness and drudgery of her life." He leaned forward and stared intensely at the crowd, his gaze searing into the hearts of those whose lives had worn them low. "Katy never gave up hope. Do you see? That was her salvation...she never gave up hope. Hope something better waited around the corner, in the next room, one more day away. She believed it, and so it came to pass."

"It is a story we can all learn from. Never give up hope. Never stop believing. Even from the worst in our lives, beautiful things can happen. I have seen it and I know it to be true. Remember my words," he looked directly into Katy's eyes. "Faith is always rewarded."

Katy slowly exhaled as if she had held her breath for days. Her eyes saw only Simon's, and within them, she saw only love. She felt a bond like she'd known him all her life and a glow warmed her from within. It would be all right. She smiled softly at him. How he came to have this gift she would never know. Why he had chosen to share it with her she now began to understand.

Her heart felt drawn to his. Part of Katy wanted to go to him, stay with him, this man she'd never seen before. It didn't make sense. At the same time, she knew she couldn't. He wasn't hers and she wasn't his. He was sending her on to someone else. Someone kind and wonderful who would give her and her family a good life. She couldn't be Simon's, for some unknown reason, so he was making sure she would be happy and taken care of, even if it was with someone else. Because he loved her and it was the best he could do for her. No, she didn't understand it, but she knew she no longer had anything to fear.

Simon felt her gratitude. More than that, he felt her acceptance of his love. She knew. He faltered briefly at the realization, his breath catching in his throat. Quickly he stood and smiled at the crowd, nodding in acknowledgment as their applause followed him off the stage. Ignoring the gnawing pain inside he motioned for another fellow to step up. He had arranged for someone else to finish off the evening with poetry so he could slip away unnoticed.

For a moment he stood off to the side watching with a full heart as Katy quietly made her way to the back of the hall. He smiled. She would have a wonderful life and know the joy of true love. Not just the ache of distant longing.

With a sigh he turned and walked away, shoulders drooping. He was finished here. The time had come to leave London once again. He had appeared in as many halls as he could reasonably manage and told as many stories as he dared. He must move on. People became more and more enlightened so quickly. A setting such as tonight's was now dangerous for him and his need for secrecy and anonymity. He couldn't take chances, despite the odd finding that by telling stories again he actually appeared to be younger than when he first appeared in that barber's shop.

Reluctantly, he would have to leave the group tellings behind. From now on it must be one on one. For people walking the street, waiting in line...wherever he found them, as many as he could find. He must move on to new territory. He would make his way to the Continent and work his way throughout Europe.

CHAPTER EIGHT

KATY moved carefully through the room. She thought only to make it out the door before being recognized by someone who announced it to the world. Nearing her goal she noticed a youth leaning against the wall staring at her. His once fine clothing patched, she guessed from the earnest wistfulness of his eyes his lot was as bad, if not worse, than her own. She smiled encouragingly at him as she reached for the door.

"You're Katy aren't you?" the lad whispered. A look of reverent awe breathed over his face.

Katy cast a panicked glance around. Had anyone heard? With relief, she realized they were still intent on the poetry.

"I knew it. You are Katy! The man's stories are true. I knew they were." He said quietly. His glance followed hers around the room as he leaned closer. "Don't worry, I won't let the others know. My name is Charlie. I wanted to tell you I'm happy your miracle is coming. Knowing good things can happen to people like us, well...it does give me hope. Just like Simon said. Somehow I'm going to make a new life, too." His toothy grin was belied by the steely look of determination in his eyes.

A sudden thought wrinkled his brow, then his eyes widened in inspiration. "Here Katy." The boy dug a grimy piece of cloth from his pocket and carefully unfolded it. "I want you to have this." He placed a coin in her hand. "This is for your mum's medicine. It will help until the miracle comes."

Katy gazed in wonderment. "A whole crown? I can't take this from you, Charlie. I know how long it must have taken you to save this and I'm sure you have need of it as badly as I. Why not surprise your own mother with it?" She tried to hand it back but he pulled away.

"My mum manages fine," he answered rather wistfully. "Anyways, I earned this money myself and I've been saving it for something special. Tonight I've found what that is. It would mean a lot to me to help you. Go on and keep it."

Katy gave him a quick hug. "Thank you so much, Charlie. Now my mother is sure to get well. When the miracle comes, where can I find you? I'd like to be able to repay you for your kindness."

"No, I don't need the money back. I get by. But say," his young face brightened again as he gave Katy a big smile, "maybe you could pass the crown on to someone else who needs it. It sure feels good inside when you help someone."

The smile faded and the boy looked down, thoughtfully rubbing his chin. "I've seen how cruel life is to poor folks when there's no one to help them. It makes me angry and I feel like I have to be doing my share to make it better. Maybe when your miracle comes I could work with you to do some of those good things for people. I'm easy to find...work right at Warren's Blacking Warehouse down at Hungerford Stairs." He wrinkled his nose in distaste. "It's not a very good place. There are lots of rats. But, my job's easy enough, I paste labels on shoe polish. It gives me a few pence, so I get by."

Katy clapped her hands together, the noise muffled by her gloves. "What a wonderful lad you truly are. I'll never forget you, Charlie. And I hate rats, too. Nothing good can come from such creatures as they. Someday, you can be sure, I'll come to Hungerford Stairs and make sure you get out of that place."

Charlie grinned in gratitude. "Come any time and ask for Charlie. Charlie Dickens."

Katy paused, looking at him intently. "There's a special quality about you, Mr. Dickens. You've the heart of a man the world will long remember." She squeezed his hand warmly and slipped out the door into the night.

Outside, she passed by a tearful mother who knelt beside her pretty daughter. "I love you, Mama," the child said. Katy smiled at them and walked on.

Unseen in the shadows of the building Simon watched Katy go, his hand pressed against the ache in his chest, a deep longing in his eyes. He stilled the voice that wanted to call her back to him. It could not be allowed. He could not pay that price again. He would accept the loneliness and the pain that went with it. Slowly exhaling the breath he'd been holding, he turned and walked away.

The clear evening sky was brilliant with stars. The air was so crisp, Katy thought she could hear it crackle as she hurried through it. She tipped her head back and took several deep breaths, savoring the coolness as it filled her lungs and cleared her bewildered mind.

Did it really happen or did she dream the whole thing? Katy shook her head in puzzlement. Out in the fresh air, on her way back to the reality of her small life, the past hour already seemed so far away and misty. Closing her eyes though, Katy could see Simon as he stood in front staring at her. 'Remember my words,' he'd said. 'Faith is always rewarded.'

Yes, it was real.

Though warmly covered, Katy began to tremble. She pulled her sturdy coat tighter and walked a bit more briskly. Her life would never be the same. In the space of one short hour, an irrevocable course of events had been set for her. It would all begin tonight. This night and that wonderful, blessed reading marked a new beginning. It was an exciting thought and she focused on that, ignoring the lingering sense of belonging she'd felt with Simon. That door was closed and Simon was gone. But he'd left her this wondrous gift.

Katy's thoughts absorbed her completely. Her hands, of their own accord, twisted and rubbed together as she replayed the evening over and over, feeling again the doubts, the fears, the joy. Who was Simon? No ordinary mortal could know such things or make such promises. Surely no demon would perform a miracle like this. She shivered again. Demons only did evil deeds and they probably used rats to accomplish them. And she definitely wouldn't have felt and reciprocated the love she experienced. *Simon must be an angel. A messenger of God to bring glad tidings.* Katy's head nodded in agreement with her thoughts. Simon was an angel. That would explain why they couldn't be together despite their love.

"Or maybe God himself?" She gasped, her hands rising to her cheeks. "No," she chided, "God surely must be too busy to bother with someone like me. But he could send a messenger. Yes, he could send an angel."

Being so preoccupied, Katy's quick steps continued

straight past her turnoff and soon led her to an unfamiliar part of town. This section appeared to house offices for the high-priced barristers and plump bankers. A coach rattled rudely by and Katy jumped, suddenly aware of her surroundings.

"Oh no. How did I come to be here?" A trembling hand flew to her mouth and Katy looked around with panic in her eyes. "I shall be so late getting home Mother will be worried sick. I'll never dare go out again."

She quickly turned around to trace her steps back in the right direction then stopped, her foot poised in mid-air. An unusual noise sounded somewhere nearby. Tilting her head first one way and then another she listened carefully. Yes, there it was again, a mix of shuffling feet and muffled groans. Curiosity and compassion for someone possibly in need overcame her fear. Katy took slow cautious steps to a narrow opening between the buildings.

"Oh!" She barely stifled the noise as it tried to explode from her lips. With a quick motion, she stepped back from the alley, praying no one had seen her. The source of the strange noises was a poor man being beaten by a pair of immense thugs. One held the victim's arms pinned behind his back as the other attacked viciously with clenched fists. The wounded man's jacket and pockets were turned out from being searched and they had stuffed a rag in his mouth.

Heart pounding, Katy tried desperately to think of a way to help. She gulped in the cool air, wishing she didn't feel so faint. She looked up and down the street with wide frightened eyes. Not a bobby in sight. There simply wasn't time to go searching for one. But then, those men in the alley wouldn't know that.

Please, please let this work, Katy pleaded silently. If this didn't scare them off she probably wouldn't make it home at all tonight. In a stroke of luck, a carriage rounded the far corner of the street. Although a distance away the sound carried clearly to the alley. *How perfect,* she thought as she pulled off her gloves. *Now it will sound real.*

Taking a deep breath, she put her fingers into her mouth and let out a loud, long whistle. A skill carried over from her childhood days learned from the boys living in the house next to hers. She pressed her back against the building front praying the men didn't come for her. Dragging in another breath, she called out as loudly as she could. "Over here, Constable! They're right down this alley!"

The carriage drew nearer and Katy hoped they would mistake it for a police wagon. Stepping into the open, she waved her arms to flag down the driver. In the darkness between the buildings, she heard angry cursing and the sound of running feet fading away. It worked.

"Driver, Driver! Please stop!" Katy cried out. "There's an injured man in the alley. I need your help."

The driver yanked in his reins, the horses and carriage skidding to a halt as Katy ran back to assist the beaten man. He lay crumpled in a heap, barely distinguishable from the piles of trash.

"Sir?" She gently rolled him face up. Taking his wrist she checked for a pulse and the gentleman's eyes wavered open. "Are you hurt badly, Sir? Can you move or should we wait for a doctor?"

He gave a small groan and pushed himself into a sitting position, wobbling slightly. "I think I'm well enough to make it home if we can somehow stop the ground from spinning so."

"Here," Katy commanded, placing a hand on his head and pushing down lightly, "put your head down for a few minutes. That should help clear it."

By now the driver, along with his passenger, hurried

towards them.

"Mr. McGuire." cried the older of the two, carriage whip in hand.

"My God, Michael. What's happened to you?" The younger man dropped to his knees and grasped his friend, his eyes reflecting his worry and concern.

Katy slowly stood up and backed away a few paces. Evidently, the injured man was with friends who would take care of him. It wasn't within her current station to intrude upon people of their class.

"Well," Michael replied, "obviously I came out to play with the cats in the alley here and tripped over an unsuspecting pile of garbage."

"Michael, this isn't funny. You're sitting here bruised and bleeding. You could very well have been left here for dead if this young woman had not flagged us down."

"You saved me?" Michael's attention suddenly turned to Katy as she stood quietly at their side. "You're the one who whistled and called out? Who scared those two robbers away?"

"Yes, Sir, 'twas me." The words tumbled nervously out of her mouth as she gave a small curtsey, her fingers knotting the fabric of her skirt. "I'm sorry, but I couldn't think of anything else to do. There was no one around and I didn't dare take time to go searching for help. Luckily their carriage came along at the right moment."

The three gentlemen stared at her in amazement.

"Do you mean to tell me, young lady, you hoped to scare those hoodlums away by yourself?" demanded the old driver.

"Correction, Sam. She did scare them away by herself," answered Michael thoughtfully. "I, for one, am not only impressed but extremely grateful. You took quite a risk with your own life, Miss, and for all you knew I might have deserved this beating."

Katy stepped forward shaking her head emphatically. "Oh no, Sir. Nobody deserves a beating like this. I only tried to do what was right."

"Well," the young friend stood up and looked at her quizzically, "we could use a few more people as concerned with doing the right thing. Thank you for coming to my friend's assistance." He gave a slight bow. "Michael hadn't arrived home and wasn't at his office so we came out searching for him. Some threats had been made against him because of a case he was working on. Now I think we better get him home and have a doctor look at him."

"Certainly," Katy stammered, stepping back apologetically.

Between the two men, they got Michael on his feet and out to the carriage. Katy found his hat and gloves strewn over the ground and quickly gathered them up. She hurried behind the men to the carriage and handed them to the driver.

"What's your name, Miss?" Michael asked out the coach window.

"It's Katherine, Sir. Katherine Torrence. Most folks call me Katy."

"Miss Katy Torrence," he dipped his head in a small bow, "please accept my offer of a ride home. This is not the time, nor the place, for a lady to walk without escort."

Relief swept over Katy's face. "Thank you, Sir. I would be most grateful."

The driver handed her up into the carriage and took careful note of her address.

The injured gentleman watched her settle onto her seat, noting her fine manners and gentle smile. Her plain clothes placed her more within the working class, though they were very well-made, and she had an air of refinement and grace about her. He suspected she came from a once fine family, displaced from their position by some cruel twist of fate. He smiled as she glanced at him.

"Although we met under poor circumstances, I feel my manners have been a bit remiss. Please allow me to introduce myself. I am Mr. Michael McGuire. This," he motioned to the young gentleman, "is my very good friend, Mr. Nickolas Brenton." Both men nodded a bow as Michael continued, "Our driver is my faithful servant and friend, Mr. Sam Kelly."

"I'm very honored to meet you, gentlemen." Katy bobbed her head in acknowledgment.

"Not half as honored as I am, Miss Torrence." Michael took her hand and kissed it gently. "I must thank you again for your bravery tonight. You truly saved my life and I am in your debt."

Katy tried desperately not to blush. A gentleman had never spoken to her in such a way before nor had one ever kissed her hand. Even so, she did not want to appear young and foolish. "Nonsense, Mr. McGuire," she replied quickly. "I did what anyone might have done.

"But it wasn't anyone, it was you. You risked your life for mine."

"I can assure you, Miss Torrence," Mr. Brenton broke in with great seriousness, "not many ladies today, and very few gentlemen for that matter, would take the trouble to assist someone in need. Especially if it meant taking a personal risk. You are to be commended, as is your mother for instilling such strength of character and compassion in you."

"Gentlemen, please stop. You cause me to blush with all this talk." Katy's hands covered her burning cheeks, for there was no helping it now. "I did what I did. The same thing I'm sure anyone passing by might have done. You can't make me believe people are in such a sorry state as you say."

Mr. McGuire smiled. This woman had a special air about her, some indefinable spark that snatched at the edges of his consciousness. "Well, perhaps we are wrong. You were hiding out there, possibly there are more." He tried to adjust his seat and grimaced at the effort.

"Are you in much pain, Sir?"

"Don't exert yourself too much, Michael. You've had quite an evening. I think rest and quiet is your goal for now." Mr. Brenton looked at his friend with concern.

"Yes, some rest does sound rather good. I'm feeling a bit worn out, though I'm sure I'll soon be back on my feet. Miss Torrence, please take my card and come to see me at my office on Monday. Say about three o'clock? I should be a bit more presentable at that time and I would like to have the opportunity to thank you properly."

He had an honest, compassionate face, making it easy to trust him. Katy looked into his clear brown eyes and felt her heart skip a beat. She knew she had no right to entertain any manner of thought about him. She vowed not to build castles out of simple gestures of gratitude. "Thank you, Sir. I'll be there," she smiled.

The carriage pulled to a stop. Sam climbed down and opened the door, waiting to assist Katy. She took his offered hand and carefully stepped out, her heart filled with joy. She helped someone in need today and what a sweet, handsome man he turned out to be. Though entirely businesslike and innocent, she would even have an opportunity to see him again.

"Goodnight, Mr. McGuire, Mr. Brenton." She curtsied gracefully.

Mr. Brenton bowed, "Goodnight, Miss Torrence. You have managed to turn this into a truly pleasant evening after all. My regards to your family."

"Miss Torrence, until Monday." Michael McGuire smiled

and tipped his hat with a flourish. "Sam, please see her safely to her door."

Katy led the way up the walk, Sam keeping pace beside her. "Miss, I can't even tell you how grateful I am for what you've done tonight. Mr. McGuire, he's a good man and I love him like he was one of my own. I can't even think what might have happened..." Sam mopped a cloth at his eyes, seemingly surprised by the moisture there. "He'll not forget tonight either. I can promise you that. He has had a sad life, but he has risen above it all and become a great man. Mr. McGuire has no family to care for him, you see. A man like him should have a family. He needs a good, kind woman to watch over him. If you don't mind me saying so, you might not have wealth but it's obvious you come from good stock. You've made quite an impression on us all tonight. I'll say no more. Goodnight, Miss."

Sam turned and strode back to the waiting coach, leaving an amazed and bemused Katy at her door. Her mind whirled. Did he give her his seal of approval? Could he actually think the two of them should be together? Blushing once again she hurried inside. Truly an impossible thought after all.

Katy sighed and carefully hung up her thick coat. As she did so, a small piece of paper fell to the ground.

"Oh dear, I must be careful not to lose his card." She reached down for it and suddenly the room spun as the realization of the night's events struck her. Slowly she sank to the floor and stared at the card in front of her:

Michael S. McGuire
Barrister-at-Law
Doughty Street Chambers, London

"I never even thought. It all happened so quickly. It's just as he said. Everything happened as Simon said it would." Her voice was a whisper, but Katy wanted to shout it through the streets. "The miracle has begun."

Barely pausing to catch her breath Katy stood up. "Praise the Saints, I must tell Mother." She hurried through the hall. "Mother. Mother, the most glorious thing has happened."

Simon took his leave of London, wandering back and forth across various countries, the years passing slowly by. In Bruges, Belgium he admired the many small canals and quaint bridges. Best of all he found a little restaurant in Markt Square, opposite the Belfry, that made the best apple strudel known to man, rivaling even the scones of old Devonshire. It became a favorite stopping place whenever he passed through the area.

He loved sitting outside under a canopied table where he could watch people meander by as he sipped from his steaming cup of tea. Accompanied, of course, by mouthfuls of warm, sweet strudel with fresh whipped cream melting over the top. This culinary dessert experience equaled sitting outside at a little cafe table in Paris, indulging in crème brûlée with his tea. Oh, the crack of that caramelized sugar on top joined with the cool, creamy custard underneath. Heaven.

In Switzerland, he came across a young boy at a train station who could not hear. Simon's heart went out to him and he prepared himself for a story. Before he spoke, he saw an oddity in the pattern of the boy's life that stopped him. He searched the lad more deeply, then examined the life threads of the man standing with him. Sadly, he realized he couldn't help the child. He could restore his hearing, all right, but to do so would destroy a thread that would save many, many others.

Simon had seldom seen such a strong connecting line. The boy's deafness would cause the doctor with him to search for cures. His advances and discoveries would find their way to a Dr. Graham Bell in America, who would use those ideas to build a machine to talk across the miles. Dr. Bell's work with the deaf would also help many. He would end up assisting a young deaf-mute named Helen Keller, who would open up a world full of possibilities for all such affected people. The end results were too important. The young boy could not be removed of his deafness. Simon turned and walked away. Even knowing the necessity of it did not quench the fire in his stomach.

In the walled city of Rothenburg, Germany, Simon walked the cobblestone streets and basked in the friendliness of its people. In Kobenhavn, Denmark, he met a young lad who had attempted to fulfill a dream by attending grammar school at the ripe old age of seventeen. Unfortunately, the cruelty of the headmaster drove him out and the young man traveled to Copenhagen with a heavy heart. Simon saw great beauty in the soul of this lad, which with very little prodding could spark forth and warm the hearts of people worldwide. There was no need to rearrange this young man's life, he just needed a push in the right direction. Simon stood next to him by the docks and spoke, storyteller to storyteller.

"So, you don't think the stage is for me then?" the young man asked.

"You've a dramatic flair right enough. But you have such a way of speaking your own words I don't think you should waste your time reciting others."

"Are you suggesting I should be a writer?"

"Mr. Anderson..."

"Please, call me Hans."

"All right. Hans, you are a writer already. It's inside you here." Simon tapped his chest. "All you need to do is let it out. Start writing down all those lovely stories your imagination churns around inside you."

"I've got no schooling to speak of."

Simon looked out at the water and pointed to a family of birds paddling there. "Look at them, Hans. When a young one is first born it's gray and scraggly. A rather ugly bird that doesn't quite fit in. You'd never suspect hiding inside is a beautiful swan waiting to grow. Don't give up. You can get your schooling here in Copenhagen. Inside of you, Hans, is a swan waiting for a chance to grow."

Hans grinned, "An ugly swan. I like that. Maybe I will try writing."

"I have faith in you, Hans Anderson. Believe me, faith is always rewarded."

Towns and countries filtered by in a continuous stream. People changed, styles changed, businesses changed. Simon remained a constant. The turn of the century into the 1900s arrived and Simon found himself desiring a chance to spread his wings even further. And maybe escape the voices in his head as well. That vast new land to the west should be well established now. He almost tingled at the thought of a whole new continent he could explore, with towns and cities full of fresh faces. He decided to return to London one final time and become another emigrant joining the mass of voyagers to America.

Within a matter of days, he wandered the streets of London, waiting for his scheduled departure date. He had accumulated quite a collection of various coins on his travels and he searched for a bank to exchange them all for pounds sterling. Easier to travel to a new world with a coin they were already acquainted with. As he walked down a lane he came across an older woman sitting on a bench. Simon stood near her, concentrating for a moment. He smiled as her life unfolded.

"Excuse me, Madam. Do you mind if I sit here?"

She smiled at him pleasantly, nodding her head in acquiescence.

He sat beside her. "Are you waiting for someone? I'm sure a beautiful woman such as yourself would not be out alone."

The woman blushed with pleasure at the compliment, smoothing some stray hairs that escaped from beneath her hat. "Thank you, young man. Yes, I'm waiting for my granddaughter. She's, well, I'm afraid she's in the pub having a lemonade with some friends. We were out strolling and happened to run into her group. They were pleasant enough to invite me in with them, but I simply had to decline." She shook her head sadly and leaned towards Simon. "It's not that they're really so horrible, you understand. They're simply so different. I would never have gone into a pub when I was a young girl. Her mother either. They seem to be such wild young things. The girls have all cut their hair off. They call it a 'bob.' That's a man's name, not a woman's hairstyle. Her mother nearly fainted when my granddaughter walked in with it."

"It must have been a great shock. I'm sure she had long, beautiful hair."

"It was beautiful, just beautiful. Now all her long, lovely curls are gone. It's such a shame," she sighed heavily.

"How difficult for you. It's never easy when young ones run off on their own and fail to heed the wisdom and experience their elders offer. It's evident you love your granddaughter very much."

"Oh, I surely do. Despite my complaining, I love her dearly. I try to spend as much time with her as she'll let me, but I'm an old woman. I don't know how much good it'll do."

"You'd be surprised. I knew a woman who had an almost identical problem with her own granddaughter, Eunice."

The old woman drew a sharp intake of breath. "That's my granddaughter's name."

"Is it really? How very odd, although it is a popular name. Maybe we can take it as a sign you'll have as happy an ending."

"Oh, I hope so. Do go on."

"Well, Eunice had been raised by loving parents who had taken time over the years to instill in her a strong sense of values, or so they hoped. However, Eunice had always been a bit of a tomboy. Never quite felt a part of the tea and embroidery set."

'That's our Eunice, too." The grandmother put a hand to her brow. "I still don't dare serve her my fine china. She invariably knocks her cup over."

Simon smiled and continued. "As she grew older, Eunice became attracted to the excitement and element of danger she found with a certain group of young people. They cut their hair, went to pubs, even put on pantaloons for outings in the country."

"No, not your young friend too? This must be happening all over."

"I'm afraid it's true. I believe it's a search for independence and their own identities. Eunice clung to her new friends and seemed to reject all the old ways and social graces she had learned."

Simon leaned towards the older woman and patted her hand. "It was almost more than her parents and grandparents could tolerate. I'm sure you can understand."

"Oh definitely. I know how they felt. What did they do to save her?"

"They trusted her."

"Trusted her?" she interrupted. "With all the poor choices these young people are making?"

"Exactly. You see, in the full scheme of things, their choices weren't so poor. The ages come and go and the passing of time can bring to an end even the things we hold dearest. But something marvelous always awaits to take their place. There are always a few folks who can see the new world ahead and help to usher it in. Eunice could. Her grandmother, although a little frightened by the changing world, could see it too.

"Fortunately the grandmother was strong enough to teach Eunice's parents to open their minds and hearts to different possibilities. They assured Eunice how much they loved her and encouraged her to follow her own path, despite society's raised eyebrows."

"That must have been difficult. Society can rule strongly in one's life."

"Yes, but when society's boundaries are pushed, tolerance is borne. Tolerance invites acceptance and with acceptance comes opportunity. Pushing the boundaries today can make opportunities for your grandchildren, or great-grandchildren, tomorrow."

The grandmother dabbed at her eyes with a handkerchief. "What a wonderful story. What became of Eunice?"

Simon looked into her eyes, "She became a wise and respected woman who taught her own daughter, and then granddaughter, to push boundaries as well. In the end the granddaughter became the Prime Minister of England."

"We haven't had a woman Prime Minister."

Simon smiled. "Not yet."

The woman's eyes widened as her hand fluttered to her mouth. "Your story. It's my Eunice."

"Faith is always rewarded, mark my words."

"I...I understand." The woman sat lost in thought for a few moments then smiled at Simon. "I think I'll have a talk with Eunice's mother this afternoon. Maybe there are some changes we need to make." She stood up and extended her hand. "Thank you...?" She waited for a name.

"Call me Simon."

"Thank you, Simon. I suppose someday England will thank you too. My future great-great-granddaughter surely will. Now, I think I'd like some lemonade." With a smile, the woman stood tall and walked towards the pub.

CHAPTER NINE

THE ship's whistle blew its parting song. For some, it made a mournful tune; a wake for the lives they left behind. For others, it heralded the triumphant start of a dream turned reality. Simon fit neither category, but he felt the excitement of sailing for the new world all the same.

He stood at the rail as the ship moved towards the ocean and watched the docks shrink away in the distance. Taking a deep breath of the fresh salt air, he turned and looked at his companions for the next several days. He could feel their excitement mingled with fear. Fear for the voyage, for the trek through Ellis Island, for their futures. They would all make wonderful subjects for a story. How could he ever choose among them? Of greater concern, in the confines of a ship over a period of several days, how could he tell a story safely? There was no place to disappear. Would he have to forego his stories on this trip completely?

His forehead furrowed momentarily as he thought, then the corners of Simon's mouth twitched. A smile bloomed on his face. There was no problem after all. He would tell his stories. He would tell them to every single person on this ship. And, he would do even more.

He nodded a greeting to some of the people around him. "Sprechen Sie Deutsch? Gut. Möchten Sie Englisch lernen? Ich würde es dir gerne beibringen. In Amerika muss man Englisch verstehen. Bringen Sie Ihre Familien in einer Stunde zurück. Verstehen?" Simon grinned at their enthusiastic response to his offer. He would teach them English, and while doing so, would tell his stories. He walked over to another group.

"Parlez-vous français, oui? Si vous voulez apprendre l'anglais, venez en deux heures. Oui?" Again he found great enthusiasm and expressions of gratitude. "Merci. Deux heures, oui, oui."

He moved on. Irish. Polish. Italian. Russian. Norwegian. He stopped and spoke to them all, arranging times for English lessons throughout the day. When this ship landed in America they'd be speaking English like they'd been born with it as their native tongue. All of them.

Simon set up his class on part of the open main deck, the only topside section allowed to the poor folk who booked passage in an area called steerage. He, himself, chose to cross in steerage rather than first or second class because he knew he'd have a captive audience of folks who could use a good story or two. They were going to the Promised Land and he wanted to be sure the promise would come true for them. He had not yet decided, however, if steerage got its name from the fact they bunked at the bottom of the ship near the steering equipment or because they were all crowded together like a herd of steers.

At the coming of the first hour, the German passengers gathered around Simon. As was to be the case with each group of people he taught, a few already had a rudimentary knowledge of the English language. But a grasp of simple basics was not good enough for them. They all seemed to possess an inner drive to understand more, to pronunciate correctly, to speak clearer. A visible demonstration of the lusty drive that placed them on this voyage to begin with.

Simon began his instruction in their native tongue. "Thank you all for joining me and allowing me this opportunity to share my...teaching skills. I'm doing this because I love words. I love the way they sound. How they form and shape in the mouth and either roll off the tongue or jump sharply from the lips. I love the way words weave and join together, blending into sentences, building into stories, no matter what language the words use. Most of all I love the stories." Simon paused and stared at the hushed group, excitement reflected on his face.

"Yes indeed, I love the stories. I'm sure you're all aware of the power of words to form mental pictures. Well, as I teach you how German words translate into English, let your mind make pictures of what those words mean. That will help you remember. For example," Simon leaned casually against the ship's rail, "let me tell you a quick story about another group of people I taught. Although very eager to learn, they did not have much time available. So, they used their hours wisely. They listened carefully, they pictured the words they learned, and they practiced with each other constantly. The result seemed miraculous. By the end of the week, they spoke English fluently."

"You see," Simon stood tall again, "they had the desire and they had the belief. If you remember nothing else, remember Simon says faith is always rewarded. They learned English in a week, and you can too."

The group nodded at him, wide-eyed, and began repeating the words and phrases he gave them. By the time the French began to gather for their lesson, the Germans engaged in small, halting conversations with each other in English. The French looked at them in amazement and hurriedly clustered around Simon.

He waved at the departing group with a grin then turned his attention to his next class. "Thank you all for joining me and allowing me this opportunity to share my...teaching skills..."

Thus, the first day passed quickly. As the sun began to drop that evening the passengers stood on the deck talking. Unlike the morning, where the differences in languages kept them separated by nationality, tonight they eagerly mingled. The sounds of many variously accented voices speaking rough English drifted in the air but with less hesitation than before. They learned well.

It was exhilarating for Simon. He looked at the mixed groups studiously practicing their new language, and all their hopes stretched out before him like an embroidered heirloom quilt. Each person added their own fabric and color to the creation, bound by the intricate stitching of their loved one's dreams. Simon reveled in its beauty, raising his eyes briefly to heaven with a prayer of thankfulness to be a part of it.

A crewman paused by Simon. "Now, what do you make of all that? Strange, isn't it?" He motioned towards the other passengers. "It seems like they started talking English all at once. Craziest thing I ever saw."

"Yes, it is rather amazing." Simon nodded his head thoughtfully. "How about this good weather? Do you think it will hold the full way across?"

The crewman squinted at the sky and shook his head. "Most likely not. This is storm season. We always hit at least one on each trip." He looked back at the passengers, his mouth puckered. "Problem with storms is most of the passengers get sick. Some aren't too healthy to begin with. I hate it when we lose some of them."

Simon turned his head quickly to face the man. "Lose them?"

"They get so sick and weak and they can't keep anything in their stomachs. Some of them aren't strong enough to take it. It kills them."

"No," Simon whispered. He scratched his ear and looked around him, then back to the crewman. He smiled. "Doesn't always happen, you know. I heard of a ship that crossed the Atlantic in the middle of the storm season and no storm ever blew near it."

"Nah."

"It's true. The weather stayed calm and balmy all the way across. Everyone had a lovely passage. The ship made excellent time, too. And," Simon leaned over and shook a finger towards the man, "not a single passenger got sick or died."

"Not one?"

"Not one."

"Not even sick?"

"No. They were all as healthy as horses."

"I've never heard of such a thing. I'd sure like to have been on such a ship. It would be nice to see them all make it like that."

Simon smiled. "Don't worry, someday soon you will. Just have a little faith."

The man clapped Simon on the back as he moved on. "That's right. Faith. If I believe, maybe even this ship will make it across okay, like the one in your story."

Simon watched the crewman walk away, then turned his gaze back to the other passengers. He nodded his head in satisfaction.

It was a gray, foggy morning when they left England. The second dawn brought blue skies and sunshine. Each day the sky remained blue and clear, with enough wind to cool. Simon held his English classes in the afternoons, the people soaking up the language like sponges. They had already learned enough that he could spend more time telling stories. Each group heard about the ship that sailed the ocean on calm waters, landing with a hull full of healthy, happy passengers. They also heard about the immigrants who landed in New York, passed through Ellis Island with no problems, and found jobs and homes, love and families.

The stories helped pass the time and fueled the people's hopes and desires for a better life. America was the new world, after all. They believed in Simon's happy endings with a desperate intensity. Their English continued to improve and many hours were spent comparing their pasts and the roads which led them to this place and time. This was contrasted with discussions of their current good fortune and the happy lives they knew would be theirs in the future.

Spirits were high. This reflected in the way all the people behaved. Kindness and tolerance seemed contagious; even societal barriers loosened. The stuffiest matriarch of high society suddenly had nothing but a kind word for the poor who traveled in steerage or the lowliest of crewmen. Social mores were not eliminated by any means. The classes did not intermingle freely, yet there seemed a softening in attitude. A sense of generosity and acceptance. On more than one occasion a buffet of succulent meats, steaming fresh vegetables, fresh fruits, and desserts was sent by the first-class passengers to the folks who bunked below to supplement their main food supply of herring, thin soup, and black bread. Each evening the ballroom doors were thrown open to allow the music to drift over the decks.

Music was a universal joy for all to appreciate.

The crew enjoyed the crossing too. Never had they had such good luck as on this trip. They buzzed amongst themselves on their extraordinary good fortune. More than once, Simon found the crewman he had spoken with looking at him curiously. He never approached Simon again, almost as if he really didn't want an answer to the questions evident on his face. The captain and crew of the vessel spent a good portion of time during the crossing whispering in puzzled voices. The expected storms never did appear.

It wasn't that they wanted a storm, but realistically they expected to get one. The radio reported several in their vicinity throughout the trip, which always seemed to miss the ship. The surprising result was none of the emigrants succumbed in some form or another to the siren's call of sickness or death. Another expectation happily unmet.

Everyone was pleased about the weather, but the people crowded into steerage rejoiced the most. If the waves were rough, crewmen sealed the steerage doors shut to keep water out and the emigrants from coming onto the deck and being swept away. A protective gesture, but the result was several hundred people trapped together in large, hot rooms with foul air retching into common buckets. An experience no one regretted missing. All on board thanked their God, their lucky stars, or whoever came to mind. No one bothered to question why. Some things were better accepted at face value.

Their last day at sea dawned. The morning sun beat hotly on the steel hull of the ship creating an oven effect in the lower quarters. Simon finished gathering his things into bundles and hurried above board to find some relief from the oppressive heat and stale air. The air was better but most of steerage, as well as passengers on the rest of the ship, had the same idea and the decks were crowded. Besides, today they reached New York Harbour. Everyone wanted to be at the rail to catch sight of their new home.

The crowd did not hinder Simon's movement. People moved smilingly aside as he made his way across the main deck of the ship. He had gained their respect by teaching them English and preserved their sanity with his wonderful tales during the long days at sea. Learning English was an unexpected gift for which they would be forever thankful. They were all fluent and smart enough to know the value of that knowledge.

"Ah, my good friend, Simon." A short man hurried up to him, sweeping the cap off his head in greeting. "I am so pleased to see you this lovely morning."

"Marco, how are you today?" Simon grinned warmly as he grasped the outstretched hand and shook it firmly.

"I'm very well, thank you. I wanted to ask what your plans were once we landed in New York." He gestured towards the horizon in front of them. It was almost surprising to note little remained of the man's normal accent as he spoke in English. It would be difficult for anyone to guess he had just arrived from Italy, and even more difficult to think only days ago his knowledge of English consisted of 'please' and 'thank you.' "I'm asking because, if you have no other plans, I would like to extend an invitation to stay with me. I have a cousin here who has more than enough room for both of us. I would be greatly honored to have a friend such as you in my company."

Simon smiled gently at the man. This was not the first invitation he had received for a place to stay. He could think of no greater compliment than to have so many willingly open their hearts and lives to him. He had enjoyed his time with all the people on this trip, though he was especially fond of Marco. He wondered if the similarity in name to his old friend had any bearing on that. It certainly had an effect on his answer to Marco's question. He would not make the same mistake twice.

"I appreciate your offer, Marco, more than you know. Your friendship has meant a great deal to me on this journey but unfortunately, mine isn't finished. I won't be staying in New York. I think I'm going to keep moving. Head out west somewhere."

Marco's face fell briefly in disappointment but the smile soon returned. "I understand, my friend. For some of us, the journey never ends. I wish you good health and happiness for all your days, Simon. You have given us a great and wondrous gift for our futures and we will be eternally grateful. God is watching you, Simon. He has put your name in a special place and He will not forget you. I will not forget you, either. If you ever return to New York, your friend Marco will be waiting for you."

A lump in Simon's throat prevented him from replying. Marco simply smiled and clasped him in a brief embrace, then walked away with a final salute of his cap. "May you find what you're searching for, my friend."

Simon turned and steadied himself on the railing, taking great breaths of the salted air to compose himself. How could the man see him so well? Equally unnerving, some of the words Marco spoke could have come straight from Liam's mouth. 'A great and wondrous gift...' Was it truly only coincidence? Mixed with the peace of knowing he again successfully fulfilled the Trust, was the old ache of longing to find an end to his quest and a way back home. If such a way even existed. Simon pushed the sad thoughts from his mind. It was wasted effort. He had work to do.

Then the cry went up.

"Land! There's land ahead!"

All heads turned to the front in anticipation. The crowd watched the distant outline as it gradually enlarged until they finally glided past land. Long Island, they called it. Simon could feel the tension and excitement in the air. But no fear. They had all started out afraid, as most emigrants did. They knew the stories of Ellis Island and of people turned away and sent back. That would not happen today. Simon's stories made sure each and every one of the people he traveled with would pass through inspection at Ellis Island with ease. The people believed him and they looked forward to a welcome reception no other group had experienced.

As Simon smiled and nodded encouragingly at different families a young voice suddenly called out.

"Look there! It's her!"

All heads turned as one and even Simon felt his breath catch. The old women and young mothers cried. The men blew their noses, remarking on the sudden abundance of sea spray irritating their eyes. Say what they might, there was no denying the power of her vision.

Liberty Enlightening the World.

"Ah yes," murmured Simon. "Give me your tired, your poor...Send these, the homeless, tempest-tost to me, I lift my lamp beside the golden door." He blinked quickly, emotions stirring deep inside him with the words, embracing them. Was the Statue of Liberty inviting him to a new home? The others, maybe, but not him. He could never really have a home again. His home and people disappeared long, long ago. She would take him in though, for it was the homeless she welcomed. Maybe she could offer him even more. The end to his journey, finally.

They had plenty of time to admire the huge statue. The ship dropped anchor and waited in quarantine until given clearance. Simon noticed disembarkment was made easier for the first and second-class passengers as the medical teams came on board to give them cursory versions of the required examinations. When the teams were assured no epidemic ran rampant on the ship they allowed her to finish easing into the Harbour. The deck overflowed with steerage passengers. The air buzzed with excitement.

By mid-afternoon, they docked at their pier in the North River. The first and second-class passengers quickly moved down the gangplanks as those in third-class waited. Someone heard steerage would have to stay on board another night and go through inspection in the morning. The others groaned but Simon simply smiled. Soon a ship's officer appeared and made an announcement. Although late in the day they received the surprising news that permission was granted for one more ship to send its passengers through Ellis Island. They could begin disembarking immediately.

A cheer went up and everyone hurried to gather their belongings. They soon discovered they didn't get to follow the other passengers down the gangplank. Instead, the people from steerage were divided into small groups who had to carry their possessions down an accommodation ladder to fill a smaller boat waiting alongside. Simon got his first look at Ellis Island as the little boat skipped along the water. The big, red brick and stone building sat on a low island in the harbour, four towers reaching up like hands imploring the heavens. As each group disembarked their boat they joined the line moving slowly towards the building's entrance. In his mind's eye, Simon could visualize the thousands of people who walked this same path before and the thousands yet to come. He was glad to be a part of it.

Following the crowded line in front of them, it took a few hours to get through the door and up the central stairs to the Great Hall. The first of the group from Simon's ship made it and began to work their way across. Steel bars guided the immigrants through a maze of inspection stations and suddenly the pace picked up. Over four hundred people breezed through without a single problem. The inspectors seemed pleased as if they had arranged for a special miracle to make such immense progress. Simon reached the line for the group of desks at the far end of the Great Hall. This was the last stop, the commissioners who had the final say on whether someone stayed or faced deportation. Finally, his turn came.

"Name please," the woman at the desk intoned, her eyes on the paperwork in front of her.

"Simon."

"Simon...what?"

He paused, unsure how to answer. He'd been known simply as Simon for so long. They had asked for his surname when he paid for passage on the ship, also. What had he told them?

The woman looked up, irritation on her face. "I haven't got all day, give your full name or it's off to deportation for you."

"My dear lady," Simon replied calmly, "I realize this position places you under a great deal of pressure but you must not let it affect you so. Let me tell you a brief story I know."

"I haven't got time for stories." She looked for a guard, intent on waving him over.

"Simon," said a small voice next to him. "Simon says, be happy."

Simon looked down to see a little girl from the ship. He had found her to be quite adorable and delighted in making her laugh with his stories throughout the voyage. He made sure she would have a very pleasant life.

"Simon says, dream pretty dreams. Simon says..." She stopped to giggle and smile shyly at him.

"Yes, Simon says," he repeated, smiling back at her. He

paused, eyebrows raised, thinking. *Of course. That's what I told them. A story that Simon said.* With another smile, he quickly looked at the woman. "My name is Simon Says."

The lady put her hand down, looking sideways at him. "All right, then. That wasn't so difficult now was it?" She flipped through the ship's manifest. "Ahh, here you are. Sez, Simon."

They completed the paperwork and Simon waved goodbye to the girl before exiting. Outside he walked down a wire-enclosed ramp to take the ferry to Manhattan. He was in America, the land of opportunity. He glanced at the paper in his hand and smiled at the misspelled name. *Sez.* It would do. *Well,* he thought, *Simon Sez, let's make the most of this. Time to settle in and become part of the New World.* He looked at the skyline of the bustling city crowded with people and the smile on his face grew until he resembled a Cheshire cat.

CHAPTER TEN

"**KATHERINE.** Katherine Torrence McGuire. Put down those papers, girl, and let's get moving. My handy time management-calendar-planner thingy you bought me for Christmas says on Tuesday, May 9, 1996, you and I are scheduled to have lunch. That's today and I'm starving."

"Meagan, why do you always call me by my full name? You sound like my Aunt Beth when I was a girl and she was angry with me. It's annoying."

"Exactly why I do it."

The petite dark-haired woman sitting behind the desk snatched up her pencil and threw it at the figure leaning against the open office door. "Just stick with the short form...Kate, all right?" Her brown eyes stared at her friend in an exaggerated glare.

Meagan leaned over and picked up the pencil at her feet.

"You're a lousy shot, Kate. Better keep practicing that wrist action."

"Ha...hah."

Meagan paused and moved her wrist back and forth as if she were flinging the pencil. She watched intently at the way her wrist bent and shook her head slowly. "Nah. Better forget what I just said. Pencil flinging requires repetitive wrist action. You'd be setting yourself up for trouble."

"Thank you for that fascinating and extremely quick medical study and report, Dr. Ahumada." Kate gathered her papers into a neat pile. She smoothed her long hair behind her ear, briefly showing a small birthmark on her neck, and grabbed her purse. "Now I'm ready for lunch. Which, by the way, we have together every day. You don't need to schedule it on your daily planner to remember." The two left Kate's office and headed for the elevator.

"I know. But it's the only thing I ever do manage to write in it. Everything else gets listed on a rather hit-and-miss basis. You should feel privileged."

"I count my blessings daily. We have to make this a quick lunch though. I'm trying to get out of here early today."

"Oh really? Got a hot date tonight, do you?"

"Meagan, I know you probably won't believe this, but I'm going to the library. Alone."

"Alone. This is supposed to be a surprise? If we were talking about me, maybe, but we're talking about you." Pondering for a moment, Meagan pushed a strand of her curly brown hair out of her eyes and smiled. "Oh, you wicked thing. I get it, you've decided you want the quiet, bookish type. Library's perfect...go for it, girl."

"Meagan, you're impossible." Kate rolled her eyes and stepped onto the streets of downtown San Diego, moving towards Horton Plaza. "There's more to life than chasing men, you know."

"No there isn't. The whole point of our lives is to find a good man. Didn't your mother teach you the rules?"

"Apparently not the same ones your mother taught you. But, in my case, it was my Aunt Beth, the best mom a girl could ask for. The only thing my real mother taught me was how to run away from responsibility."

"Oh, touchy subject. Sorry about that, Kate."

"No, it's really not. Any sadness or anger I felt towards my mother stopped long ago. It wasn't worth the energy they took from me. I loved my Aunt Beth. She gave me a great life and she loved me like I truly was her daughter. I was very lucky."

Meagan reached out and squeezed Kate's arm. "I'm so sorry you lost Aunt Beth last year. I loved her, too. She was such a sweet woman, And, she made the best brownies."

"She really did. I have her recipe, at least. I miss her so much. She was Dad's oldest sister and the closest thing to having him. I guess she filled in for both my mom and my dad. So, when I lost her, it was a bit like losing him all over again." Kate cleared her throat and wiped her eyes. "I'm sorry. I still get emotional sometimes."

"They're worth getting emotional over." Meagan grabbed her friend in a bear hug. "That's a lot of loss to deal with and it will always be with you in one way or another. But, your aunt and your dad will be with you, too. Love like that doesn't die. That's the kind of fairytale I like to believe. And, I'll be with you to give you a hug, or to make you laugh, or to steal your cat. Whatever the situation calls for."

Kate laughed as her friend let her go and wiped her eyes again. "You can't have Chewbacca, Meagan. We've already settled that. But thank you for the rest. It means a lot. You really are a wonderful friend, do you know that?"

"Of course I do. That's why I keep reminding you, so you don't forget...and so you'll give me your cat."

Kate laughed again and gave Meagan a playful jab. She looked up and noticed the restaurant next to them. "Hey, let's stop here and have the soup and salad bar."

"I refuse to diet this week."

"Diet? Are you kidding? They've got the best blueberry muffins there. Double chocolate ones too."

"Twist my arm and lead on."

The two made their way down the long salad bar, Kate piling her plate high with the assorted greens and toppings. "Broccoli and cauliflower, kidney beans, chickpeas, tomatoes and cucumbers...I love it. This always makes me feel so healthy."

Yeah, until you got to the end. You blew it with all the cheese and croutons, not to mention that ranch dressing, Kate. You have any idea how many calories you just dumped on your healthy plate?"

"But they're good calories. Tasty calories. This still has to be better than a greasy hamburger and fries. All those fresh raw vegetables must balance it out somehow."

"Whatever you say. I won't even bring up that big blueberry muffin drenched in butter."

"Appreciated. Besides, I did get an unsweetened iced tea." Kate shrugged her shoulders and headed for a table. "You said you didn't want to diet, I remind you, so stop complaining. We're eating healthy junk food today."

They ate for a while in silence, conscious of their need to finish and get back to the office. Meagan gave her friend a scrutinizing look and finally spoke up.

"So," she waved her fork, "why are you going to the library? I thought everyone gave that up with college."

"You mean you don't go to the library? Ever?"

"Are you kidding? Why would I want to go there?"

"Because libraries are full of information. Anything you want to know about you can usually find an answer there.

They have hundreds of novels to enjoy, cookbooks, how-to books, biographies, newspapers...everything. I can't believe you don't go to the library."

"You sound like a commercial for crying out loud."

"Well, you sound like a bimbo."

"I am not a bimbo."

"I know, I know," Kate apologized. "But don't knock a community resource you obviously haven't taken the time to know anything about. You should come with me sometime. It can be a great tool for work too."

"I'll think about it. Maybe I'll trade you a night out having fun with people for a night in with your books. There is life beyond work and libraries, you know."

Kate smiled faintly. This wasn't the first time they'd discussed her preference for a good book and her cat to a night out on the town.

"Okay, I'll ignore your strategic silence. Let's go the infomercial route. What are you getting at the library tonight?"

"Tonight I'm continuing the search for my roots."

"Really? Like Alex Haley?"

"It's a bit different." Kate frowned at a stubborn chickpea that wouldn't hold still for her fork, finally plucking it up with her fingers. "My life's history, although it has drama, isn't quite as dramatic or groundbreaking as his, except for the Simon stories. I mean, 'Roots' was a monumental work. Serious, important stuff."

"So," she gave Meagan a wink and teased her, "probably not enough fluff for your reading entertainment. None of that staring deeply into each other's eyes, followed by the kissing and the hugging, and then the handsome man with his bare chest sweeping the fair maiden with her heaving bosom up into his arms and carrying her away to the bedroom..."

"You read that book, too? Wasn't it great? My favorite part is when he sees her standing on the balcony in the moonlight, and he climbs up the vines to reach her and he kisses her, and then she rips his shirt open." Meagan's face was bright and animated with the memory.

Kate stared at her a moment, then shook her head. "I'm afraid I missed out on that one, I am so, so sorry to say."

"That's okay. You can have my copy."

"Trade you for my copy of 'Roots.'"

"Nah. I watched the mini-series. Well, most of it."

"You, my friend, are a bastion of culture. A credit to enlightened women everywhere." Meagan smiled at her happily. Kate took a breath that exhaled as a chuckle. As clueless as her friend could sometimes be, or pretend to be, she more than made up for it in other ways...her unwavering friendship, her boundless love, her intense loyalty, and an enduring sense of faith that everything, always, would eventually work out for the best.

Kate smiled back. "So, returning to our previous conversation, I'm only putting names and places together. It's fun to trace your ancestors and see who your people were and where they came from."

"A library has that stuff? You mean I can go and look up Ahumada in the file and read all about my family?"

Kate raised her eyebrows and chuckled again. "It's not quite that simple. There's a lot of research involved. You start with yourself and your parents, go backwards to your grandparents, then your great-grandparents, your great-great-grandparents, and keep working your way backwards. Sometimes, you can find some older relatives that have information or stories. If you're really lucky, they'll come up with an old family Bible or letters or photographs." Kate swallowed another quick bite. "Eventually you have to resort to books and records of births, deaths, marriages, even ship's logs to trace and match names and places. Depends on how far back you want to go."

"Sounds boring. I know my parents and grandparents, and I know I came from El Cajon, CA. That's far enough back for me."

"Ah, Meagan. You're so...so..."

"Shallow?"

"Uncomplicated. What you see is what you get. No pretense. It's so refreshing."

"That's why you hang out with me. I balance out your brain power, keep you focused on the real world. Otherwise, you'd never have any fun. Hey, if you're not going to eat that last muffin, toss it my way."

Kate handed it over with a shake of her head. "I'll never understand where you put it all."

"In my mouth, dear. It all goes in my mouth. Say, on this family thing, how far back have you gone?"

"Well it took some doing but I've made it into the 1790s on my mom's side and I'm getting into the early 1600s on my dad's."

Meagan stopped eating and stared at Kate in surprise. "The 1600s? My God, did they have people back then?"

"Not only did they have people, they also had the original Katherine."

"No, another one? You actually found an ancestor named after you?"

"Well...she was named first, and it appears there were two of them. Both on my father's side. The first was Katherine Peterson Torrence, in the 1600s. The second was Katherine Torrence in the early 1800s. She married an attorney in London and became," she paused for emphasis, "Katherine Torrence McGuire, or Katy for short."

"Wow. Another you. Does it feel weird to know someone else has your name?"

"They both died a long time ago, Meagan. Besides, I like being named after my ancestors. Creates a bond. Like we're all linked in some special way. I'm trying to find out more about them. Not only because of our names, but because of this strange family fairytale."

Meagan was inhaling the crumbs from her fingers and paused briefly. "A legend? Like they were witches or queens in exile? No, I know. Lady pirates with buried treasure. We'll be rich."

"Sorry, no hidden treasures. Not in that sense anyways." Kate looked at her watch and jumped up. "We should be back already. Looks like I won't get out quite as early as I hoped."

"So we run. But what's this strange story? I'm dying to know."

The women rushed off, dodging people on the sidewalk, Meagan straining to hear the puffed words trailing back.

"Well the second Katherine, or Katy as they called her, started with a good life but somehow the family lost all their money; then the father died, and she ended up with a poor sad life. She would have ended that way, too, except one day this man, a storyteller, came to town. The strange part is, apparently this man's story was all about Katy. He told her future, how her luck would change and she would marry a wonderful man, end up happy, and have money. It all came true. Or so they say."

"Who says? Where is this guy, I want to meet him."

"He's long dead, Meagan. This was in the early 1800s, remember? His name was Simon and he supposedly had some mysterious power. At least that's how the story goes. I guess they believed in things like magic back then. I'm afraid that's all I know about it."

The two reached their building and pushed into the elevator. Meagan punched the button for the seventh floor and looked at the clock.

"See? We did it. You can still get out early tonight."

Katy was staring at the clock, a thoughtful look on her face. "The really strange thing is, I got this letter from a great-aunt back east, and she not only told me the Katy story, she said the same thing happened to the first Katherine, too."

"No." Meagan looked at her, eyes wide.

"That's what she says. Katherine Peterson Torrence and a storyteller named Simon." Kate shook her head. "This aunt's an old woman, like 100 years old, and I kind of wanted to pass it off as simply getting the two names confused. You know, the same story but getting it mixed up between the two Katherines."

"Yeah, I'll bet that's it."

"Not exactly. She sent me copies of some old family papers and they said Katherine Peterson and she married a doctor, not a lawyer."

Meagan stared at her friend, temporarily silenced, her mouth twisting in contemplation. "Well, at least your namesakes have a history of marrying well. You should take a lesson."

"Meagan."

"All right, all right. Not another word. But while you're researching, check out that Simon guy. If he's got a descendent around today, I'd sure like to know about it."

Kate's eyes widened and she grabbed her friend. "Meagan, you're a genius."

"I am? Why?"

The elevator door opened and they continued towards their respective work areas.

"Because that's what I'm going to do. I'll not only see if Simon might have existed back then, but I'll also try to trace him up to some present-day people. Wouldn't that be a kick?"

"Well, if you do, I already told you I want to be there," Meagan called after her friend's departing figure.

Kate practically waltzed back to her office. Wouldn't it be amazing to meet Simon's descendants all these years later? Almost like a family reunion. Would they have stories about Simon and the Katherines too? At least Simon. They must have some information about him.

She sat down at her desk and aimlessly shuffled the piles of papers around. Suddenly her hands paused in midair. What if the stories were true? What if this Simon actually had the power to see into people's lives... past and future? Could that power pass through generations? Is that how there were two stories, two hundred years apart? Is there someone out there now who could look at a person and really know them, unlike anyone had ever known them before?

Maybe most importantly, Simon, whether the original or a descendant, had apparently twice found her ancestors named Katherine. Could that mean there is a Simon now searching for her? Some secret bond that keeps pulling the Simons and Katherines together? The thought gave her a chill that made her shiver. Somehow, there must be a way to find the answers to these questions.

She sat at the library later that day amidst a pile of books on her table. One lay open before her but she paid it no heed, her eyes staring blankly. A figure quietly approached from the rear and gently laid a hand on her arm. With a small cry, Kate leaped to her feet and spun around, eyes wide.

"Boy have you got good strong reflexes. Why don't you give me a karate chop for good measure?"

"Meagan! You scared me to death."

"Shush. You're in a library, remember? Everyone's

staring at us." She paused briefly, patting her hair. "Yeah, everyone is staring. That's perfect. Any good-looking men? You play this game better than you know."

Kate rolled her eyes as she sat down and motioned to the chair next to her. "What are you doing here, Meagan?"

"I was invited. By you, if I remember correctly."

"I'm just surprised you took me up on it so quickly."

"Well," Meagan shrugged, "I thought I should at least see what this place looks like. Great stonework by the way. Love the big staircase. Now if it ever comes up in conversation again I shall reply 'been there, done that.'" She leaned forward conspiratorially, "Besides, I wanted to see what guys hung out here. See if they're all nerds wearing plaid shirts and glasses, or whether there might be a few surprises, you know?"

"Now that's the Meagan I know and love. Did any pass muster?"

"Actually they all seem pretty darn good. I didn't expect them to be so normal looking. Especially that one," she motioned casually with her head, "over there by the window. I'd rate him above normal." She batted her eyelashes at her friend.

Kate chuckled. "All right, you can go talk to him. I have a little more to finish here anyways." She shook her head as Meagan sauntered towards the window then looked back at her book. Clearly, she wasn't going to get anything done here tonight. Her mind raced with thoughts of Simon and the two Katherines. She closed the book and began gathering her papers up. By the time she finished returning the books to their shelves, Meagan waited at the table for her.

"Ah, I know that look. It's the same look my cat has when I treat him to a can of Fancy Feast Wild Salmon Dinner. Chewy loves the fish dinner. I take it your stroll was successful?"

"Well, I do have a date for Friday night."

"Friday night? Meagan, you don't even know this guy. I've told you before, make the first couple of dates for lunch. It's safer that way. Lunchtime is nice and bright, lots of people around, and your date knows you're expected back to work in an hour. It's a perfect safety net."

"Trust you to be thinking about safety nets when it comes to men."

"Well, it's just the way life is, Meagan. Better to be safe than sorry. I hope you at least told him you'll meet him at the restaurant instead of giving him your home address."

Meagan bit her lip and looked away, "Say, isn't that a row of books over there? Let's go look at them."

"Meagan. You gave a complete stranger your home address."

"He's a nice guy, Kate, really. Besides, who sounds like an angry mother now? I'm a grown-up. I can take care of myself."

"I know you can. I just wish you'd be more cautious because you're my best friend. I care about you. There are some mean people out there. Promise me you will be careful?"

"I'll be careful. Now give me a quick tour and let's go. Talking about that salmon dinner made me hungry. You got any more Fancy Feast stuff at your place?"

Kate made a face, "Meagan, it's cat food."

"Chewbaca won't mind. We're pals."

"Forget it. I'll buy you a pizza."

When they arrived at Kate's home later, Meagan immediately curled up in a chair with Chewy. "Hi there, baby," she cooed softly as she rubbed under the cat's chin. "Are you ready to come home with me yet? I'd feed you wild salmon dinners every night."

Kate smiled as she sat on the couch by a box of papers.

"Sorry, Meagan. You still can't have Chewy."

"But I love my little Cougar."

"So do I. Besides, your landlady won't let you have pets. You already have full visitation rights. That's the best I can do."

"I know," Meagan sighed. "At least I'm his Godmother. You sure are a beautiful tabby, aren't you, my precious." She stroked the silky orange fur. "Do you think he ever gets confused with all his names?"

"Apparently not. He seems to know who he is."

"That's because he's the smartest cat in the world. Aren't you, Cougar." She scratched behind his ears.

"These are the letters I was telling you about," Kate pulled the box of papers onto her lap. She had contacted every relative she could get a name and address for during her ancestral search. Digging through the box she located the small pile of correspondence received from her Aunt Nancy in Arizona. Chewbaca left Meagan and jumped on the couch to playfully bat at some loose pages and then flopped down on top of them. Kate smiled and scratched the cat's chin. He purred deeply in response.

She turned her attention back to her aunt's papers. Although bits and pieces of Katy's story had circulated among her family for years, she'd always assumed it was a romanticized fairytale version of the truth. These papers showed the facts. She held up the pages her Aunt Nancy had sent for Meagan to see.

"These are copies from an old family Bible. It shows a family tree starting in 1702 and traces marriages, births, and deaths up through 1854. You wouldn't believe what an enormous help it's been. Now," she pointed her finger at a spot low on one of the pages, "look here at these names in 1825."

Meagan moved over to the couch for a closer look.

Among the last of the listings was Katherine M. Torrence, wed to Michael S. McGuire, Barrister.

"Wow. Katherine Torrence McGuire. Just like you said." She shivered as Kate shuffled through the papers on her lap again. "It's weird to see someone else with your name. I wonder what else you two have in common."

"Not much, I'm sure," Kate said distractedly as she held up the aunt's letter and skimmed it again, looking for notations to show the names and stories about Simon could have been easily confused. "See here. My aunt said Katy married a lawyer exactly as Simon's story said she would. The Bible entry seems to bear that out. But is that really any proof Simon existed?"

Meagan gave an exaggerated shrug. "Got me. I wasn't there. What did that New York lady write about this Katy and the other Katherine?"

Kate shuffled the pile again and picked up the newest letter she had received from a great-aunt in New York. "She tells a very interesting tale. Katy was her grandmother and she heard her story about Simon directly from her. And, she remembers her family saying a Katherine Peterson was given a story by Simon in the 1600s, and as foretold married a physician by the name of Torrence. John Torrence." She dropped the paper back into the box in bewilderment. "See? First-hand knowledge. According to Great-Aunt Edith, the names are different, the dates are different. It's two separate women and two separate stories."

"No, no. It has to be a simple mistake. Most likely there was a storyteller court-jester kind of guy in Katherine's time. You know, back in medieval days they believed in wizards and dragons and things."

Kate made a face at her friend.

"Really. They had those knights in shining armor and everything. I've heard about this stuff. So he told a story that turned out to be similar to what happened to Katherine. She probably thought it would be fun to tell the kids the story that brought her and her husband together. I mean, I would have done that."

Kate chuckled and pushed a stray hair from her face. "You almost make sense, Meagan. The story probably got told so many times through the years people started mixing the two women up. It'd be a logical mistake. Maybe Katy even encouraged it since it was such a great story."

"See what a good friend I am to have around? Can I solve your problems or what?" She stood up and stretched. "But enough good deeds for one night. I need to get home to bed."

Kate stood and walked her to the door. "Thanks, Meagan. You are a good friend. Drive carefully," she called out before locking up for the night. Taking the box of papers, she turned off the living room lights and entered her bedroom. Putting on the old t-shirt she slept in, she curled up on her bed and pulled out the old aunt's letter again.

Made-up story or not, Kate would always treasure this letter in its fragile handwriting and the copy of an old battered paper that recorded her family history on her father's side from the 1600s. As Great-Aunt Edith had said, there under the year 1632, was noted the marriage of Katherine A. Peterson and Dr. John Torrence. The letter, of course, told the miracle stories of the Katherines as recalled by Edith.

"I remember Nana Katy with great fondness, though she died when I was still young. Pawpaw Michael, I'm afraid I can't recall at all. But, I distinctly remember the stories she told of Simon. Mother and Uncle Gordon told all of us the

stories for years also. Uncle, who was Nana's son like my father Sheldon, insisted every word of it was true. Simon, the magic storyteller who foretold Nana's and Pawpaw's meeting and marriage, never returned. They often heard rumors of strange and wonderful things happening across the lands, though, and they would smile and know he was still at work."

"Nana said she could remember her grandparents and other family members telling about a Great-Great-Great-and-so-forth-Grandmother who was also named Katherine. Katherine Peterson. She was said to also have met a Simon who told her story. Because of it, she met and married John Torrence who was a well-respected doctor. This was back sometime in the 1600s, so the story is quite old. But it was so special it was told to their children, then their grandchildren, and so on until it reached Nana Katy. Then Nana had her own story to add to it, and she told her children, and they told me, and I told my children. Thus, it has carried through the years and now resides with you. So it falls on you and your cousins to take it into the future, for it is a story worthy of remembering. It is a source of great hope. Have faith in the future for as Simon said, 'faith is always rewarded.' "

"I can't say if it was the same Simon telling both stories. Although considering how miraculous they were it almost wouldn't surprise me. But part of the first Katherine's story said near the end of her life, she had become concerned the rumors of the mystic storyteller had ceased for several years and worried the mysterious man had disappeared."

"Considering he was older than her to begin with, some assumed the logical explanation was the gentleman had simply passed away. That would mean a different Simon, a relative perhaps, gave Nana her story. Quite honestly, part of me hopes Simon was the teller of both tales and he continues to live on. Still, if he hasn't, one gets curious as to what manner of an ending would come to a man such as him."

Kate wondered too. If someone really possessed all that power, surely he wouldn't simply lie down and fade away. No, an incredible event would have to happen; one that let people know a momentous loss had occurred. She must remember to check out any major events around that time. Just in case. Maybe it could help her locate Simon and the time of his death.

She sighed, wanting to believe a magic storyteller named Simon had really existed. If only she could've been there, been a part of that wonderful, mysterious time. How must it have felt to have one's life instantly directed in the most glorious way? With surprise, Kate realized she was jealous of her ancestors. At least one of them met the mysterious man, while she could only use her imagination.

Oh, to have been part of the magic. To have met someone like Simon. If it'd been me, I would've wanted him, not some other guy. A sigh escaped her lips. *If only the stories could be true. What would it have been like? What did Katy and Katherine feel and think as each saw her life take shape as Simon said it would? Maybe having him appear in my life wouldn't be so bad, after all. Certainly nothing to be afraid of.*

Kate closed her eyes and leaned back, letting her mind drift away. The two stories played out in her head, seeming both familiar and real. By letting her mind just go, it felt as if she were there, feeling the wonder, experiencing the love shared between each woman and Simon. As if it was her living each woman's life. Kate could remember how they wanted him, how he wanted each of them, as well. But he couldn't belong to either one. So, Simon did the best thing he could do. He gave them a marvelous love story where they could live happily ever after...without him. *Next time, I won't let him go. I want the happily ever after, but only if it's with him.* Half-asleep, she smiled and pulled her blanket up over herself. Chewy settled comfortably on her stomach, purring himself to sleep.

CHAPTER ELEVEN

IT was the appointed day and hour, and Katy Torrence found herself standing nervously outside the address listed on the card. She read the numbers again, to be sure she had the right place, but there really was no need. Painted there on a wooden sign were the words:

Michael S. McGuire
Barrister-at-Law

Katy smoothed her skirts and looked nervously around. No one paid her any heed and she chided herself for behaving like a youthful schoolgirl. Taking a deep breath she stepped forward and opened the door.

The reception area was as elegantly appointed as she imagined it might be. Mr. McGuire did not appear to be hurting for clients. No, his pain came from other areas, the physical side being the least of them. She looked over the beautiful dark wood furniture and upholstery of fragrant leather. With pleasure, she noted the accent pieces of rich brocade and the exquisite, yet tasteful, artwork carefully scattered about the room.

Katy let out a small sigh. Things such as these were no longer meant to be hers. As true life went, Mr. McGuire, with very sincere appreciation, would probably offer her a position to clean these beautiful offices, and a good offer it would be. A fine job in these hard times and most likely the pay would be handsome too. As much as it pained her, Katy knew she would accept. She had a family to support.

"May I help you?" The natty young man queried from behind a tidy desk, his eyes carefully trying to hide his opinions.

"Yes," Katy faltered, pushing the card at him. "I've an appointment to see Mr. McGuire."

"Ah." The man's face brightened for a moment. "You must be Miss Torrence."

Composure regained, she stood tall and lifted her chin. "That I am."

"I'll let Mr. McGuire know you've arrived. Excuse me." He passed her and entered another room.

Katy smiled to herself and counted her blessings. She really was fortunate. It was a shame Simon's story couldn't be true; her mother set her straight on that. This was, however, an opportunity to improve life for herself and her family. She wouldn't let it pass by. She would keep her head on straight and be practical about this, as Mother had said. All the same, she would have liked to believe Simon.

"Miss Torrence, thank you for coming." Mr. McGuire strode forward, stopping to give a polite bow as he reached her. Katy inclined her head slightly and returned his warm smile.

"So good to see you under better circumstances. Please," he motioned to his office, "come in and sit down. Mr. Curran, have the tea brought in to us."

As Katy entered his private office, she noted with satisfaction that it exceeded, if possible, the understated excellence of the waiting area. There was no doubt this room belonged to a barrister. The large desk had several neat piles of papers on it and shelves upon shelves of law books took up most of the walls. To the side lay a sitting area with deep leather chairs placed before a warmly crackling fire. This was where he led her.

A mature, friendly-looking woman wheeled in a brass tea cart as they took their seats. Katy tried to hide her amazement at the wonderful array of pastries and sweetmeats piled upon the serving trays. The ornate cups and teapot filled with steaming, fragrant tea made her heart sing. It brought back such fond memories of life before her father died. She finally got to have an extravagant tea again, no pretense necessary.

"Miss Torrence," her host spoke, "I'd like you to meet Mrs. Kelly, my Housekeeper."

The smile froze on Katy's face. Of course he'd already have a Housekeeper, as well as other staff. The place couldn't stay so neat and tidy on its own. Mrs. Kelly looked so motherly and stable though, Katy wouldn't have wanted to take her position, even if she could have.

"Mrs. Kelly is Sam's wife, my driver whom you met the other night." Obviously, he was very fond of the couple.

"How do you do? I'm pleased to meet you, and I can't tell you how happy I was to see your husband drive up that night."

"Oh Miss, it's we who are happy you were there. You're the one who saved our good Michael. That's why I insisted on coming over and setting up this nice tea for you. He's been like a son to us and I can't even imagine what might have happened if you hadn't come along." She wiped at her eyes with a napkin.

"It was nothing, really. It all happened so fast."

"Tch...nothing she says. Have you ever seen such modesty?" She prepared to pour the tea and looked at Katy. "Do you take cream and sugar, Miss?"

"Yes, please." She took the offered cup and noticed Mrs. Kelly prepared Michael's tea with just sugar.

"Well, you two eat up, don't let these sweets go to waste. I'll be sitting by the door there so you can talk privately. I'll come back in a bit to see how you're doing, but let me know if you need anything." Mrs. Kelly paused and patted Katy's shoulder, "God bless you, my child."

Watching her cross the room and sit, Katy briefly thought how relieved her mother would be to hear they'd been properly chaperoned. She looked at Michael and shook her head in wonder. "I don't understand all the fuss that's been made over this. I did what had to be done, there was no time to think..."

"About the danger you were putting yourself in? I'm sure it must have crossed your mind but you didn't let it stop you." Michael reached for a small plate on which he placed a flaky pastry filled with rich custard. He handed it over to Katy. "Try that one and see how you like it. It's always been a favorite of mine."

"It looks delicious. Are you having one also? If I'm going to be dropping flaky crumbs down the front of me, I think it only fair that you do so as well."

His laughter was heard even in the reception area. Mrs. Kelly leaned further into her embroidery to hide her smile and cast a knowing look through the doorway at Mr. Curran. Speaking under her breath to herself she said, "My Sam was right. She is perfect for him. Now, all we have to do is get them to see it."

Time and conversation moved along, the teapot was empty and the trays mostly crumbs. Both were surprised at the lateness of the hour when Mrs. Kelly stood once again. "Excuse me for interrupting, Sir, but the light's fading outside and I'm afraid her mother will be getting worried about Miss Torrence."

"Oh heavens. Is it that late already?" Katy stood up. "My mother will indeed be concerned."

"Forgive my thoughtlessness. I should have paid more attention. Mrs. Kelly, please arrange for Sam to drive her home."

"Certainly, Mr. McGuire. Will you be escorting her?"

As a gentleman, he could not refuse. Even so, his initial look of surprise quickly turned to pleasure. "Most definitely. If she doesn't mind the company, that is."

Katy tried to ignore the sudden burning in her cheeks. "Your company would be most welcome, thank you kindly." They had talked so comfortably throughout the afternoon, she was caught off guard by the thoughts now hanging in the air and felt a wave of shyness. She quickly dropped her gaze from Mr. McGuire's face and made quite a chore of gathering her things together. Michael, as well, felt it necessary to clear his throat and adjust his jacket, looking anywhere except at her.

Mrs. Kelly left the room with a very satisfied smile.

The drive home felt awkward and they tried their best to keep the conversation on the business arrangement they had made. Katy had accepted employment as a Companion to an elderly neighbor of Michael's. She was a noblewoman, well-known and wealthy, with a reputation for being fair and kind. It was a marvelous position. Not only because of its respectability, especially for a member of the poor genteel, or even for its very generous wages. It was because Katy admired and respected the woman so much for her exceptional philanthropy. It was more than she had ever dared hope for.

"I can't thank you enough for securing this position for me. I'm looking forward to meeting Mrs. Compton."

"Please don't thank me. It was the least I could do to repay you. Plus, you are particularly well-suited for this, with your warm personality and kind heart..." his voice faded and he paused, looking quickly out the window. Clearing his throat, he abruptly continued, "Which will certainly keep me in Mrs. Compton's good graces."

He smiled brightly at Katy who glanced shyly back, and they both turned promptly to the windows again. Sam smiled and shook his head. Wasn't young love grand?

Once more Sam carefully handed Katy down from the carriage. But this time her escort to the door was Michael.

"Do come in and let me present my mother. She's most anxious to meet you."

Michael hesitated, wondering with slight irritation why this introduction made him nervous. It was only proper that he should meet this woman's mother. He had secured a prestigious position for her and could now be considered a guardian or benefactor of sorts. He was an attorney, after all, used to dealing with people and situations. Things must be kept in perspective. This was only business. Clearing his throat, he followed Katy into the cottage.

"Mother. I'm home, Mother," she called. Turning to Michael, she placed her hand briefly on his arm. "I'll go get her, it won't be but a moment. Please make yourself comfortable in the sitting room," she nodded towards the cozy room to their side.

Michael followed her with his eyes as she left, his hand touching the spot on his coat hers had just vacated. He shook his head slightly, as if trying to clear it, and glanced quickly about the room. It was small but tidy. Although obviously not much money there, he could see it was furnished with an eye to comfort and good taste. A room that welcomed people and invited friendly conversations and pleasant times. Katy's home, indeed.

He strolled about, looking with interest at the homey little touches, wondering if Katy might have made some of the things herself. At the very least, he was sure she must have helped select and arrange them. Glancing out the window, he noted with pleasure how the tiny flower garden was situated so as to show well from either inside or out. Someone had definitely taken much time and trouble to create this haven.

His reverie shattered at the sound of approaching voices. Michael quickly cleared his throat again, adjusting his jacket and smoothing his hair. His heart hammered in his chest, and while his mouth went dry, he could feel the moisture surface on his palms. Taking a deep breath, he dried his hands and smiled as the women entered the room. Katy and her mother glided confidently through the doorway; a younger girl hesitantly slipped in behind.

"Mother, this is Mr. Michael McGuire, the gentleman I've told you about. Mr. McGuire, this is my lovely mother, Mrs. Torrence, and my younger sister, Elizabeth."

Michael stepped towards them and gave a formal bow. "Mrs. Torrence. Miss Elizabeth. It's a pleasure to meet you both. Miss Torrence told me how wonderful her family was, but I can see now she was being modest even in this."

Elizabeth merely dipped her head lower and slid further out of sight behind her mother. Michael's quick glance at Katy showed pity the girl was even more timid than she had mentioned. Life would be far more difficult for her. Mrs. Torrence, however, broke out in a merry laugh that caught him off guard.

"Ah, you are definitely a member of that venerable society of legal men. The pretty phrases roll off the tongue so easily."

The color rose in his face as Michael stood speechless before the chuckling woman.

Katy had no such problem. "Mother. How can you say such a thing."

"No disrespect intended, I assure you. I was simply meaning it is a profession where one must think quickly and be prepared to smooth the path with a," she paused, "kind word. But, I can see I've made the poor man blush. Which is a good sign," she added under her breath. "So, let me welcome you to our home and offer my thanks for the good things you've done for us and our Katy."

"I simply mirrored the good thing she did for me."

"Now, don't start me on that one." Mrs. Torrence led the way to some chairs where she motioned for everyone to sit. "It was a courageous thing my girl did and I am proud she didn't hesitate to help someone in trouble. But, when I think of what could have happened to her..." Mrs. Torrence grasped her chest, rolling her eyes.

"Exactly. That's why I felt setting her up in as comfortable a position as I could was the least she deserved."

"Too right," the mother stated.

"Mother," Katy started again.

"Now don't hush me. I'm an outspoken woman. Always have been and not likely to change now. Mr. McGuire has heard worse, I'm sure."

"Outspokenness, in general, I hear plenty of. But direct honesty, such as yours, is rare and refreshing. Please don't hold back on my account." He smiled at the older woman, relaxed now and truly enjoying the exchange.

"See now, I told you it didn't bother him. He comes from

strong stock, Katy. Just like you."

The talk continued with Mrs. Torrence making the two of them recount the whole story again together. She interjected with gasps of horror and great clutching at her heart. Then they moved on to Katy's new station and the wonderful opportunity it presented.

Elizabeth sat with them and although she didn't join in the conversation, she did manage to look up and even smile. Suddenly she leaned over and whispered in her mother's ear.

"That's a splendid idea, child." Mrs. Torrence looked at them brightly, "Elizabeth has suggested we invite Mr. McGuire to join us for some tea. Would you care for a cup, Sir?"

"I would love a cup. Thank you, Mrs. Torrence. Miss Elizabeth," he replied graciously.

Katy's heart seemed to stop beating and she could feel some of the color drain from her face. She knew she should be happy Elizabeth had made an effort to join in, but all she could think of was the wonderful tea in Michael's office and how scanty their offering would be. For the first time with him, she felt ashamed.

"Maybe we should postpone tea for another time. You're looking rather pale, Mother. You haven't sat up this long with company in months and I don't want you to wear yourself back down."

"Forgive me," Michael stood. "I enjoyed our meeting so much I entirely forgot how ill you've been. I've overstayed my welcome. I do apologize."

"No, Mr. McGuire, I'm fine. Just somewhat tired. Company does me good so I hope you'll return again."

"Thank you, I will. It's been a great pleasure." He looked at Mrs. Torrence with a side glance at Katy. "Truly."

"I'll never doubt a word of yours, Mr. McGuire. I know a good man when I meet one." She nodded approvingly.

Katy escorted him to the door and said goodbye. Ashamed at her earlier reaction, she regretted forcing him into leaving. With surprise, she realized if she could, she'd keep him there forever. Maybe the realization showed in her eyes, for as she looked up at him he smiled.

"Don't worry, I'll be back. In fact, I'll accompany you to Mrs. Compton's house Monday morning to make introductions. That should help to allay any concerns and make your start easier."

"Thank you. I am a bit nervous about meeting her."

"You shouldn't be, she can't help but love you." He paused and the silence clung to them like silk, Katy afraid to even breathe. Michael left the unspoken words hanging there. "And, the next time I'm invited to tea, I fully intend to have it. I don't care how it's served or what is or isn't served with it. The company is what counts."

Katy blinked, startled. "But how did you know?" she sputtered.

Still smiling he took her hand and kissed it. "It's all a matter of keeping things in perspective. The trick is deciding which perspective you want to view it from." Bowing, he departed without another word, leaving a very flustered woman staring after him.

Sam had the carriage door open. "You were in there for a bit, Sir. Did you have a pleasant visit?"

"Yes, actually. I did. But rather strange as well. At first, I was so nervous I was tempted to come right back to the carriage and leave. Then I relaxed and found myself wanting to say the most curious things. I think I would have stayed forever if I could have," he mused.

"Bless my soul, it's about time." Sam climbed into his seat. "Martha will be well pleased."

"Whatever are you talking about? Time for what?"

Sam turned full around and looked at him with a

twinkling smile. "You're thirty-nine years old, Michael. It's about time you fell in love."

"Love?" Michael sat back heavily. Yes, love. He had already admitted that possibility as he stood in Katy's doorway fighting the urge to sweep her up into his arms. That was the proper perspective. A smile grew over his face.

"Well Sam, maybe it is about time. I wonder what excuse I can come up with to see her again soon."

As luck would have it the opportunity arose two days later, when Mrs. Compton requested Katy's presence for tea and an introduction. She wanted a chance to get acquainted before Katy officially assumed her duties and volunteered Michael to bring her. He had no hesitation in accepting the task, which Mrs. Compton shrewdly observed. On the selected afternoon he showed up much too early at Katy's door. They hoped he would do so and the whole family was ready, just in case. They spent a lovely afternoon entertaining their guest until Katy's appointment time with Mrs. Compton.

The future unfolded before her, and in her heart, Katy knew Simon had told the truth. It could be no mere coincidence. Some day, after she and Michael were happily married, she would tell him the story of how they were destined to meet. It would be a lovely, hopeful tale to pass down through their children for years to come.

She would not forget her promise to Charlie, either. First thing she'd do would be to rescue him from that awful factory and get him back to his family. He had so much inside him to give the world she could fairly sense him ready to burst the night they met. They would find the right outlet for him and Charles Dickens would unleash his own magic for the poor and downtrodden. She was sure that was the truth, too.

CHAPTER TWELVE

SHE had decided then. Kate had four weeks of vacation saved up and she would use them all. She would go to England and track down Simon. If anyone asked her, which many of her friends did, she couldn't say exactly why she needed to do this. It seemed crazy. There was such a strong urge, a longing that pulled from deep inside her, impossible to put into words, but it was there and it wouldn't die. She had to go. She had to find out what happened to Simon.

"You know, Kate, when I said you should track this guy down I was kidding. If anything, I thought you'd check through those library books you love so much. Not go chasing halfway around the world." Meagan planted herself, hands on hips, in the doorway of Kate's bedroom watching her friend pack.

"Well, I am going to use library books, in part. Except,

I'm going to be using the ones over there. They're more likely to have some of the information I need. Besides," she stopped packing to look off into the distance and smile, "I want to see the country where Simon and my ancestors lived, maybe walk down the same roads they once walked. I get goosebumps thinking about it."

"Okay, I admit it. I'm jealous. I want to go with you. Why don't you put me in one of those suitcases and take me along? I'm small." To emphasize her point Meagan climbed into the nearest Pullman and tried to curl up into a ball. It didn't quite work.

"Meagan, there are parts of you sticking out everywhere. You're not exactly the Pullman type, you know. Why don't you just buy a ticket?"

"I don't have that much money laying around," she whined. "Not all of us are the coupon clipping, savings account types like some people in this room."

"Don't tell me you don't have a savings account."

"I have a checking account. The kind you hand out signed pieces of paper from when you buy everything you see. That way, you have no need for a savings account."

"No need? What about the future? What if you have some big unexpected emergency, like you get sick, or lose your job?"

"I'm resourceful. It would work out."

Kate rolled her eyes. "Didn't I read a story about this? The ant and the grasshopper?"

"Not those yucky chocolate-covered ones, I hope. I mean, I know they're considered gourmet and all that, but I have to draw the line at eating bugs."

"Never mind, Meagan. Let me sum this up for you. I'm going to spend four weeks running around Europe, and you're not."

Meagan climbed out of the suitcase with a thoughtful

look. "Yeah," she said, "Yeah."

The plane from San Diego touched down at LaGuardia Airport in New York City. Kate only had a two-hour layover and she spent almost half of that getting to the proper gate. Once there she still had an hour to kill and settled down in a chair with her Diet Pepsi and a box of Crunch n' Munch. The butter-toffee kind.

She had decided to forego all the suitcases and settled on a large backpack that met the plane's carry-on requirements. After reading 'Europe Through the Back Door' by Rick Steves, she decided she really didn't need as much as she first envisioned. Actually, it gave her a sense of freedom to travel so lightly with all her belongings right next to her. No hassling with baggage claims, no worry about lost luggage. Most importantly, she could keep all her research papers with her. She wanted to take no chances they might disappear en route.

As she chewed the time away, Kate pulled some of the papers out and scanned over them. Her mind drifted away on thoughts of the mysterious Simon.

Walking down Arthur Avenue in the Bronx on that very same June afternoon, Simon busily observed the crowds. He loved seeing the changes time brought and the 1990s were certainly different. What would the turn of the century bring? Suddenly he stopped and tilted his head, looking into the distance. He could feel the pull as someone reached out to him. It was a completely different type of feeling than those distant voices that sometimes still echoed faintly through his mind.

His brow creased in puzzlement and he glanced quickly

about. No, the thoughts did not come from near at hand. Somebody...somebody out there searched for him. He had felt for a while it might be so, but the feeling was so far away he couldn't be sure. *Far away...San Diego? Yes, they started in San Diego. But the pull I feel is much closer. They're here in New York.*

There was no doubt in his mind. Someone definitely looked for him and they'd traveled some distance to find him. With a small smile, he continued on his way. He had no idea if this coming was good or bad. He only knew that if it concerned his destiny, he had no control over it and must simply accept what was to be. One thing he did feel sure of. Whenever this Searcher actually found him it was certain to be a momentous occasion.

Her plane took off only forty minutes late and Kate tried to get at least a couple hours of sleep. The time passed quickly. Now she looked out the plane window and felt a shiver of excitement pass through her. Only a few hundred feet below she could see the winding River Thames as it flowed amidst the great city of London. She had really done it. She was here. The older woman sitting next to Kate, prim and proper in her tailored suit, cheerfully played commentator for the sights laid out below them.

"Is that London Bridge?" Kate echoed the remarks of other passengers.

"The big one? My no, the one next to it is London Bridge, dearie. You're looking at Tower Bridge, and that's White Tower there on the bank. Probably the oldest building you can see well from up here. Although, you most likely know it as the Tower of London. I'm sure you've heard tell about it with the Crown Jewels and all."

"Really? I've heard about them since I was a little girl. I can't believe I'll have the chance to see them in person. Oh," Kate pointed below. "What's that one? The building along the river that looks almost like a fortress?

"That would be the Houses of Parliament. The books still call it the Palace of Westminster. Look there at the end."

"It's Big Ben," Kate laughed. "I can't believe I'm actually seeing Big Ben. It looks so clean and new, see how white the clock face is?"

"We take care of old Ben, no question on that."

"I've always read how crowded it is here, but there's really a lot of green isn't there?"

"Green's important to us, dearie. We love our gardens and we love our moors. It's been bred into us to love the land for hundreds of years." Her sudden seriousness dissipated as she glanced back out the window. "Right there, dearie, look over at that dome right there."

"Over there? Yes, I see it. What building is that?"

"That's Saint Paul's Cathedral. I know you've heard of that one. That's in a part of London they used to call 'The City'."

"The City?" Kate's eyes opened wide and she peered close. "I know about that. I mean, I've been reading quite a bit about it lately. That was the original old London, wasn't it?"

"Yes, it was. At one time they called it Londinium. But a lot has changed since way back when. London outgrew those old walls and tore most of them down. Mostly now it's all business and law and banking."

"Are there many original buildings left?" Kate pressed close to the window, trying to keep the fading buildings in sight as the plane circled for landing at Heathrow Airport. She was certain everyone on the plane could hear the echo of her pounding heart.

"Which original are you referring to? London goes back almost two thousand years, dearie. Not much original from those days, except the rocks maybe."

"I'm sorry. I meant early to mid-1600s. Anything left from then?"

"Not much, I'm afraid. Didn't you study your history, dearie? First, there was the Great Plague in 1665 followed by the Great Fire of 1666. Almost everything within the walls of The City burned to the ground, including the original Saint Paul's. Had to start pretty much from scratch. But no wood this time, only stone and brick allowed. Didn't want to provide kindling for a blaze like that ever again."

Kate sat back, her breath escaping her lungs as she stared blankly at the seat in front of her. Her body felt numb. Gone. Everything from Katherine's time gone. She had forgotten the fire.

The woman stared at her, a bit taken aback. "Now don't go looking like you've lost your best friend. Trust me, there are plenty of old things to see in London. The same streets still run through it, in better condition than they were then. Though not by much. There are wonderful historical buildings and there are the museums too. The British Museum near the University of London has lots to see. Started in the 1700s I think, and it even has a wonderful old library. That's where I'd start, dearie."

A smile reappeared on Kate's face. "The 1700s you say?" At least she could find out about Katy.

The plane touched down and Kate gathered her jacket and bags together as she thanked the woman for her kindness.

"I enjoyed it. Now have you got someone waiting for you, dearie? Or are you on your own from here?"

They continued talking as they left the plane and walked

through the airport. "I'm on my own. I was going to stay at Hazlett's in Soho..."

"Ah yes. William Hazlett's old house."

"Excuse me?"

"He was an essayist in the 1700 or 1800s. It's old, I'm sure you'll enjoy it there."

"Well, I'm not actually staying there after all. I was about to say a friend recommended the Hotel Ravna Gora." Kate smiled, "I liked the sound of it. Kind of rhymes with that Eagles song, 'Hotel California?' An equal number of syllables so they flow the same."

"I don't know about any song, but the Ravna Gora is a lovely place to stay. Used to be Mr. Holland's mansion. Nice Yugoslavian family runs it as a B&B now. They've got some lovely roses out front and there always seems to be a kitten running about. It's an excellent choice."

Kate paused and looked at the woman in amazement. "How do you know all these things? You're like a walking encyclopedia."

"Actually, I was a tour operator here in London for years. I've researched and repeated this information so many times it's all committed to memory. But, I'm retired and now I'm the one doing the traveling."

"Well, I'm glad you have the opportunity to be on the other side for a change. I hope you enjoyed your visit to the States."

"It was wonderful. And huge. I never understood how big America really was. So much to see and such variety. I'm already planning my next trip, but all the same, I am glad to be home again. Do you know how to get to the Ravna Gora?"

"Take a taxi?"

"I recommend the full London experience. Take the Tube, it's quick and it's cheap, only a couple pounds will get you a day pass. Piccadilly runs right from the terminal into central London, you'll probably want off at Holland Park. Only a short walk to the Ravna Gora from there."

Kate wrote the names down. "Wonderful. You've been such a help. To be clear though, is the Tube your subway?"

"Subway? I should say not. That's much too far for a subway. Who'd walk it anyways? No, dearie, the Tube is the Underground."

"The Tube is the Underground?" Kate stared for a moment. "We're talking about trains, right? Underground trains?"

"Well of course we are."

"Good. That's what I thought you meant...a subway."

Now the woman looked vexed. "You Americans and your strange speech. Most certainly not the subway. Subways are for pedestrians to cross under a road. I'm talking about the Piccadilly."

"The Picadilly's the Underground...which is the Tube."

"That's what I said in the first place, dearie. Do have a good time on your visit, but I wish you'd brought a friend along to help you get about." The woman turned towards the entry line for U.K. citizens.

"Thanks again." Kate called after her. As she threaded her own way towards the Visitor Immigration line Kate muttered quietly, "I probably should have learned English before I made this trip."

Shortly thereafter, having successfully navigated her first excursion on the Tube and was careful to 'Mind the Gap,' Kate found herself exiting the Underground station onto Holland Park Avenue. She had managed to discover and purchase Capitalcards from the Underground ticket station at Heathrow and now had almost unlimited access to bus, Tube, and British Rail services during her stay. With a sense of accomplishment and anticipation, she checked her map and headed east.

The hotel was a couple blocks to the left of the station, on the opposite side of the road. Simply crossing the road turned out to be interesting business. The cars drove in the wrong direction. Out of habit, Kate looked left and almost stepped out into the lane, only to find the cars came from the right. She finally managed to cross and climbed the stairs to the hotel's entrance.

Checking in was quick business. Kate found the owners, Manda and Rijko, to be friendly and helpful. They welcomed her to London and were very interested in hearing about San Diego.

"We can always tell the Californians," Rijko stated.

"Yes," Manda agreed, "Californians are such friendly Americans. More 'laid back' you call it?"

They chatted a few minutes more. Finally, Manda threw up her hands. "We're keeping you talking too long. You must be tired. It's a long trip from California." She went into an office off the foyer and returned with a key in hand. "I'll give you a room on the first floor. My other opening is on the third but I don't want to make you climb that far." She motioned to the wide spiral staircase winding upwards behind her. "Your room is off to the right at the top of the first flight of stairs. The toilet and shower are in the main hall on each floor." She handed over the key with a smile.

"Up the stairs? We're not on the first floor already?"

"No, of course not. This is the ground floor. This is where you'll have your breakfast in that room back there. First floor is one flight up."

Picking up her backpack, Kate moved to the bottom of the stairs and looked up the middle of the spiral. "Wow. That's a good hike. Thank you for only making me go up one floor." The owners laughed as she began her trek up.

The room was plain but clean and comfy. Kate went to the window and slid it open. Fresh air poured in with the sound of traffic and people laughing. She looked outside to see a red double-decker bus drive by and suddenly wanted to dance. London. She never believed she'd ever go anywhere and here she was in London. She loved it already.

Quickly unpacking her things, she headed towards the bathroom where a long, hot shower called to her. According to her watch, it was almost two a.m. in the morning San Diego time. She had managed to get some sleep on the plane, but was it enough to help her body adjust to ten a.m. in London? Maybe she should make it a short shower and get outside where the magic of the city could do its work.

Kate followed her own advice. Soon she was back on the Tube heading deeper into London, her tour book clutched in her hand. When she got off, she wandered the streets a bit to look and listen to the people. Finally, she waved down a double-decker bus. She had looked forward to this for weeks. Now, she could personally start tracing Simon's life and look for his descendants. When she completed her task, or maybe mixed in with her search, she would be a typical tourist. There was so much to see.

"Thanks for stopping. Are you going to the British Museum? I'm not sure I'm reading this schedule right."

"British Museum, Miss? Is that where you be headin' now? Why would you be wantin' to go to the British Museum?"

"Well, I wanted to explore some of the history of London and its people and that seemed a good place to start. At least, that's where I was recommended."

"You were, were you? Well, this be a good place to start, too. British Museum's only down the road a wee bit. Lots of historic buildings and things along the way. You could probably be walkin' it with no problem."

The bus driver looked perfectly serious.

"Well...thanks for the suggestion, but if you're going that

way I'd just as soon ride." Kate leaned closer. "You see, you have a wonderful bus here and I'm dying to ride in the upstairs of a double-decker like this."

"Well, why didn't you be sayin' so in the first place? Could have saved us all a bit of trouble." He turned to the passengers waiting patiently. "She would have walked, you see, but she didn't want to be passin' up a chance to be ridin' topside. The lass has good taste."

The group murmured their assent, save for one fellow in the rear who called out, "Why don't you quit talking and take a seat so we can get moving."

The bus driver ignored him and waved her on in. "I suppose I'll go on and be takin' you to the British Museum then. Seein' as it's on my way and all." He patted the coin box next to him but Kate pulled out her Capitalcard. "Planned ahead, did we? Well go on up and get your seat. I've got people to deliver." He turned away but not before Kate caught his little wink.

She'd better get used to their brand of humor, too, she realized. With a smile, she hurried back and found the staircase. It was a small spiral fixture and she barely managed to grab the rail as the bus lurched forward. Weaving and wobbling, she made it up and found a seat by the window. Her bird's eye view of the streets and buildings was wonderful. She would have to take a whole morning and just ride a bus around. They stopped and started a couple of times, but on the next stop, she heard a bellow from down below.

"Somebody go tell that lass up there that I won't be takin' her any farther. She's goin' to have to be gettin' off here."

A boy's head popped up the stairwell and looked at her. "Sorry, Miss. Driver says you've got to get off."

"Me? I have to get off? But why? I've got a pass."

"I don't know why, Miss. You'll have to ask him."

Kate climbed back down the stairs, her face flushed a subtle shade of red. "Did you say I had to get off the bus?" she asked the man at the wheel.

"That I did, lass," he replied without looking at her.

"May I ask why?"

"Did you not ask me to be takin' you to the British Museum?"

"Well yes, but..."

"And did I not say you could easily be walkin' there?"

"Yes, but we agreed..."

"Well, then. There you have it."

Kate was thoroughly exasperated. "Just what is it we have?" she asked, hands on her hips.

"The British Museum. Right there." He pointed behind her.

Kate turned to look. "Oh." She paused a moment to collect herself. "I didn't realize it was so close."

"See, lass? Didn't I say you could be walkin' here?" He grinned very broadly, now.

"Yes. You did say that. Thank you for all your help." Kate stepped off the bus onto Great Russell Street, her cheeks burning as the sound of laughter drifted back from the departing bus. With a sheepish glance around she smiled. At least she was creating some good stories to tell back home.

She turned her attention to the museum and gasped. It was remarkable. Hurrying towards the large building, she looked in delight at the huge entrance pillars and the building's wings, which seemed to stretch out in all directions. Picking up a brochure at the door, Kate vowed to return when her work was done. She couldn't pass up the opportunity to enjoy collections that included Egypt, the Orient, and Medieval Europe. Although billed as one of the world's finest museums there was no entrance fee. Kate shook her head in amazement. She could easily spend several trips exploring its treasures. But, first things first.

Following the signs, she picked her way downstairs and found herself in an immense reading room, oval in shape, perimeter walls lined with hundreds of books. Seated at long tables in the middle of the room were crowds of people thumbing through their selections. Moving forward, Kate noticed that all along the wall, doorways into small display rooms interrupted the shelving. As she examined some of these, she was impressed to find such things as a 4th-century Bible, several authors' original manuscripts, and even a first folio of Shakespeare's plays. Kate found the last item particularly interesting. She carefully touched the display case with her fingertips in awe, overwhelmed at seeing some of his original works. She was sure she felt his spirit there and kept checking the shadows for his presence. *Shakespeare's house,* she thought, *a definite must-see.*

Back in the main room, Kate started searching through the books. After a few inquiries, she found that to trace individuals, as through birth and death records, would require a trip elsewhere. But, she was directed to a cased section containing several manuscripts and journals from individuals living in the London area from the 1400s through the 1800s. Looking at a few of them might give her a good idea of the flavor of that era.

Through the glass she skimmed through several of the open pages, finding the language tedious and their outlooks and beliefs rather astonishing when compared to her own enlightened times. Finally, as she itched to move on to material more substantial for her purposes, she came across a journal entry that grabbed her attention.

"Th nite turnt owht tu b most rewarden howe evr wen a Eirish storitellr apeered bi th naim ov Simun. He toad wundrus talz ov majik that had th stranjest affekt on us awl. I no i lef thar lik a nu man ful ov glorius hop fore r futur."

She had found him. Kate could scarcely breathe, she was so excited. Reading on, she found as with her ancestors, Simon told a story that reflected the life of one of his listeners. Like Katy and Katherine, he foretold a bright future that would be shared by many. It was a story the writer claimed came true and it happened because "Simun sez fath iz awayz rewarded."

Kate hurried to a docent and did some quick persuading. She needed to know the date of the writing. It had occurred on May 17, but of which year? Was it 1630? The same year as her family's story? Or maybe 1824? The docent brought a staff member who opened the case and carefully handled the journal with gloved hands. He turned the pages and pointed.

Kate gasped in shock. Fifteen hundred and twenty-five. "Surely that must be a mistake. He must have meant 1625. Please check the other pages."

The staff member shrugged and gently turned more pages. Fifteen hundred and twenty-five. More pages, and at the end of the journal now. Fifteen hundred and twenty-five. Kate backed up to a chair and sat down.

"Is that sufficient, Miss?"

She looked at the man and blinked. "Oh, yes. Thank you. I wasn't expecting such a find. It will help my research immensely. Thank you so much for your help." Her voice seemed to come from far away. The man nodded in satisfaction and replaced the journal, locking the case behind him.

Feeling dizzy, Kate left the museum. Outside, she took large gulps of the cool air. Her head grew less fuzzy as she tried to make sense of things. She had made excuses for her relatives and ancestors as confusing their stories about the two Katherines, and that only one had possibly met Simon. How could she explain this away? It was a totally unrelated source and an unrelated time.

She knew it couldn't possibly be the same Simon. Even if the stories did seem identical. Assuming he had been, say, twenty years old in 1525, that would make him one hundred and twenty-five in 1630. Kate laughed. Remarkable even for 1996, let alone back when life expectancies were so much shorter. That left one conclusion.

Her Simon was the son, or more likely the grandson, of the first Simon. It was the only logical explanation. Apparently, the gift did pass down through the family, along with the ancestral name. If not too diluted it might be present even today. She could imagine one of them walking down the Strand and getting a sudden premonition from a passerby. Probably pass it off to an active imagination and ignore it. Or, have a reputation among their neighbors as being slightly touched in the head.

She smiled, happy with her resolution, and walked off briskly. It was late afternoon and she hadn't eaten since the plane. Time to partake in the local delicacies.

CHAPTER THIRTEEN

HER guidebook offered several suggestions for eating spots. So many, in fact, Kate had no idea which restaurant or pub to choose. But, help was close at hand. Coming down the street on his bicycle was a genuine British "bobby", tall helmet and all. Her reading told her these men carried no guns. They kept the peace with truncheons, a sort of baton, and their wits. They were also great sources for advice and information. She flagged him down.

"Can I help you, Miss?"

"I hope so, Constable. It's not an emergency or anything. I arrived from the States today and I'm starving. Could you possibly recommend a good place to eat nearby?"

The Constable chuckled. "This is the kind of problem I like...easy question, easy answer. There'll be plenty of good eating around here, Miss, but," he looked at the watch on his wrist, "it's almost 3:30 p.m. now. Most of the pubs close at 3:00 p.m., don't open again till 5:00 p.m. They're the best if you want some real English food. Pub grub they call it."

"Pub grub?" Kate laughed. "I love it. That will definitely go on my list of things to experience."

"And well it should. Best food of the nursery variety...good plain cooking. For your immediate needs, the hour is such I would recommend the other British staple that every visitor should try. A nice Afternoon Tea."

Kate's eyes widened and seemed to glow in the sunlight. "Oh, yes. I've always wanted to do that. Where do I go?"

"One of my favorites, Lascelles Old English Tea House at 2 Marlborough Court, Carnaby Street. It's not far, just the other side of Soho near Regent Street. Would you like to take a hackney?"

"A what?"

"Sorry. A taxi. There's one coming now. Shall I hail it?"

"Please do. I think I'd enjoy a taxi trip. I hear those cabbies can talk up a storm."

They were on the sidewalk of Bloomsbury Street with the southern-facing traffic. The cabby drove north on the opposite side of the road. The bobbie blew his whistle and raised his hand to the cab, setting off an incredible scene that made Kate's heart pound.

Completely ignoring all other vehicles on the road, the cab made an immediate U-turn. The driver was impervious to the screeching tires and honking horns surrounding him.

The officer nodded his head with a grin and motioned to the car pulling in front of them. "Turn on a sixpence, they can."

"Will I be safe with him?" Kate eyed the vehicle suspiciously.

"Perfectly. Best cabbies in the world and they're a proud lot. Not just anyone can drive these things, you know. Takes them almost four years doing the knowledge. Have to study, get registered and all." He opened the door for her then leaned down to the driver, "Take her to Lascelles for Tea, if you don't mind."

"A privilege, Constable." They saluted each other as the car moved away.

The car was noisy, but that had no effect on the cabby's ability to converse. He kept a running monologue the whole drive, shouting over his shoulder through the six-inch gap in the glass partition.

"Constable's right, don't you know. Can take up to four years doing the knowledge. Of course, I did it in less than three and a half. Always was a bit on the quick side. Pick things up real easy like. I rode my bicycle through every back alley of this city, clipboard hooked to my handlebars, till I knew every route and every building they even thought of putting up. We cabbies have our hands on the pulse of the city, as they say. Nothing you could want that we don't know where to go and how to get there. Ask me for anything and I can tell you where it is without even stopping to think. Take two of the best views in the city. One, go to London Bridge at dawn and watch the rising sun as it hits Tower Bridge. Two, over at St. Paul's, you know the cathedral, climb up to the Golden Gallery at the topmost spire. Not many make it up there, but the view of the city is spectacular. Now, where to get the best ice cream soda the world has ever seen? Over at Fortnum & Mason, needless to say, 181 Piccadilly, fourth floor. All the food's good, but the ice cream sodas are jolly nice. Suppose you want to see some local color. Plant yourself on one of the park benches in Chelsea. On the one hand, you'll have the pensioners. Old men sitting in their long red jackets with their rows of medals and their black hats. Retired war veterans, they are, and we make sure they're taken care of at the Royal Hospital there. On the other hand, next bench over you'll have the local punks with their fluorescent mohawks, black leather, and ringed noses. Study in contrasts, I always say. Well, look here. We've made it to your Tea in no time at all. Jolly good choice, I think. Have a cuppa for me, will you, luv? Thanks for the tip. Did you know what the word tips means? To insure prompt service. Good one, don't you think?" With a grin, he touched the brim of his hat and drove off.

"Heavens," Kate said, watching him go. "I don't believe he stopped to breathe once."

Inside the Tea House, she settled into her chair and ordered a steaming pot of apple spice black tea to start. With it came a three-tier stand of traditional treats including madeleines, custard tarts, and finger sandwiches. She especially enjoyed the cream scones slathered with rich clotted cream and jam. The tea was spicy and delicious and soon gone as Kate munched away. She passed up the rich Dundee fruitcake, choosing to finish with a slice of Victoria Sponge and a cup of English Breakfast tea to go with it.

She doubted they'd ever heard of Coffee Mate here, which was fine with her as she preferred to use milk anyways. Kate was oddly pleased to learn milk and sugar was also the preferred British way to make a decent cuppa, though it had to be milk and not cream which could mask the tea's flavor. She sighed and leaned back, looking happily around the cozy tea salon. It was one of the most soothing afternoons she'd experienced in her life.

When she roused herself enough to leave, Kate decided a walk was in order before going back to the Ravna Gora. Not only would she be able to see the sights, but she could walk off some of those rich foods, too. She walked down Regent Street admiring the many stores and shops and found herself at Piccadilly Circus. She had to laugh at the appropriate name. In a way, it was a circus, indeed.

Gigantic neon signs dominated this traffic triangle, or roundabout as they called it. Pepsi, Kodak, McDonalds, Panasonic, Sanyo...she read them off as she took in their flickering glory. Surely, this must be the Times Square of England. The British version of a neon jungle. It was crowded and busy, full of shopping arcades, fast food, and fast people. A good place for pickpockets, and she instinctively held her daypack tighter as she moved through the masses.

Since she found herself in the area, she did stop and manage to force down an ice cream soda at Fortnum & Masons. It was as good as the cabby promised. After working her way up a few more streets, she located a Tube station and headed back to Holland Park. She was so tired, the Ravna Gora looked as good as home ever did. She collapsed into bed without another thought.

The next morning found her much refreshed. After her turn at a quick shower, she went in search of a good English breakfast. It waited downstairs, included in the cost of her lodgings. Exchanging warm smiles with the other guests, Kate sat down at one of the long tables. Rijko immediately appeared.

"Good morning. Would you like coffee or tea?"

"Tea, please. I've always liked the smell of coffee but the taste never quite measured up for me." She wrinkled her nose.

"Then, I'll bring you tea. How do you like your eggs cooked?"

"I like them fried over hard. I like them completely dead, no runny life left in them," she stopped as she saw his eyebrows raise. "I'm really not a violent, difficult person. I just sound that way in the morning."

"You're from California. You're different, I know," he smiled. "I'll be right back with your tea. If you'd like a bowl of cornflakes or some water, it's here in front." He motioned to a table as he walked to the kitchen. Kate could see Manda and another woman beyond him, cracking eggs into a large pan. He soon returned with the promised pot of strong brew and a rack of toast. Kate had barely poured a cup when her plate of eggs and meaty bacon was placed before her.

"Dead eggs," he intoned. Kate flashed him a smile as he moved over to a young couple sitting down. "Good morning. Would you like coffee or tea?"

She ate quickly and walked to the now familiar Holland Park Tube, ready for the day's work. The efficiency of the transit system was a wonder to behold. A giant underground spiderweb that could get her anywhere she needed to go, especially with the coordinated bus system. A couple quick switches and she exited at Tottenham Court Road, only a short walk back to the British Museum.

It seemed like a good place to start from again. Inside, she enquired about further record research from a friendly docent.

"Sorry, Miss. We don't carry those types of records here. What you want is the Public Record Office down on Chancery Lane. That's the best place to look for what you're needing. Only problem is they limit such access. It's usually reserved for scholars and official researchers." She paused a moment in thought when she saw Kate's disappointment. "Tell you what. I'm going to write a quick introductory note for you and attach my card. Maybe that will be enough to make them happy and gain you entrance. Shall we try that?"

"Yes. Definitely, yes. Let's try that."

Soon Kate was on her way again, hopefully clutching the letter and card that might take her further along on her quest. She found the Office building and with pounding heart presented herself to Reception. The man at the desk seemed impressed with the introduction provided by the docent, more so when Kate showed all her research papers. She was deemed legitimate enough to use their resources.

The morning passed quickly as she went through books and microfiche, verifying births and deaths and marriages of ancestors she had already researched. When she came to the period in which Katy lived, she began searching for some clue to lead her to Simon. Without a last name, she feared it would be impossible.

On a whim, she checked under Simon. Who could say that wasn't his last name? She found such a listing on a census, and surely it was his for there was no other name included with it. No reference to his birth or death either, just a name to show he had been there.

Although such a listing wasn't unheard of, Kate found herself strangely unnerved. Especially after yesterday's reading. She dug some more, checking now in the records for 1630. There he was again, Simon. Taking a deep breath, she tried one more time. Fifteen hundred and twenty-five. Simon.

Sitting back in her chair, Kate laughed silently at herself. It couldn't be the same man. For some reason, the family preferred to use only their surname. No first names. Never mind the lack of marriages or births to carry on this family. The records were old, mistakes happen. But...just for the heck of it...she pulled out random dates.

Fifteen hundred and seven, Simon at Norwich. Fourteen hundred and eighty-two, Simon at Chester. Sixteen hundred and forty-three, Simon at Alnwick. Thirteen hundred and eleven, Simon at Amesbury, the location of Stonehenge. Stonehenge, for God's sake. Kate stood up abruptly. It was too bizarre. She returned the research materials and left the building feeling the need for some fresh air.

Her watch showed a little after noon, so she walked down Fleet Street to a pub she'd heard about, Ye Olde

Cheshire Cheese. The name alone made it worth a stop, and she determinedly forced Simon from her thoughts. She looked over the blackboard menu by the bar, passing up the bangers and mash to try their shepherd's pie.

It was hot and tasty, a steaming bowl of minced meat and onions with gravy, topped with mashed potatoes broiled golden. She washed it down with a Shandy, a mix of half bitter, their traditional draught beer, and half lemonade. It was an unusual but refreshing taste sensation, perfect for an unusual day. She ordered a second.

Even with the bitter, she couldn't figure out the information she had found. From what she understood, families in those days stayed pretty much in one area. They didn't go hopping back and forth all over the country. And yet, this Simon appeared in central England, the north, the south, and back again. Through hundreds of years. It didn't make sense.

And, there was the gap. She last found the name Simon in 1665, then 'poof' he was gone. For a couple hundred years, absolutely nothing. She would have thought the family had died out, but that left Katy unexplained. Except that in 1824, Simon suddenly reappeared in London, as if he, or his family, had been hanging around in hiding the whole time. There was no reasonable explanation. It was all too impossible.

Irritated, she decided to drop the whole thing and forget about it. She'd be just another tourist and enjoy all the wonderful things London and Great Britain had to offer. Resolved, she headed down the street to Sir Christopher Wren's masterpiece, St. Paul's Cathedral. Impressive from the outside, breathtaking from within. High vaulted ceilings were laid with mosaic designs of beautiful angels, arms outstretched almost as if supporting the center dome. The dome itself had eight different scenes from the life of St.

Paul painted on it. The choir area had wonderful wooden carvings of fruits, leaves, flowers, and angel heads. The high altar, made of Sicilian marble, portrayed Christ Triumphant and four golden angels. She didn't find it hard to believe it had taken almost one hundred years to build this amazing structure.

She meandered through the building and visited the American Memorial Chapel, dedicated to the 28,000 Americans who died in Britain during World War II. Tears came to her eyes as she read down the long list of names on the Roll of Honour. Tears of sadness for the many lives lost, and also tears of appreciation for this foreign country's remembrance of them.

Kate moved on to the Whispering Gallery, where a person supposedly could hear a whisper one hundred feet away. She tried it out with some other visitors, sharing a giggle to find it amazingly true. Could Sir Christopher have known the acoustics of this room's design would produce such a result? Or, was he as surprised as everyone else when the oddity was discovered? She shrugged. It didn't matter. It was good fun either way. Before she left, she climbed the unending steps to the Golden Gallery, eager to see the view. The city lay open before her stretching in all directions, old and new mixed in a wonderful hodgepodge. Two points for the cabby. He was right again.

From St. Paul's, Kate moved farther into 'The City.' She wandered down streets with names like Cheapside; and Bread, Milk, and Wood Streets. It amused her to find all these areas whose names reflected the trades once housed there. She felt like she was part of their history, walking the old streets, hearing in her mind the merchants calling out to their customers. She walked through Poultry and Garlick Hill, and finally down Cannon St...one of the few names that were changed from the original. It used to be Candlewick, home to the local candlemakers.

There she found the Monument. Built to commemorate the Great Fire of 1666, it was two hundred and two feet high...the exact distance from the stone base to the house of the King's baker on Pudding Lane. The place where the devastating fire originated. Kate admired the relief showing the King and his citizens fighting the blaze. The plaque said it lasted five days and consumed four hundred and fifty streets, eighty-nine churches, and thirteen thousand houses. Shuddering, Kate moved on. The only good she could imagine that came from it was it helped put an end to the Plague.

Finally, she came to the Tower of London, notorious for its executions. Here was where Henry VIII beheaded two of his wives and had Sir Walter Raleigh led through the Traitor's Gate to his death. Kate looked in amazement at the fifteen-foot-thick walls, marveling at the construction of the fortress. Once inside she went straight for the Crown Jewels.

As she waited in line, one of the Yeoman Warders, in their traditional Tudor uniform with the big white ruff collar, entertained them all with a tale. "We're the Beefeaters you've heard tell of. Why the name Beefeater, you may ask? The Yeomen were established in the 1400s as the personal guards of the King. As such, they were allowed to eat as much beef from the King's table as they desired. A rare privilege, I assure you. Thus, we became known as Beefeaters."

"We were also tasked as the official 'Guards of the Tower,' originally guarding prisoners and the Crown Jewels. We're more ceremonial now, though the Crown Jewels are still stored here and we do keep an eye on them. So watch yourselves as you walk through, because we'll be keeping an eye on you. too," he stared at them with exaggerated sternness.

"As Guards of the Tower, we do take our role quite seriously." The Yeoman managed to stand even straighter, if it were possible, and took a quick step forward as he pointed to the wall above them. "That's why we take such good care of those black birds you see flying and sitting about here and there. Legend has it this fortress, and the crown, will stand only as long as the ravens live within its walls. Of course, we know it's only a legend. But it's an old custom we cherish and preserve. And, it doesn't hurt to be careful...just in case." His face creased as he gave a little wink and a hint of a smile.

Kate smiled back as she hurried to catch up to the line moving ahead of her into the Jewel House. This is what she'd been waiting for. She bounced on her toes in excitement, then bounced across the threshold as her turn to enter came. She blinked while her eyes adjusted to a darkened room. A slideshow of the famed jewels was being shown along one of the walls. She figured she'd better take a good long look at the pictures since she probably wouldn't get any closer to the real things. They were impressive. If only they showed them with a common object so she could gauge the actual sizes of everything.

The slideshow started over and the line moved on. Kate followed along but hesitated as they passed through a large, thick metal door. She tipped her head and examined it, puzzled. It looked like the vault door she'd seen at a bank once. Why would they have such a thing here? The answer presented itself as she turned the next corner.

The Crown Jewels, live and in person. Kate gasped, wide-eyed. She had no words for the feelings that overwhelmed her as she gazed at the various crowns and scepters in the glass cases. She stepped onto a moving sidewalk that slowly took her past the exhibit. It wasn't enough. She circled around the walkway and took the moving sidewalk on the other side of the exhibit, just for the full effect. The jewels were enormous. She couldn't imagine them being real. How did they keep such large heavy looking crowns on their heads? Imagine the head and neck aches afterwards. To think they were still in use, albeit sparingly.

The afternoon grew late and Kate decided it was time to head back towards her room. She took the Tube but got off near Trafalgar Square instead. Her guidebook said it was a must-see. She strolled through the pigeon-filled square, admiring the beautiful fountains, huge lion statues, sculptures, and the tall Nelson Monument. A local filled her in a bit on the history of the sea victory at Trafalgar, and of the square itself. Somehow it seemed appropriate that England, with its dry humor, should have designated a round stone lamppost on the southeast corner of the square as its smallest police station.

"And not only that," said the chatty local woman, "but they say the French Crown Jewels are buried beneath this beautiful square, as well."

"They say? Hasn't anyone ever tried to dig them out?"

"Now, why would we want to ruin this lovely view.? It's Madame du Barry, mistress of the deposed King Louis XV, who's said to have hidden them here. What if we were to dig and there were no jewels? It'd ruin a perfectly good story, it would. Not to mention our square." Kate chuckled as she walked on. She wasn't sure she agreed, but it seemed perfectly logical to the chatty woman.

Continuing up Charing Cross Road by Covent Garden, she found a group of bookstores. This was a real treasure, considering how much Kate loved books. There was still some time before closing, so she browsed, hoping to find some good reading for the evening. Or perhaps, a nice antique collectible to take home.

She passed by a couple of the larger stores, preferring the

crowded intimacy of the smaller second-hand antique shops. She worked her way through a couple of them, and at the third a large round woman cheerfully offered assistance.

"Lookin' for anything particular, Miss?"

"Not really, just something old and interesting."

"Well, we've plenty of that. Look around and see what catches your fancy."

Kate did just that and found two books she considered buying. One was a novel written in 1902, the other a small history of the plague in London during the 1600s.

"If you'd like, Miss, I got those three big boxes on the table there from a couple boot sales. I made it to both the St Augustine's School and the Tottenham car boot sales. Haven't had time to sort and set them out yet, but if you feel like rummaging, you're welcome to it. Got a good deal, I did." She placed her hands on her round hips and nodded her head for emphasis. "Let you have anything in the boxes for three quid each."

Kate blinked. "Quid? I...I'm afraid I only have pounds. I don't know how much a quid is."

The woman let out a roar of laughter, slapping her thigh with one hand while all the rotund parts of her body joined in the merriment. After a minute she patted her chest, taking a few deep breaths to settle herself. "I thought you might be American, lass." She wiped a moist eye. "Bless, that was a priceless bit. You're as bright as a button. A quid is the same as a pound, love. Just a different name for it."

Kate's face was hot and she knew it must be red. So much for being well-prepared so she didn't look like a bumbling tourist. "Oh. Sorry about that. Guess I gave myself away there. I've only seen the word 'quid' in books. They never said how much a quid was." She shrugged sheepishly with a small involuntary giggle.

"Don't worry, lass. It took me a while to figure out how

much a 'buck' was. You're doing quite well for a Yank. Besides, I really needed that laugh today. So," she waved an arm at the boxes, "have a look and find something good. Save me a bit of trouble, it does." She winked, "Less to put away."

The offer was too good to refuse; even worth a little embarrassment. Three pounds was a good price for antique books. To her disappointment, Kate saw why the woman had gotten such a good deal. They all seemed to be dry histories and boring biographies of unknown people. Well, unknown to her, at least. She didn't want books simply for show, she wanted to enjoy reading them.

As she was about to give up, she caught sight of an old leather binding shoved to the bottom. Intrigued, she pulled it out and found what appeared to be an old journal. Now, that could be interesting reading. She looked at a date and her heart jumped. Sixteen hundred and sixty-five! What a find! She grabbed four other books from the box to go with her treasure, in case the lovely bookseller should see the journal and have second thoughts about that great price. Besides, she felt like she should pay the woman a little extra.

"Well, now, you found something after all. The better for both of us. Let's see, these five from the boxes, that's fifteen quid...or pounds," she looked at Kate with a grin. They both giggled this time. "Were you taking these other two, as well?" At Kate's nod, she continued her arithmetic. "Then, we've got another twelve pounds thirty, and nine pounds eighty. That makes...let's see, thirty-seven pounds ten. Right?" She glanced at Kate and then back at the books, recounting. "Yes, that's right, thirty-seven pounds ten shillings."

Kate handed over the money, "Here's thirty-eight quid." They both laughed again. While the woman got her change, Kate quickly put all her purchases in the open shopping bag sitting on the counter. She took it, and the coins, thanking the seller as she made her way to the door.

The woman beamed at her. "Very nice meetin' you, love. Been a good day for both of us, I dare say. Come back again, why don't you? We ship to the United States."

"I just might do that," Kate smiled back and gave a little wave. Outside, and out of view of the bookseller, she pulled the extra four books from the bag and placed them on one of the tables in front of the shop. She could sell them to someone else.

With the hour getting late and eager to begin reading, Kate hurried to Holland Park, stopping at a little takeaway for an order of fish and chips. She watched as they took pieces of golden battered fish and a good portion of chips, larger cut french fries than she was used to, and sprinkled them all with salt and vinegar before wrapping them in newspaper for transport. She hurried back to her room, pleased at the thought of trying another new British experience.

Sequestered away, munching fish with one hand and holding the journal with the other, Kate read. It was not long before the food sat beside her, forgotten. Transfixed, she read as quickly as she could, shock and disbelief fighting for first place in her head. She read about Simon. Her Simon. The Simon. The journal was the long-lost writings of Marcus, rescued from the Great Fire by the Innkeeper's wife, passed down through the years to people who either didn't read it, didn't care, or didn't understand what they had. But Kate read it. And, she understood it.

What were the odds of her coming into possession of this book after hundreds of years? Pretty much impossible. Yet, here it was. Almost like someone wanted her to have it. Wanted her to learn the truth. All the suspicions and nagging doubts jumped at her like hungry dogs. This was her Simon, alive in 1665. And in 1630, as well? And if alive in 1630 and 1665, why not 1525 and 1824? Why not 1996? Her head hurt at the concept. It couldn't be true, but...? The questions hung unanswered.

CHAPTER FOURTEEN

WELL, they were gone. Simon puzzled over how someone could manage to come so close to finding him and then just leave. He felt them move farther and farther away. Who was it? Why were they searching for him? How did they even know about him? He had been quite careful all these years not to leave too obvious a trail.

There were the people whose lives he had touched with his stories, of course. But, that kind of thing easily gets labeled as legend, or coincidence, or wishful thinking. He carefully spaced out the timing and areas where the stories occurred and almost never signed anything or left a paper trail. All purchases were paid for in cash.

It was an interesting puzzle for certain. He dwelt on it throughout the next couple of nights, his thoughts periodically interrupted by some mental connection with that distant search. He paused momentarily as he felt their concentration focus in on him, then it faded into the air. Where had that search taken them? What were they waiting for?

The next morning Simon fixed himself breakfast. Not just a bowl of cereal, but a good old full Irish fry-up. It had been a while since he last indulged in one, but for some reason, it was stuck in his mind. He pulled out his big frying pan and filled it in succession with some potatoes and onions, a couple slabs of back bacon, pork links, tomato slices, and two eggs. As they were frying, he warmed up some baked beans and put a couple slices of bread in the toaster. He made himself a pot of tea, setting the table with milk and sugar, butter and marmalade.

He eagerly dished up his meal and sat down. *Umm, this is good.* The aroma and taste brought back so many memories. As he washed the meal down with plenty of hot tea a name suddenly came into his mind. *Marcus.* He paused. It must be because of the meal. He and Marcus ate breakfasts like this almost every day.

Tonight's story for Katherine hurt Simon deeply. I think he actually loved her himself, though I don't recall having met her before.

His fork clattered onto the plate and Simon actually looked around as if expecting to find someone standing nearby. "Marcus?" No one was there. They were his words, without a doubt. Nobody else knew about Katherine but the woman herself. But why was he hearing them now? He cautiously took a sip of tea, his mind trying to focus on this distant voice.

I told Simon how unbelievable it was that with a simple change of appearance, he became virtually invisible to everyone he met.

This time he stood up. "Who's doing that?" He took a

few steps, looking around. No, of course, there was no one here. He closed his eyes and concentrated. The thoughts came from far away. It was the Searcher. They were in London and had found something. Something that had long been hidden.

Simon pushed further. *A journal...Marcus' journal. Somehow the Searcher found it and is now reading his words. I didn't even know Marcus kept any writings.* He wasn't often surprised, but this discovery caught him off guard. Had Marcus kept a record of their entire time together? How did the Searcher come into possession of it when he hadn't even known it existed? What were the odds of that?

He sat back down at the table and picked up his fork. There was nothing he could do about it. He had no power to change anything that affected him personally. Besides, the way this Searcher was able to follow his trail seemed as if it was meant to be. Certainly, no one else had been able to find him throughout all these many years. He might as well finish this fine breakfast for soon the Searcher would know many of his secrets. They were closing in and would be coming for him next.

Simon finished eating and poured himself another cup of tea. He took it into the living room and sat in the old rocker by the front window. He sipped it while gently rocking, looking absently out at the sky. He knew he hadn't much time left. If the Searcher had found their way to London, it wouldn't be long before they discovered he had emigrated to America. Right now they were reading all the things Marcus wrote about him, and Marcus knew a lot.

Soon this person would return to the States. If they had the ability to track him in Europe, finding him here should be no problem. He contemplated the issue for several minutes, slowly looking around his home and then back out the window. With a nod of his head, he again stood, his mind decided.

He would meet the Searcher on their home ground. He would go to San Diego. Perhaps it might catch them a bit off guard to realize Simon knew and was expecting them. Maybe he'd have a chance to figure out who they were and why they searched for him. What would happen then, he couldn't say. Were they friend or foe? Did they want to control him and his powers? Or, would they finally be the end of him? *My end,* he sighed. *Finally. Now, that would be momentous.*

No sense in putting it off. If the Searcher was truly able to track him, then let them track him back to the West Coast. The feeling there wasn't much time left was insistent. He must go give his notice immediately. He took a deep breath and headed towards the apartment door marked 'Manager.' Mrs. Carozza was going to love this.

She opened the door on his second knock. Mrs. Carozza was tiny and wiry, but ferocious. The whole block was scared of her. Even Simon trod carefully. She stood there and looked him up and down as if she were assessing whether he was worth her time or not.

"So?" she said. "Not rent time. What brings you to my door, Simon?"

"Mrs. Carozza, I'm sorry to bother you. I wondered if I might come in and have a word?"

She stared at him a moment then took a step back. "Might as well join me in the kitchen, then. I just made a fresh pot of tea. I assume you smelled my cookies baking a little earlier, didn't you."

Simon smiled and followed her. He always knew she had a soft spot for him, despite her gruffness.

"I actually did need to speak with you." He stepped into her kitchen.

"You just like my cookies, that's all. Can't fool an old bird like me."

"I wouldn't even try."

She seated him at the tiny kitchen table and set out another cup. "Help yourself, no formality here as you well know." She pushed the cookie jar within his reach and sat down, staring intently. "Not a social call, is this? I see that look in your eye, so you might as well state your business."

Simon smiled as he pulled out a cookie. "Nothing slips by you, Mrs. Carozza. I'm afraid I've come to tell you I'll be leaving. Tomorrow."

"Hmmph." She sat back with narrowed eyes, her lips puckered with disapproval. "Not much notice. Not any notice, really." She stared at him a moment then her body relaxed and her features softened. "But, you have been an excellent tenant, even paying your rent early. Can't complain about that. I know you've kept your place clean and in good shape, shouldn't be too hard to get it rented back out."

"The furnishings are yours, of course, but I have a few items of my own I won't be taking with me. Some books and plants and such. Could I give them to you to either keep or distribute to our neighbors?"

Her eyebrows arched in interest. "You leaving that picture in your living room? The big Irish landscape?"

"I'm afraid I'll have to."

"Well," she smiled generously, "I'll be glad to help you out and take the extra things off your hands." She sipped her tea. "Where you going?"

"I thought I'd give the south a try for a spell." He covered his tracks out of habit. "I hear Florida's pleasant for old folks."

"Good enough, I suppose. Too much sunshine for my taste. You're not old enough for Florida, anyways. Got family there or something?"

"Something like that, yes."

"Well, best of luck, young man. I hope you find it worth the bother."

He finished his cup and stood to leave. "I hope so, too. I really do. Goodbye, Mrs. Carozza. Don't get up, I'll let myself out." He paused and took another cookie to go.

She smiled at him. "See? I knew you came for my cookies. Old family recipe. Take another one or two with you. It's your last chance to enjoy them." She paused, surprised by emotion. Clearing her throat she continued, "Well, goodbye, Simon. I believe I might miss you."

Simon stopped at the door, looking back at her lined face. "Mrs. Carozza? Live happily ever after."

"Hmmph." Mrs. Carozza stared after him as he closed the door, thoughtful. "What an odd thing to say. Funny, though, now I think of it. I do feel happy. How odd." She shrugged and shook her head as if trying to clear away the strange sensation.

Back in his apartment, Simon sat again in the rocking chair by the window. He liked the way it creaked as he slowly moved back and forth. A soothing, homey sound. He would miss it. *There are so many things here I'll miss,* he thought. *But then, there always are.* He looked out the window, blocking the feelings of loss and loneliness. Throughout his long life, they continued to be problems he couldn't resolve. He had always hoped time would harden his heart, protect him from the pain. It wasn't to be. Couldn't be, he realized.

He needed those feelings of pain and joy, longing and sorrow. It was those emotions that kept his humanity, his ability to empathize, alive. They kept him in touch with the people around him. Gave him the desire to keep searching, keep rewarding.

He rose suddenly, shaking his head. *Best not to dwell on it. Better to just do what needs doing.* With determination, he crossed the room and took a small bag from the closet.

He filled it with his few articles of clothing and toiletries, a box of good Irish tea bags, the remaining small pouches of gold and coins, and a novel he read by a boy he once crossed paths with. He looked at the worn cover. 'Great Expectations,' it was called. He smiled and patted the book with satisfaction.

Lastly, he gently tucked in a small cloth containing a couple old mementos. One was a plain gold ring that once belonged to his dear friend, Marcus. The other was a small worn cross on a chain. A gift. The first he had ever received, given by the only person who had ever searched him out to thank him. His heart still warmed at the thought. If anyone was going to do such a thing, it would be Katherine. Of course it would. He knew her heart, so it shouldn't have surprised him, but it did. The short meeting left him simultaneously grateful, happy for her, and saddened once more for what could never be his.

These two precious items he found to be the only things really worth keeping. He had learned so much since the sacrifice of his people had brought an ending to the Druids, yet sometimes he felt as if he knew nothing at all. Even so, the fact he continued to go on led him to believe his feeble attempts met with his ancestor's approval. Despite his mistakes, he must be accomplishing some good. Simon felt a sense of satisfaction for that. *Maybe,* he thought wistfully, *fate will smile on me and let me go home.*

Bag packed, Simon walked slowly through his little apartment. He smoothed the blanket on the bed, straightened the clean towels in the bathroom. He aligned the kitchen chairs evenly around the table and stacked the dishes neatly in the cupboard. He watered the plants in the living room, gazing one last time at the busy street outside his window. *Why prolong the inevitable? This home is no longer mine. There's no reason to stay another night. Time to go.*

He picked up his portable belongings and opened the door. Pausing, he looked once more at the home he left. A sigh from deep within escaped his lips as he slowly pulled the door shut.

CHAPTER FIFTEEN

"**NEXT**," the woman called out, motioning him forward.

Simon approached her, nervously licking his lips. "These are safe, aren't they? I mean, how often have they fallen?"

The young woman smiled kindly at him. "It's your first flight, isn't it?"

"I'm afraid so. Maybe, I should take the train."

"There's no need really. Airplanes are an extremely safe form of travel. One of the lowest accident ratios for any form of transportation. Go ahead, give us a try."

"Well," he smiled weakly, "I've been curious about it ever since da Vinci first drew those pictures." The ticket agent looked at him strangely and Simon waved the words away. "Never mind. What I mean is, it's probably the only thing I haven't done yet in my life, so I might as well do it now. Give me a window seat on your next flight to San Diego, please.

Non-smoking."

Grasping his ticket, he wandered off to find his gate, muttering to himself. "Maybe I'll get lucky and it really will crash. Probably be the only one to survive and then wouldn't there be questions to answer? All those poor people on board. No, no. Can't let that happen." The agent's concerned gaze followed after him.

Simon's plane didn't leave for three hours. After locating the point of departure, he decided to explore the mini-city they called a terminal. It was fascinating, saddening, deplorable, and exciting, all mashed together. Much like the city it served. Overwhelmed, he entered one of the over-priced restaurants and ordered a cup of tea.

From his seat near the window, he could see a small boy sitting lonely in a chair, face smeared with dirt, clothes encrusted with filth. Simon's heart contracted as he looked into the child's eyes. *Abandoned. Unloved. Living loose in the terminal. Begging for money. Digging through garbage. Don't stay too long. Keep moving. They'll send security. Never catch me. Police, security, social services. No one can catch me.*

Simon managed a smile at the boy's pride in these accomplishments even an adult would find difficult to maintain. He knew very well that simply staying alive was a monumental task.

"I'm sorry, Sir."

Simon looked up to see the waitress motioning out the window.

"We keep shooing him away, but sooner or later he just comes back." She crossed her arms and shook her head with pursed lips. "Imagine the nerve, the pesky little rat. I'm sorry he's disturbing your visit to us. I'll get rid of him for you."

She took a step forward, her face stern, but Simon quickly put his arm out and stopped her. Jaw tight, he forced a smile. "How thoughtful of you. But, considering how busy you are, why don't I handle it this time."

"Really, Sir, it's no trouble. I consider it my job, and my pleasure."

Ignoring her, Simon got up from the table and headed out the door. The boy watched the exchange. Eyes riveted on Simon, he poised for a quick escape. The older man paused a comfortable distance back.

"Must chase you off a lot, don't they?"

The boy shrugged with mock disinterest and looked away.

"How'd you like to play a little trick on them?"

His small eyes narrowed carefully as he turned back to look at Simon, his gaze shifting between the restaurant and the man.

"Why not be my guest and walk right inside that restaurant with me? We'll sit at one of those shiny tables and order a double stack of pancakes and sausage. If you think you can manage that much food."

"What's the catch?"

"No catch. We'll even sit by the door so you can make a quick escape if you feel the need. I just think those folks should learn how to treat a young lad properly. And, we're just the ones to teach them. Besides, I know this terrific story about a little boy that you might find interesting to hear."

Trying not to appear too eager, the boy shifted in his seat and kicked his feet along the floor. He looked up at Simon. "I'm not a little boy, ya know. But, I s'pose somebody oughta teach em. An' I know old guys like you have a hard time gettin' people to set for their stories."

"Indeed."

"They won't let me in, ya know. Not someone like me. They'll call the badges."

"I can assure you. They will let you in today."

The little fellow wiped his nose with his hand, which he rubbed on his pant leg. He stared into the restaurant, watched the plates of food being carried out and onto the tables. Mesmerized, he licked his lips.

"So, it's a deal?" Simon asked, watching the lad closely.

"I s'pose. But, we hafta set by the door. Just in case."

"Agreed."

The pair walked towards the waitress waiting inside. Her mouth, at first hanging wide in astonishment, began to move furiously as she motioned to someone across the room.

The distressed manager appeared just as Simon and his companion entered. He stepped in front of them to block the way. "Excuse me, Sir, but you can't bring that...that child in here."

"I didn't realize you had a ban on children. Is that posted somewhere?"

"Children, we allow. Vagrants, we do not." His nose wrinkled in anticipation of a foul odor he expected to drift his way.

"I see. You've misunderstood." Simon chuckled. "This young man is my guest. I'm buying him breakfast."

"That's a thoughtful gesture, I'm sure, but..."

"I don't think you understand." Simon still smiled, but his gaze locked with the manager's. "He's a fine little lad in unfortunate circumstances and I'm buying him breakfast this morning. Here. In your restaurant. We must all contribute however we can. A kind man such as yourself would have a soft spot in his heart for those in his position. You would willingly offer whatever comfort and sustenance were within your power. In doing so, you would feel fulfilled and happy, with a new sense of purpose to your life. Your kindness will help so many."

"I told ya, I'm not a little boy," the child broke in sternly, arms folded across his chest. Simon patted him on the shoulder but did not look away from the other man.

The manager's eyes blinked rapidly and a smile worked its way across his face. "You know, I couldn't agree with you more. Those of us with homes and jobs should be thankful to be so fortunate. It's our responsibility to help others who aren't so lucky."

He nodded his head happily and glanced over at the speechless waitress. "What are you staring at, Jenny? We have customers here. Don't you think you should get back to work now?"

"But, Sir. You told me to never..."

"Never mind what I told you before. I'm telling you now to wait on these people promptly. Consider them my special guests." The manager walked away humming. "And give them their choice of dessert. On the house."

The waitress's mouth snapped shut, cutting off the reply that hovered there. With a forced smile, she turned to the pair. "Please be seated. I'll bring your menus."

"Wow!" The boy's eyes shined with admiration. "Ya sure taught them good. How'd ya do that?"

"Do what? I didn't do anything except tell them we were here for breakfast. Sit, please."

The boy sat, his eyes never leaving Simon's. He grinned. "Yeah, but when ya talked, he jumped like a startled cat an' did just what ya said. An' she," he nodded his head towards the scowling waitress, "had to do just what he said, 'cuz he's her boss. Does that mean yer his boss?"

"Of course not. I've never been here before. He simply acquired an enlightened look on life." Simon took the offered menus and began to busily examine one.

"Yeah, right. Ya know what I think? I think ya could be everyone's boss if ya wanted."

Simon paused, the menu lowering as he met the youth's bright gaze. Humor glinted in his eyes, tickling its way across his face. "I think it's time to order, Paul...and to evaluate the possible repercussions of sharing my stories with one so insightful."

Paul slid back in his seat, eyes wide. "Huh?"

Kate got very little sleep that night. She read through the whole of Marcus' journal, astonishment growing with each page. She finally dozed off a bit before dawn, convinced she held the answer to a puzzle the world remained unaware of. It had to be true. A feeling burned deep within her soul, one she had experienced on rare occasions before, that told her so. Based on what she discovered so far, she could extrapolate Simon was, indeed, still alive. And telling stories somewhere.

She awoke with a start, fearing she'd wasted too much of the day. Panic set in when she saw it was 1:30 p.m. Hurriedly dressing, Kate rushed from her room. A young woman looked up from a pile of sheets as Kate entered the hall.

"The Records Office. What time does it close?"

"Excuse me, Miss?"

Kate took a breath and tried to slow her racing mind. "Do you happen to know what time the Public Records Office closes?"

"Oh, let's see." The woman paused, running through a mental list. "I believe that's 5:00 p.m., Miss. You can ring them to be sure, though."

"No," Kate nodded her head. "I think you're right. I remember seeing it posted there yesterday. I've still got time to make it."

"Are you well, Miss?"

Kate hadn't bothered looking in the mirror. She'd no idea how pale she seemed, or how dark the circles under her eyes were. "Yes, I'm fine. I just didn't sleep much last night."

"Well, then, just have a seat downstairs. I'll bring you a bracing spot of tea. It's just the thing to get you going on a day like this."

"No, really. I've got to get to that office and research something."

"That office isn't going to disappear in the next five minutes. Trust me, you need this cup of tea, and well sugared, too. Come with me and set yourself down and I'll be back in two shakes of a lamb's tail. The kettle's already hot. You'll feel worlds better."

"Thank you," Kate followed her downstairs obediently. "That does sound wonderful, actually." It was probably better if she had a few minutes to gather her thoughts and think this out. Didn't want to go running through the streets like some crazed woman. Even though she wasn't sure she wasn't crazy at this point. "Why did you say you'd make the tea 'well sugared'? Does that mean something special?"

"Well, when you're feeling overwhelmed, or poorly, or have a lot to do, or you just need an extra boost for some reason, it helps to put more sugar in your tea. I remember my nan and my mum both doing this. Most likely, everybody's nan did this. It's something to do with the mix of sugar energy and caffeine to keep you going, and some wet to keep you hydrated. It really does work."

"Okay. I do feel overwhelmed and I definitely need a boost. Well sugared tea, it is."

Kate took a seat in the dining room as the young lady went on to the kitchen. She soon returned and set a fragrant steaming mug before her, along with a hot bowl of oatmeal. Kate looked up quizzically.

"We had some porridge cooking. Just the thing when you need some soothing. I was in the mood for it myself."

"I guess I look like I need this more than I realized. Thank you. It looks wonderful, and I'm actually quite hungry now I think about it. I didn't eat much dinner last night, either."

"Help yourself, please. I know it's past breakfast, but sometimes there's nothing more comforting."

Kate took a big mouthful of the hot cereal, topped with brown sugar and cream. It did inspire a comforting, homey feeling. Halfway through the bowl she paused, spoon in mid-air. Visions of Simon flashed through her mind, sitting as she now sat. Both of them eating a bowl of steaming porridge in a foreign room far from home. It was an enlightening moment.

Last night she saw only the magic. The exhilarating glamour of an ongoing miracle. This morning she saw a man alone in a neverending world. No place to call home and no one to share it with. Giving up your life for others didn't always mean you had to die.

"I don't know if it will help, or if this is more for me than for you. But, I'm going to find you, Simon. Somewhere there's a trail, and I will find you."

The man with gray-streaked blond hair paused, teacup at his lips. A look of consternation crossed his face as words echoed through his mind.

"Well, find me then, and let's be done with it!"

"What're ya talking 'bout, Simon?" Paul returned from the restroom looking like a new boy. He had washed his hands and face and smoothed his hair down. Standing by their table, ladened with empty dishes, he waited for Simon's answer.

"Nothing, Paul. Old men just like to talk to themselves. Don't you look splendid."

"Ehh," Paul said, kicking at the chair leg, "good 'nough, I s'pose." He turned his head so Simon wouldn't see the flash of pride cross his face or the little smile on his lips. "Ya know, yer really not an old, old man. I've seen 'em with wrinkles, an' no hair, an' bent backs. Yer not old like that. Yer just kinda old. So, that's not so bad."

"Well, thank you, Paul. That's very kind of you." He put a hand out to ruffle the boy's hair, paused, and patted his shoulder instead. "I'm afraid I'll have to be catching my plane soon. But, you remember my story, Paul. It's very important to remember what Simon says."

The boy broke into laughter.

"Just what's so funny?"

"Simon says...Simon says." His laughter rang again. Simon's brow crinkled up as he looked at Paul in confusion.

"Ya know, the kid's game. Simon Says. If ya do what Simon Says, ya win. Now I know where it comes from."

"Not from me, certainly. That's an old game."

"And you're an old man. Well, sorta old. But don't worry, it was a pretty cool game."

Simon gazed beyond the boy, distracted. "My, what a nice-looking woman. I wonder what has her worrying so."

Paul turned and looked out the restaurant window. "I don't know, but I don't like the look of the creep behind her. Ya gotta watch yerself 'round here."

"You'd know better than any of us. Paul, my plane's going to be leaving. Why don't you keep an eye on things, until she's safely out of here."

"Yeah, I think I'd better." He took a few steps then paused. "Simon? Thanks. Ya know, fer the food, an' the story an' stuff. I...I wish ya could stay an' be my Pop."

"That would be so very nice, Paul. You're a special boy. But, don't give up hope; there's a dad out there for you. And a mom."

The boy rushed into his arms. Simon embraced him, savoring the moment, part of him wishing he could stay.

"You get going now, Paul, and take care of yourself. Faith is always rewarded. Simon Says."

Paul nodded and trotted off with a teary smile. He could do something to show Simon his gratitude. He would catch up to that woman Simon worried about and make sure she stayed safe. Just as he approached the lady, the creepy man following her lunged forward and grabbed her purse. Paul lunged too, sliding right between his legs and knocking him to the floor. The purse went flying. Paul scuttled after it, turning quickly to prepare for any attack. With relief, he saw the creep running down the hall, a nearby security guard in hot pursuit.

"Young man, are you all right?" The woman crouched next to him, placing a gentle hand on his shoulder.

He looked into her concerned green eyes and thought he was in heaven. She was so beautiful and kind.

"Yes, Ma'am. I'm fine." He stood, suddenly worried. "Are you okay? He didn't hurt you, did he?"

"No, I'm fine, too. Thanks to you. You saved me. That was an awfully brave thing to do."

Paul beamed at her.

The lady's gaze drifted to the people around them. "Where are your parents? I'd like to tell them what a wonderful thing you've done."

Paul shifted his feet, unwilling to meet her gaze now. The lady looked at his downcast eyes. Her mind registered the condition of his old, dirty, ill-fitting clothes. He had made a recent attempt to clean himself up, at least. But, if what she now suspected was true, it was a futile effort. Her heart grew heavy as she gently lifted his chin to look into his eyes.

"You're alone, aren't you?"

Paul nodded, unable to speak. From the corner of his eye, he thought he saw Simon watching them, a smile on his face. It irritated him a little Simon felt this embarrassing moment warranted a smile. But, he didn't dare turn his head for a better look.

"Do you have any idea where your parents might be?" the woman asked.

"No," Paul managed. "My mom's dead. My pop," his jaw tightened and he looked down again for fear he'd cry, "my pop left me here a couple months ago. Said I was in the way." His chin quivered uncontrollably, which made him angry. He focused on the anger, hoping it would stop the tears from falling.

"My name's Louise. Louise Chandler." Her heart broke for this courageous little boy and his valiant struggle. "Can you tell me yours?"

"Paul Smith." His eyes lifted, his emotions under control again.

"Paul, I'd like you to come home with me. I have a big empty house just crying out for a special boy like you to fill it up. Would you consider that?"

Paul's eyes widened. He barely dared breathe lest she discover she'd made a mistake. "Won't I be too much trouble for you?"

"Not even possible, Paul. You'll be a joy for me. If you like it there, we can see about you staying permanently. I don't have any children of my own. I've been waiting to find a special fellow like you."

Understanding dawned in Paul's mind. He looked quickly around. Simon had gone. But his story was here, and it was true. Paul would have a new family and a joyful life filled with love and happiness.

"I'd like more than anything to go home with you, Mrs. Chandler."

"You can call me Louise."

"Could I call you...Mom?" Paul glanced shyly up at her.

"I think I'd like that, Paul. Wait until you meet Andy, my husband. I hope you like sports because he teaches math at the high school and he goes to all the school games."

"I love sports!"

"That's wonderful. How about fishing? My dad goes almost every weekend and he's been wanting someone to go with him."

"Is he like a grandpa?"

"Definitely a grandpa. Every week he asks me when he's going to get a grandson."

"I love fishing, too. Well, I haven't actually gone, but I've always wanted to!" Paul gave a little bounce of excitement.

"Wonderful." Louise slipped her hand into his and they walked down the corridor towards the baggage area.

"Is it okay for a white boy to live with black folks?"

"Of course it is. Andy's rather pale himself. We're all just people, honey. What does it matter what the wrapper's like? Inside we're all the same. We all want love and joy and happiness and acceptance. If they haven't done this kind of adoption before, they will now. Did I tell you I was an attorney? I can find all kinds of laws and cases to convince a judge."

"I'm convinced already." He leaned his head against her arm. "Let's go home."

Simon leaned back in his seat, smiling. Take-off had gone well, and he actually found it rather interesting. He discovered he liked a birds-eye view of the world. Everything in general seemed good right now. Paul was well taken care of. One of the best stories he'd done in a long time. Helping children proved especially gratifying. Maybe he should focus on them more often.

He looked out the window again, watching the plane's shadow jump among the soft clouds. Definitely one of the better forms of travel he had used. One hundred times better than the bumpy horse and carriage he'd ridden for so many years. The word *'ship'* formed in his mind. Yes, he had taken a ship across the Atlantic. It had been rather pleasant, as well, once he got his sea legs.

A little crowded, perhaps, and the food wasn't exciting. They had expected steerage to survive mainly on herring and brown bread, but Simon and his stories managed to arrange for a better selection a couple of times. However, he hadn't touched that type of fish since. All the same, the trip was worthwhile. Those people held such hope. From the youngest child to the oldest grandparent, they all believed that a brighter future awaited them. Their spirit and their joy had been like a soothing elixir for his soul.

When? When did he make the voyage? Which ship was he on? The questions floated by, puzzling Simon. It seemed as if someone else was asking them. He looked carefully around, but no one paid him any attention. *Well*, he thought, *it must be the Searcher. At any rate, I certainly do remember well enough. It was on the Servia, sailing May of 1900.* He sighed. *It really was a most worthwhile trip.*

Kate stood in front of shelves piled with old ship logs. To her side were drawers of microfiche, all categorized by ship and date. For all the good it would do her. A headache already formed behind her eyes, and she closed them, rubbing her temples. Simon's name had stopped appearing in the records and a kindly man suggested that maybe her person had taken a ship to America. Near the end of the century, it seemed half the population in Europe had emigrated. Maybe he had, too.

Now, she faced the impossible task of locating his name among the thousands listed here. If he had even taken a ship.

Yes, he had taken a ship across the Atlantic.

Kate stopped, surprised. "That was quite a definite thought. Where in the world did that come from?" She looked back at the books, still not knowing where to start. "When? When did he make the voyage? Which ship was he on?" she cried out in frustration. Almost immediately words formed in her mind.

On the Servia, sailing May of 1900.

Kate sat down hard in the nearest chair. No one was around her, but she could have sworn someone had whispered in her ear. She flagged over the man who had escorted her to the logs.

"Was there a ship by the name of the Servia?"

"Oh, yes." His face lit up. "Beautiful ship, the Servia. The first all-steel passenger liner to cross the Atlantic. Maiden voyage was in 1881, I believe." He grinned. "Steel ships were stronger and lighter than iron or wood, you know. Quite the advancement."

"Could you direct me to her passenger lists?"

"Right over here. Got it on Microfiche, I believe. Which year do you need?"

"Well, I'd like to see 1900...May 1900."

"Very good. Got it right here. So, you think you've tracked down your emigrant then, have you?" He pulled out a transparent sheet, handing it to Kate with a flourish. "Do you know how to use this?"

"I do. Thank you very much." She took the sheet with trembling hands and inserted it into the machine. Snapping on the light, she moved quickly to the 'Si's'. There was no Simon. She leaned her head against the machine in bitter disappointment. It had been too good to be true for the ship's name to just pop into her head like that. She should have known better.

On one last slim hope, she backed the list up. Maybe they put a single name like Simon at the beginning of the 'S's'. She looked through the names, carefully working her way up the list. Suddenly, her hand froze. She stared at the name for a full minute, wondering if it could possibly be.

"Sez, Simon."

Wasn't that how he ended the stories she read about in Marcus' journal? Didn't he say the same thing to her ancestors?

"Simon says."

"Simon says, Miss?"

Kate turned to see the bastion of ship trivia still hovering near.

He continued, "Is that like the kiddie's game? You know, Simon says do this, Simon says do that?"

A smile started across Kate's lips, growing rapidly. It all made perfect sense.

"That's it. Of course...Simon says. Simon tells a story, and you do what he says. That's probably where the game came from in the first place. It's so obvious. This has to be him."

The little man backed away, obviously thinking her quite daft. Kate was ecstatic. Surely she had the right man, and he was in America. She dashed for the door, then skidded to a stop.

"That ship was going to America, wasn't it?"

"Yes, of course. Ellis Island to be exact."

"Ellis Island? How perfect. He went to New York." She started running again. "I've got a plane to catch."

The landing was a little rough. The airport sat right in the middle of the city, and those tall buildings seemed a bit too close for Simon's comfort. But, they got down all right. Soon after he checked into a pleasant hotel with a name that sounded like it belonged in Hawaii, the Hanalei. It was clean and comfortable and the staff seemed friendly. A good home base until he decided exactly what he would do next.

His Searcher seemed to be gone. Simon couldn't pick up anything out here no matter how hard he concentrated, so could only assume they were still in England. It was just a matter of time, then. He was certain he would be able to tell as they moved closer. They were linked somehow, even if he had no control over the situation. With that link, the Searcher would more or less announce their arrival. He was ready.

Kate made her way through LaGuardia for the second time in a week, overwhelmed by the enormity of her task.

"How will I ever find him?"

"Find who, honey? Did you lose someone?" Two clerks standing beside the American Airlines counter stared at her.

"Excuse me?"

"Sounded like you lost someone. We were just about to take our break, but I'd be happy to help you first. Don't want no lost people running around this place."

"Oh, thank you. But I didn't lose him here. I lost him in New York City. I think."

"Lost in the city? Honey, I don't think there's much help for you. Who is it?"

"Uh, my grandfather. Simon...Simon Sez."

"Simon Sez?" The other ticket agent perked up. "You say his name is Simon Sez?"

Kate dropped her bag, heart pounding. "Yes. Do you know him?"

"Not really, but I sold him a ticket just yesterday." She leaned forward. "Nice man. A little different, but a nice man all the same."

"Honey, how can you remember one passenger out of all the people that go through here?"

"Because, like I said, he was different somehow. Not to mention that catchy name. He was a good-looking gentleman with grayish hair."

"And blue eyes?" Kate asked breathlessly.

"Yeah, prettiest blue eyes I've ever seen. Anyways, he was a little nervous. Never been on a plane before. Said some strange things."

Kate moved closer. "Like what, exactly?"

"Said something about Leonardo da Vinci, almost like he'd met him before."

"Hah!" Kate jumped exuberantly. 'It's him. I know it's him. Did he tell you any stories?"

The two women looked at her strangely. "You must be related, honey. You're a little different yourself."

The other ticket agent broke in again. "You should probably know, he said something about the plane crashing, too. Almost like he wanted it to."

Kate froze. "The plane didn't crash, did it?"

"Well, of course not."

"Good...good." Kate took a deep breath. "That's good."

The two clerks exchanged looks.

"So, where did he go? Where did he buy the ticket for?"

"Oh, I'm not supposed to give that information out."

"For crying out loud. It's my grandfather." Kate threw up her hands in exasperation. "I've got to find him."

"Tell the girl, Liza. You told her everything else."

"Well, just don't say you heard it from me. He bought a ticket for San Diego."

"San Diego? Oh, my God, San Diego."

"Don't have a hissy fit, honey. What is it now?"

"I live in San Diego. What if he's looking for me?"

"So what if he is? He's your grandpa, isn't he?"

"Yes." Kate forced a smile, her fingers fidgeting. "Yes, he's my grandpa. And he's in San Diego. Thanks for your help. I'd better go change my ticket."

She picked up her bag and hurried to the purchase counter. Worry etched her face. "I've found him and he's in San Diego. Why is he in San Diego? He knows about me, that's why. He knows that I know. He's probably upset. Kept this great secret all these years and then I come along and blow it." She stopped. "Maybe I shouldn't go home."

She started again. "Yes, I should. I've gotten this far. I can't stop now. I have to meet him, speak to him...he's a living miracle. Whatever the consequences, I have to meet him face to face."

Glancing around, she noticed people staring at her. "Okay," she told them, "I'll stop talking to myself. Just remember, though, talking to oneself is either the mork of a genius or a madman. I'll let you take your pick." Some folks responded with laughter, and Kate moved forward to take her turn at the counter.

"I have a ticket for San Diego for three weeks from now, but I'd like to exchange it for your next flight there, please."

"I'm afraid there'll be a service charge."

"That's fine. Just get me on your next plane. Grandpa's waiting.

CHAPTER SIXTEEN

SIMON sat on a bench at the boardwalk admiring the boats in the marina. The whole place really was quite lovely. Seaport Village was a tourist attraction, and it certainly had more than its share of folks running around. But, that was part of why he liked it so much. Such a wide variety of people to watch, to tune in on, to select from. It was a veritable shopper's paradise. Tomorrow he would have to try the historical Old Town. *I really do enjoy checking out all the local sights. After all, I'm a tourist, too.*

The smile on Simon's face suddenly froze in place, his eyes focusing into the distance. The Searcher was coming. He could sense the person now. Their progress was so much quicker than he had anticipated. They apparently had returned from England, picked up his trail in New York City somehow, and now the Searcher headed west. Directly towards him.

How could this person know to follow me to California so quickly? Who can this Searcher be? "Well," he stood up, "so be it. Probably better that we get this over and done with. Should be a very interesting meeting."

Kate arrived in San Diego late at night and was exhausted. She wasn't good at sleeping on planes, even with one of those inflatable neck pillows. As she disembarked and walked towards baggage, It felt like one part of her was literally dragging the other half of her along behind. What a relief to be home. She was eager to get to her own bed and have a decent night's sleep. Still, she questioned every airline and terminal employee she passed on the way out. No one could recall the man she described. Hundreds of people passed through these halls, they reminded her.

Outside, she tried one last time as she approached a couple of waiting cabs. "Hey, either of you guys working here yesterday afternoon?"

"Why you wanna know?" One of the men stepped away from his car.

"My grandfather arrived yesterday afternoon and I don't know which hotel he's staying at. I hoped I'd run into the person who gave him a ride."

"So, an old dude, huh?"

"Yes, kind of. He has grayish hair and striking blue eyes."

"No kidding, blue eyes? And...and a kind of crinkly face and gray hair? Is that your grandfather?"

"Yes, that sounds like him," Kate answered with excitement.

"Well, guess what. I never laid eyes on the old man." He

broke into laughter.

Kate scowled. "Thanks for nothing."

"Don't mind him, he thinks he's some comedian." The other driver stepped forward. "I'm sorry, but I didn't work here yesterday afternoon either. I am working now though, so if you need a ride?"

"Hey, she's my fare." The first man interrupted.

"I am definitely not your fare. There's no way on God's green earth I would even consider putting foot in your cab." She brushed past him towards the second driver, who hurried to open the door for her.

"Hey, I said that's my fare."

Kate stopped and turned slowly. "Is it ears or a brain you lack? It's almost midnight and I've been traveling non-stop from England. As a consumer paying for a service, I will choose who provides that service. I choose cab number two. You seem to be suffering from a severe case of cranial-rectal inversion. I suggest you get immediate help." She looked up at her driver who was laughing behind his hand. "Shall we go?"

She was soon home in bed, and the sun had long risen by the time Kate opened her eyes again. She stretched out, resembling her cat Chewy waking up from a rest. "Tea," she mumbled. "I need my cup of tea. Maybe two. And, well sugared." Throwing back the covers, she padded with bare feet towards the kitchen and put a mug of hot water with a tea bag into the microwave. She chuckled as she watched the water heat. Surely the good English folk would cringe at such a sight. Certainly not a proper cup of tea, but she'd happily drink it nonetheless.

"Okay, agenda. Tea, shower, food, Simon. Sounds like a plan."

She accomplished the first two easily. Number three was a problem. Having planned on being gone a month, not much food was left at the house. The solution seemed obvious. Casa de Bandini. It was definitely time for a Bandini Burrito. She had to find Simon, of course, but not on an empty stomach. Even he would have to agree with that.

Kate quickly dressed in shorts and a t-shirt and ran a brush through her hair. She stepped outside, found it to be a beautiful day, and decided to walk down to Old Town. Her little house on San Diego Avenue was only a few blocks away and the exercise might counteract the calories awaiting at the other end. She strolled along enjoying the sun and soon entered the historic state park. She had always liked the ambiance of the place.

As usual, she took the back entrance into the garden courtyard of the restaurant, preferring to eat outside and listen to the mariachis. The huge burrito was excellent, as was the Vallarta, a drink that tasted like a strawberry piña colada. If Simon proved amicable to their meeting, she'd have to bring him down to experience this. With a contented sigh, she leaned back in her chair and closed her eyes, listening to the peaceful splashing of water in the fountain mingling with the singer's guitars.

Simon was ready for lunch. He spent the morning browsing through the many interesting little shops in Old Town and now needed to select a restaurant. He stopped in front of one, reading the sign.

"How interesting. Used to be their family home." He stepped back and admired the wide verandas that appeared to go all the way around the house, both first and second floors. "I could enjoy sitting in a rocking chair on that porch, soaking up all this sunshine. But, fine day that it is, I'm afraid I don't wish to eat lunch inside your home. This is a day to stay out in the fresh air. Sincere regrets, Mr. and Mrs. Bandini."

He nodded his head and moved on towards Bazaar Del Mundo. There had been a pleasant outdoor restaurant in there, the Casa del Pico, and he liked the thought of sitting under one of those big, bright umbrellas. Simon walked on eagerly. He had told a couple of stories already today and definitely felt the need for some replenishment.

Kate listened to the music a few more minutes before getting up. She was full, but even so, vowed to have a churro to round things out. She walked the long way from Bandini's to the Bazaar, hoping that would justify her desire. The Mexican bakery sat near the entrance, and Kate happily noted the line wasn't too long. She waited her turn, eagerly accepted her warm churro, and then wound her way through the crowd, almost running down an older gentleman.

"I'm sorry. Excuse me," Kate told him as she slipped on by. Two steps further she paused and looked back as the man continued walking away. She shook her head, laughing. *Get a grip, girl. You're letting your imagination run wild. Graying hair does not a Simon make. Besides, he was nowhere near old and withered enough.*

As she moved on the gentleman stopped. He glanced around quizzically. Then he turned to stare at her departing figure. His hand instinctively pressed his chest against the sudden racing of his heart. *My God,* Simon thought, *it's the Searcher. And she's a woman.*

He moved slowly after her, keeping his distance. He

wanted a chance to judge who she might be and whether she was alone. *No harm in simply following her. Just to be sure the time is right for our meeting.*

He could feel that distinct bond between them just as he had sensed several times before. He focused on her intently but was unable to see anything. He nodded as if expecting it. *Yes, our lives are definitely intertwined. Never did have the power to see lives that were too closely linked with my own.*

Kate walked down San Diego Avenue towards her home with a growing feeling of discomfort. She looked up at the overcast sky. Funny, it looked like it might storm. Strange since it started out as such a beautiful day. She gave a little shiver and moved on. That feeling again. It was crazy. She was sure someone watched her. She glanced casually around. Nothing unusual. But the feeling persisted.

At the next shop, she paused and pretended to look at the display in the window. As people passed by, she stared at their reflections instead. No one even glanced at her. "Damn! What's going on here?" she muttered. Lightening reflected off the window and she jumped as thunder suddenly crashed.

Kate sagged against the building, taking a deep breath. "It's my imagination working overtime. A little bit of jet lag goes a long way. Of course there's no one following me. Reading too many mystery novels, that's all." She straightened and walked on. Rain began to fall. It drummed a steady heartbeat on her face.

Kate's mind whispered, trying to convince her all was well. *You're doing fine. It's just rain. Nothing's going to happen. A few more blocks and you're home. You're fine.* Despite the words, Kate felt the hair on her neck prickle. She walked quicker. They were close. Who would want to follow her? No one. No one except...

"Simon," she breathed as she quickly turned. Kate stood

face to face with the gentleman with graying hair.

Simon felt his heart stop, his breathing stop, his body frozen in time and space. He stared at her face, looked into her brown eyes. And yes, there below her ear was the small familiar birthmark. *It can't be! How? How could this be possible? Am I given another chance? Or is this to be one last torture?* His eyes grew moist and suddenly he was glad for the rain. A buzzing grew in his ears and he sucked in a breath, the air finally releasing him.

"Simon?" It couldn't be him. Simon should be old and gnarled. Not the handsome youngish man standing in front of her, staring with the most beautiful blue eyes she'd ever seen.

"At your service," he replied with a sweeping bow.

"Oh my God." Kate's legs sagged. She staggered to a low stone wall and sat down. Simon reached out a hand to help, but Kate flinched away. "Don't. Please, don't."

He backed off a couple paces, hands up to show he meant no harm. *She's frightened. I suppose I must be quite the surprise. But, then, so is she.* Distant buried memories fought their way into his mind. Crystalline splinters that had never quite been crushed pricked at his heart. He looked down, almost expecting to see blood on the shirt plastered wetly to his chest.

"I don't believe it." Kate pressed her hands to her face, taking several deep breaths. Her eyes never left the figure standing there. Lightning lit up the sky. The thunder seemed almost a constant roar. "Are you doing that?" She motioned upwards.

"I think, perhaps, we're doing that. Maybe if we calmed down a bit?' He smiled gently.

"You look just fine. You don't even look old. I'm the one freaking out over here." Kate talked with her hands as much as her words.

"Trust me. Inside, my world's catapulting. I didn't expect...you."

"You do know then. That I know about you."

Simon nodded slowly.

"Are you angry?"

"No. Just puzzled. And, surprised."

"You and me both," she gave a faltering smile, pushing the wet hair back from her face. "I can't believe it's you. That you're real. That you're alive. That you're standing here in front of me. I don't know whether to hug you or run away." Her hands continued to move of their own volition.

"I think I'd prefer the hug," he smiled. "Do you mind if I sit down?" Simon motioned to the stone wall.

Kate nodded, unconsciously sliding further away.

He lowered himself, adjusting his seat for comfort. "I'm sure you're shocked. I knew you were coming and I was still surprised. But, if you know who I am and what I've done, then surely you know I'll not harm you."

Color flushed up her cheeks and she looked down. "I'm sorry. I should know that. It's just..." She tried again, "It's just that..."

"I know. It's all right." He gave her that soft smile again then looked up through the light drizzle. "There, now. The storm's easing."

Kate didn't follow his gaze. She stared at him, her brow furrowed, wondering why he made her feel this way. Why did he smile as if he'd seen her before? What was he, really? If she could only...she hesitantly stretched out her hand towards him. He glanced at her and she stopped, hand hovering in mid-air.

"It's okay," he said softly, nodding to her. She leaned forward until her hand gently rested on his cheek. He barely dared breathe. She slid closer and raised the other hand to him, feeling his face. It took all his strength not to take her in his arms and clasp her to him. *Can she see it in my eyes? God, please don't let her see.* Her hands dropped to his shoulders, then to her lap, brushing his chest as they fell. Their warmth seared through to his heart.

The rain trickled away to nothing, the sun beginning to peep from behind the clouds.

"You are real," she finally said. "I almost wasn't sure. But, you're flesh and blood. I could feel your heart pound. I could see your soul in your eyes, and..."

"And what. What did you see?" he whispered.

"Pain. I saw pain, Simon, and longing."

He turned away, a smile fastened stiffly on his face. "Yes, well. I've had plenty of time to cultivate both." He stood up and turned towards her. "You have me at a disadvantage. You know who I am, yet I don't know who you are."

"You don't? Kate tipped her head, puzzled. "You look at me as if you know me."

"I know you are the Searcher."

"How can that be? You always know. You can...wait...I remember." She closed her eyes, recalling Marcus' journal. He had mentioned Simon had no power over him because of their friendship. "That's right, I do remember. I'm too involved in your life now. I'm blocked off somehow."

Now Simon looked puzzled. "How do you know so much? Did..." his face suddenly brightened, "did Liam send you?"

"Who?"

"Never mind." He shook his head sadly. "Just someone I once knew." He looked back at her, tenderness shining in his eyes. "I have seen your face before, however. Your very spirit. Please, what is your name?" He held his breath, almost afraid of the answer.

She looked into his eyes, unable to turn away. "I'm Kate McGuire. It's short for Katherine Torrence McGuire."

His eyes closed briefly, his breath released in a small sad chuckle. *Katherine Torrence McGuire. Of course, it had to be. Of all the people in the world to search for me, it would be the descendent of the only two women I have ever loved.* "Kate," Simon smiled. "I thought so. Now, I understand. I suppose you know something about who your ancestors were, about where your name came from?"

"Yes, I do. I know about both Katy and Katherine. I didn't believe the stories about you, at first. I certainly didn't believe you met both of them, two hundred years apart." Her hands flew to her cheeks again. "How can you be alive? How can you even be here?"

"It is a very long story. But, I can tell you both your ancestors were very remarkable women. I believe you have inherited their spirit. Perhaps the best of both. You certainly have inherited their appearance."

"Have I?"

"Yes. If you don't mind me being forward, you're even more beautiful, if possible."

Kate felt her cheeks grow warm as she blushed, her heart echoing the pounding of his. "I don't really know how to answer that. Thank you? But, Simon," she grasped his arm. "I have so many questions. So much I need to talk to you about. I can't believe this is all true and you're really here."

He laid his hand on top of hers, feeling the warmth of her touch, ignoring the feelings that ignited from the contact. "I'm surprised you've figured out as much as you have. Shocked you could actually track me down. I suppose we both have a lot of questions." He looked at her and then down at himself. "Of course, you realize we're soaking wet. We should get dried off. Our talk is bound to be quite lengthy."

Kate looked at both of them and laughed. "I knew it was raining. It seemed rather secondary to meeting you, though.

I live just up the street," she motioned to the left. "I've got some old sweats you can wear while the clothes dry. We'll be able to talk without being disturbed. Nobody even knows I'm back in San Diego."

"You live right up there? Now, isn't that an odd coincidence? This must be fate." He laughed as Kate raised her eyebrows and looked at him sideways.

They lapsed into silence as they walked up the street, sneaking guarded glances at each other. They were especially careful not to touch again, both reluctant to acknowledge the electricity such contact generated.

He looked so much younger than Kate ever expected and so handsome and vibrant. She couldn't imagine the things he must have done and seen through all those years. He would probably be an infinite source of knowledge. Yet, he seemed so vulnerable, too. Kate snuck another look at him. She'd never believed in love at first sight before, even if it did feel like she'd known him forever. But why'd it have to be him? He could have anyone. Probably been with queens and contessas and all sorts of beautiful and exotic women. She could never hope to hold the interest of someone like him. She took a breath and let it out in a sigh.

Simon heard the sound and glanced at her quickly. *She's disappointed now she's met me. She probably expected some wise old sage who could solve the problems of the world with a wave of his magic wand. Instead, there's just me. I suppose I'm not even very much to look at. Not like her. She's so beautiful. She radiates with energy and passion and kindness. A woman like her could have any man she wanted. I'm crazy to let myself imagine any kind of life with her. I know better than to even think of having a relationship.* He shook his head in resignation.

Kate broke the silence. "My house is just up ahead on the left-hand side of the street."

"Which one?"

"Right there. The place painted Navajo White with the red Hibiscus near the door. That's the requisite California house color."

"Very nice. But, it doesn't really look like it's a white house. It's more like a pale..."

"Orange?"

"Yes, exactly."

"I did say it was a California house color and in California, everything gets blended together. When I had the place painted, I actually asked about why it was called Navajo White, when it really wasn't white at all. I was told it was more of a pastel yellowish-orange, but it got its name from its similarity to the background color of the Navajo Nation flag. I liked that, so I went with it."

"It's very nice. Good choice. I like all the plants, too. Especially the red flowers." Simon stopped in front of the house, which was partially situated up the side of a hill, and nodded approvingly.

"Those are the red Hibiscus. They're the requisite California yard plant." Kate laughed. "But, they do look especially good with my Navajo White house. So, let's go up."

He followed Kate up the flight of stairs to her door and turned to look back at the view. "How beautiful That's the San Diego Bay, isn't it?"

"Sure is. Luckily, the other side of the street built further down the hill. Left me with a great view." She unlocked the door and stepped inside. "Come on in. This is home, sweet home."

Simon walked in and looked around at the cozy furnishings, the paintings on the walls, the photographs of family and friends, and all the decorative touches and little collections that so obviously reflected Kate's personality. He closed his eyes as if deep in thought and a smile appeared on his face. He nodded his head. "Yes, home. This has the feel of home. It's wonderful to be able to stay somewhere long enough to put down roots and truly make a place your own. It's been so long since I've felt it this deeply." He opened his eyes suddenly and looked at Kate as if realizing what he'd just said.

She smiled reassuringly at him. "Good. I like people to feel comfortable here. I've always mixed and matched whatever odds and ends I've found and they seem to blend well together. My eclectic collection. I prefer things that have aged a bit, you see." Her voice faltered and she dropped her eyes quickly from Simon's face.

He jumped into the silent gap. "Clothes. Did you say you had something dry that might fit me?"

"Oh, of course. I'm sorry. I can't believe I'm letting you just stand there in those wet things. Just a minute." She hurried into the bedroom and soon returned with a pair of sweats. "They're a little old, but they're huge on me so they might come close to fitting you. The bathroom's the first door down the hall and there are fresh towels inside." She motioned behind her.

Simon stepped forward and reached out for the clothes, his hand closing over Kate's fingers. The electricity of the touch stopped both of them short. Kate looked into Simon's eyes in surprise. The smile faded from his lips. Time slowed to a heartbeat. They stood close enough to feel the heat of each other's bodies.

He swallowed hard, his breath shaky. Kate nervously wet her lips. Simon's eyes followed the circuit of her tongue and he gazed longingly at her moist, soft mouth. Kate could scarcely breathe, the air escaping in ragged little gasps. She tried to speak, but her lips moved soundlessly. Her head tilted up towards him, her eyes dark and wide. It was more than Simon could bear. His head slowly, hesitantly lowered towards hers.

Something pushed against his ankle. Simon paused, then continued moving towards Kate. It pushed again. Puzzled, he looked down. An orange tabby rubbed against his legs.

"Oh, it's my cat." The spell broke. Kate nervously shoved the sweats into Simon's arms and reached down to scoop up her pet. "This is Chewbaca. Or Chewy for short. Although he answers to Cougar for Meagan. He'll even come if you just call him Cat. He's very smart. Do you like cats?"

"Usually." Simon breathed deeply, trying to regain his composure. "Actually, I'm very fond of all animals. I must say, he is an especially pretty cat." He reached out and scratched behind Chewy's ears, careful to avoid touching Kate's hands.

"Yes, he is. Well, the bathroom's just down the hall. I left a towel out for you. Luckily, it's turned back into a nice sunny day, because I'll have to hang your things on the back porch to dry. I'm afraid my dryer gave up the ghost just before I left for England. "

"Most things do, sooner or later."

"Yes, most things. Except for..." Kate hesitated awkwardly.

"Except for me?" Simon smiled wryly. "Yes. I suppose you think that a blessing? It is not." He turned and walked to the bathroom, closing the door without another word.

Kate buried her face in her hands. "You fool," she whispered. "What an awful thing to say. I've hurt him. How could I be so stupid?" She shook her head in disgust and walked into her bedroom. She dried off and changed quickly, mentally searching for the right words to mend her mistake.

Simon stood at the living room window looking out to the bay when she returned. She stepped up behind him and gently put her hand on his shoulder. "Simon, I..."

He turned abruptly at her touch and pulled away as if burned. The feel of her hand left a searing heat that tore through him. "Don't do that."

"You are angry with me. I'm sorry."

He smiled. "No, I'm not angry. I wish I were. Mere anger is a feeling I could understand. Something I would know how to deal with."

"I don't understand."

Simon shook his head. "Never mind. It's just as well you don't. At any rate, I should be the one apologizing to you. I have been behaving poorly. It must be the shock of discovering you."

"Oh, me too," Kate said, relieved. "I have all these thoughts and feelings rolling around inside of me and I know I'm doing and saying all the wrong things. If I act stupid or say something insensitive, please forgive me. I don't want to offend or hurt you. And I certainly don't want to drive you away. Not when I've just found you."

Simon chuckled. "I've no intention of going anywhere. Not when I've just found you. I'll forgive your stumblings if you'll forgive mine. Deal?"

"Deal."

"In that case, how do you like my outfit?" He turned around and showed off the worn old sweats.

Kate giggled. "So, they're a little small and have a few holes. They're comfortable, right? And, they're dry."

"Was I complaining? I think they're perfectly marvelous."

"Good. Why don't you have a seat and I'll brew up some iced tea. Then we can talk." She motioned to the couch as she walked towards the kitchen.

Simon sat down and got comfortable. He lifted his arm to his face and inhaled the scent of the shirt deeply. It smelled like Kate. He laid his head back and closed his eyes. *Oh, God. Why did you bring us together? Why allow me to again fall in love with someone I can't have? How can I just sit here and pretend I feel nothing? How will I ever be able to walk away and leave her? I don't think I can do it again.*

Kate stood silently in the doorway watching him. She could see the pain on his face and it puzzled her. She fought the desire to go to him and hold him, caress the lines of worry away. Why did this desire for him keep reappearing? Of all the men to fall in love with. She gave herself a shake and stepped into the room.

"Tea will be ready in a moment."

Simon's head snapped up, his face a careful mask to hide the turmoil inside. If he had to leave her, if the longing became too much and he had to walk away, there were things he must know first.

"How did you find me? Even with your ancestor's stories, how did you know I might still be alive?"

"I didn't believe it could be true for a long time. Not until I found this." She pulled out an old book from a drawer in the end table and handed it to him.

Simon opened the book and began reading. He drew his breath in sharply and looked up at Kate. "It's the journal. From Marcus. How?"

"I don't know how. I stumbled across it by accident in an old bookstore in London. Must have been fate." She smiled.

"I can't believe it. Marcus." Simon caressed the book tenderly. "My dear old friend. I have to read this. Do you mind?"

"Of course not. Go ahead. I'll feed Chewy and get us that iced tea. I'm sure it's about ready."

A couple hours later Simon closed the journal. His eyes were misty, but he smiled. Kate put Chewy down and stood up from a chair by the window, stretching.

"Are you okay, Simon?"

"Probably better than I've ever been since Marcus died. Reading his words has helped resolve some questions I've carried for a long, long time."

"What questions are those, if you don't mind me asking?"

Simon smiled again. "I suppose for once I don't mind someone asking. Heaven knows Marcus tried. But, I wasn't ready to give answers to him."

"Are you ready now?"

He looked at her as if measuring her soul, his words releasing slowly. "Yes, I think perhaps I've reached a point where it's necessary to share my story with someone else. Maybe even imperative. I feel strongly that I should share it with you in particular. Why this is, I don't know. But with the kind of life I've led, I've learned the value of trusting such strong impressions." His eyes dropped back to the journal. "This could take some time. Are you up for it?"

Kate's heart picked up its pace in anticipation. "Time, I have. I'm not expected back to work for over three weeks yet."

"Well, I hope that's long enough. It'll get us started anyways."

"Just how old are you, Simon?" Kate whispered, almost afraid to hear his answer.

"I was born in the year 380 A.D. in a country you know as Ireland."

Kate sat down hard on the floor, her legs too shaky to hold her. The unwavering gaze of her wide, startled eyes never left Simon's face.

He looked back at her intently. "Ahhh. You expected old, but not ancient. You do believe me, though, don't you? This is going to be a hard tale to swallow regardless of what you thought you already knew. I have to know you can be open enough to hear it."

She quickly shook her head. "Please. I...I want to hear it all. I've had enough outside confirmation to be aware your life has exceeded any mere mortal's. I expect to hear things that are beyond belief. I promise I won't make any judgments. Although...I do have one request of my own." She reached out a shaking hand to the end table where there was a pad of paper. "I'd like to take notes. I swear I won't do anything with them afterwards unless I have your permission."

"You want to record my life. Marcus did too, I guess. What little part of it he was aware of." Simon pondered a moment. "No harm in taking notes, but I will hold you to your word. I trust you to keep this private for now. I am feeling my age of late, despite my stories. I think you could tell my tale not too far in the future without fear of it hurting me."

Kate had the pad and a pen now, settling on the floor near the coffee table where she could write. She hesitated as she felt a shiver go down her spine at his innuendo. "Are you saying you're going to die soon?"

Simon noted with surprise her face had drained of color at the thought. "You're skipping ahead to the end of the story, Kate. I hope you're not the type to read the last page of a book first. We must start at the beginning."

"I was born on the night of the winter solstice, at the moment when the full moon reached its zenith on its journey across a black satin sky. That was looked upon as a most fortuitous sign. In honor of this sign, I was given the name Síomón, or Simon. An unconscious title among my people. It means 'he has heard' or 'listening intently.' An important skill for a storyteller. Especially one who listens to people's hearts and souls."

"Who were your people, Simon?"

"They were those who have become the source of legends. We were a very private people who kept no written histories." He smiled at Kate's paper and pen. "All knowledge was passed down through the spoken word and memorized. Therefore, what information exists of us today is mostly speculation and piecework. I am the last of the old Druids."

Kate's mouth fell open despite her best intentions. "Druids? I didn't think they were real."

"They are. Or, rather, they were. Liam and the others knew our time was ending and the memory of our existence would fade. That is why they sent me. I am their last gift to mankind. All that remains of my people I carry here, inside of me." He touched his hand to his chest, right where the heart was.

"You're the very last one, Simon? Carrying all the knowledge and memory of your people alone? How heavy a burden that must be."

"How do you know it's a burden?"

"I told you in Old Town. I can see it in your eyes. How have you survived all these years? What keeps you going?"

Simon's shoulders sagged and he rested his head in his hands. "I have asked myself those questions many times over the years. I have asked them even more of late." Sadness settled on the man like a cloak until he seemed to shake it off of himself. He straightened back up and smiled.

"You know what? I'm beginning to get hungry. Any chance you have something around here?"

"I'm afraid not. I cleaned out my refrigerator for my trip. But, since we're stuck here for a while with your wet clothes, how about I order a pizza? It could be here in half an hour."

"Excellent. I don't think I've had pizza in years."

"Ham and pineapple okay with you?"

"Ham and pineapple? On pizza?" Simon looked thoughtful. "All those things I've heard about California food must be true." He shrugged, "Why not? Ham and pineapple it is."

He watched as Kate walked across the room to the phone, admiring her lithe movements. Her gracefulness reminded him of a sleek and elegant cat. Then, he looked down at the book laying on his lap and gently caressed it, his eyes misting up again.

"It's a miracle. I didn't even know Marcus had started keeping a journal. For it to have survived all these years and end up in your hands..." He wiped a hand across his eyes. "Those were difficult years, but I wouldn't have traded them for anything. After Liam and the others were gone, Marcus was the first true friend I had. All the pain was worth it."

Kate placed the pizza order and kneeled back on the floor beside the table. "Marcus thought the world of you, too. I know he didn't regret his choice at all. Is he the last friend you've dared to trust?"

"No," Simon smiled. "You are."

"Me?"

"Yes, you. Reading Marcus' journal and reliving the memories of our time together made me realize how precious it was. Despite losing my friend in the end, despite my pain. It was all worth it to have known him. I wouldn't give that up for anything."

"But what does that have to do with me?"

Simon slid forward on the couch until he was close to Kate. "I've never told anyone the whole story of my life. Not even Marcus. But I'm going to share it with you. I'm trusting you. It's all so different now. My time is finally ending."

"Simon, no. Please." Kate felt her heart thudding as a sense of desperation grew within her.

"It's true. I can feel it. I'm not quite sure how, but I believe part of our coming together is because I'll need your help."

"I don't want to help you die. Simon, I've just found you. I want a chance to be with you for a while. I mean, you don't even look old. Not like I pictured you. You're more like Sean Connery."

"Hmm, really? He does seem to go on forever, doesn't he?"

"Yes, and he looks great doing it. And so do you."

"I looked much older after Marcus died. I secluded myself away. I stopped telling stories for a very long time." He pulled at his chin, thinking back. "I aged very quickly then. Surprised even me. When I started storytelling again, I found it alleviated the aging process." He looked at Kate with a shake of his head. "Apparently, as long as I keep telling stories, I'll keep living." He sighed and looked away.

"Then tell your stories, Simon. For a few more years at least. Give me a chance to get to know you. For us to know each other. Everyone needs a friend."

"And now we each have one. In those early years, I had another friend back in Ireland. His name was Tadhg. We were born minutes apart. I came first, and just after the moon crested Tadhg came. We were inseparable all our lives. Although sometimes I had the feeling he stuck close to me just to make sure he would reach whatever goals we set first. I used to tease him that he always tried to beat me to make up for having been born second. He didn't always laugh. Near the end, I think saying goodbye was hard for him. He seemed distant. Still, he was my best friend. I miss him. I miss them all."

"It must be hard to always leave people behind."

"Yes, well, they warned me about that. I wasn't completely blind when I chose this path. In fact, I think they tried to train me throughout my life for what lay ahead. Liam must have known from the beginning. He was the Chief of our clan and also my friend." Simon's eyes glazed as his memory searched back. "I used to believe they thought me lazy, which was why they always made me assist the elders doing their work. Every day as I helped them, I learned their trades and listened to their tales. I learned a lot from my laziness." He chuckled as he shared the stories of his youth.

The delivery man showed up twenty minutes later. Kate brought out paper plates and napkins and cans of soda. They stuffed themselves, talking rapidly in between bites. Simon found the mix of toppings to his liking and ate almost twice as much as Kate. As she cleaned up afterwards, Simon stood awkwardly. He shuffled his feet back and forth and cleared his throat, uncertain of what to do or say. A rare moment. He fought an odd desire to laugh, like a nervous schoolboy.

"Well, I'm sure my clothes are dry. I suppose I should get back to my room. I have lodgings in the Hotel Circle area."

"You're going to leave?" Kate stopped working and brushed off her hands.

"I have to, sooner or later. I don't want to take up too much of your time or get in your way."

"You're not. Really. I...I hate to let you go like this. It's too soon.

"I don't have to go. I just thought maybe I should." He knew he definitely sounded like a schoolboy now and mentally kicked himself.

"Do you want to go?" Her voice remained calm and even, but her eyes reflected stronger feelings.

"No." Truthfully, he began to think he never wanted to leave. But those were foolish thoughts. Nothing could ever happen between them. That's not how these things worked for him. They had simply been brought together to accomplish a specific purpose. When successfully completed, they would go their separate ways. In between, they would share the joys of friendship.

"Then don't. In fact, why don't we go get a few of your

things, or all of your things, and you could just stay here? For a while, at least. I have an extra bedroom."

Simon smiled, not quite sure why his heart sang. "I have a better idea. You haven't had a chance to go shopping and get food yet. Why don't you bring some things and stay with me tonight? We can have breakfast in bed." His face reddened and he quickly added, "Two beds. There are two beds in the room. We can have breakfast in two beds."

It was Kate's turn to smile and her laughter floated like a melody. "Sounds great. It's rather daring to go to a hotel room with a man I've just met, but I think I can trust you. It'll take me only a minute to get ready. I never unpacked from my trip."

Simon carried in his clothes from the back porch, locked the door, and headed back to the bathroom to change. He glanced at the cat as he walked by him. "Do we need to bring Chewy?"

"No, my friend, Meagan, will be coming by to take care of him. I set it up before I left for Europe. Now that I think about it, that definitely makes going to your hotel the better idea." She glanced quickly around the room, making sure everything appeared to be in place. Her eyes darted to the clock. "In fact, Meagan should be here within a half hour. We better get going. Otherwise, the whole world will know I'm back. And especially that I'm with a man."

"Is that such an unusual occurrence?"

"For me, yes. Meagan would have hysterics and it wouldn't be a pretty sight. Let's enjoy some peace and quiet before you have to be exposed to that." She went to her room, stuffed her toiletries back in her pack, and zipped it up.
Simon appeared in her doorway holding the sweats. "What do I do with these?"

"I'll just stuff them back in the drawer. I doubt Meagan will notice." She put them away and carried her pack to the living room, looking at the spaces as she walked. "I think that's the last thing. Everything in the house looks in order."

"Then let's go." Simon took the backpack from Kate and put it over his shoulder. Kate bent down and rubbed Chewbaca's chin, murmuring to him softly for a moment before she followed him out.

They got Kate's car from the garage and made a quick drive to Simon's hotel. They entered his room, one behind the other, careful not to accidentally touch. They were here to share a story, nothing more. But there was no sense in inviting that electricity to spark between them again and bring to mind other reasons for being together.

Meagan entered the house and turned on the lights in Kate's living room. She stopped and looked at the cat on the couch. "Why are you just lying there, Cougar? All week long you've come running and meowing when you heard my key. You were so happy to see someone to play with." She sat down next to him and stroked his back. "You're not getting sick are you?"

She went to the kitchen and looked at his dishes. "What? Your food and water dishes are full. Haven't you touched them since yesterday? Poor baby, maybe you are sick." She paused and sniffed the air, then hurried back to the cat and looked him in the eyes. They were nice and clear. His nose was cool and moist, and his tongue looked fine. Meagan scrunched her face in thought.

"Well, you don't look sick, but something doesn't fit. Does it smell like pizza in here to you? Cats can't order pizza, can they? Maybe that's what happened. You played with the delivery guy and filled up on pizza. But how did you pay? Do you have a charge account?"

She sat down on the couch again and pointed the remote at the television. "I'll just keep you company for a while and make sure you're okay. I'd take you home with me but you remember that mean old landlady of mine. Last time I had you over she threatened to throw me out. It's not my fault she's allergic to cats. If she'd stop snooping into other people's apartments she wouldn't swell up like a pumpkin. Did you save any pizza for me? I'm starving."

CHAPTER SEVENTEEN

SIMON and Kate sat and talked into the early morning hours, sharing their lives and their dreams. Kate was lying on her stomach in the second bed and pushed herself up on an elbow. "See?" she said sadly. "We have more in common than we realized. We were both abandoned."

"Yes, but I had a choice in mine. I was an adult. I chose to let the clans leave me. You were a little girl. How can a parent just walk away and leave their child? Especially as pretty a little girl as you must have been."

Kate looked at him in surprise, then smiled. "Thank you, Simon. I think you're rather dashing yourself. As far as my childhood situation, I guess my mother didn't feel capable of taking care of a child after my father died in that accident. I suppose it was a blessing; she obviously wouldn't have been a good parent. My father had a reason for not being around.

At least he maintained the honor of the Torrence McGuire name, even if my mom didn't."

The color rose in Simon's face and he fought the urge to pull her close and wrap his arms around her protectively. "I just wish I had been there. I could have changed your story for you. I could have made sure you had the life you deserved."

"Simon," Kate shook her head, "no you couldn't have. It's sweet that you want to protect me, but stop making everyone's burdens your own. There is no possible way for you to correct all the wrongs in this world. That part of my life wasn't fun, but my Aunt Beth was there to take care of me. I had other aunts and uncles and cousins to love and include me. There were plenty of good years that helped make up for the bad ones. And, my Aunt Beth was a wonderful mom."

"All in all, I think I turned out all right. Who's to say I would be this same person if my life had gone in another direction? The bottom line is, either you couldn't have helped me because our lives were meant to intertwine, or you would have helped me and we would never be together today. The choices worked themselves out."

Simon sighed. "I suppose so. Certain things must happen sometimes, even though it's painful to let them. There are always choices that must be made and some which require wounding in order to reach an ultimate good. I've had to make those choices before myself. It's hard to stand by and watch the hurt when I have the power to change it."

"You are a good man, Simon."

He looked at her, startled. As much as she respected his power, clearly, she was not over-awed by who or what he was. She truly saw the man inside and had feelings, at least of friendship, for him. The mystical parts of him she accepted as being there, but it seemed to be the man she cared for and truly admired. He couldn't speak for a few moments and cleared his throat more than once to get rid of the sudden lump there.

"Thank you," he said quietly. He looked at the clock and sighed. As much as he enjoyed her company, the night grew late and his eyes were heavy. "Well, I guess we should call it quits for the night. It's been a pretty exhausting day for both of us."

"Hear, hear." Kate yawned for the fourth time in a row. Her watch showed it to be after 3:00 a.m.

Simon stood. "I'll change in the bathroom. You can stay here."

"Great." Kate got up and tossed her backpack onto the bed. Suddenly, she walked to Simon and embraced him. His eyes widened and he managed an awkward pat on her back. His heart beat like thunder in his ears and his skin seemed to burst into flame as he felt her press against him.

"Why did you do that?" he gasped.

"Because I don't think you've gotten many hugs in your life, and everyone needs to be hugged. I just wanted you to know how much I appreciate you and that I'm glad fate brought us together."

The look of amazement on his face was replaced with one of consternation. "I'm pleased as well, but I don't think it's a good idea to be doing a lot of this hugging."

"Not hug? Why?"

"Because...because it's dangerous, that's why." He turned and practically ran into the bathroom and shut the door.

"Dangerous?" Kate laughed and shook her head as she walked back over to open her pack. "First time I've heard that one. The only way a hug could be dangerous is if..." she turned around to look at the bathroom door with a smile, "he likes me." She could feel the rhythm of her heartbeat increase and she licked her lips. If only it could be true. She hurried into her nightshirt and crawled into bed. He liked her. She couldn't help smiling as she pulled the covers up cozily around her neck and let her mind drift away on the possibilities.

She hugged me. I knew she cared about me. Simon paced the bathroom floor nervously. *I just hope she doesn't do it again. She's so sweet and beautiful. I don't think I can be strong for much longer if she touches me again. Oh God, I wasn't supposed to fall in love with her.* His pacing stopped and he sat on the edge of the bathtub as a thought settled on him like a butterfly on a flower. *Was I?*

Hope flooded him at the open possibility. He didn't know the route his own path took; who could say that the threads of their lives weren't meant to be woven together? "It might be okay. It might work," he whispered. Emotions whirled inside him and he stood up to pace some more until he could calm down. By the time he finally came out of the bathroom, Kate was enveloped in a dream full of Simon and hugs and other dangerous things. He smiled tenderly at her as he climbed into his own bed and soon drifted into dreaming himself.

Kate smiled and took the bite of grilled halibut from the fork Simon held out. 'Ummm. Perfect. I didn't know you were a master chef, too.' She reached out for him, the setting sun reflecting off the shine in her eyes.

Simon knew he could lose himself in those eyes. She was the most beautiful woman he had ever seen. Her beauty ripened with every passing hour until he thought he could no longer bear to look upon her face. But he did look for he could not turn away. He leaned down and kissed her deeply, his fingers trailing through her long, dark hair...

Flash!

The sand was hotter than the sun. Too hot to stand barefooted. Kate wondered how Simon could manage it. He must have dug his feet down into the cooler layers. She stretched a leg off the blanket and kicked some of the brown crystals at him with her toes. Without a word, Simon scooped her up from the ground and walked into the azure blue water. They both laughed as they slowly sank into the cool liquid.

He did not let her go. Kate shifted to face him, wrapping her arms and legs tightly around his body. He felt so good. He belonged in her embrace. She stroked his face tenderly.
'You are the best thing that ever happened to me, Simon. You are the miracle in my life.' Her soft mouth pressed hungrily against his.
Simon kissed her back with equal passion, holding her close to his heart. 'I love you,' he whispered against her lips. 'I'll love you forever...'

Flash!

They stood together on a green hilltop next to a big oak tree. Kate's ivory dress was simple yet elegant. Simon wore a kilt and had a large sash draped over one shoulder, both woven in the plaid of his clan. They held hands as they looked into each other's eyes and smiled. The sound of bagpipes drifted across the wind, a haunting melody that lingered in the soul.
'Are you sure, my love?'
'More sure than I have ever been. This is the path I've waited to follow for hundreds of years.'

'Then I am sure too. My life has waited for yours.'

Simon removed a ring from his right hand and gently slid it onto Kate's finger...

Flash!

Kate clamped her jaws together, determined not to scream, not to give in to the pain. She felt as if she were caught in a huge vacuum that squeezed and pulled at her. Her eyes closed as the pain subsided and when she opened them again Simon leaned over her.

He brushed her damp hair away from her face. 'It's almost over. You're doing a beautiful job.' He squeezed her hand and helped her lean forward as the pain rose again. 'Push! Push! That's it! Push!...'

Flash!

Simon stood alone on a cliff overlooking the sea. Kate stopped her approach and stared, drinking in the beauty of this man who loved her. He turned towards her and her breath caught. They smiled at each other and Kate crossed the remaining distance to his arms. 'My heart still beats wildly every time I see your face,' she said.

'You think mine does any less? If possible, my love for you grows more every day. I couldn't bear the thought of not being with you.'

A shadow spilled up the hill.

Kate's face creased with worry. 'Simon, there's still so much to do. You must go on, no matter what happens.'

The smile slipped from Simon's face. 'What do you mean? What could possibly happen? Everything is as it should be. Everything is fine.'

'Always remember how much I love you, Simon.'

The shadow fell between them and suddenly Simon could not see Kate in the darkness, could not feel the warmth of her touch. 'Kate!' he cried.

Her voice faded through the blackness, 'Always remember, I will love you forever...'

Flash!

Simon's eyes quickly blinked open into the darkness and he looked around with fear, searching. Kate suddenly sat up in bed with a sobbing moan.

"Kate." He moved to her quickly, without thinking, taking her in his arms. "I thought you were gone. I thought you were lost forever."

"Something tried to pull me away, Simon, but I didn't want to go. I never want to leave you, Simon. I love you. I always have and I always will." Her tears fell on his bare chest as she clung to him.

"Shhh. It's all right now. We're both safe, my love. Nothing will separate us. I never doubted your love for me." He stopped as she stiffened in his arms. Awareness sprang to life and understanding spread across his face. He looked around the room...his hotel room. He pulled away and they stared into each other's eyes.

"It was a dream," he whispered. "They were all dreams."

"All dreams," she echoed, the tears still wet on her face.

He squeezed his eyes tight against the sudden loss he felt. "But, it seemed so real. I thought that you...that you really...I believed it to be true." He knew he sounded a fool but the love he felt in that dream was real. Love he had waited all his life for. Why did fate so cruelly taunt him with it and then snatch it away with the opening of an eyelid? Kate was not his, yet he wanted her so badly he could scream. He turned his head away.

Kate reached up and turned his head back, her hand gently caressing his face. "I believed it, too, because it is true. You said yourself there's a bond between us. We were in those dreams together. Those were our wishes and desires. I'm almost thirty-five and I've never married. I know that doesn't seem old to you, but it is to me. People look at me funny. I've waited all these years for the right man."

Simon could barely breathe. "Kate, what are you saying?" he whispered.

"You know what I'm saying, Simon. Perhaps those dreams were real. Perhaps we really lived those lives with each other. What are the chances of two people sharing the same dreams at the same time? I believe what I felt in those dreams and so do you. To put it simply, you're the right man, Simon. You're the one I've been waiting for."

Simon bowed his head, closing his eyes against the sudden flood of emotions. "It wouldn't work. I won't even mention the obvious age difference, that's really not the issue. It's because of what my life is...or isn't."

"It worked with Marcus, didn't it? You said his friendship was worth it. Wouldn't mine be?"

"Of course." He raised his head and grabbed hold of both her hands. "The thought of being with you is so wonderful it's almost more than I can bear. I've wanted this too. For longer than you can imagine."

"Then why deny it now? You've given so much, why not have something for yourself?"

"Because it wouldn't be fair to you. Look in my eyes, Kate. Really look. My body may appear acceptable, but inside is the tired soul of a very, very old man. I go on because I don't know what else to do. I need an ending."

Kate looked at him, her chin and lower lip trembling. "I wish it weren't so, Simon, but I heard it even from Marcus' words, and that was 400 years ago. You've given more than any man should have to. I'm being selfish."

"No more than I." Simon pulled her into his arms to comfort her, savoring the feel of her body. Their dreams draped around them, flooding their thoughts with memories of how it might have been. Kate wrapped her arms around his neck and suddenly their lips were pressed together. Simon felt as if his entire body was engulfed in flames.

"Oh my God...oh my God," he whispered as Kate's lips traced the contours of his face. His breath came in ragged gasps. His body felt ready to explode. He pulled away abruptly.

"I...Kate, I can't. I can't do this." His whole body trembled. "Oh, Kate. You're the woman I've longed for all these many years...but it can't be. I can feel that my time is finally almost up, and I can't hurt you this way." Still, he wanted her, wanted this one last gift. He wanted to fully experience love, however fleeting, before he left this earth. All these long years of denial. Would it be so wrong to have it now?

She put her arms back around his neck, laying her head on his shoulder. Softly stroking his hair, she listened quietly.

"Kate," his voice shook with emotion, "this is a unique situation I find myself in. I'm treading on unfamiliar ground. I, who've treaded all life's paths for over sixteen hundred years." His eyes drifted up in thought, then back to hers.

"I thought I had done all I could, all that was allowed for me. But now, you're here." He haltingly took one of her hands, stroking it gently, overwhelmed with his emotions. "There is a bond between us, unlike anything I've ever known. I'm willing to admit this. But, it frightens me. I don't know whether to run from it or towards it."

Kate straightened up so she could look him in the face. "Oh, Simon, run towards it. Don't ever lose a chance to love out of fear."

"Our time is so short. It isn't fair to do this to you..."

"And so, you'd deprive me of the opportunity to enjoy this love while I can? The love's already here, Simon. If we weren't willing to admit it before, we have to now. We shared the same dreams as if we had really shared each other's lives. You can't protect me from that. I've never felt this way before. I doubt I ever will again. Don't leave me wondering and wishing for the rest of my life."

He gently released her hand. "I'm so terribly old, Kate."

"Simon, you're so much older than me it's ridiculous to even bring it up again. You're older than everyone...and it doesn't matter. I love your wisdom, your intelligence, your dry humor, that wonderful giving heart. And yes, I love the mysterious, mystical aura around you that's allowed you to live all these years. I wish I'd been a part of it. Part of the magic, part of the miracles, a traveler through lands and time."

She grasped Simon's hands tightly in her own. "Please, Simon, don't deny me this little part I have in the closing of one of history's greatest dramas. We can make those dreams our reality."

He swallowed hard. "Kate, I've never...I don't even know how..."

"Shhh. It's okay. I'll show you." She ran her fingers through his hair, caressed his face, traced the outline of his lips. She kissed him softly. Her hands gently stroked his neck and chest. Simon's breath caught as her fingers ran over his hot skin. She could feel him trembling under her touch.

He stared at her with wide eyes, barely breathing. Kate

removed her nightshirt and Simon inhaled sharply. She was so beautiful. He lifted a hand towards her and hesitated. With a smile, she took it and placed it gently against her breast. He touched her tenderly, reverently. As her lips nuzzled him again, he let out a low guttural noise, a painful sound escaping from the depths of his soul. Kate guided him down onto the bed. He kissed her hungrily and felt the moist pressure of her tongue. His mouth opened and he kissed her deeply.

They took their time as their hands and mouths explored and caressed each other's bodies. With a mutually growing passion intensifying with each touch, Kate moaned and spread her legs, pulling Simon on top of her. He sucked in his breath as she used her hand to guide him into her and showed him the pleasures of a deep, enduring love. All his long-denied needs and desires finally broke free of their self-imposed prison. Eventually, Simon cried quietly in her arms, unable to express this new flood of emotions in any other way. Kate cried with him, holding him tight. It was the most perfect moment of his life.

They lay in each other's arms for a long time. Simon kept looking at Kate, stroking her skin softly. He smiled. "I had no idea that this..."

"None? You had no idea at all?" She raised up on her arm to look at him.

"Well, a slight suspicion, perhaps. I've seen animals procreate. But no practical knowledge." He smiled again, his cheeks coloring. "Definitely no idea it would feel so..." he searched for an adequate word, "so amazing. So pleasurable. So perfect." She leaned over to stroke his brow, kissing his face tenderly.

"Well, you're a pro, trust me. I've never felt more loved in my entire life."

Simon's smile widened. "I think you're magnificent,

Kate. Absolutely beautiful. Maybe who you're with and what you're feeling makes the difference. This probably sounds silly, but I want to thank you. You're so much more than I ever imagined. I'll take this memory with me forever."

"So will I," Kate murmured, laying her head against his chest.

"I love you," he whispered.

Kate's breath caught this time. She looked up at him and a tear rolled down her cheek. "I love you, too."

They slept in each other's arms until long after the sun had risen. When Kate awoke this time, it was with a shy smile at the man lying next to her. Simon's eyes were open, as they had been for some time, enjoying the peaceful beauty of her sleep. She smiled again and he leaned over to kiss her.

"Thank you," he said.

"For what? I only smiled at you."

"I've always wanted this. To wake up with a beautiful woman, have her eyes rest on my face and light up with love, and then I lean over and kiss her. It's a dream I never thought would come true."

"It's been a night full of wonderful dreams." She snuggled closer to him, her breath warm in his ear. With a fingertip, she traced his lobe, down his jaw, and around his lips. She wrapped her leg over his and kissed him firmly on the mouth, her body pressed against his. It was another hour before they finally climbed out of bed.

Most of their waking hours were spent sharing their thoughts and feelings. Kate quizzed Simon about where he was and what he did during different periods of history...the Fall of the Roman Empire, the Invention of Printing, the Magna Carta, the American Revolution and the signing of the Declaration of Independence, whether he'd ever met Leonardo da Vinci. Simon's memory was long and remarkable.

"Leo was an amazing gentleman. I spent many enjoyable hours in discussion with him. Even posed for one of his paintings, though heaven knows where it is now."

They stood at the end of a street in La Jolla overlooking Pelican Rock.

"Leo. You called him Leo?"

"Well, he wasn't the stuffed shirt you'd think he'd be. I was his sounding board for a piece. He had a rough go of it, used to get very discouraged by the response of the scientific community over his ideas. I had to assure him more than once that he was on the right track, although it would take a few years for everyone to catch up with him."

Kate laughed with excitement. "I can't believe you knew Leonardo da Vinci. Did they think he was insane with all his ideas? Or, did they believe him? Was he just another starving artist? How well-known was he back then? Did he live in a little flat above a cafe?"

"Hold on, hold on. Too many questions. I'll tell you everything you want to know, I promise. But first, we must get a closer look at the birds. Is there a way across all those rocks?"

"All right, I'll be patient." She pointed over to the side of the road. "Those stairs lead straight down to the rocks and then we just have to start climbing. The tide's pretty low so we can get out quite a ways."

"I'm game if you are."

"Let's go." She started down the stairs and led the way onto the rocks. "So, just how many famous people have you known?"

"A few."

"A few? You've met them all, haven't you?"

"Definitely not. Most of mankind has done fine on its own. Without me interfering."

"Humph. I'll just bet."

Simon pointed to a large puddle of water caught in the rocks. "Look here. There's a starfish in the water."

"It's called a tide pool. Every time the ocean tide goes out, it leaves pockets of seawater and life behind."

"How wonderful. Look, there's another puddle." He hurried over to peer into it. "Crabs. And some big slug thing. Like a giant snail without its shell."

"Yep. It's called a Sea Slug." Kate observed him with squinted eyes. "William Shakespeare."

"What?"

"William Shakespeare. Did you know him?"

Simon sighed, "Yes."

"Aha! Charles Dickens?"

"In a roundabout way. Never met him personally."

"Right. Sigmund Freud?"

"Never laid eyes on him. Are you satisfied?"

"Not yet. Leland Gaunt."

Simon paused and looked at her in surprise. "Leland Gaunt? I hope you're not feeling 'needy' today. Let's just say I've done some cleanup work behind that one, or those of his type."

"Okay, how about Adolf Hitler."

Simon shuddered. "Definitely not."

"Well, that's one you should have met. Now, there was a man who badly needed some influence from you in his life." She smirked at him as if she had gotten the upper hand somehow and climbed onto the edge of another rock. "Now we can see the birds better. Look at all of them sitting there."

Simon climbed up beside her, the smile on his face as much for her as for the view. "This place was aptly named. I've never seen so many pelicans. Or such a vast quantity of bird droppings."

"How romantic of you to point that out." Kate took his

hand, laughing, as he leaned over and gave her a peck on the cheek.

"You want romance? How about this? I'd do anything for you. If you want the moon, the stars, just ask me. I'll get them. If you want bird droppings, I'll get them too. Just say the word and I'll jump in that water without hesitation."

Kate looked at him, one eyebrow arched in disbelief, as she laughed again.

"You don't believe me?" He hopped down the rocks.

"Simon, are you crazy? What are you doing?"

"I do this for you, fair maiden. For love." He stepped into the water.

"You are crazy," she laughed.

"Crazy for you," he stepped further and the water reached his knees. "I will prove my worth and my abiding devotion. I will bring you the sacred bird droppings."

Kate scrambled down the rocks and perched at the water's edge. "Simon, come back. I believe you. I believe you would go out to the Pelicans and scrape up some of that disgusting white gunk. But in all honesty, I'd rather have a flower."

He paused, eyebrows raised. "A flower? Such a simple request, so lacking in peril and danger and devoid of white gunk." He studied Pelican Rock and then turned and studied Kate. "But truly a delicate gift to match your own delicate beauty. I will get you the flower." He waded back to dry land. Two young women who stopped to watch the scene play out clapped their approval. Simon bowed gracefully then took Kate's hand and led her towards the stairs.

They passed another couple just as the glowering woman snapped, "Why don't you ever do anything like that for me, Tom? You never get me flowers, let alone go in the water for bird droppings. I'll bet it never even occurred to you to ask if I wanted you to go out there and get me some..."

Simon and Kate smothered their laughter and hurried on.

"Poor Tom," Kate said when they were back on the street, "He'll never live this down. I don't think she'll stop until he scrapes some of that gross white stuff up for her."

"If he does, can't you just see it sitting on the coffee table in a little crystal dish?" They didn't bother to hide their laughter this time.

The tide was scheduled to be lower the next day, so Kate took Simon out to see Cabrillo Monument on Point Loma peninsula, then over to the tide pool area down the side road. This was a much flatter spot than the area at Pelican Rock, easier to walk over and explore. They searched out the trapped pools of water and examined different anemones and crabs, another starfish, and even found a small abalone. They wandered around hand in hand, laughing and talking. More than one person commented on the couple, so obviously in love.

As the tide started coming back in, Kate stood alone at the end of a little jetty of rock. The rising water slowly covered it until it looked as if she was walking on water. She stood there, the expanse of water stretching out around her. Alone. Isolated. Separated from everything else. An incredible feeling of loneliness and loss washed over her. Simon felt it too. He stood back on the dry rock and watched her, suddenly feeling the passing of time again. His time. After all those centuries, now that he wanted more, there was not much of it left. The span of water between them loomed like an impassable gulf.

She turned and looked at him, fright showing in her eyes. He stepped towards her and held out his hands. She carefully made her way to him, neither seeming to breathe until she was safe in his arms.

"That's what it's going to be like, isn't it." Her muffled voice stated it as fact. "Sooner or later you'll have to go, and

I'll be the one left behind this time. I'll be stranded in the middle of an ocean with a rising tide."

"I don't want that for you, Kate."

"I know you don't." She straightened and looked down the shore. "Come with me. I'll show you one of my favorite spots." She led the way up from the tide pools and along a grassy path at the top of the hill. They walked on for a while until they reached an area of rocky cliffs and crashing waves.

"Here. This is where I come when I need to find some peace and strength."

Simon drank it in, contentment washing over him. The sounds were old and familiar. "It's beautiful. I see why you would choose this place. I grew up next to the call of crashing waves. It's one of the most soothing sounds I know."

They settled on the ground together and watched the sea and the sky as the sun lowered on the horizon, the ocean symphony playing their heart's melody.

Each day they explored someplace different and shared memories. They drank in every new experience, memorized every expression on each other's faces. They lived a lifetime with each other in a matter of days. At the end of one such day, after visiting the small-town charms of Julian, the two shared a light meal in their room.

Simon finished a little story in between bites of his grilled chicken salad. "So, it was either the fish or the balloon. There wasn't much choice so I let go of the balloon. It drifted up into the sky just as the fish flipped out of my hand and back into the water. I lost them both," he shrugged. Kate looked up at him through her eyelashes with a low laugh. She was breathtaking. His heart wanted to burst with joy and love.

"How do you do this to me?" he whispered. "With a look, with a touch, you bring me to my knees. Never has anyone had such power over me. I would do anything you asked.

Until I met you I never really understood love. Everything I've done before is nothing compared to this. This is where the true power and strength of mankind lie. I love you, Kate."

"I love you, Simon. I'll love you forever."

The expression on his face clouded. If only he could always be here to protect and watch over her. He pulled his chair closer to hers and placed his arm protectively around her shoulders. "I'd fight the darkest shadows to keep you safe. I would die for you."

Kate knew Simon remembered. The strange shadow in the last dream they shared had haunted her thoughts more than once. The dream had terrified her, but not nearly as much as what she feared it might really mean for them. Strangely, that was not what frightened her now. She put an arm around his waist. "You would die for me, Simon, as I would for you. But, would you live for me, as well?"

Her eyes watched his until he turned away with a sigh. "I do not think that is something I have a choice in anymore. The voices call to me, their words almost a chant now. I don't think I have much time left. These days with you are my dream come true. But all dreams end, and sooner or later the dreamer must awake."

Her arm around him tightened, but her voice sounded resigned. "I know. I don't want to lose you, but I knew the end was in sight when we met. You told me from the beginning you couldn't stay. I just wish...I wish it could be different. But, since it can't, I will do everything I can to make these last days happy ones for you."

"Simply being with you has fulfilled all I've ever wanted. Leaving you will be the hardest thing I've ever done. If only these blasted voices would leave me alone. They call and call, but they tell me nothing. If I could just know how or when. If I'm supposed to do something, why don't they just tell me?"

She looked at him sadly, wanting to help him, wanting to keep him. To do one would mean to negate the other. "I wish I knew the answer to help you. I honestly do. I love you enough to let you go, though it will break my heart."

Simon felt the muscles in her body suddenly go taunt. "What is it, Kate?"

"I do, Simon. I do know the answer." She moved back and looked at him. "I'm taking you to Ireland, Simon."

He looked at her in amazement. "To Ireland?" I've never gone back there. In a sense, she banished me years ago, when they drove the Druids out. Why go back now?"

"To finish the story, Simon."

"No. That chapter closed long ago."

"Simon..."

"No, Kate. I can't go back there." He sat back, staring into the distant east. "I don't go where I'm not wanted. I appreciate your help, but let's just forget about this part of the conversation."

She nodded reluctantly, her mind still racing. Ireland was the answer, she was sure of it. They finished their meal discussing what joys Julian would hold during their Apple Festival in the Fall. They sipped cups of black tea, wishing for apple pie, and watched the lights twinkle on outside. A love song played on the radio.

"Ahh, a beautiful love song for the beautiful lady. May I have this dance?" Simon moved out of his chair as he swept her a bow and held out his hand. With a soft smile that set his heart racing, Kate moved into his arms.

They swayed together, their hands caressing each other's backs. Simon kissed the top of her head, and as she looked up, he kissed his way down to her mouth. The swaying stopped as their kisses grew more intense and their hands began caressing new areas. Fingers worked at buttons and buckles, clothing tumbled into a heap. Giggling like school children they moved to the bed. After more kissing and touching they begin to sway to a different beat.

A new day dawned and Kate stretched as she awoke. She smiled at the figure next to her and whispered, "Did you dream of Ireland, Simon?"

"Why would I?" He rolled over and looked at her, the morning sun warm on his face.

"I just wondered if you thought any more on my suggestion."

"No. All I've thought about is you and that old comedy bit from last night. 'Who's on first? I Don't Know. Third Base!' Boy, I sure do love those guys. Abbot and Costello were a great team. One of the best. Just like Laurel and Hardy."

"You're changing the subject." Kate traced a finger down his nose and chin, then poked him in the ribs.

"Then, to politely change the subject again, let me suggest we go out for some food. Didn't you say El Torito's has a great Sunday Brunch?"

"Yeah, yeah. Food and sex. Sex and food. I never thought you'd be so typical."

"Lest you forget, I was a sixteen-hundred-year-old virgin. How do you expect me to act? Especially around one so enticing. At least be grateful I saved myself for you."

"All right," she smiled, "I am. You know we've got at least another hour before they start pouring champagne at El Torito's. I have an idea of how we could pass the time. Are you up for it?"

"Heh, heh, heh," he gave his most menacing chuckle. "I thought you'd never ask."

Two hours later they drove onto Harbor Island all fresh and polished, small smiles hidden behind innocent glances at each other. They managed to get a window table and helped themselves to the buffet. The array of food overwhelmed, everything from make-your-own tacos and tostadas, eggs and chorizo, to house specialties and a finale of caramel-drenched flan, all washed down with plenty of Mimosas. They worked their way through the line twice each until their stomachs felt swollen. As they sipped tea looking out at the harbor after their meal, Kate brought up Ireland again.

"Simon, I know you don't want to hear this, but I really have a strong feeling that you need to return to Ireland."

"We've discussed this. I've told you, I can't go back. I had to leave Ireland." Simon's voice sounded resigned.

"If you've kept up on your Irish history at all, you know whether from war or famine or economics, Ireland's people have always been forced out...forever a Flight of Earls. But she loves her children and her arms are open to welcome them home at any time. And Simon, you're still a child of Ireland, are you not?"

He sighed. "Yes, I suppose I am. Ireland was my first love. But what good is it to go back now?"

"Simon," Kate looked at him, laughing. "It's so obvious. That's where it all began, that must be where it all ends."

Simon stared into the distance, thoughtful. Slowly, a smile grew on his face. "Of course. Of course. Back to the fire. I left Liam and the others there, that's where I'll find them now."

"Oh, Simon, it all fits together. I knew you were supposed to go back."

His smile abruptly faded. "No. They wouldn't want me back there. I can't go."

"Who wouldn't want you back?"

"My people. It's too late."

"You don't know that. And you'll never know if you don't go and find out. It's the fish and the balloon again. What choice do you truly have, Simon? You know you can't go on forever. You've already told me you have a strong sense your time is almost up. Are you going to do yourself in or just wait till you drop on the street somewhere?"

He looked taken aback as the words washed over him. "I...I hadn't thought about it like that. Neither of those options sounds particularly appealing."

"Of course not. We need to go to Ireland. If I have to let you go, I want you to go with the honor you deserve. It should be in a beautiful place where you can rest with the people you came from." She grasped his hand. "Please, Simon, humor me. I have to take you to Ireland. I need to take you."

He patted her hand gently. "All right, Kate. We'll go to Ireland. I'm not sure we'll find what you expect for me, but I agree it does make sense. I've missed her so much all these years. However the end comes, at least I'll see my homeland one last time."

THE trip overseas proved uneventful. Simon obtained his passport with little trouble. He simply presented himself in person, and after a brief conversation, the clerk issued him the magic booklet. Now they traveled the unfamiliar winding old roads of Ireland, Simon directing her like a homing pigeon. The roads were all new as far as Simon was concerned, but he could feel the directions they needed to take as if he followed a trail of breadcrumbs.

"Here. Stop here."

Kate parked the car off the road and turned to look at Simon. "Are you sure?"

"Yes," Simon smiled, looking into the land beyond her, "we are near the place. I can feel their presence. They're waiting for me."

Kate gave a little shiver. "This is all a little strange, but I can feel something too. It's kind of spooky."

Simon opened his door. "Come, Kate. There's much to do and little time left. Tonight's the full moon. Our traditions required these ceremonies take place at the full moon because we believed the moon's zenith released greater powers." He shrugged. "Must have been something to it. That's when I was sent on and the others disappeared."

Kate climbed out of the little car and followed him into a broad field that rose up into a large hill. "How will you know what to do, Simon? They didn't give you instructions before they died."

"That's just it, they're not dead. Not really. Can't you feel the life in them? I never understood before...they bound their essence to me, but their souls are still here. Waiting."

"After all this time? What are they waiting for?"

"For me. They're waiting for me to make it safely home." Simon stopped and looked up at the sky as he took a deep breath. The exhalation became a sigh. His excitement made him seem younger somehow. "I never knew how this would end. I began to fear I would just have to go on and on, forever."

He looked at Kate and a glint of his old weariness showed in his eyes. "I've seen enough of this world. Although I've found much good, I've also found much to grieve over. I don't have the strength or desire to deal with it anymore." His look softened. "Now then, lass, if I'd had someone like you by my side all these years, it might have been a different story. I might have enjoyed living forever."

Simon allowed himself to visualize how it could have been. It was a pastime he gave up long ago, realizing that longing for what could not be his only brought pain. But for this one last time, he would ponder these thoughts and enjoy their bittersweetness.

He could see himself as a young man again, strong and

full of life. There was Kate, walking beside him, working beside him, sleeping beside him, raising a family together. The thought made him grin like a Cheshire cat. They fit well together, an indefinable bond mingling their spirits. He could feel it, knew she felt it as well.

But for all the joy and comfort her presence brought him, the fact remained he was a very old man on his way to prepare for his own death. Their spirits mingled, briefly, but there could be no future. Every fiber of his being screamed his time was finally up. He welcomed that realization at the same time he mourned its inevitability. An old familiar feeling prickled at the back of his neck and wormed its way down into his soul. A thousand tiny voices whispered in his ear. He had heard the voices so often before, but never really understood. He was overdue. He had passed beyond the boundaries of his stay, and he must return to his clan.

He glanced at Kate and frowned. She was the conduit allowing that return. He couldn't explain it, wasn't sure how he knew it, but it was true. He would not have come home, could not have come home, if not for her. She enabled him to fulfill the end of his journey. But it was the trade-off of one dream for another that twisted in his gut. He would have to leave Kate behind. Could he be that strong? Did he really have a choice anymore? *If only I had met her sooner, had more time with her...*

"Simon?" Kate called him back. "I wish I'd met you sooner." He was only vaguely surprised at her echo of his own thoughts. "If I'd been either of my ancestors, I would have gone straight for you. Forget the other guys." She paused, searching through her memories. "Sometimes I think I was both my ancestors. I remember things. I don't know if I read them somewhere or if they're really my own thoughts. It's a little bizarre, but that's kind of par for the course lately. Anyways, I would have chosen you. I do choose you. Always."

She tipped her head and smiled at him. "I know it sounds crazy, but I would've liked to have been part of this strange life you've led. I can't even begin to imagine the things you've seen. And all the lives you've changed for the better...it's just incredible."

Simon stopped abruptly. All the lives he'd changed. His face burned with a shameful memory and his lack of honesty. He couldn't leave without Kate knowing the whole truth about him. "They weren't, you know." His voice was gruff and he glanced quickly away from her. The presence of his past clan seemed to grow cold in the air around him. His heart sank as he again feared they would not want him back. He had broken the Trust...he was outcast.

"Weren't what, Simon?" Kate stared intently at him, sensing the turmoil he experienced.

"They weren't all for the better." His eyes could still not meet hers and he stepped a pace away. "I couldn't bear to tell you before. And I was so excited coming here I almost forgot." He turned towards her now with a look, almost of panic, burning on his face. "I didn't mean to. I wasn't thinking. I simply reacted."

"Simon," Kate hurried to him, frightened by what she heard in his voice, "what are you talking about? Whatever happened, I'm sure it's not as bad as you think."

"It's worse. I broke the Trust, Kate. The whole purpose of my existence, the reason they sacrificed their lives. In a moment of anger, I destroyed it all." His shoulders hunched over and he looked with resignation back down the hill they had climbed, every inch now a tired old man. "There will be no welcome for me here."

Kate barely breathed out the words, "What did you do, Simon?" His pain was so palatable, she listened for his answer with dread. Was it really so horrible he truly could never go home?

They stood for several minutes before Simon could speak. "It was London, during the Great Plague. As you know, I had allowed Marcus to become very close to me." He looked at Kate sternly now. "I was very careful those hundreds of years to maintain my distance, to not let any attachments form. But Marcus...," his eyes and thoughts drifted away and she knew he was seeing his old friend once more.

She thought back. "His journal, it ended very abruptly. On your arrival to London, in fact." Kate looked at Simon, concern in her eyes. "I know how good a friend he was to you, Simon. Marcus died in London, didn't he."

"Well," he cleared his throat, "Marcus was like the son I would never have. For those few wonderful years, I felt as if I had a family...and I loved him dearly." His voice broke and faded away, his eyes glistening. "Marcus died of the Plague. There was nothing I could do to help him. Oh, I tried. Dear God, I tried." He shook his head sadly and walked a few more paces, struggling. "There was nothing I could do."

"I wanted to give him an honorable send-off. He deserved that much from me. Unfortunately, some drunkards stumbled onto us and desecrated the burial."

"Simon, no." Kate hurried to him and grasped his hand, sharing his pain and fear.

"They didn't realize what they were doing, I know that now. But I was so angry, so full of hurt. I wanted them to hurt as well. I wanted to punish them for defiling Marcus' resting place." Simon looked into her eyes with great sadness. "I put the Plague on them, Kate. I sentenced three men to die a slow, painful death worse than anything Marcus had experienced."

Kate let out a small noise, her hands clasped at her mouth. "Couldn't you have taken it back, Simon? Couldn't you have changed it?"

Simon shook his head, obviously disgusted with himself. "By the time I realized what I had done, they were long gone. It was several more days before I heard anything about their whereabouts and could track them down. It was too late. They were in great agony but held onto life because of my edict. All I could do was end their suffering and let them pass on."

"I'm so sorry." She reached out for him and held him tightly in her arms.

They stood clasped together on the hilltop near some woodlands. There was no traffic on the road to distract them. Folks avoided this area if at all possible, local legend having spirits haunted the hill and its woods. Enough curiosity seekers had enough strange experiences here it was taken as truth. The area remained secluded and unchanged. As Simon and Kate stood willing for the strength and wisdom to continue their journey, no one disturbed them.

Finally, Simon looked across the shades of green stretching before him. The view soothed him somewhat. Kate almost thought she could hear the haunting melody of a bagpipe in the distance. She lifted her head and looked around wonderingly. Though her eyes searched, she could see no one else around. "Did you hear that?"

"No. It was probably the wind. It can play tricks in these woods. I'm just soaking in the view." It was good to finally be home, regardless of the outcome of today's venture. He turned and nodded at the woods. "We need to go through the trees. There should be a clearing with a large old oak tree near one end." He took her hand and led her in.

They had walked for some time when Simon stopped, his body tense. He pointed ahead. "There it is. You can just make out the clearing and the tree beyond. That's where this all started." He stared at it with a small smile. "What a wonderful old oak. So much larger and gnarled than I remember. Isn't it beautiful?"

The smile faded. He turned suddenly and started back the way they came, ignoring the voices pounding in his head. "I can't do it. I have no right to go back."

"Simon stop!" Kate hurried after him. "Wait. Just wait a minute, Simon." She stepped into his path. "What happened next? After the men died, Simon, what did you do next?"

"I ran away," he answered harshly. "For two hundred years I hid from men. Self-imposed exile to punish my crime."

"And then?"

"Then?" he paused and his face softened. "Then I joined the world again, my desire and belief in helping people strong once more. I thought, somehow, I could make amends. I worked hard to make life go right for as many people as crossed my path." He smiled. "It was very tiring."

"There!" Kate interrupted joyously.

Simon looked at her, his face furrowed in puzzlement.

"Don't you see, Simon?" Kate practically jumped with joy. "You paid your debt, you did make amends. You restored the Trust, Simon."

"Restored, no, Kate." He tried to step around her.

"Yes." She stopped him again and looked him squarely in the eyes. "Simon, you may be a Druid, and you may have incredible powers, but the fact is you are still human. And humans make mistakes. No one, not even you, is perfect. Your leaders weren't perfect either. Otherwise, they would have seen this was far too much to ask of any one man."

She smiled gently and touched his care-worn face, "You have done so much more than they probably ever thought you could. You've made beautiful changes in the lives of thousands of people. One mistake can't erase all that. You've already punished yourself more than anyone else would have. Let it go, Simon...forgive yourself. Believe me, you have fulfilled the Trust."

He dropped his head, his shoulders quivering. Kate wrapped her arms around him. "What a burden you have carried for the human race, Simon. How very tired you must be. Your people should never have made you think the fate of the whole world was your responsibility."

Slowly, Simon raised his head and looked around. He appeared to be listening to something distant. "Yes, I am tired. Take me home, Kate. I don't think I would be allowed to leave this place again anyways.

Kate scanned the area worriedly. "Not allowed to leave? By whom? What do you mean?"

"I mean, one way or another it ends tonight. Whether I die or I go with them. I can feel the truth of this, and like everything that affects me personally, I cannot change it. My only choice might be which of those two endings I prefer. If I get a choice." He looked at Kate and gently caressed her face. "I'm so sorry it has to be this way."

Kate didn't trust her voice to attempt a reply. Instead, she smiled bravely and held out her hand. Arm in arm, they turned and moved back towards the clearing and sacred oak. The closer they got, the stranger Simon felt. Younger, lighter somehow.

"Ahh, the rocks. See all those sunken areas of rocks? Those used to be the entrances to our homes." They walked closer. "Looks as if time has done them in. They were built underground, you see."

"Underground? Why was that?"

"Practicality. The earth protected us from the outside...wind, rain, cold...prying eyes. We protected her and she protected us. It was a good exchange."

"Which was yours, Simon?"

He pointed at his feet. "Here. This was my home."

They kicked around at the rocks for a little bit, looking for a piece of his history. Kate quietly let Simon reminisce. Finally, he broke the silence.

"We'd better go on down. There are some things I think we'll need to prepare." He motioned to a faint, overgrown trail. "This was the path they led me down all those years ago when they gave up their lives. I never dared hope I would walk down it again to give up mine."

Still, he hesitated. Kate took his hand, nodding encouragement. "They'll be so happy, Simon. You'll see."

With pounding heart, Simon started the descent. It was Kate's belief in him that allowed him to go on, for deep inside he still feared his kinsmen wouldn't let him come home. Not here, not with honor as he desired. They might allow him to die, but in shame as an outcast. They might have called him back to condemn him. All the same, there was only one way to find out for sure. He would do the ancient ritual once more. If indeed their spirits still waited, he would face them once and for all and know the truth.

CHAPTER NINETEEN

SIMON looked over at Kate with a weak smile. "In the old days, we walked down this path deasil." He saw her questioning look and continued. "That was what we called our special formation for making an impressive entrance and exit. It was used for all formal ceremonies. Supposed to reflect the path of the moon, the changing of the seasons."

"Most of our customs honored some tie-in to the earth and the stars. Our lives came from the land. We believed we had an inextricable bond to it and an obligation to honor and protect it." He chuckled. "That was actually one of the beliefs we shared with our fellow Irishmen. We all knew how important the land was."

"Well, it is a beautiful land, Simon. And everywhere there are signs or people saying 'Céad Míle Fáilte.' I mean, how special is it to be told 'One Hundred Thousand

Welcomes' everywhere you go? There's such a sense of peace and tranquility here. I almost hate the thought of having to leave it and go home. I wish I could stay here forever.

Simon looked at her sharply, thoughts racing through his mind. "What if..."

She looked at him with a smile. "What was that? Sorry, my mind was wandering. Were you saying something?"

"No," he shook his head and looked away. "I didn't say anything."

"This has been some of the most incredible countryside I've ever seen. No question in my mind why they call Ireland 'Land of the Forty Shades of Green.' Every single plot stretching into the distance really does seem to be a different variation of green. So gorgeous. And how did they get those fences to look that way? All the light shining through them is just beautiful. They seem so open and airy, like lace. So, well, artistic isn't the word I'm looking for, but it gets the general idea across. They don't seem real, somehow."

"They use no mortar. The stones are simply stacked one on top of the other."

"But, how do they stay? There are miles of them, perfectly intact."

"As you said, it is an art. Passed down through the years from father to son. Those fences stand up well through the years. Ireland is an old country and she maintains a lot of the old ways." Simon looked at his surroundings with great satisfaction. "I might not have been able to come back before but I've kept my eye on my native land. Some think she should leapfrog into the modern world, and in some matters maybe she should. But for many of us, it's her quiet old worldliness that we cherish. It's that tranquility, that tie to roots hundreds of years old that draws us in and charms all the world-weary travelers looking for a piece of home."

"Simon, that's it exactly." Kate's eyes glistened with

happiness. "That's exactly how I feel…like I've finally come home. As if I've gotten a more grounded perspective on life now and can see what's important and what's fluff."

They were almost at the clearing but Simon paused to look at her. "What is important, Kate?"

"To know where you come from and where you want to go. To live an honest life that enriches others as well as yourself, leaving the world a little better than you found it. To not be afraid to embrace life passionately and to love fervently. Even if it seems impossible. Even if it can only be for a few weeks, or days, or hours." Her voice trailed softly off, but her eyes remained on Simon.

He stared at her for a moment, then his mouth lifted into a contented grin and he traced his finger along her cheek. "You're right. For all I had accomplished before, my life was not complete until you brought love into it. You were the last missing piece." His smile slipped. "Of course, that means the puzzle of my life is complete, doesn't it? And when a puzzle is finished, who doesn't sweep the picture away and empty off the table?"

She rushed into his arms before the words faded and they held each other tightly. "You were right," she mumbled against the cloth of his jacket. "That first day we met, you were right. You said that sometimes we have to allow the choice that brings pain in order to reach the right end." She looked up at him with tears in her eyes. "Well, this hurts worse than anything I've ever lived through, and yet I know deep in my soul that it has to be. It's as if there were little voices inside telling me that we must finish this. That you must be sent back."

"You can hear them too?" He looked down at her, his face troubled.

"Sense them more than hear. But the same thing echoes through the wind and the whispering grasses. The same words you told me at the top of the hill and that shine in your eyes. You have to go back. Tonight. You can either leave with them or die alone."

Simon exhaled slowly and buried his face in her hair. The clouds drifted by as they clung in each other's embrace, trying to hold onto their strength and composure for the task that lay ahead. When he lifted his face again, he noticed the sun.

"We have only a short time left and work that must be done. It's a sad irony that when my longed-for time of leaving this earth finally comes, I'm also given that which I'd desired most throughout all these lonely years. Love is painful, indeed."

He looked at the clearing, Kate's eyes following his gaze. In the center of the grassy field was a bare dark brown patch of earth in the rough shape of a circle. "The fire site," he murmured.

A wave of panic washed over Kate. She knew it wasn't possible, but a part of her wished they could just turn around and walk away. If they'd only stayed in California they might have escaped this. But that wasn't true either. Whatever force lived here, it had reached around the world and used her as a tool to bring Simon to this place as surely as if she'd been following a script. There was no doubt in her mind tonight was the night. If they'd stayed in San Diego, it might have been a bus as he crossed the street. At least here there was some rightness to his going. A sense of completion. He deserved that.

She saw pain in Simon's eyes and realized he was aware of her thoughts. She tried to give him a reassuring smile. "I knew from the moment I met you I wanted to be with you. I know now the purpose of my finding you was to bring you home. This is the way it's supposed to be, Simon. We both know that. Even though I wish it could be different, it's not."

"We tasted true love, which is more than many people get. Now I'm here to see that your life ends with the dignity and love and compassion you deserve. I'll be all right," she told him even though that part wasn't completely true, "because you'll always be with me here," she pressed her hand to her heart. Impulsively she wrapped her arms around him and squeezed him tight a moment, wishing it could be forever, before releasing him. Gathering all the inner strength she possessed, she walked into the clearing. Looking around with a bittersweet resignation she asked, "How do we start?"

If she could be strong, so could he. For her sake. Holding his own emotions in check he replied, "We must prepare the bonfire." He approached the still-dark earth with interest. "How strange that nothing has grown here after all this time."

The earth was soft and undisturbed. He prodded at it with his foot, first on one side and then the other. His face creased in thought.

"What are you looking for?"

"Nothing, I guess. Just remembering. Trying to figure out how to start tonight's fire properly. Ideally, the fire should be started with the Druid's Eternal Flame. The Sacred Fire of Be'al, our Supreme Being. I know it's long gone, but I couldn't help but hope..." he gave the soft dirt one more good kick and his foot hit something with a thud. Quickly he dropped to his knees and started digging at the hard object. With a whoop of exultation, he pulled loose a dirt-blackened stick and cried, "...hope that it was saved somehow."

As he held the burned rod aloft, free of its earthly prison, it ignited. Both Simon and Kate jumped in surprise, Simon dropping the burning stick. Even so, the flame continued.

"My God, Simon. How did it do that?"

He was smiling broadly as he picked it back up. "It's the Eternal Flame. After the passing of the Druids, I thought it had been completely consumed by the bonfire. Never did I imagine it might actually have survived."

"This is good?" she asked, examining the fire more closely.

"Yes, this is very good. I had my doubts about the success of lighting a sacred bonfire by flicking my Bic. But to now find the Eternal Flame has been waiting here all this time. Yes, I have the highest of hopes for tonight's success. Maybe this will work out all right after all."

"How can you still have any doubt, Simon? Deep in our hearts, in our very souls, we know this is meant to be." She reached out a cautious hand. "May I hold it?"

He handed the torch to Kate, whose eyes grew wide as she gripped the wood. "It...it almost feels alive. As if there were a current of electricity or the beat of a heart within." Shuddering, she quickly handed it back.

"It's the Druid magic," he said. With a swift movement, he embedded the base of the staff into the dirt. "This will stand as our watchfire while we prepare for the midnight hour. We'd better start bringing the wood."

"You were right when you told me we probably wouldn't find much wood laying around here. Good thing we stopped and got some branches and peat along the way."

It took them each a couple of trips to carry everything down from the car. When they finished, there was a good-sized pile in the middle of the dirt, suitable for a small bonfire.

"Will it be big enough, Simon?"

"I think so. There's nothing more we can do now except wait for the moon's zenith. Why don't we pull out the basket of food? I could sure use that bottle of wine right now. Almost wish we'd brought something stronger." He looked at

Kate, grinning nervously.

"I know what you mean," she agreed.

They sat in the grass, sharing sandwiches and fruit, washing it down with wine. There was the almost audible sound of a clock ticking their time away. They avoided the subject, talking of Kate's life, the beauty of Ireland, anything they could think of. Finally, Simon pulled a small package from his pocket.

"I've been meaning to show these to you." Carefully, he unwrapped two small items. "This ring belonged to Marcus. And this," he held up a very old cross on a chain, "belonged to your ancestor, Katherine Peterson."

"Oh, it's beautiful." Kate touched it gently. "How did you get it?"

"I told you she was a very special woman. Of all the people I've told my stories to, she was the only one who searched for me afterwards to thank me. And to give me this." He smiled tenderly at Kate. "It appears that tracking me down runs in your family."

"As does good taste."

Simon took her right hand and carefully placed both mementos in it. "I want you to keep them now. I've carried them with me for hundreds of years. They hold special memories of special people. They'll keep me close to you."

"Simon..." she whispered.

He held up his hand. "One more thing." He reached into his other pocket and pulled out a small silver object. "Do you know what this is?"

Kate shook her head no. "Well, yes it's a ring. But I've never seen one like it before."

"It's called a fáinne Chladaigh or Claddagh ring. Legend is it was first made by an Irish prince as a wedding ring for his beloved. The hands are for friendship, the crown is for loyalty, and the heart...the heart is for love." He took her other hand and slipped the ring on her finger.

"When it's worn this way, with the crown on the outside protecting the heart on the inside, it means you've given your heart to another. I do love you, Kate. Perhaps more than you'll ever know."

"I love you, too. More than can be measured." A tear crept down her cheek. "It's absolutely beautiful. I'll always wear it, Simon. To me, we are married, bound together forever. I won't forget you." Her hand unconsciously caressed her abdomen, a smile flickering through her mind. *A part of you will always be with me.*

"I know you won't. And I'll never forget you, my Wife."

They embraced, tasting each other's mouths and the saltiness of tears. The thick grass cushioned their bodies as they lay down and loved one last time. The minutes continued to tick and sooner than either imagined the full moon stood high above them, reaching the zenith of its journey across the dark sky.

Simon stared at it. "The moon is in position. It's time."

Trembling, Kate stood up. "This is going to be harder than I thought, Simon. I hope I can be strong enough for you."

"You've already shown me how strong you are. Still, I almost wish you'd stayed at the hotel. I don't feel good abandoning you at night in the middle of nowhere like this."

"I know, but I needed to be here. I have the map to get back into town and there's nobody up here to bother me. I admit I'm a little scared, but I needed to be here."

He sighed. "I needed you to be here, too. I don't think I could have faced this on my own."

"Simon, we've avoided talking about it, but do you think tonight is what that last dream meant? The darkness that would separate us?"

For a moment, Simon's eyes narrowed. "I wish I knew for

sure. It almost felt as if there were a different meaning, but it seems tonight's circumstances meet the qualifications too. Here, in the dark of the night, we will lose each other. That's nightmare enough for me." He squeezed her hand firmly. "I have to trust that you'll be okay. So, let's start the bonfire."

They walked to the torch and Simon held it aloft repeating words Kate took to be spoken in Gaelic. With a swift motion, he hurled the staff into the pile and the bonfire leaped into flames. Kate's heart pounded, but the feeling of Simon's strong grip held her steady.

He glanced quickly at her. "Be brave, my precious Kate." Then his voice boomed out again, reciting the ancient words.

She could recognize the pattern of sounds when he repeated different sections but she couldn't understand them. Her heart began to pound harder and the wind seemed to pick up. She could hear the roar of the waves as they crashed on the cliffs beyond. All the sounds seemed amplified. Was a storm coming? She looked up in confusion at the calm sky.

The noise around them increased. She could barely hear Simon. I'll love you forever. Did she call out the words or had he? Maybe they said them together. Or thought them? The wind whipped across her face. She felt the night closing in on her. Constricting her chest. Closing off her lungs.

The fire's intensity grew as well. She was afraid she would be burned alive. If the noise didn't crush her first. It echoed through her brain. The waves. The wind. And the voices. Voices? Yes, hundreds of voices rising in a crescendo. They were here. Kate didn't think she could take it much longer. It seemed they would crush the very life out of her.

"Simon," she screamed, covering her head. Her knees gave out.

And Simon was there, falling to the ground with her.

Putting his body over hers. Protecting her from the onslaught. Everything went dark.

"Wake up. Come now, children, open your eyes. You're safe."

Kate's eyes flickered. She was lying on the ground, but she didn't feel Simon's weight on her.

She moaned, trying to sit up. "What happened?" Her eyes finally focused on a strange man's face peering cautiously into her own. She scooted back in alarm. "Who are you?" Then she focused beyond the man. With amazement, she saw she was surrounded by people. All dressed in earthy brown cloaks.

"I am Liam, the Stallir of Simon's clan."

"It worked," Kate whispered, fear and awe mingling in her voice. "You've all come back for him." Sudden panic filled her. "Where is he? Simon," she called out.

She turned and saw a young man lying in the grass near her. She crawled closer, barely daring to breathe.

"Simon?"

"He'll be awake in a moment. This took a lot out of him," Liam said. "Quite literally, I suppose."

"But, he looks..."

"He looks just as he did. We are all just as we were when the Ending came."

"Well, he may look the same to you on the outside, but he's gone through an awful lot on the inside. Do you have any idea..."

"Yes," Liam interrupted softly, "I do." There was moisture in his eyes as he looked down at Simon's quiet figure. "See if he will wake for you."

"If his body has reverted back," Kate paused, uncertain how to express this new fear.

"Don't worry, he will remember you."

Hesitantly, Kate placed a shaking hand on the man's face, stroking his forehead. He looked to be near her age now. He was still a good-looking man but so different from the Simon she knew. When he woke up would he really be her Simon? Or, would he be a stranger like the rest of them?

"Simon. Simon, can you hear me? Wake up. They're here, Simon. It worked. Wake up."

Slowly the figure stirred, drawing in a deep breath. Kate stared fearfully into his eyes as they opened, letting out a sigh of relief. They were Simon's eyes.

"Kate?"

"Yes, Simon. I'm here."

He reached for her then noticed the figure standing behind her.

"Liam," he shouted, trying to jump to his feet. He wobbled as he rose, his legs feeling like rubber. He would have fallen if two figures hadn't rushed to his side, supporting him. "Diarmuid. Sliabh. You're all here. I can't believe it. Where's Tadhg?" He hugged the men to him, laughing. Suddenly it seemed everyone was pushing forward, wanting to hug him, to welcome him home.

All save for one lone figure who scowled, then stepped back into the shadows. "It should have been me. I should have been the one chosen. The one honored. All that power, all that glory...what a waste. It should have been me," Tadhg growled under his breath.

Kate put her hands protectively over her head, pushing through the crowd. She broke free and found herself standing alone at the edge of the clearing. *I'm happy for him. I really am.* She saw his joy at finding himself truly home again and knew it was the right thing. She was glad she helped him. Still, part of her felt like crying, even screaming out her anguish at all of them.

She listened to their laughter and excited chatter with a sad heart. *It's happened just as it should,* she thought. *They're so glad to see him. He had no reason to fear after all. This is what Simon needed. I told him they'd want him back.* She turned from the joyous reunion and looked in the direction of where the car waited. The two of them had said their goodbyes earlier. Simon was with his people again. Maybe it was time for her to go back to hers. She glanced back with tears in her eyes and started up the path.

"Kate!"

She could barely hear the voice above the cacophony of noise. She paused as it came again. Now, the crowd was parting.

"Kate, wait. Don't leave."

The space between the people opened wider and she saw Simon stumbling through.

"Don't leave me yet, Kate, please." There was anguish in his voice that made Kate's heart want to break and sing simultaneously. He had them all back, and still, he wanted her. She rushed down the path and into his arms, tears rolling down her cheeks.

There were tears on his own face as he held her. "Kate, you were going to just leave? Without even saying goodbye?"

"We said our goodbyes, Simon. And all these people pushed in and they were happy and you were happy. You're home, just like you wanted. I thought my part was finished, that I was just in the way." She almost felt annoyed with herself that she couldn't stop crying.

"Oh, my sweet Kate. You're the one who made this possible. I never could've done it without you. I owe you so much."

"You don't owe me, Simon. I did it because I wanted to.

Because I love you."

They held each other, heads close. "I love you so much," Simon whispered.

He straightened up, smiling, but there was sadness in his eyes again. "Come, I want you to meet Liam and the others."

They moved back through the group, hand in hand, until they reached the fire again. Simon introduced his friends to her.

Liam surprised her with a strong, though brief, embrace. "Ah, our own Caitrín. We are all so pleased to meet you. You are exactly as I imagined you."

"Caitrín? What is that? What does it mean?"

"It is the Irish Gaelic form of your name, Katherine. So very fitting for a woman such as yourself. It means pure and innocence, you see."

"Oh well...I'm not really all that innocent. Or pure." Her face felt hot and she knew it was turning a blotchy red. "I mean, I think I'm a good person and I try to..."

"Trust me when I tell you, your spirit is indeed pure and innocent," Liam said. "And yes. You are a good person." He smiled at her

Simon gave her a squeeze. "Yes, she is, Thank you, Liam." He turned as a figure approached them.

"Ah, here is my good friend, Tadhg. I didn't see you earlier, Tadhg. Where were you?"

"I was here, Simon. Just biding my time." He took Kate's hand and kissed it, looking into her eyes. She shivered involuntarily. "How beautiful you are, Caitríona. How lucky Simon is. Again." He smiled at them both, a smile that didn't reach his eyes, and slowly released her hand.

Kate fought a strange desire to wipe it clean on her pants. *This is Simon's best friend. There's no reason why I shouldn't like this man. Yet there's something almost frightening about him. And dangerous.*

Liam raised his arms to quiet everybody and gain their attention. "On behalf of all of Simon's friends and our fellow clans, I thank you, Katherine Torrence McGuire.." The Stallir bowed to her and everyone followed.

Thank me? I don't understand. What for?"

"When we sent Simon out we really had no clear understanding of exactly what would happen. Simon knew the risk he was taking. Yet, he chose to go anyways as a means of helping the world and preserving our very essence. A Druid's life is normally longer than the average human's and we did expect Simon to live even longer because of our Joining. But we had no idea we had sentenced him to go on for hundreds and hundreds of years with no hope of an end in sight."

He turned to Simon now, placing a hand on his shoulder. "I never would have asked you, Simon, if I had known what I was condemning you to."

"It's all right, Liam. Everything worked out well."

"Yes, but you've paid a tremendous price for it. We were aware of all your pain and doubts. We know what you had to endure and what you had to give up." He looked at the other Stallirs. "Even so, you managed to accomplish more than we ever dared hope for. You have fulfilled our Trust to the highest degree."

The color drained from Simon's face. "I'm sorry, Liam, but...I haven't." He forced himself to maintain eye contact. "I broke the Trust, Liam. I used my powers to hurt." His voice broke.

"Simon," Liam repeated gently, "we were aware of everything. In all those hundreds of years, you made one dreadful, sad mistake, which you did your best to remedy and which you paid for. We never expected you to live this long. How you managed to maintain your sanity is beyond us. If there is forgiveness to be sought, it is we who seek it from you. You have proven yourself more worthy than any of us. You are the wind, Simon."

"You were there." Simon choked back more tears, releasing once and for all the terrible burden he carried. Kate squeezed him, smiling.

"And that brings us to why we thank you, Kate. Simon's time had to end. We were determined to free him one way or another. The bond that held him was to be severed tonight. Our first choice was to have him return to us, welcomed home with love and honor. If he had not come, he would have died instantly and been lost to us forever."

"But, we knew his heart. Simon would never have come home on his own. It was your love and determination, your willingness to sacrifice,...your pure and innocent spirit...that brought him back to us. We are in your debt." He smiled at her, but Kate saw his eyes contained sadness, too. Liam looked up at the sky, watching the moon. "Our time grows short," he told the others. "We must prepare."

As everyone moved into their circles, Kate looked at Simon in panic. "Simon, I don't want you to leave. I can't pretend anymore. I don't want to go through the rest of my life without you."

Simon held her close, his own heart pounding with dread. Why could he never have what his heart desired most? Why was he always called upon to make these terrible sacrifices?

"Kate, I wish...I wish..."

"What Simon," Liam interrupted, his gaze locking on them. "What do you wish?" Simon stared at him. "Quickly now. Tell me what you wish for, Simon."

"I wish Kate and I could stay together."

"And you, Kate? How do you feel about this?"

"I want more than anything to be with him."

Liam's face softened into a smile. "Then stay."

Meagan looked out the window of Kate's office, a single tear falling down her cheek. Another office worker popped her head in as she walked by. "Hey, Meagan. What are you doing in here?" When she got no reply she stepped closer. "You're crying. Meagan, what's wrong?"

"It's Kate. She's not coming back."

"What do you mean? Of course, she's coming back."

"No," Meagan shook her head. "Don't ask me how I know, but I do. She's never coming back." She picked up a pencil from the desk, smiling sadly as she remembered how many times Kate had thrown it at her. She clutched it to her chest and moved past the other woman towards the door. "Wherever she is, she's loved and happy. And she won't be coming back here."

"Simon," Liam was saying. "You still have the power. Hold her tight and she will stay with you.

Simon looked at Kate. "Are you sure this is what you want? What about your life back in San Diego?"

"You already know, Simon, the only thing I'll miss is my cat, Chewy, and my best friend, Meagan. And Meagan has always wanted Chewy, so they'll take care of each other. This is what I want, Simon. To be with you. I just wish I could let Meagan know I'm all right."

"We're taking care of that, Kate. Welcome to your new family." Liam hugged her. Then he motioned for her and Simon to follow. "We must take our places in the circle. Our Leaving is at hand."

"What's going to happen, Simon?"

"I think we're going to pass into another realm."

"But I can't. I'm not a Druid."

"Hush, child." Liam stepped in front of her, his gaze penetrating her soul. "You must believe for it to work. Simon, hold her tightly in your arms. Don't let go no matter what happens." Liam lifted his voice to the others. "Join hands. Those of us closest must place our hands on this very special couple. They must pass through with us."

He looked back at Simon and Kate. "We will join our powers with yours. Kate will cross over with us." He said it as a statement of fact.

They were all in position now, hands and spirits joined together as the chanting began. Kate and Simon looked into each other's eyes, fear replaced by love and joy. The wind howled once more, the voices growing, the very air pressing in on them. Nothing could pull them apart or break their locked gaze. They were going to be together. Kate smiled and leaned close to his ear. "Simon, I think we're going to be parents."

As the new day dawned a light rain started, putting out the last of the fire's embers. The clearing was empty and the falling rain soon washed even the footprints away. Hundreds of footprints that showed no coming and no going. The air was calm and still, no restless spirits left to disturb it now.

Meagan walked through Kate's house, gently touching things here and there, lost in memories. She had no proof, but deep inside she knew the truth. Something wonderful had happened to Kate. Something she had wanted more than anything else, and she definitely wasn't coming back.

Meagan felt sorrow, but only for her own loss. Chewbaca rubbed against her legs and she picked him up, stroking his fur softly.

"She didn't even say goodbye, Cougar. We were like sisters. I'd have thought she'd find some way to say goodbye to me."

Meagan entered the bedroom. Almost immediately her eyes were drawn to an old book on the nightstand, propped up against the lamp. She was sure it hadn't been there before. She set the cat on the bed and picked the book up, examining it. It was an ancient diary. There was a chain dangling like some sort of page marker, so she opened the diary there. The chain was attached to a beautiful old cross. Even as she lifted it in her hand, she knew it had been left for her.

"I knew it. I knew she'd find a way to say goodbye to me." Meagan clasped the cross to her heart and read the page it marked.

'He always keeps it with him. He will not take much else as we move from place to place, but he keeps the cross. No one ever bothered to thank him before, even with all the miracles he has done for them. Katherine Peterson Torrence was a rare breed. Only a strong, beautiful spirit could draw Simon in. It is a shame he cannot find someone like her for his own.'

'He is a sad man, for all the joy he has brought others. Oh to be sure, he finds contentment in his work and companionship with me. But I see well enough. He longs for the kind of life that has been denied him. He wants a woman to love, a woman who will love him back so hard she would not think twice about making a sacrifice for him.'

'And, he wants to go home. But Ireland and love, the two things Simon wants most, are the two things he cannot have.'

Meagan closed the book and sat heavily on the bed.

"Simon. That's what happened." She looked at the cross again then slipped it over her head.

"This belonged to Simon, given to him by Kate's ancestor. Now, how would Kate have gotten hold of it unless she found him somehow? And how did it get back here for me to find? She addressed her questions to the cat, but Chewbaca merely blinked his eyes and stared at her.

Meagan scrunched her nose, trying to think.

"Okay, Cougar. Somehow Kate found this guy, Simon. And somehow he was still alive. They fell in love, she teleported this message back to me, and then they went off to live in Never-Never Land. It makes perfect sense." She stood up, nodding her head to herself, still holding the book.

With a wistful look around, she picked up Chewy and moved towards the front door. "I'll miss you, Kate. You were the best friend I ever had." She shook her head in regret. "I knew I should have stayed in that suitcase. No telling where I could be right now."

She left the house, locking the door behind her. She stroked the cat reassuringly. "You were supposed to be my cat anyways. If the landlady still won't let pets in my apartment, I'll move. Maybe into Kate's place. But you know what I'm going to do first, Cougar? I think I'll go open a flipping savings account."

THE
END

Meet the Author

Linda Williams Stirling, being somewhat nomadic for most of her life, has had several careers including a Catering Director for a hotel chain, a Senior Law Clerk, an Executive Director for a Non-Profit, and a Foreign Service Officer (Diplomat) for the U.S. Department of State. She has lived in multiple locations in New York, California, Illinois, Virginia, Washington, DC, Southeast Asia, Central America, and the Middle East.

In between work and raising her three beautiful children as a single parent, she kept writing; publishing articles, essays, and poetry. Now that Linda is retired, her children are adults, and she has four beautiful grandchildren, she has returned to her first love... writing fiction. She currently lives in Upstate New York with an insufficient number of pets, in the same small town from which she started her life's journey.

Linda has a number of chronic illnesses, autoimmune diseases, and chronic pain conditions that are disabling. Her hope is that by sharing this information, others like her will realize they can accomplish more than they might think. It will take longer, it will increase pain levels for a bit, and it will be more exhausting than if they were completely healthy, but it is possible for one to find the thing that makes their heart sing and do it.

Simon Says is Linda's debut novel and, believe it or not, is inspired by an actual event.